Dear Shelia,

Carmine's Angel

In the beginning, MANY years ago, you read the 1st draft of Carmine's Angel!

A Novel

Your feed back was so helpful and appreciated. Thank you.

Rosemary Montana

In loving,
Rosemary

Cover design by Trish Weber-Hall.

Balboa Press books may be ordered through booksellers or by contacting:

Balboa Press
A Division of Hay House
1663 Liberty Drive
Bloomington, IN 47403
www.balboapress.com
1 (877) 407-4847

Print information available on the last page.

ISBN: 978-1-5043-8061-4 (sc)
ISBN: 978-1-5043-8063-8 (hc)
ISBN: 978-1-5043-8062-1 (e)

Library of Congress Control Number: 2017908305

Balboa Press rev. date: 04/27/2018

In loving memory of Kathe Montana Kirrene,
my beautiful, feisty, passionate sister
without whose constant nagging and encouragement
this book would never have been completed

PART I

Chapter One

Carmine was pissed. She had forbidden her daughter, Cassie, to use that word, but there was no better way to describe how she felt about her headache. Okay, well, how about enraged? That was better. Enraged about the worst, most intense headache she ever had. But it wasn't going to stop her. Not now!

After almost eighteen years of putting her life on hold to raise Cassie, tomorrow she would start the fall semester at California State University, Los Angeles to finish the one year she had left for her business degree. Cassie was now eighteen years old and attending University of California in Santa Barbara, paid for by Cassie's father, a man Carmine had been briefly married to in order to give Cassie legitimacy. The agonizing years of waiting, planning and plotting the life she wanted to lead had finally arrived. She had managed to take enough courses over the years to have enough credits to graduate in the spring, which raised her usual impatience with delays to a level that was barely tolerable. She was so ready for this new life to begin.

Carmine had meticulously envisioned what her new life would be. After graduation she would find a position with a congressperson or another political organization and use that experience to follow her passion for being a voice for women's issues and helping underprivileged women to become self-sufficient.

Yeah, a cranky internal voice chimed in. *We all know what happens when you plan your life!*

Carmine stuck out her tongue and shook her head as though the thought would disappear. The shaking only made her nauseated, like a vise was squeezing her head and her brain was going to explode. She had been fighting it for two days now and nothing she did stopped it.

It's only a headache; it's not going to impact your life, so get over it.

To make herself feel better, she thought of how she had spent the weekend cleaning out any residue of her "old life," including clothes, files and anything else that was tainted with the past. When school started tomorrow, it would be a rebirth of the life she was supposed to have. In spite of the pain, she hugged herself in anticipation of her destiny, as she saw it.

Yes, yes, yes! Carmine repeated to herself. At last! She loved her daughter, but life with Cassie had often seemed like cycles of hell punctuated with stints of purgatory during those agonizing teenage years. Cassie had finally reached some level of maturity, thank goodness, but now she was at college and what Carmine didn't know, wouldn't bother her! Right? Carmine silently said a prayer that all was well with Cassie.

Cal State was starting its fall session in August, one month earlier than usual, due to a construction project that was scheduled over November and December. School would be closed for classes during that time. Just thinking about those six weeks off at the end of the first quarter made Carmine's overwhelming anxieties subside to an almost manageable level. She'd have time to rest and adjust before the next quarter began.

Maybe the headache was a reaction to the potential stress she was imagining. After all, starting college again at 37 while working a full-time job would give anyone pause, wouldn't it? She evaluated that thought. *Breathe, breathe, breathe; let go, let go, let go.* She waited for the headache to disappear as she held her head in her hands. But her head still throbbed like a pounding drum making her miserable!

Carmine wistfully thought about going to bed and how good the crisp white pillow case would feel on her head. But, sighing instead, she reluctantly began to lay out her clothes for the next day. A pair of deep blue stretch jeans that snugly fit her 5'4" well-proportioned figure along with matching sandals with short cork heels. A mint-colored t-shirt and a matching short jacket completed the outfit, which she placed on her bedroom chair.

She took a glimpse of herself in the bathroom mirror. With so much pain she was experiencing, Carmine was surprised to see that she still looked the same. Short dark-brown straight hair with a side part and bangs, large brown eyes that looked even larger in her small heart-shaped face stared back at her with only minute evidence of what she was feeling. And thanks to her Italian heritage, she had the olive skin that didn't show wrinkles easily. *Thank you, great grandma!*

Maybe the trendy outfit, a good night's sleep and hair tucked back behind her ears, would knock off several years of her age and she could look closer to 30 instead of 37. Blend in with "the kids," as she thought of them. *Yeah, sure! Dream on, Carmine!*

She would go to bed early, be rested and ready for the first day of her new life! This is what she had been waiting for since Cassie was born; the freedom to do what she wanted. There was no husband or even a boyfriend. She had become so disillusioned that she only dated men with whom she couldn't possibly get involved or didn't date at all because she had too many other priorities.

Carmine performed her evening ritual preparing for bed. She took off her make-up, took a long, hot bath filled with bubbles and aromatherapy oils. After applying moisturizer, eye cream and whatever was the "in" cosmetic for that week, she practiced her yoga exercises. They didn't take that long and she always felt more relaxed and balanced. Then she did twenty to thirty minutes of meditation.

Neither the yoga nor the meditation helped the headache. It was still there, angrily throbbing and pounding in her head like a baseball bat hitting a hard wall. Carmine crawled into bed. She was nauseated; possibly as much from the many remedies she had tried to quell the headache as from the headache itself. She was so exhausted that she fell asleep within minutes.

Sometime during the night, Carmine awakened suddenly. The headache was gone; absolutely disappeared. Carmine felt like she was floating, and she was almost giggling with joy.

What is going on? I haven't had these feelings since I was a little girl at Christmas. She felt herself leave the bed and looked around. There seemed to be a light coming from somewhere in her condo, but she knew she didn't leave a light on. When she turned around to switch on the ceiling light, she gasped, stopped breathing, froze and was unable to move. There was a huge man in her bedroom. She wanted to scream, but no sound came out. Her ability to speak had disappeared, strangled with fear. She opened her mouth to scream, but only ugly small sounds came out of her throat, like a small dog trying to gargle. The man did not move.

Finally, her voice high and breaking, she asked, "Who are you and what are you doing here?" *Great defense tactic, Carmine! I'm sure he is going to identify himself and then tell you that he is here to rape you, harm you, take your money, and whatever else appeals to him.*

Carmine felt behind her for the base of the small lamp on the table near her bed.

"Oh my dear Carmine, you are not going to need that lamp where you're going," came a softly whispered response in somewhat of an English accent. "Forget it."

With a loud, belligerent voice laced with acute fear that made her sound shrewish, a tone she had been trying to rid herself of for years, Carmine shrieked, "Who do you think you are and what are you doing here?"

"Carmine, Carmine, don't you recognize me?" The reply sounded almost distressed. "I've been with you all your life and on a few occasions, you have even seen me. I'm your Guardian Angel, Laurence."

Carmine started giggling. She knew it was stupid because the guy could attack her at any moment, but she couldn't help herself. Not only did she have a man in her bedroom, but a crazy one at that.

"No, Carmine, I'm not crazy."

Now he was reading her thoughts!

Carmine felt her body become hot. She felt rivulets of perspiration form especially on her face and the fear became more crushing and intense. She crossed her arms and hands tightly over her chest as though protecting herself.

Carmine shook her head, tightly closed her eyes, clenched her teeth, and then opened her eyes again. He was still there.

Then it came to her. Of course, she was having a lucid dream. Carmine just had been reading about these types of dreams. People were actually dreaming, but awake enough to recognize that it was a dream and allow it to run its course.

Carmine felt her body slump with relief as she exhaled her breath. *I'll just wake up and everything will be back to normal.*

"No, Carmine, you're not having a lucid dream. Carmine, look at your bed. Who do you see in it?" The man's face was kind, but his implication was horrifying.

Carmine faced the bed and started shaking. She was in it. How could she possibly be in the bed and here, too? Her body felt the same as she uncrossed her arms and felt surreptitiously up and down her arms and legs. She looked in the dresser mirror, moving her head from side to side, lowering and raising it. No image appeared! She went rigid with fear and felt so hot she had to stop herself from removing her nightgown.

"Carmine, Carmine, don't be frightened. You're out of your body. It's time to go home! I am here to escort you. Really, Carmine, I'm your Guardian Angel, Laurence."

"What do you mean, 'home?'" She leaned towards him, her teeth bared as if to attack. With her hands back protecting her chest, she snarled, "This is my home, you brute, and if you don't get out of here right now, I'll … I'll … call the police. Go! Get out of here! Get, go, go get!" Her mind urgently searched for anything that would convince him to leave.

Almost hyperventilating, she finally spit out, "Or you'll be sorry."

Somehow that was not the threat she had hoped for.

And then she thought of what else he said. "What do you mean, out of my body?" Carmine whispered.

"Carmine, you know that headache you had for the last two days? Well, it wasn't so much a headache as an aneurysm in your brain and it ruptured last night. You've actually left your body."

"Left my body?" Carmine became a statue, hardly breathing, thinking of the implications. "You mean that ah, ah, ah I'm DEAD?"

"Where I'm from, we don't consider you dead, Carmine. We call it a transition from one reality to another. Technically, you are still you. You haven't changed. But the world you have lived in, space and time, have changed. That's all.

"Look at your bed, Carmine. Your body is still there. But how you feel, think, and act are still you. You have just changed from one form of life to another. Don't you still feel like yourself?"

"Oh, God, please help me." Carmine couldn't follow everything Laurence was saying, but what she did comprehend was absolutely terrifying.

Carmine, now shivering, wrapped her arms around her chest for warmth, fell heavily on the carpet, and sobbed softly.

"This is the absolutely the worst dream I have ever had. And I can't wake up."

In a shaky, but belligerent voice, Carmine lashed out, "Listen, what I discussed two weeks ago in a hypothetical conversation about what happens when anyone dies is one thing. It's another thing to have it happen when you're only 37 years old and about to start the life you always wanted. And I have a daughter who needs me. I can't believe I'm having this conversation." She started hammering the rug with her fists. "I hate you. This can't be happening. No, no, no!"

Carmine looked up with one eye closed and the other tentatively open, hoping that he would have disappeared.

It didn't work. He was still there.

"Look, Carmine, it's time to take you to the Director. We've wasted a lot of time. I wanted to do this a little differently from the usual routine. I thought with your spiritual background you would understand more than the others. I thought you would want to be aware of what was happening as you made your transition, and would be appreciative."

Laurence sighed, closed his eyes and shook his head. "The Director said I was making a big mistake, but I was convinced that you would be different. So I made the choice to have you conscious during the process."

Carmine became quiet. Her breath was very slow and she felt herself very calm. It seemed he was making sense.

If what he said really happened and she was dead, then what was taking place was actually what she had always thought would occur when death came.

Carmine didn't know what questions she should ask first. "Who is the Director? Wasted time? What does that mean? Usual routine? Why, me?"

Lancelot? Leonardo? Leonard? Something with an "L". What did he say his name was? Carmine asked herself as she opened her mouth to ask the questions.

"Trust me, Carmine; your questions will be answered in good time. But we are really late and I need to have you where you are supposed to be now." There was a flash of bright, white light and a swooshing noise that made her stomach feel as though she was on a Ferris wheel just before it goes down from the top. She closed her eyes, gritted her teeth and screamed.

Chapter Two

When Carmine opened her eyes, there was the most ethereal, pastoral scene she had ever seen in her life. Or her last life, she noted, as she breathed a heavy sigh. She saw she was standing on a small hill before what seemed to be a tiny, very white English cottage with green vines and rambling pink and red small roses entwined around the structure.

The cottage was surrounded with thick, green grass and a variety of flowers and trees growing in great and wild profusion. The foliage burst forth in the most intense, glorious colors – magenta, cerise, tangerine, rose coral, crocus, lilac, fuchsia and nuances of colors that Carmine had never seen before.

At the bottom of the hill was a small lake that reflected the sky, making the water a kaleidoscope of muted, soft rainbow colors of blue, white and sunshine. The air was filled with the scent of the flowers and the warm air caressed her face. Melodious music of bells, harps and what seemed like hundreds of the sweetest heart-wrenching violins drifted from the cottage.

Carmine forgot the emotional pain of her death and, to her amazement, and, seemingly without her will, one foot took a step, with her other foot following, then another until she found herself gracefully swaying to the music's compelling rhythms.

"It's like a scene from a fairy tale," she told herself. She stopped suddenly, looked down at herself and realized that she was still wearing her old heavy cotton nightgown. It had small holes in it and stain spots from when she had cooked food in it. Thankfully, it had long sleeves and at least covered her. It was even white. How appropriate! Carmine just laughed at herself and thought of it as Angel attire. She should've been embarrassed, but wasn't!

Carmine stopped dancing and started rubbing at a few of the many dirty spots that were sprinkled on the nightgown. *There is no way I could feel this way on Earth. It should be bothering me and, instead, I'm just accepting it. Very strange!*

"Don't stop, Carmine! I enjoy seeing you dance and I'm glad you like the music. And don't worry how you are dressed, it makes no difference here," said a voice.

Startled, Carmine turned around, and there he was. She had temporarily forgotten about him with all the other distractions. She couldn't think of him as any name, well, except, the "brute." Thinking of him as, as Lancelot, Luigi . . . or was it Laurence? Yeah, Laurence! Her Guardian Angel? It was all too frightening.

Seeing Laurence reminded her of the despair and hopelessness she felt earlier. She started angrily to demand to be returned to Earth immediately, but she stopped suddenly when she really looked at him.

He was very tall—definitely the size of a very, very tall basketball player. *The Lakers could really use him the way they were playing lately, especially without Kobe Bryant!* His hair was long, blonde, and almost white. His skin was very smooth and seemed almost translucent. But his large, hypnotic eyes were what held her attention. They were a deep, deep luminous turquoise, almost like a mirror, and she felt he could see right through to her soul. No matter what she said or her tone of voice, his eyes radiated such love and understanding she was almost ashamed of herself. And she felt such peace and comfort in his presence.

Laurence's expression duplicated the pictures of spiritual icons such as Buddha or Christ that were done by the revered artists of history and he had such a melodious tone to his voice when he spoke, but with a very soothing English accent. He was dressed in something that looked like a combination of a Karate outfit and a sweat suit. It was all of a creamy white color with the same color sash around his waist.

"That's the way you are supposed to feel, Carmine. Being at peace is the most wonderful feeling in the world."

"So you can read my mind, aren't you clever?" as she tossed her hair and gave a haughty shrug. "But if you don't tell me why I am here and why this happened to me I am going to do something really desperate. And if I remember right, you are my Guardian Angel!"

"Everything will be explained to you, Carmine. Have patience."

"If God had wanted me to have patience, he would have given it to me. I don't have patience; never have!"

"Carmine, Carmine calm down! I don't know how many times I have told you that in your last life. But it never seemed to help. I really feel I've let you down." Laurence heaved a great sigh, heavy with sadness.

"I'm confused. What do you mean, 'in my last life?'"

"I have been with you since you were born into your last life. I was with you at every moment and I always tried to help you."

"Oh, yeah! How come you didn't help me when I married that jerk I was married to for two years? And what about the time that I took the 'job from hell?' And what about the time...?"

"Carmine, Carmine! I did try to help you before you got married. The night you became pregnant, I tried to stop you from going to him. Remember when you had the flat tire on your red Volkswagen? But you were so intent on seeing him that you 'borrowed' your parents' BMW." A small knowing smile played around Laurence's mouth. "Remember, you got into trouble with your parents because you took their car without permission and you also got pregnant. Then you decided you had to marry him. It was your choice. I could only do so much." Laurence shrugged his shoulders and sighed.

"Wait a minute, you could've stopped me. Angels are supposed to have all that power and magic."

"Oh, no, Carmine. You have free will! We can't stop you from doing what you want. We can try to influence you, but we can't decide for you. That's what life on Earth is all about! And I've done everything I can within my Guardian Angel's Code of Ethics to help you. But you don't listen very well, Carmine. You're so intent performing your will instead of God's." Laurence heaved another heavy sigh.

Carmine heaved a sigh of impatience at Laurence's reaction and continued asking questions.

"Hey, you just said I had free choice. So why can't I do my will?"

"You have free choice but it should always be in conjunction with your highest good, which is God's will. That's what Guardian Angels are for! To help you clearly see that your will and God's will are in harmony."

Carmine curled her upper lip so high it showed all her teeth and snarled, "This is a bunch of you-know-what! What am I waiting for? Where are we going? And, by the way, where am I? If you're my Guardian Angel, then you reverse this dying episode and return me to my life. I insist!" She tried to give him her most powerful look. "Immediately!"

Laurence shook his head and sighed loudly. "Carmine, Carmine what you call 'your life' has just changed. Right now, you are outside of what we call the Designation Cottage where it will be decided what your next step will be on your spiritual path. What that will be depends upon your behavior in your last life as well as how much spiritual knowledge you gained and earned during that lifetime."

At that moment, the cottage door opened and out came a tall woman dressed almost the same as Laurence. The only difference was the woman wore a crimson sash around her waist and appeared to have long, floating, blond-white hair that was draped in a loose bun at the nape of her neck.

The music that Carmine had been hearing became louder and Laurence raised his hands together to eye level as in a prayer pose. He bowed slightly. "Peace to you, Mother." The woman mirrored his pose and bowed to him.

"She's your mother?" Carmine looked intently at Laurence. "I thought there was a resemblance."

Laurence tried to hide a smile, and then started chuckling quietly, bursting out in loud laughter.

"No, Carmine, that is what she is called. She is not my mother. The title 'Mother' describes all the attributes that an Earth mother is supposed to have; love, compassion, sympathy, sensitivity, forgiveness and the ability to listen to what is really meant instead of hearing words! She gives the unconditional love and understanding that all mothers are created to give. The same qualities that you give to your daughter. She's to assist those of you who pass through here in their transition from one reality to another."

"Carmine," Mother said. "You have had a very messy transition, which is Laurence's doing." Her voice was so melodious, so commanding and compelling that Carmine stood transfixed, not entirely understanding what the woman said. It stopped Carmine from saying anything more. Though at the mention of Laurence, Carmine was ready to castigate him for his role in the chaos she was feeling.

Instead, Carmine started crying again and couldn't stop. Everything was suddenly very clear. She was dead. She was going to be assigned to a level of consciousness in this reality that she had earned in her current Earth lifetime and this was someone to guide her in that journey.

"Carmine, you are much more knowledgeable than most people about the transition between your Earth life and this life. You studied about it and practiced many of the concepts that are done here. So, why are you so upset?" Mother queried kindly.

"Because it is not my time!" Carmine burst out, holding back her tears. "If you are really here to help me, then please let me go back to Earth and my life," Carmine begged with her hands in prayer. "I can't die now; it's the wrong time. I was just beginning to live the life that I should've lived eighteen years ago. I just know you made a mistake."

"No, Carmine, we have not made a mistake. As you can see, the dates are very exact." As Mother was speaking, what seemed like an enormous computer screen arose between them. The screen highlighted Carmine's name and a date beside it.

Carmine looked. But, as she looked closely, she noticed there were two dates; the second one was under the first one and was not highlighted, but was for forty-five years later.

"Then how come there are two dates here? I can't die twice, even in this reality. Huh? Huh?" she asked, with her hands on her hips, pouting vehemently. Carmine swallowed hard, knowing how audaciously she was behaving—with Angels no less. But she couldn't seem to stop herself. And where was Laurence, HER Guardian Angel, when she really needed him? Carmine frantically looked around. Why didn't he support her? When her eyes found his, she saw him frowning and shaking his head, mouthing the words, "No, no, no!"

Mother looked too and a frown also appeared between her eyes. "I'm not quite sure about this, but there is a very obvious explanation. Some research needs to be done and I'll speak to the Director. Stay with her Laurence," and she immediately disappeared, leaving Carmine staring at the computer, mesmerized by the two dates and the implications of what they meant.

She was jolted back to the present when Laurence started speaking to her, "Carmine, your behavior with Mother was appalling. I can't believe . . . ."

Before he could reprimand her further, she started an angry barrage of questions. "Why did you take such a risk with me? What were you thinking of? How could you be so stupid and do this to me? Why aren't you helping me more?"

Laurence winced as though he had been hit with a sledge hammer. "I – I wanted to see if an Earth human who has read and researched about what to expect when it left the Earth plane could make the transition without going through the usual ritual."

Laurence was looking everywhere except at Carmine, picking imaginary lint from various parts of his robe and speaking quickly. "And I know you so well. After all I've been with you since . . ."

"You made an experiment of me?" Carmine's voice was so shrill and loud, she was sure it could be clearly heard on Earth. "I'm here because you wanted to see what would happen?" Her eyes glared with anger and her chin jutted as she pointed and waved her finger at him.

"Listen, you, you, you simpleton! If you were working for me, you would be fired with no unemployment benefits because you didn't follow the darn rules. How did you ever get this job? And where do I complain? And …"

"Carmine, Carmine, you're out of control again. You were supposed to make your transition today, or die, as you call it. I didn't change any of that. I just changed the way it is usually done." Laurence was puzzled by Carmine's reaction. After all, she considered herself enlightened.

"Unbelievable, Laurence. Just change me back to the Earth plane as you call it. And then leave me alone for the rest of my time there. With an Angel like you, I hardly need the devil. I can't believe any Angel with the name of Laurence could be such an incompetent, uh, uh…" Carmine couldn't think of a name strong enough to call him. "You are the antithesis of an Angel," she finally sputtered out.

And before she even knew what was happening, she burst into tears once again. Leaning on Laurence, Carmine sobbed pitifully into his arm.

"Oh, Laurence, I can't believe this is happening. I'm so sorry. I know I shouldn't blame you and my behavior is abominable, but how would you feel if everything you lived for was going to start tomorrow and then it's taken away from you?"

Before Laurence could reply, Mother appeared. She was accompanied by another very tall Angel with the same Karate-sweat suit. His differed from the others because he was wearing a heavy gold satin sash around his waist and was more regal in his bearing, but had the same long white hair and luminous turquoise eyes as Laurence. But besides the love and peace emanating from them, there was such compassion, understanding and kindness. He bowed to Carmine with the same hand posture the others had used and Carmine bowed back. But this Angel didn't seem as approachable as Laurence and Mother. Carmine was not afraid, but certainly she would not think of yelling at him as she had at Laurence.

"This is the Director, Carmine," Mother said.

Carmine surreptitiously wiped her nose and eyes with the sleeve of her nightgown. Holding Laurence's hand tightly, she sniffed herself into an upright position facing the Director.

Seemingly not to notice Carmine's appearance or behavior, the tall Angel said in a kind, very low, tenor voice, "Carmine, it seems as though there has been a small mistake. And, of course, we will correct it, if it is possible. However, it depends upon the answers that you give me now. So, let's . . ."

"I knew there was a mistake," Carmine interrupted. "I knew I shouldn't be here. Laurence just needs to take me back. Come on, Laurence," as she beckoned to him with a wave of her hand. Laurence was trying to quietly shake his head and again mouthed the words, "no, no." He was covertly waving his hand, signaling Carmine to stop.

"Just a moment" the Director's voice commanded. Carmine took a step backward and with a bowed head, immediately stopped her agitation.

"I said a slight mistake. What happens, whether you stay or go back, depends upon your answers. You see, the last time you were here, you were absolutely outraged that your life had ended at that particular time. Actually, your behavior was about the same as it is now," he said with an amused, kind smile.

Carmine bowed her head again and felt her face become very red. She opened her mouth to defend herself, but the

Director continued speaking. "But before I explain what happened then, I need to tell you what previous lifetimes led to this peculiar dilemma."

"Previous lifetimes?" Carmine's eyes became very wide. "Then it's really true that we reincarnate life after life." Carmine was talking to herself, forgetting everyone else. "There were so many people who ridiculed that belief. I was pretty sure, but, you know, it's nothing that you can prove. I mean . . ."

"CARMINE!" Laurence's frustrated voice brought Carmine out of her reverie, back to where to where she was. "The Director is speaking to you! Pay attention!" Laurence hissed. Carmine glanced out of the corner of her eye at Mother, who was shaking her head at Carmine but with an understanding smile on her face.

"I'm so sorry, Director." Carmine bent her head in apology, but scowled at Laurence when she looked up and mouthed an "I'm sorry" to Mother.

"Let's talk in Earth terms, Carmine." The Director seemed impervious to both Carmine's behavior and Laurence's interruption.

"Twenty lifetimes ago, in a place which you now call China, you ended your life by your own hand, which is absolutely forbidden as you violated the contract you committed to and you still had work to do before returning here. The consequences don't end when you step out of your body. A body is only on loan for the person to use during its lifetime.

"The body is like an automobile that you use on your planet. You use the automobile to transport you from place to place, but it is not you. When the auto wears out, you buy another automobile, which is not necessarily the same type of auto you had previously. But you are still you. You don't change just because the automobile has changed, no matter what type of automobile you use for transportation.

"The soul, which is the true you, uses the body in the same way that you use an automobile. It houses the soul and uses the body only as a vehicle for the soul's journey through a specific lifetime. The type of body given you depends on many complex components having to do with your past lives, your next lifetime and so on.

"When you leave here to enter another lifetime, you make a spiritual contract or curriculum, as we call it, with yourself that includes the spiritual lessons you need to learn in that particular time. It specifies what you want to accomplish and when you should return here. Then, that contract is approved or revised by a Council of higher souls."

Carmine looked like a marionette as she kept opening and closing her mouth, trying to interrupt the Director. But furtive glances at Laurence stopped her, as the look on his face warned, "Don't you dare!"

The Director, giving no reaction to Carmine's conflict, continued.

"However, should an individual take his or her own life before the contract is completed, then each time the soul must return for another twenty lifetimes as a penalty."

"Ah, ah, ah!" Carmine placed her hands on her throat hoping that would help get the words out. It didn't. She then opened her mouth very wide along with her eyes. No words. Finally, in a voice that did not seem to come from her, it was so emotional, Carmine hoarsely whispered, "I would never take my life. It's just something I would never do. I have always tried to live a spiritual life. Not that it was perfect, but certainly I did the best I could." Mother nodded when Carmine spoke, as though agreeing with her.

Carmine put her hands on her head, closed her eyes and then shook her head. With a more confident and stronger voice, she said, "No, I still think you have made a mistake."

"I'm not finished speaking, Carmine," the Director said kindly. "There is much more. May I continue?"

Carmine, too upset to be mortified by the soft reprimand, nodded her assent.

"Yes, Carmine, you have learned your lesson. You would never take your life, again. However, in your last lifetime there was an accident. You were drowning and Laurence thought you were taking your own life again. So, instead of waiting to see what would happen, he had you make your transition at that time. He thought it would look as though it was your scheduled time to leave your body.

"It really was an accident and you would have been saved. You still had a few years to live on Earth before you were supposed to return here and you did return earlier than you were scheduled.

"So it was decided that, in this current lifetime, you would not leave until you accomplished all that you contracted to do and there would be no further imposed penalties.

"This is where the error occurred. The first date was the one that you were originally scheduled to return, that should have been deleted, and replaced by the second date. But for some reason the first date was never removed. Hence, you are here now."

"So, it was Laurence's fault? Laurence, how could you do that to me?" Carmine wailed with her hands on her hips.

Turning to the Director with a questioning look, Carmine said, "What an incompetent Angel. How was I so unlucky to get him for all these twenty lifetimes?"

"When a soul doesn't fulfill its curriculum for the current lifetime, then the Guardian Angel feels responsible for that and agrees to stay with the soul until it has completed its twenty lifetimes. So the Angel remains with the soul until the soul learns its lesson.

"Laurence was penalized for your last lifetime fiasco and has been working hard to learn that lesson. He had to retake and pass many of his Guardian Angel classes, which are extremely difficult. He also could not be promoted to the next level of Guardianship until you finished the twenty lifetime penalty."

Carmine glared at Laurence as the Director spoke. However, Laurence refused to look at Carmine and seemed very intent on either examining his fingernails in minute detail or staring at something of great interest in the distance, although his face was now a unique color of red.

"Serves him right! When I think what I could've accomplished in this lifetime, if I had only. . ." Carmine felt tears of frustration fall on her face as she thought of the life she had just lost.

"Ahem, Carmine. May I have your attention, please?"

Carmine gulped and nodded.

"Now, because of this date error, you are here once again. And before we can make decisions on what to do with you, I need to ask you some simple questions. May I do that?"

Carmine seemed to have the same feelings she had in her human form because she felt dejected, weary and angry. "Do I really have a choice?" she asked herself bitterly.

"Yes."

Chapter Three

The Director asked Carmine to be seated. Three tall golden chairs appeared immediately in front of the cottage, with high backs and what appeared to be very deep thick cushions. When Carmine sat, she became as high as the Angel, even though she was much, much smaller.

The Director noticed her puzzlement and explained, "No one here is to feel intimated or not equal to the rest of us. The cushions automatically adjust themselves to the correct height.

"I'm going to ask you some questions regarding the spiritual contract that you made when you started your current life. I want you to answer yes or no. Do you think you can do that?"

Why does he think I can't do that? Does he think I'm stupid? Carmine thought, but answered, "Well, of course."

"One of your main priorities was to guide individuals, not in the flamboyant or high profile manner that you did in one of your previous lifetimes, but in a way that would guide them living their day-to-day life. You wanted to motivate humans, to understand their uniqueness and help them attain their contractual agreements."

"I've always liked helping people . . ."

"No, Carmine, remember, you have to answer yes or no to the questions and I haven't finished."

Carmine closed her eyes and sighed with irritation. *This is becoming ridiculous. Angel or not, big mucky muck Director. Just get on with it!* All types of caustic remarks were going through Carmine's mind, but she just replied with a fake smile, "Okay."

"I know this seems slow to you Carmine, but you need to understand how important these questions are."

Carmine gave what she now hoped was a sweet, accepting smile, but the glower from Laurence made her feel she hadn't succeeded. She glowered back! He shook his head. She silently mouthed the words, Help me! He closed his eyes and pretended he didn't see her.

"Carmine! Laurence! Stop it."

"Now, the first question. Have you helped humans in the way that was just described to you?"

"Huh, mmmm, hummm. Well, I've been in human resources for most of my career and, many times, employees would come to me with problems about their personal lives. I would do all I could to respond to their needs and give them assistance."

"Not quite as she was supposed to," Laurence responded. "She did help many, many individuals with her suggestions or encouragement or advice, when they asked and sometimes unbeknownst to her, just by being there at the right time has been helpful to many. But she became sidetracked when her daughter was born. Her daughter wasn't originally scheduled to be born until several years later. As a result, Carmine couldn't do what she had promised herself to do, at least not to the great extent that she had contracted for."

"So, Laurence, is the answer No?"

"Wait a minute," Carmine interrupted with a rude tone, "what does he have to do with it? This is my contract, my life and I decide what I have accomplished."

"Not exactly," the Director admonished. "You see, each Guardian Angel is very much a part of a human's life. The Angel is there to help humans accomplish their contracts and to guide and lead them. Laurence must be very objective in his evaluation of your life because he is also evaluated on how he did with his responsibilities."

"You have helped, very much, Carmine, but not in the specific way you contracted to. That's because you had your daughter and you couldn't do what you had planned to do, so you fulfilled only part of your contract." Laurence gave Carmine a tender, compassionate look of understanding.

"I could argue with you, but obviously your word is better than mine," Carmine sniffed.

"Carmine," the Director said her name kindly, but with authority. "Don't allow your feelings to stand in the way. This is strictly an objective evaluation.

"Another part of your spiritual contract was to love and find what you humans call your soul mate. What that means is someone who is not only your friend, mentor and lover, but makes a commitment to you, as you do to him, to give loving support in all areas of each other's lives; emotionally, physically, mentally, and spiritually. There is an attunement in all these areas, but the basic one is to realize each person's soul potential and to search for God together. Soul mates are also together to help each other find their true path in the current lifetime. Did this happen?"

"God, no," Carmine replied. And then caught herself with a grimace. "Oops! Sorry, I didn't mean to phrase it that way. But the jerk that I married was the farthest thing from a soul mate one could find. Talk about a spiritual path! The only things he ever worshipped were his companies and the money they generated. You sure helped there, Laurence," Carmine said with disgust.

"Carmine," the Director said with a slight impatience in his voice, "you must answer these questions either yes or no. And stop blaming Laurence. He was just your Guardian Angel. He didn't make your decisions, you did. Take responsibility for your actions. There were many components that went into that marriage. You had an old Karmic debt to pay that soul and you did. Now that is over!"

"You did not find your soul mate, then, Carmine? Correct?"

Carmine, with apparent impatience, replied. "Yes, that is correct."

"Now what about love to others and yourself? Have you given the type of love that benefits and assists others so that they are confident, joyful and feel strong enough so that they can go forward in life? Have you helped others in ways that they could fulfill their spiritual contracts? And most important, have you loved yourself?"

"I'm not sure about love to others. I mean I love Cassie and I loved my parents and relatives, but maybe not so much others. And there are so many things I don't like about myself, that it has been really hard to love me. So maybe the answer to both of those questions is no.

"But I have done volunteer work; lots of it. I've worked with individuals and groups preparing them in all areas helping them to find jobs and to meet any other needs they might have in the workplace. And I volunteer three or four nights a month feeding the homeless. But I am not sure about helping them to fulfill their spiritual contracts." Carmine wrinkled her forehead as she pondered the question.

"Laurence?" the Director asked.

"She is correct about the first two questions, Director, the answer is no. But she has truly helped a few individuals achieve their spiritual contracts. Of course, not as many as she had planned, but some."

"You also said you would help a specific soul to find its path in its current lifetime; one that would enhance humanity. Have you done this?"

"Director, I can't answer that."

"Actually, Director, she has. It was her daughter. Her daughter is on her way to becoming a very fine artist, which she wouldn't have done this lifetime if it wasn't for Carmine. And her art is going to enhance humanity and the world!"

"You mean Cassie is going to be a great artist? I always knew she was talented. I gave her art lessons as soon as I became aware of her interest. This is great! Fantastic! I'm so happy. Thank you, thank you, Laurence." She threw him a joyful kiss.

Carmine hugged herself with delight and made small happy noises with that revelation while Laurence tried to send her a silent message warning her not to interrupt the Director.

"So, that's yes?" the Director confirmed, with Laurence nodding in agreement.

"Now this question is very important, Carmine, so please answer it as accurately as possible. Did you take pleasures in the beauty of Earthly life? For example, did you really see the beauty and brilliance in all the flowers and trees? Did you truly look at the sky at its most magnificent moments with its changing colors; or at sunset, when the sky is streaked with radiant hues? Did you stop when you saw rainbows and delight in that phenomenon? Did you smell the grass after a rain and walk in the sand by the ocean, or walk in the mountains in the crisp clear air, seeing the splendor of the forest vegetation and the animals that dwell there? Did you delight in each day with its unique gifts and changing beauty to savor and enjoy?"

Carmine felt herself become flushed and bent her head, as though she could hide from the answer. She heaved a big sigh, took a huge breath and blurted out, as fast as she could, every excuse she could think of.

"Director, I tried many times to take a quick look. But between working and raising a daughter and all the other activities needed just to maintain a home, time was scarce. And after I was divorced for the first two or three years, my ex-husband was very slow on child support or didn't pay any and I had to work two or three jobs. And then there was technology and that was a huge time user; e-mails, social media, computer crashes, webinars . . . It never stopped.

"Then there are more people and more lines for everything now, so you have to wait more and the freeways are a mess because there are always more people using them, again adding extra time to the day. And I was always on the phone or writing letters to my HMO because of Cassie's health, and was constantly fighting with them about something, almost every month. I had to squeeze in exercising and making sure I recycled, voted, and, anyway . . . there just wasn't any time for those kinds of things. I really tried and did some of those things, but not as much as I wanted. But I tried, honest!" Carmine said with her last ounce of breath, slumping down in her chair, relieved of the effort it took to answer the simple question.

As Carmine was speaking, the Director's face went from serene and composed to one that seemed to be struggling in holding back a great deal of laughter. His face was red and he placed his hands over his mouth by the end of her recital of excuses.

He looked at her in a way that reminded Carmine of her father when he had caught her in one of her creative stories on the many occasions she disobeyed or rebelled against family rules she didn't agree with.

He seemed to compose himself. With an unreadable look on his face, he asked, "Laurence, what is your response?"

Laurence look embarrassed and simply said, "It was always the lowest of her priorities, Director. Everything else came first."

"So the answer is No?"

"Correct, Director."

Carmine gave Laurence a scathing look. *With friends like you, I don't need enemies.*

"Carmine, one of the reasons humans are on Earth is to take rest in the beauty that is there. Working is always very important in order to care for and feed the body, but your life on Earth is really of the soul; to enhance it by giving it opportunities to grow and learn so that it can complete the curriculum that it agreed to when entering that reality. This is one way of realizing your spiritual divinity and oneness with the Universe and God. Enjoying and savoring whatever Earth or nature has to offer takes you out of yourself and puts you in touch with your higher, loving essence."

"Not to make Laurence out to be embellishing the truth, being an Angel and all of that, but I did take time. If you look at the percentage of time that I had to use to work and do all the other maintenance chores, I am sure you would find that the percentage I spent equaled those of others who had more time." Carmine gave Laurence a smug smile, feeling she had successfully overcome the Director's criticism.

"Rubbish, Carmine, you can't use that kind of comparison. Everyone has the same amount of time. It's how you used it. This was part of your spiritual contract, which by the way, is in all spiritual contracts. It's one of the basic requirements for Earth life.

"So, in summary, Carmine has not really fulfilled most of her spiritual contract or curriculum. There is much left for her to do to accomplish her goals for this lifetime. Correct, Laurence?"

"That is correct, Director."

"Then, I think you, Mother and I need to talk about this situation with the Council."

Carmine waved her hands and arms in great agitation. "Hey everyone, stop. How about my input? After all, this is my life you're discussing and I think I can add some insight. After all . . .!"

"No, Carmine, this is not something you can negotiate!" And immediately after speaking to her, all three of them disappeared.

The music that had been playing in the background seemed to be more melodious and Carmine felt herself become very calm and serene; a feeling she seldom had in her Earth life. "Maybe being here is not that awful; maybe I should stay." She snuggled deeper in the gold chair and closed her eyes. "Why am I struggling? This is so much better than Earth."

Suddenly, the music stopped and she sensed activity around her. She opened her eyes and there stood Mother, the Director and Laurence.

The Three Musketeers. Carmine smiled at the thought.

"I'm glad we amuse you," Laurence said with a grin on his face.

Carmine felt herself blush. "Uh, it was just a thought! I forget you can read my mind."

"It's nothing to worry about, Carmine."

The Director began, "We have discussed and analyzed the situation with the Council. You have not fulfilled most of your spiritual contract, as you still need to meet your soul mate and assist others in achieving their potential. There are Earth people who need you and cannot go forward without you. But most of all, you have not taken the time to enjoy the true simple beauty and pleasures of Earth. You will live out the balance of your life as designated in the Record Book and you will be returning forty-five years hence. And, of course, Laurence will be with you."

"Oh, thank you, thank you Director and Mother," Carmine said with great excitement; "you have made the right decision. I have felt the peace and love that is here, but I really need to return."

"And to have my very own Angel. And what I'm going to be able to accomplish. It's limitless. And now that I know about this place and what really happens here, everyone on Earth will want to do better and . . ."

"Carmine, you don't understand," the Director said with a deep frown on his face. "When you return, you will not remember any of this. It will be like a dream that quickly fades upon awakening. Very few individuals are allowed to remember the transition."

"Wait a darn minute, Director, are you telling me I am not going to remember any of this? After you and Laurence bungling everything for the last <u>two</u> lifetimes, you're going to take this away from me?" Carmine's voice reached a pitch that it would have drowned out several running Harley motorcycles if they had been nearby.

Laurence interrupted, "Carmine, you are incorrigible! Please, remember where you are. You can't dictate to the Director. And besides, you should be pleased that you are going back."

"I need to be compensated for that last lifetime where I was returned here earlier than planned," Carmine said angrily, with tears in her eyes. "And for going through this mess this time. With so many screw-ups, you would think Government was in charge, not Angels!"

"How do you want to be compensated, Carmine? We are not in a court of law, like you have on Earth," the Director asked in a puzzled voice.

"I want to remember what happened here and I want to be able to talk and see Laurence. That is the least that you can do. This way I can help others better and assist them in understanding about dying and reincarnation and all the other spiritual bits and pieces that took me so long to learn."

"Carmine, that is not possible. First of all, individuals have to find their own path in seeking spiritual truths and each level of spiritual knowledge must be earned by the way the individuals live their lives. Secondly, what you have learned here cannot be shared with anyone unless the Council gives its permission, which it rarely does."

"Look, let's analyze this on an unemotional level," Carmine continued as though the Director had not spoken. "One, you shortened my life the last time around because of a mistake; your mistake, not mine. So, maybe if I had stuck around like I was supposed to, I would have done better in this lifetime.

"Two, this last lifetime you dragged me here; you made me go through this, this inquisition and, again, because of your mistake, not mine. As long as I am here and learned about these things, then I believe, most emphatically, that I have the right to take this hard-learned knowledge and apply it to the rest of my life. And think how it would help others to live a better life, because they will know how they live will affect their next life, which, by the way, will help me fulfill my spiritual contract."

"Carmine, I can see why you were what is called a 'lawyer' in one of your lives, you certainly can argue well."

"A lawyer," Carmine repeated to herself as she basked in the thought. "I always knew that I had some background in the law; in fact, sometimes, I thought of becoming a lawyer this lifetime."

"This needs some interpretation." Turning to Laurence and Mother, the Director nodded and then simply disappeared.

Carmine returned to her soft cushion. Serene and happy, she knew she was going to win. She just felt it and her intuition on Earth had always been very good.

Just as she closed her eyes, the trio returned.

"Carmine, we have taken your request to the Council and it has been decided that yes, you can have your compensation as you call it, but there are some restrictions and limitations."

"Yes!" Carmine clenched her fists in triumph and then gave her most gracious smile to the Director.

"First, you will be able to see and communicate with Laurence. This will help you facilitate your life and helping others. However, in no way, can you use Laurence to help you personally succeed, make money, or be famous or do any other intervention of that type. In other words, you cannot use him to enhance your life or anyone else's in any measurable way. You will be able to give assistance and aid in such a way that will help an individual to realize his or her potential. You can influence individuals and use Laurence's help in that way, but nothing else. In addition, you cannot interfere if it is someone's time to make the transition here. Is that understood?"

"I can't win the lottery through Laurence or become rich or famous or anything else. I get it, if I understand you right."

"Or help anyone else in that way, but yes, that's correct."

Carmine was disappointed, but thought it was probably in her best interest to agree. Maybe she could get around them when she got back to Earth.

"In addition, there are three other points that you must understand and acknowledge."

Carmine held her breath wondering how many more restrictions and rules she was going to have to live with.

"There may be a time when you will feel there is no more need for you to have Laurence available to you, as you now want him. It is your decision and you have permission to do that; it will have no repercussions. Laurence will then be returned to you as before you made this transition."

"I can hardly believe that I would let an Angel leave, but, okay."

"The second point is you will not be able to remember what date you will return here. That is information that no ordinary human should know or could handle well. Is that agreed?"

"Of course! It would really affect my whole life knowing when I'm going to die. I can't imagine anything worse. Knowing what a beautiful place this is compared to Earth, I know I will want to return, but not right now. Earth is my home, even though it has been so difficult living there with so many problems. But maybe I can make it a little bit better, just by knowing that there is a better place and I can give people hope."

"Yes, Carmine, here is a much better place to be than Earth. Earth is sometimes a very hard school; there is much to learn there. But you are doing well, so go back, my child, and do what you went there to do. With Laurence to guide you, you will fulfill your spiritual contract.

"The third point is that you cannot tell anyone about Laurence or anything about your experience here or what you have learned. This contract will immediately be suspended and the consequences to your life will change accordingly with severe penalties.

"You should also understand that Laurence may exhibit very human behaviors due to the different energy and vibrations of Earth that will impact him because of his visibly manifesting himself to you."

Carmine looked at all three of them, and nodded slowly, "I promise not to discuss my experience here with anyone and I understand about Laurence." She crossed her fingers behind her back and hoped she would be able to do it.

Then she asked, almost hesitantly, "What do you mean by consequences to my life and severe penalties?" As Carmine spoke, the Director looked at Mother and Laurence and there was an almost indiscernible nod from Mother.

Carmine started to become very sleepy. She started saying something about how nice it was to meet everyone and she had some more questions to ask, but it became very hard to articulate her thoughts. There was another swooshing noise and another round of a Ferris wheel whirling and everything went black.

PART II

Chapter One

Carmine awoke slowly and stretched and yawned. That was the deepest contented sleep she had ever had. It was absolutely delicious. She smiled and noticed the headache had disappeared.

Wow, that was quite a dream, I should write it down. It was definitely something to share with my support group.

She lay on the bed thinking about it when she glanced at the clock and noticed it was almost seven. "Seven o'clock," she screamed. "Today is the first day of school. What am I doing in bed?" She jumped hurriedly out of bed and ran into the bathroom to take a quick shower. "How am I going to get to school, find a parking space and my classroom all before nine o'clock?" she asked as she soaped herself. "I can't believe I slept that long."

Chastising herself for not getting up earlier, for sleeping through the alarm, and for sleeping so late, Carmine could always find a list of things to beat herself up about and make herself feel bad. It was a terrible habit and made her feel worse about herself. She had even worked with a therapist to try to overcome it. But she couldn't seem to stop criticizing herself when she fell short of her ideals. The negative self-talk was so debilitating. Her therapist had given her an exercise, which she called compassionate self-forgiveness that released and forgave any judgments against her that caused emotional upset. But it was an old habit and hard to break.

"This would be a good time to have an Angel nearby," she said aloud as she thought again about the dream. "Maybe he could give me a good hair day for once and ensure there is no heavy traffic for another."

"Is that what you need, Carmine? Stop reprimanding yourself when things don't go as you think they should. It only makes you feel bad. No one should do that to themselves."

Carmine felt the soap slip from her fingers as she fearfully turned around to find where the voice came from. She could see a form through the shower door. She very slowly opened it, ever so slightly, and peeked out.

There, all seven feet of him, stood Laurence.

She closed her eyes very tightly for a quick second; then opened them. He was still there.

"That wasn't a dream?" she whispered hoarsely. "It really happened?"

"Yes, Carmine. It really happened!"

"Couldn't you have given me a bit more notice and introduced yourself in a less shocking way? After all, I'm taking a shower and . . . Oh, my gosh, I don't have any clothes on!" she gasped. Bending down as low as possible to hide her body, she grabbed a towel from the floor and wrapped it around her. Her short wet hair was plastered on her head and she felt the steam from the shower waft around her body.

"You should at least have the decency to turn around," she snapped at him.

"Carmine, Carmine, your impatience again! Why do you always react with anger? I will never understand you, even after twenty lifetimes together."

Carmine started to defend herself against that remark when Laurence interrupted her and continued speaking. "Angels do not see humans in the same way as other humans appear to each other. We see the soul and the energy of a human—its essence. The body is just something that is wrapped around the soul. Almost the same way you are using that towel to cover your body. Whether a human is a male or female in each lifetime is decided based on its spiritual contract. If you give me permission, then I can see you as you appear to other humans."

Carmine just stood there motionless, with her mouth and eyes open wide. *Amazing! I am standing here, soaking wet, and he is telling me these incredible pieces of information that thousands of people would love to know and I understand everything he is saying.* She shook her head and just stared.

"Wait a minute," Carmine looked at him accusingly. "How come you appear to me as a male Angel? And I'm certainly not going to give you permission to see me as I am on Earth; at least not now."

"Because humans see each other as male and female. You see Angels in the same way."

Carmine closed her eyes. *This can't be happening. I am an intelligent, rational person who does not use drugs or any other type of stimulant that could be manufacturing this illusion.* Then she looked again. He was still there.

Finally, because there was nothing else she could do and she was becoming cold, she stepped out of the shower, with the towel still around her, picked up her white terry robe, turned her back and put on the robe. Whether he saw her as an entity or not, she was still a woman with a strange man in her bathroom.

"Can we go into the living room and talk more about this?"

"Of course, Carmine, but aren't you concerned about arriving at school on time? I know this is your first day and . . ."

"Yikes, school. I completely forgot about it. What am I going to do? My first class is at nine and if I'm not there, they'll give my place to someone on the waiting list," she said as she ran to her bedroom, shed the bathrobe, ran her hands through her damp hair and picked up the clothes she had waiting for her on her chair and hastily began to pull them on. Jeans and t-shirt on, she grabbed the jacket and tied it around her waist. Even though it was the end of August and very hot, she knew she would need it in the air-conditioned classrooms. Rushing back to the bathroom, fumbling through her makeup, she took another two minutes to slap on some moisturizer, sun screen, and a light layer of foundation and then applied mascara and lipstick. Amazingly, her hair had dried to a quite an attractive style. As late as she was, she paused and looked again.

"Wow! That has never happened! My hair looks great and I haven't even run a comb through it."

"Well, Carmine, you did ask for a good hair day, didn't you?"

Carmine had almost forgotten Laurence. But there he was, right there with her in the bathroom.

"You did this?"

"Yes, and if you will get into your car, I'll assist you in arriving on time to your class."

"Let me check my phone. I have a traffic app – it will tell me how bad traffic is." She hit the icon, typed in her destination and found that the traffic pattern was red going less than 12 miles an hour. Carmine moaned, "What am I going to do? I will never get to school on time."

"Carmine, go to your car! Now!"

Carmine ran to her large rolling burgundy backpack, which she had filled the night before with her books and all her essentials for the day. She adjusted the handle, snatched up her car keys, ran out of the condo with the backpack trailing behind her, locked the front door and bumped her way down the three flights of steps to the garage, feeling that was quicker than waiting for the elevator.

She opened the front door to her white Honda Accord and threw the backpack in the passenger seat. Simultaneously, sliding into the front seat, she started the engine and closed the door. As she backed out of the garage, she turned around to see if Laurence was there and he was, sitting in the front seat, holding her backpack.

"Can anyone else see you, Laurence?" she asked as she deftly made her way to the freeway.

"No, Carmine, just you."

Carmine felt herself inhale and exhale very deeply. This was going to be one unforgettable day as she looked at the car clock and saw that it was eight o'clock.

Chapter Two

Carmine reached the freeway on-ramp, which was a few minutes from her condo. Luckily, the light was green on the transition road to the actual freeway. "There is no way I can get to school on time," she said out loud, not expecting a response. "I can't believe I did this to myself on the first day of school."

"Carmine, don't continue to chastise yourself. I promise you that you will arrive at your class on time. Forgive yourself for the error, even though the error is more about your interpretation. It happened. You are always too hard on yourself. Humans seem to think they should be perfect, but it is irrational. You can strive for excellence, but don't judge yourself. Even Angels are not perfect 100% of the time, so how can you humans expect it of yourselves?"

"Laurence, I'm not up for a philosophical discussion at this time of the morning," Carmine's voice was so loud that Laurence put his hand to his ears. "Just help me to be on time when my first class begins, please!"

"Carmine, haven't you noticed that the traffic is lighter than when you checked for traffic this morning?"

Carmine was so intent upon the time and trying to drive faster than the speed limit, while at the same time looking out for police cars that she hadn't noticed. But when she looked around at the other lanes and ahead of her, there were not many cars. *Maybe an accident occurred before I got on the freeway and all the traffic behind me is blocked.* She saw Laurence shake his head no.

"Are you telling me, Laurence, that you are responsible for this lack of traffic?" she asked incredulously.

"Well, even though I can't overtly interfere with other lives to help you with yours, I can influence the flow of vehicles. Hence, the light traffic."

"Oh, bless you, Laurence, I'm not even going to ask how you do it; I am just going to be grateful and keep my fingers crossed that we will arrive on time."

Carmine kept up her rate of speed, knowing that Cal State Los Angeles campus was only thirty minutes from her home in Studio City, on weekends, when traffic was considered minimal, at least for Los Angeles. On a Monday morning, even in a summer month, it would take at least forty-five minutes or more, plus the nightmare of finding a parking space. Though she had paid for reserved parking, so had everyone else. It was "first come, first to find the parking spaces." The prized parking spaces, of course, were the ones closest to the campus. These were always taken by the students who had the 7:00 a.m. classes, a time when Carmine would not even think about having a class.

Carmine had made a preliminary trip from her condo to the campus earlier in the month to know what to expect when school actually began. Knowing she had a 9:00 a.m. class meant that she could expect to park as far from the campus as possible and still be in a campus parking lot. It would take her at least twenty minutes to get to the campus and her classroom.

The traffic continued to be light as she turned off the ramp for the campus. "I'll head straight for the farthest parking lot; hopefully, there will be some spaces left yet." She glanced at her clock on the dashboard and gasped! It had only taken her 25 minutes to reach the campus. A true miracle!

She glanced at Laurence, sitting there with what she felt was a very smug smile on his face. As she was about to tell him that he shouldn't look that smug, at least for an Angel, he interrupted her.

"Carmine, don't go to that far parking lot. Turn in here, very quickly please."

"Laurence," she started to argue with him, "You think you're in Heaven because there is no way there is going to be a parking place there now. No one leaves school this early and opens a parking space."

"Carmine, turn right now and don't argue. You are the most stubborn human I have ever been assigned to."

The car turned quickly in the parking lot, almost without her help. She turned to Laurence, with her eyes flashing. "You realize that if I don't find a parking space, I'll be plenty late for my class and they will give my place away. If that happens, you are out of my life – zap, bingo, gone."

"Carmine, stop it. Look over there. Is that not a large enough space to park your vehicle?"

"It's probably a handicapped parking space," Carmine sighed, but looked anyway. Her eyes grew very large and she looked at Laurence out of the corner of her eyes. She felt her face grow hot because there was a perfectly good parking place a driveway away from the campus and close to where her first class started.

Laurence did not look her way. He started humming, to her incredulity, *Amazing Grace.*

"Okay, Laurence, I apologize," she said jeeringly. Then she changed her tone of voice and said humbly, "I do apologize, Laurence. Thank you for this space."

She grabbed her backpack from him, jumped out of the car and locked it. She forgot Laurence until she started running towards the Campus. *Oh, my gosh, did I leave him locked in the car?* She turned around to look and ran right into him.

"Are you following me?"

"Carmine, Carmine I am your Guardian Angel. I go everywhere with you and always have. You can simply see me now."

"This is not the time or place to have this discussion. I need to be in my class immediately," she snapped loudly at him. She noticed that people were looking at her and realized that no one else could see Laurence.

I must look so crazy! Maybe everyone will think I have a cell phone that they can't see. She put her hand up to her ear. *Anyway, it doesn't matter, this is Los Angeles. I won't seem all that strange,* she smiled at that comforting thought. *I must pretend that Laurence doesn't exist and totally block him out of my consciousness when I am with other people.*

Carmine mused on the impact that Laurence would have in her life now that she knew he existed, could speak to him and have him reply. Thinking about how different her life would be with an Angel beside her all the time made her dizzy, lightheaded and almost frightened. She was so focused on Laurence and what a difference he would make in her life, she missed her building and had to turn around, walk back and then run up the three flights of stairs to her classroom.

I am so grateful that I made a preliminary run last week. Otherwise I would still be looking for the building.

She reached her class at exactly nine o'clock. Glancing at the door to ensure that it indeed was the right room, English 102, she grabbed the first seat she could find and literally fell into it. *After everything that has happened to me in the last twenty-four hours, I can't believe I made it.* She whispered a prayer of thanks. And heard a voice say, "You're welcome!"

She looked up. Laurence was standing right beside her. "You, again! Go away," she hissed out of the corner of her mouth, hoping no one would see her. "I don't need you now."

"I'll stand behind you, Carmine, so you can't see me."

"Yes! Please do that quickly," Carmine said with her mouth moving as little as possible.

She noticed the woman seated next to her was looking at her very curiously. She smiled what she hoped was a sincere, welcoming smile and said, "Hi, my name is Carmine Craig. It took forever to get here and I guess I'm just talking to myself trying to get myself to relax."

"Hi, Leslie Lani."

And before Carmine could say another word, Leslie continued without, seemingly, taking another breath. "I know it sounds like a Hollywood name. My parents thought that as long as I was born in L.A., I might as well have a name that would look good on a marquee.

"And they had four boys before me and had their heart set on what they felt was a feminine name. Can you believe that? Actually, I really want to be an actress, but I thought I'd finish college, just in case. I'm majoring in Theater Arts, but this is a required course, so I have to take it. My boyfriend thinks I'm crazy to finish my degree, but I want to keep my options open. The teacher isn't even here yet!" Leslie finally paused to take a breath.

While Leslie was speaking, Carmine couldn't help staring at her. *She certainly could be an actress. She not only would look good on a screen but on any magazine cover, including Vogue or W, not to mention any of the sports magazines.* Besides being young, maybe nineteen or twenty, she had gorgeous thick dark brunette hair, the most wonderful flawless skin, a nose that Carmine would have happily traded her car for—straight, narrow, and very thin—and huge blue eyes surrounded with eyelashes that were so thick she wondered how she could see out of them.

And what Carmine could see of her figure was enough to make anyone stop and stare! Leslie seemed very tall seated in the desk with a nicely developed chest. But with all her beauty, she seemed very friendly and there certainly was nothing she was hiding from anyone. Carmine laughed quietly to herself. *I have learned more about Leslie in three minutes than I learned from some friends in six months.*

Just as Carmine was going to respond to Leslie, the teacher walked in. He was average in height, about 5′ 9″ but very well proportioned with large shoulders, on the husky side. His hair was a deep reddish brown, with strands of silver in it. His eyes were a blend of hazel and brown, surrounded by numerous laugh lines. His nose was in proportion to his face, but hooked somewhat; but, strangely, added to his appearance rather than distracted from it. His lips were full with a generous wide mouth that gave him a friendly, outgoing appearance and he had a small reddish beard growing around his lower jaw and chin. His overall countenance was that of a happy, relaxed person and the way he walked and presented himself immediately gained everyone's attention. Carmine thought he was very attractive. She had always been captivated by men with beards and red hair. As she was looking at him, a thought occurred that she had known him from somewhere, but she couldn't seem to make the connection. She shrugged the thought off, sat up in her seat and gave him her undivided interest.

He introduced himself as Jake Steiner, gave the usual preliminaries about how important the class was and what he expected. The list of expectations was going to require a lot of time. Looking around the class, Carmine realized she was definitely one of the oldest people there, with the exception of the teacher . . . maybe! *I should have taken this class years ago,* Carmine was angry with herself for not tackling this class sooner. *Not that I know everything about writing, but this is going to take a lot of time and I already write pretty well.*

"Carmine, why do you berate yourself like this. You did the best you could, as all individuals do, most of the time. Use compassionate self-forgiveness on yourself as you have been taught. Perhaps there is a higher reason for taking the class now instead of earlier, did you ever think of that? You are choosing to view life with a very narrow lens. When you look at the world as you feel it should be, and not as it is and form judgments about the mismatch, then you are limiting your interpretation of reality."

"I forgot about you, Laurence," she said snottily, trying to speak without moving her lips. "Just what I need is to have you reminding me all the time how and what to think."

"No, Carmine, I am not doing anything different. I am trying to help you revise the negative self-talk and reframe it into positive alternatives. Angels are always there giving encouragement."

As she was going to reply, she noticed Leslie looking at her again. She smiled quickly and said through closed teeth, "Scram, Laurence, I'll talk to you later."

Professor Steiner spoke about the assignments, the tests that would be given and what the due dates were. He took roll and, when her name was called, he paused and looked at Carmine for what seemed like forever. He smiled a smile that made the lines around his eyes crinkle and looked back to the roll sheet to continue calling roll.

He's probably wondering how much older I am than everyone here! This could be really depressing. Come, on, Carmine, stop it. Laurence is right. Be happy that you are here and can finish your degree this year. Be positive!

After giving a homework assignment, the teacher let everyone leave early so they could buy books if they hadn't and so he could help the students who still needed to enroll in the class if there was room and answer questions about the course work. Carmine and Leslie walked out together. As Carmine turned, she saw Professor Steiner looking at her, with a strange look on his face. Before she could comment, however, Leslie continued their earlier conversation as though there had been no interruption and Carmine forgot about mentioning it.

Well, I was right. She has legs as long as I am tall. Leslie was pretty close to six feet with a superb figure to match. *If she acts as good as she looks, she should get every part she auditions for.*

Leslie finally paused to take a breath and Carmine asked, "Leslie, how tall are you, if you don't mind me asking?"

"With or without my shoes?"

"Without."

"Five feet eleven and one-half."

"Has that ever bothered you? The reason that I would like to know is that I am so short and it bothers me. I was wondering how it feels from your standpoint."

Leslie grimaced. "Actually, it bothered me when I was in the sixth grade and was the tallest one in the school, including the boys. I was five feet nine inches and gradually added the other 2 ½ inches after that. But my parents were very supportive. They gave me dance lessons and a modeling course, which led to a modeling career for several years.

"But then my chest developed and I didn't have that many calls and I got bored. I never gave up dance—jazz and ballet are my passion. And, of course, acting. Right now, I do a lot of commercials. Usually background stuff. I'm going to be the greatest actor; that's my goal. To do theater; really great theater. And of course I'll do movies and TV, but only if I can do continue to do great theater. My boyfriend, Bart, says I am really stupid to do the theater. I should just go for the movies and TV."

Carmine realized that Leslie had mentioned her boyfriend often during the conversation, but always with some negative remark he had made. As far as Carmine could tell, he seemed to criticize many things she did or said. *Sounds like a creep.*

Laurence started saying something about her judgment, but Carmine gave him a look that stopped any comment he was going to say.

Carmine had some time before her next class. "Hey, Leslie, how about a something cool to drink from the cafeteria before the next class?"

"I have time. I'd love it!"

After getting their iced tea and finding a shady table to sit at outside, they both gave a sigh of pleasure to be able to relax a few moments.

"Tell me about your boyfriend, Leslie. Is this someone serious or what?"

"Oh, well, I'm not sure. It's serious to me. I don't date anyone else and he says he doesn't, but sometimes I wonder. But he is in the acting business, too. He works as a waiter at the Ivy in Beverly Hills. Makes lots in tips and is able to work in commercials. He just wants to make it big. Movies, TV, whatever there is. He has a great body and is really handsome. Girls are always drooling around him. I'm lucky he is interested in me."

"Gee, Leslie, I would think he would be lucky you are interested in him. You obviously have a brain, you're breathtaking beautiful and you have an incredible figure. Do you realize you said 'not sure' about him twice now? It sounds as though you are 'not sure' about this relationship."

Leslie blushed and Carmine realized she was in her Human Resources role and thinking of Leslie as an employee. She was analyzing a situation that really was none of her business.

"I'm sorry, Leslie, I apologize. I am somewhat opinionated and being older than you . . ." Carmine shrugged and stopped speaking.

"Oh, that's all right, Carmine. My family says the same thing. They think he takes advantage of me. You were pretty sharp to pick that up in the short time we've been together."

"It's part of my work, Leslie. I've been in the human resources field probably as long as you have been alive. After a while, you get instincts about a situation. It's the only way you can survive, using your gut or intuition, to be honest. And we all have it. Most people don't pay any attention to it. I picked up on something you said earlier about not being sure about Bart. Maybe that is your intuition speaking to you."

"Carmine, wow, I never thought of that. Guess I need to think about what it is trying to tell me."

"And do not forget about having your Guardian Angel to help you," Laurence whispered.

Carmine turned around quickly to see Laurence behind her, smiling. With all the distractions of the day, she had completely forgotten him. With Leslie right beside her, she couldn't say a thing, but glared instead.

"Is something wrong?" Leslie asked as she saw the expression of Carmine's face.

"I just remembered that I forgot to do something this morning that I needed to do. Oh, well, nothing I can do about it now."

"Look, I have to run to the bookstore before my next class. I'll see you in class next time. It's been great talking to you, Carmine. I hope we can do this again," Leslie said as she picked up her backpack.

"Me, too."

As soon as Leslie was out of sight, Carmine turned to Laurence. "I can't believe you spoke to me when she was right here. And in class with everyone around. Do you want everyone to think I'm crazy?"

"Well, Carmine, I think this is hard for both of us. We are not used to seeing each other and when we do, it becomes confusing for both of us. Remember, you can always change your mind about this arrangement where I would not be visible to you."

"Don't worry, Laurence, I will definitely manage! There's no way this arrangement is going to change. It's just a matter of adjusting and being flexible. Which, you know, I'm not that good at."

Carmine was watching how she spoke and who was around her. She needed to be careful. "Listen, Laurence, why don't we agree that you'll speak to me and I'll just listen. Then if I have any comments or need to talk to you, I can do it later or when there's no one around."

"Okay, let's try it, Carmine. This is new for me, too."

Carmine looked around again and found they were alone for the moment. She was too curious to wait for an answer to a question that had been shouting inside her mind. "Laurence, tell me. Were you the only Angel in the class or was everyone's there?"

"Each human always has an Angel by its side at all times. But whether the individual pays attention to the message of the Angel depends upon the spiritual level of that person. For instance, the more attention paid to the Angel's guidance, the easier it is for the Angel to be heard. And the more attention that is paid to each message, the clearer each succeeding message becomes. This manifests itself in what you humans call intuition. It is usually associated with an uncomfortable feeling or discomfort or something that makes the individual think about the decision that is going to be made. That is why some individuals seldom make errors in judgment; they are very highly attuned to their Angels' messages.

"But if a human does not pay attention to the Angel's guidance and continues to ignore the Angel's help, then the Angel's impact decreases. The messages become obscure no matter how loudly the Angel speaks. It is almost like the Angel is wrapped in a heavy material that can't be penetrated. Even though the Angel is giving guidance, the individual can't hear it.

"You humans have a saying 'Use it or lose it.' That is exactly what happens when a human ignores the Angel's help. Sometimes humans call it their conscience or they had a 'feeling.' It is very sad because the less attention that is paid to the Angel, the less help is received. Then when a human has a serious challenge and asks for help, it can't hear the answer, even though the Angel is guiding the human as usual.

"You have very good intuition, Carmine, because for the most part you listen and you listen to what your body is trying to tell you. Your meditation assists you significantly. Have you made the connection yet that when you meditate on a regular basis, your intuition is increased? Conversely, the less you meditate, the less intuitive you are?"

"I guess I would have if I had thought about it. But I haven't until now. It's certainly an incentive not to miss meditation!"

Carmine looked at her watch and realized that she was going to be late for her next class unless she ran. Laurence was proving to be a terrible distraction.

"The class is right over here," Laurence said, as she looked around. "You won't be late."

Carmine sprinted towards the building, with Laurence right behind her. She had managed to have all her classes on the same days so she could handle her work life efficiently. She had a regular schedule with all her consulting clients, which she loved. In addition to the English class, Carmine was enrolled in Principles of Marketing and a Business Communications class. She had taken the easier classes this quarter so she could adjust to the school environment. However, next quarter she had to take her final required courses, Business Statistics and Business Finance; classes she was dreading and loathing. Numbers intimidated her to the point of nausea. But if she wanted to have her Bachelor of Science Degree in Business Administration she had to take those courses.

Oh, well, like Scarlett, Carmine thought as she ran to her next class, *I'll worry about it tomorrow.*

Carmine went through the next two classes without meeting another classmate and certainly the instructors didn't look at her as the English teacher did.

There seemed to be more older, or mature students. I didn't feel that I was the oldest one, which is nice. It gives me a feeling of belonging, she thought as she walked to her car.

"I'm exhausted," she said to herself as she flopped into the hot car. And almost flopped out of it when she sat down, the seat was so hot.

"Careful, Carmine, you forgot to put the window protector up this morning."

With all the activities, excitement and anxieties about starting school and keeping his promise to stay out of her eye range, Carmine had again forgotten about Laurence.

"I can't believe that I forget about you. It has been a day," Carmine sighed. "Laurence do something to traffic so

I spend a minimum amount of time on the road. I'll bless you for that."

"I think I can honor that request, Carmine."

Carmine turned to say thank you and her eyes and mouth became very wide. "Laurence," trying to suppress her giggle, "what are you wearing?" He no longer was wearing his white Karate attire, but had changed to a gold jersey with the numbers 888 on the shirt and matching gold shorts.

Turning a slight color of red, Laurence put his head down a little when he replied. "Well, you said something about playing with the Lakers so I thought I would dress the part. It is not something I can do usually, but since this situation with you is unique, I thought it would be an interesting experiment for me."

Carmine shook her head in disbelief and only said, "It's fine, Laurence. Let's Go!"

As promised, the traffic home was light for the time of day. "I don't know how you did it, Laurence, but thank you," Carmine said as she drove into the condo garage. She dragged herself and the backpack out of the car. Somehow she had managed to get through a day that was unsurpassed by anything she had experienced in the past or probably any time in the future.

First Laurence, then school, all the homework. Her thoughts trailed off. It hurt too much to think. *I want to go to bed, put the covers over my head and suck my thumb.*

She walked into the condo, which was unbearably hot, but she opened the sliding glass doors in the living room that led out onto a terrace of trees and a border of flowers that were surrounded by a tall, redwood fence, covered with ivy, giving the condo privacy. Immediately a soft cool breeze swept through the living room, cooling it. She then switched on the air conditioning and within a few minutes, all the rooms had cooled considerably. *Thank goodness for this side unit with no walls attached. I have fresh air from two different directions.*

She threw all her paraphernalia on the round kitchen table and went into the living room. She tiredly plopped down on her deep burgundy couch, tossed her head back to rest on the large cushions and stared at the ceiling. Laurence sat along with her.

After a few minutes, he tentatively asked, "Carmine, are you all right?"

"I guess so, Laurence. I think my system is having a hard time with everything that has happened today. Talk about changes taking place in a life. I don't think my body has had time to assimilate everything. I feel so overwhelmed." As Carmine spoke, tears started forming in her eyes. She sniffed several times, trying to stop.

"Carmine, what would you have me do?"

Trying to control herself, she bit her lip and closed her eyes. Giving a last big sniff, she replied listlessly, "Nothing, Laurence, just keep out of my way for now. I have to make something for dinner and then hit the books. I also have to work tomorrow and prepare for that, too." A deep sigh escaped her lips.

Carmine thought about work. Trying to make herself feel better, she tried to think of everything positive about the situation. *It won't be too bad. I have Tuesdays with one client and alternate Thursdays with two other clients. Then I have Fridays free to do my image consulting work and to schedule in any other clients that may want my assistance or catch up with my homework. The three regular clients have promised, as much as possible, a year's commitment. This way, I won't have to do marketing. Just focus on the work and this way I can do the homework without worrying too much about money.* She would be okay, if everything worked out as planned.

"Carmine, you should never worry about money. Don't you know your needs will always be taken care of?"

"Laurence, please, leave me alone. I don't want to hear about this now."

"Of course, Carmine, but let me ask you something. Has there ever been a time in your life when you needed something that it had not been provided? Now I am talking about need, not want."

"Laurence, pleeeasse!" Then Carmine raised her eyebrow, shook her head from side to side. "Actually, my needs have always been provided for, sometimes very surprisingly."

"That's right, Carmine. You have to have faith along with positive thoughts. You know the mustard seed story. There is pure truth there, as there are in many of your sayings.

"In fact, Carmine, there are two different sayings that all humans on your planet are aware of, but few realize that they are basic universal laws. If truly followed, your planet would be extremely different. One tells you how to live and the other tells you what to do in order to live well. And you do both, Carmine, on many occasions."

Carmine jumped off the couch, faced Laurence with her hands on her hips, leaning as close as possible to him and yelled, "Well, what are they, Laurence are? I can't bear this suspense."

"These are phrases you have heard all of your life, Carmine, but never thought much about them."

"Laurence" Carmine snarled in a low menacing voice, "What are they?"

"Carmine, Carmine, patience," Laurence directed. However, after one look at Carmine's face, he began speaking quickly.

"They are said in many ways throughout your planet, but the meaning is the same. The first one is 'Do unto others as you would have others do unto you.' Think about it,

Carmine, if everyone followed that law and behaved in that way, would it not be better for everyone?"

"But Laurence, everyone knows that saying," Carmine said with disappointment in her voice. "It's quoted all the time and everyone seems to agree with it. I mean no one says they don't believe it."

"But how many people follow it and incorporate it into their daily lives?"

"You know, just to be positive, I think people try, but, obviously from what is happening in the world, it is not the first priority or thought about that much. But you are right, if everyone practiced it, the world would be a much better place!" Carmine balanced from one foot to the other with her hands on her hips, her head moving from side to side, thinking about the implications of everyone following that simple saying.

"Okay, Laurence, what is the second one?"

"This one tells you how to live abundantly in every area of a human's life. It is 'as you give, so you shall receive.' The more you give away, the more you have. And this is not meant only for financial needs, but for all your needs. If you want more friends, then you have to give friendship; if you want more love, then you have to give love; more understanding, then you must give understanding. This is a very powerful universal law, Carmine, and it is hard to understand why so many of you humans ignore it.

"For instance, in the area of what humans call money, and there are so many who want to have a great deal of this commodity, the more money you give away, the more you will have. Think about it, Carmine. The times that you have given away money, has it not always returned to you and even more?"

"You know," Carmine said thoughtfully, "I always give to various charities on a regular basis and I never seem to have less because of it. On many occasions, in fact, I seem to have money come to me in unanticipated ways or expenses diminished unexpectedly.

"Other times I have given more than I thought I truly could afford to give, to friends, or even employees, always anonymously of course, who were having a hard time. Yet I never seemed to have less money because of it. I never gave it much thought before, but I guess it's true."

As Carmine sat pondering what Laurence had just told her, she exclaimed, "Laurence, are you telling me that if I want more money, or more of anything I guess, that's all I have to do is give more of whatever I want?"

"Yes, Carmine, that is exactly right. And the Universe, especially in the area of money, looks not at how much is given, but how much the person who is giving is able to give. For instance, if someone on your planet is considered very poor because of a lack of what you call money, but still gives even a small amount, then the results of that giving will be very large. Is it not written in one of your wise books about the 'widow's mite' who gave, in comparison to others, a tiny amount, but because it was all she had, she was rewarded abundantly? And if someone who has much and doesn't share in proportion to his or her wealth, then the results would be disappointing. The Universe is very exacting and very fair!"

"Laurence, I'm so fascinated by what you are saying. I mean these laws, as you call them, are known by everyone, but it certainly does not seem as though many people practice them.

"I have to take time and think about what you've told me. It's so amazing and so simple. Is there anything else that you would like to share with me about this giving? Please! I am so intrigued!"

"I don't think so, Carmine, as it is very simple and easy to do. Like anything else, however, it does take time for the accumulation of that giving to take effect so one shouldn't expect to give one day and obtain results the next. You, Carmine, give financially on a regular basis so the accumulation process is already in place. As you give more, then it speeds up the results for you."

"This is so amazing, Laurence. And it certainly inspires me to give more in everything in my life." *What if everyone in the world gave to one charity or someone in need? The world would be so much better and so much happier.* Carmine spent a few minutes in silence thinking about what Laurence had just told her.

Laurence can answer anything I need to know. Smiling to herself, Carmine promised that she would access Laurence's knowledge to whatever extent he would allow her.

Carmine tried to bring herself to the present by shaking her head and the rest of her body. "Hey, Laurence, I'm impressed. And appreciative! But you're also a distraction and I'm not focusing on my homework. Could you please be silent for a while so I can work without thinking about you?"

"Of course, Carmine."

Carmine did all the usual things needed to be done at the end of the day, all the time thinking of what Laurence had told her. She took care of all the "weed patches," as she called them, which needed her attention. At last at 7:30 in the evening, she found herself finally ready for her homework.

"How disgusting. All this homework and I have to work tomorrow too. How am I going to do all this? School work, regular work, maintenance?" Carmine clinched her mouth shut to stop herself from sobbing.

Then she did what she always did when she was down. She did some perception checking and talked to herself so she could feel better. "Carmine, you're whining! Don't look at the forest; take one branch of one tree at a time and focus on that until you are done. You are organized and very focused and you have scheduled your days to support what needs to be accomplished that day. You will be fine!" Sniffing a little and trying to ignore the part of her that was filled with self-pity, looking at the positive, she started on her homework.

At 9:30, she was rethinking her decision to return to school. *Was it worth it?* As she stretched and yawned, she decided it was too big a question to answer and closed her books, threw everything in one pile and walked away. Maybe Laurence would finish her homework, she thought with a big, hopeful smile. Glancing at him for an answer, she saw him shake his head. Pointing her nose in the air, she ignored him and decided she would ignore her usual nightly routine of yoga, and take a long, hot bath adding almost every oil and bath salts she had to the water.

"This is heaven," she sighed contentedly.

"Heaven is considerably better than a hot bath, Carmine."

Carmine shrieked! Hurriedly grabbing a towel and pulling it into the bathtub over her body so it covered her from the neck down, she yelled. "Out, out! Who gave you permission to come in here? Can't I have any privacy? Get out, now!"

Laurence gave her a puzzled look. "Remember what I told you this morning; that Angels just see the energy of the person, not anything else and I am with you twenty-four hours a day every day of your life."

"Well, I don't care. Things are going to change and when I am in the bathroom you are not allowed. That is ironclad Rule Number One. Understand?!"

"Certainly, Carmine, all you have to do is ask. Yelling at me like a child is uncalled for." And Laurence haughtily left the bathroom.

I think he sulked out of here. Is that possible with an Angel? I guess the Director was right when he said Laurence might display human traits. Then feeling a little remorseful, *I'll have to make it up to him I guess.*

After her bath, Carmine went out to the living room where Laurence stood, staring out the sliding glass doors.

"Laurence, I'm sorry, I didn't want to hurt your feelings. It is so hard to remember that you are with me and that you know everything I do and think. Please, give me a chance to become used to everything. This has been a very stressful twenty-four hours with you becoming part of my life, school beginning, making adjustments. Come on, Laurence, you know how I am – I become so tense and stressed over every small thing and now I have you and you are a big, big deal."

"I'm not angry, Carmine. I guess I had my feelings hurt. Yes, even Angels have feelings, in this reality. In the past, every time I tried to help you and you didn't listen, I felt that I had failed you. And it made me feel bad. Now, because you can see me, I want to help you as much as possible. You have an advantage in life that others don't have and I want you to make the most of it."

"Of course, Laurence. I know! I know! I am so blessed. But, please, can we discuss it some other time? I am so tired! It's hard to make sense about what you are saying. I need to go to bed, right this minute! So, thank you and goodnight, Laurence. See you in the morning."

"Goodnight Carmine."

Carmine nodded her thanks and walked into her bedroom, turning off the light, with Laurence trailing behind. Meditation was not an option tonight. She knew she would fall asleep in the chair.

"Carmine it is never useless to meditate. What better way to fall asleep than thinking of God?"

"Laurence, will you please shut up and leave me alone," Carmine snapped impatiently, raising her voice.

"Yelling again," Carmine reprimanded herself, "just what I need for a peaceful night's sleep and I know better. I might as well meditate now, since I woke myself up with that yelling and probably couldn't fall asleep no matter how hard I try." Then feeling guilty about yelling at Laurence, she sent him a silent apology, which he acknowledged with an understanding look on his face.

Carmine proceeded to meditate when she, indeed, almost fell asleep in her meditation chair and had just enough energy to go to bed and fall into a deep, deep sleep.

Chapter Three

I can't believe that it is seven weeks into the quarter. Carmine looked at the Outlook calendar on the computer. *It has gone so unbelievably fast.* Working three days a week, with another two full days of school, and a few clients she juggled in-between for her image consulting side of her business, she felt she was on a never-ending treadmill going at an uncontrollable breakneck speed. Her days were filled with studying whenever she could find a moment, maintaining her life and home with the never ending routine errands and tasks and trying to fit Laurence into her life in such a way that it didn't detract from everything else.

Managing her life with school, work and living took all Carmine's time. She had given up almost all her extra-curricular activities with the exception of feeding the homeless; even ceased seeing friends or her support group so she could manage her daily schedule. But Laurence was now a huge event in her life and he took up time she really didn't have. So although it shouldn't have felt like an intrusion, it certainly seemed like it.

Carmine always had to remember that Laurence was with her every moment of every day. The first week she was ready to give him back, so to speak, and return to their former existence. She was always surprised when she saw him, and, would be resentful when he answered questions she asked herself when she did not expect answers and she became absolutely livid when he would, in her mind, reprimand her when her actions or behaviors weren't exactly what he thought they should be.

They had many arguments over that issue and Laurence had finally made Carmine understand that the only difference from the past was that she now saw him when he was speaking. Prior to their current existence, she had assumed that all the thoughts that came to her mind were her own only. Now she knew that many were, in fact, from Laurence. But the new arrangement was an adjustment for both of them because Carmine's reactions and perceptions of Laurence now could affect him.

They finally decided that Laurence would try not to respond to any of Carmine's thoughts or actions unless she requested his assistance or if something would harm her. After all, he told her, he was her Guardian Angel and still had his work to do.

Whoever would have thought that having an Angel with you all the time would sometimes hamper your life instead of making it perfect? Carmine thought to herself one Saturday morning. She was dressing for a distant cousin's wedding on her deceased father's side. Since the ceremony didn't start until 1:30 that afternoon, she was taking her time while trying to clean her house, wash clothes and do all the tasks that she should've done during the week.

Carmine was looking forward to this event. It was her first fun activity since school started. It would be attended by many relatives she hadn't seen for some time. It would be good to catch up. Cassie, much to Carmine's disappointment, wasn't going to be able to attend because she was taking an extra class that required her to be at school on Saturdays and she was afraid she would miss too much.

Carmine had even bought a new dress to wear when she was shopping with a client at Saks Fifth Avenue. Gossamer silk, in a deep rich ruby, swirled with threads of silver. It had spaghetti straps that attached to a deep V-neckline. The dress molded to her body, ended mid-calf at the hem on one side and had a slit to above her knee on the other. The matching gossamer shawl was a perfect cover-up for the ceremony. Worn with very high heeled strappy silver sandals and a small silver clutch, she felt it was perfect for both the church ceremony and reception, which was being held at the old Biltmore Hotel in downtown Los Angeles.

Carmine finished doing her makeup and hair, put on her strapless bra and then carefully pulled the dress over her head without touching her hair or makeup. Pulling on her silver heels, she looked at herself in her full length mirror. Trying to be objective, she rated herself a B, for overall attractiveness. She thought the dress would look better without the strapless bra, as she hated wearing it, but felt she was far too old to go without one.

Those were the good, old days, Carmine thought nostalgically. *No bra, little makeup and I still looked great. Now it takes me an hour to do my hair, makeup and all the 'extras' to give me the illusion of youth. There must be some advantages of aging,* Carmine thought as a way of comforting herself. *But our society makes it hard to appreciate the older woman.*

"Carmine, I'm sure you always look beautiful. And there are so many advantages of being older than younger. It is strange how you humans, especially those of the female gender, are so unhappy when they live many years on Earth," said a voice.

Laurence, again! Would he never learn that he was only supposed to respond when she asked? Even though he had told her she had the ability to communicate with him by thoughts, she didn't feel comfortable or advanced enough to do so because she thought he would not understand exactly what she meant.

She hurriedly arranged the décolletage of the dress so not too much of her chest would show and went out to the living room with a disapproving look on her face.

"I know, Carmine, I'm not supposed to say anything, but you are always so hard on yourself. I see you are very attractive; probably more so than when you were younger. You reflect a depth and wisdom now that you didn't have when you were younger. And so many women seem to feel the same as you; it is completely puzzling to me."

Carmine took a deep breath and spoke almost furiously, "Well, look at our society, especially here in Los Angeles. Youth is idolized, emulated, copied, treated as royalty! Age, even after only thirty, in certain circles like the entertainment world, is thought of being decrepit, disgusting, repulsive, and sickening. If you ever mention your true age, and it happens to be over thirty, you are immediately ignored!

"And women do everything possible to disguise the reality of their years, truly believing that there is eternal youth. Look at the thousands and thousands of products at the cosmetic counters, legions of plastic surgeons, the flourishing spas, and the myriad of other youth-seeking businesses that inure women to the myth that they can stop the aging process. They spend countless hours of their precious time and hundreds of thousands of dollars on everything and anything that promises youth. And I'm not immune. I go right along with it. In fact, I'm probably the first in line for any new product that screams 'Instant Youth.' It's truly ugly!"

By the time Carmine's tirade had peaked, her voice was hoarse and her face deeply flushed from anger towards herself, other women, and all the manufacturers and the media that so insidiously made women feel that youth was all that mattered and that aging was not only to be disguised, but totally rejected and denied.

Laurence stared at her, with his mouth open as though he was trying to speak. If there could be anything as a stunned Angel, Laurence embodied it.

Finally, shaking his head as though he could understand what Carmine said better, Laurence said, "I'm not sure what to say, Carmine. But I'm sorry you feel that way. Every age has a great deal to offer and it is very sad if others don't recognize the gifts that come with the various ages of life."

"Well, there is nothing that you can do, Laurence. But I appreciate you listening; thank you! I can't tell you how much better I feel. I guess this was something that has been bothering me for a while. Especially since I'm back in college with people, for the most part, who are far younger than I."

Then Carmine grew intent, "Laurence, can you see me as I really am? Not this nonsense with the energy fields or pattern?"

"Yes, Carmine, but, remember, only with your permission."

"Okay, I give my permission. I want you to tell me how I physically look to you and how I compare to other women. I am sure, throughout history, you have seen many beautiful women."

"Yes, but only when they reach the other side, unless some special instructions were given. In those few cases, it is at the age of their choosing, usually their youth."

"See, even on the other side, everyone chooses young. It's maddening."

"Carmine, each individual is beautiful; there is not one that is not."

"Yeah, yeah! Forget the spiritual mumbo-jumbo on this one, Laurence. I want to know how you think I look – you, Laurence, understand?"

"Of course, Carmine."

She saw Laurence look at her; then he was on the other side of her and then back to the front.

"What can I say, Carmine, you are as lovely as a Christmas Angel on a Christmas tree, and you could compete with any one of the women in history who were thought of as beauties for their time; Cleopatra, Josephine, the Mona Lisa . . ."

Carmine was laughing so hard when he finished that she was holding her sides with both hands. "Laurence", she said in between gasping for her breath, "I am sure that it is blarney, but it makes me feel good. Thank you for indulging me." Giving him her widest smile, she continued, "You have made me a happy woman. I feel I look pretty and it is nice to have someone validate that feeling."

"By the way, Carmine, what do the men wear at this event?"

"Oh, I don't know. The men wear a suit with a tie and the ushers usually wear tuxedos, which are like suits but more formal, and most of the time black with a white shirt and bow tie. But sometimes the colors are coordinated with the women's dresses. Why?"

"Just curious!"

"Oh, God, it's 1:00; I'll never be able to get to the church in Hollywood on time. It's on Sunset Boulevard and, with traffic, it will take at least a half hour to get there. Why do I always do this?" she whined to herself.

"Carmine, don't worry, we'll get there on time! Remember, I'm with you."

Carmine ran to her car and started off without even glancing at Laurence. She was finally getting used to having him with her and not worrying about him keeping up.

She quickly drove out of the garage and hastily made a left hand turn onto the street. *That was a fast turn,* Carmine thought, a little scared at the speed she was going. Laurence was right; all the lights were green. *Having an Angel is definitely equal to winning the lottery... in some ways.*

Carmine was congratulating herself on the negotiations with Mother the night she "died" ensuring that Laurence could be an integral part of her Earth life. "Excellent, excellent," Carmine thought, as she arrived at the church with ten minutes to spare.

Turning to Laurence, she started to thank him and stopped. He was wearing a tuxedo with a white shirt and a ruby bow tie. Every once in a while, he would change his usual attire and she was getting used to it. She smiled at him and said, "You look very nice, Laurence; I like that you added the ruby tie to match my dress." She finished thanking him; then she continued in a warning voice, "Now, Laurence, remember, stay out of my way and do not say anything to me unless I ask you first."

"Of course, Carmine. However, Carmine, I'm still seeing you as you are, not in the energy pattern mode. Do you want me to continue that way?"

Carmine paused a second to reflect on the question and replied with a little hesitation, "Yes, but when I do something personal like go into the ladies room, change to the energy pattern. Okay?"

"Yes, Carmine."

As Carmine entered the small church, she was escorted down the aisle by one of her second or third cousins; she wasn't quite sure. She smiled to some of her relatives and blew kisses to others. She sat down by another family of distant relatives. *This is going to be so much fun.*

Carmine took a quick look around her to see who else was there. There was a man behind her whom she didn't recognize and who seemed to stare at her. She felt herself shiver and knew she was going to stay as far away as possible from him. Sometimes that happened to her with people. She could never figure out why, but she was almost always correct. *Umm, I must ask Laurence about him.* "But not now," she warned, just in case Laurence was going to respond.

She stopped her cursory viewing of the congregation as the wedding music began. Both sets of parents were escorted down the aisle by an usher: the groom's first and then the bride's. Carmine noticed that both mothers were dressed in beautiful designer ensembles; simple, but extremely elegant.

The sole attendant on the bride's side was her sister Chardonnay. Carmine always giggled to herself when she saw or heard Chardonnay's name. Chardonnay was exactly eighteen years younger than her sister, Chloe, 34, making her, Carmine calculated, 16 years old. Her parents had dropped Chloe off at college eighteen years ago, had helped her settle in and then had gone to dinner. It was a bittersweet evening as there was a sense of loss and sadness because their only child had left and they knew it was the end of an important and beautiful era in their life. However, they also saw it as opportunity to do all the other things couples put off when there were children involved, including traveling much more often and seeing exotic places they had always wanted to visit.

He was going to semi-retire from his own very profitable construction business, so there were no financial concerns and they were now free without obligations. They soothed themselves with a bottle of Chardonnay and then celebrated with a second bottle. That night Chardonnay was conceived. So when Chardonnay was born, that was the name they gave her.

"I bet Chardonnay is glad they weren't drinking Anisette or Whiskey," Carmine chuckled quietly to herself.

Chardonnay was a beautiful young woman with very white skin and blonde hair and large blue eyes; the coloring her father attributed to Northern Italy where his parents were born. She slowly walked down the aisle in a very short daffodil crushed taffeta strapless dress with scalloped hem and very high strappy matching sandals, which Carmine recognized as Jimmy Choo's. Carmine happened to glance at the man who earlier had given her the shivers. She noted that he watched Chardonnay with a look on his face that reminded her of a tom cat. She gave another involuntary shiver. *This guy is trouble.*

She heard Laurence mention "seeing the loving essence of each individual," but before she could respond, the wedding march began and Chloe started down the aisle with her father. She looked the exact opposite of Chardonnay; olive skin, black, black hair and eyes to match. Dazzling beautiful and elegant in a strapless crème-color gown made of heavy silk with the fabric crushed from the bodice to the hip where it then tucked into a wide band of pearls and crystals that circled her hips, then draped into a long V-shape in the back.

The train was very long, outlined with the same pearls and crystals. So was the short puffy veil held on Chloe's head by a crown of baby white roses. She held a small nosegay of white and yellow baby roses with tufts of white hydrangeas. Chloe smiled happily at her groom, who winked back at her. This made her laugh, as well as all the guests, so the wedding started on a happy and relaxed note which continued all through the short, but beautiful and moving ceremony.

After a long and lingering kiss at the altar with the guests clapping loudly, the bride and groom strolled out into the garden of the chapel where they greeted their guests. There was much hugging and kissing and laughing among the guests and the bride and groom.

"So what did you think, Laurence? I must say, you behaved quite well in there; I never saw you and you were quite good at keeping your opinions to yourself while I was thinking." Carmine thought about what she had just said and shook her head, *Here I am complimenting an Angel on his behavior.* She cringed at the audacity of her statement.

"I don't mind, Carmine. Angels are here to make humans happy and to make their lives easier. Each soul has made a spiritual contract or curriculum to accomplish certain goals while on Earth so that the soul can grow as well as experience much joy and love. However, many, many challenges await the soul because Earth has so many distractions.

"If a soul achieves all the objectives in the spiritual contract, then the soul can continue its upward spiral until it no longer has to return to Earth, having learned all the lessons it has needed to learn. But, alas, there is much forgetfulness once a soul is on Earth and that is why there is so much conflict and strife here." Laurence's earnest tone struck a contrast to the day's levity, but Carmine joined his thoughts.

"Well, I guess there is a lot of forgetfulness," Carmine said in a caustic tone. "Look at the state of the world. It's a wonder any one can sleep at night—there are so many issues to worry about. Politicians, who are out for themselves, a government that is supposed to be run for the people is run for the government's or lobbyists needs. Corporate ethics seem non-existent, crime is high, AIDS and other diseases are rampant, drugs are out of control, wars and the terrorists and their attacks that take place all over the world. There is such a feeling of hopelessness and fear felt by everyone; it is hard to stay focused and positive. And there doesn't seem anything the people can do to make things better." Carmine realized that she was having a conversation with Laurence and that no one could see him. She turned her head in every direction to see if anyone had noticed her behavior. Everyone seemed oblivious to whatever she was doing and she said a thankful prayer as she blew out the breath she was holding.

"Even though what you said is all true, Carmine," Laurence said sadly, before she could interrupt, "but there is also much good and happiness generated by humans. In fact, there is much more good taking place and that is where you and all others must focus. Sometimes humans have limiting interpretations of reality and focus on what they see, which is many times the negative. One of the challenges of the spiritual contract is to maintain the positive focus and the joy and positive energy in the soul's life. Every time there is a positive thought, contribution, service by any individual, it uplifts the whole world. And more and more individuals are enlightened, as you call it, so the world is actually being shifted to a higher energy."

Carmine nodded her head. "You know, I never thought of it that way. It is something to think about. But not now. This is a wedding! A happy event! We'll talk about it later." And Carmine walked back to the chapel and the merriment, only to find there was a long brigade of cars lined up behind two limousines set to parade downtown to the Biltmore Hotel.

Carmine ran to her car and managed to slip it into a space close to the front of the line. She noticed that same man who had given her the shivers, right in front of her. He even waved to her as though he knew her. Carmine ignored him even though she knew it was rude, but he gave her a terrible feeling and she always went with her instincts about people. She knew she didn't want anything to do with him. She felt Laurence start to comment on her thoughts about "seeing the loving essence" again, but she said softly

"Don't you even start" and saw him struggle at trying to say nothing.

The short ride downtown following the limousine was fun with the honking of horns and everyone smiling and laughing. Carmine knew that Cassie would have loved it. *Maybe I should have insisted she be here. After all, a wedding is an important event.* As Carmine was berating herself for Cassie's absence, Laurence started in with the continual, "Carmine, you are too hard on yourself" speech.

"Not now, Laurence," Carmine warned him.

"Well, why don't you learn, Carmine? Anytime something doesn't go the way you think it should, you blame yourself instead of looking at the circumstances objectively. These small things are not at all important and they take so much of your energy. If you have clarity of intention of what you want to manifest, you will see a shift. The Universe will support and help you achieve those manifestations. Not just you personally Carmine, but anyone. As you learn to focus on your positive thoughts and energy, your knowing of what is possible will change. At the same time, accept what is and know that all is well. It all works in a cycle! The clearer your intentions, the more you create, the more connected you are, the more you will manifest."

"Laurence, PLEASE, please be quiet."

Carmine sneaked a look at Laurence after she said that and it seemed as though he was pouting. *Impossible, it must be the lighting.*

Carmine felt as though she had returned to heaven when she walked into the room where the reception was being held, for it was a fantasy of flowers, candles, and fragrance. White and yellow roses with huge white chrysanthemums were the tall centerpieces on the tables along with baby's breath, with long strands of ivy with fern entwined around the centerpieces. Two sets of tall candelabras sat on each side of each centerpiece. Hundreds and hundreds of votive candles glowed everywhere, giving the room a shadowy, magical feeling. Trellises placed at each side of the room were adorned with the same flowers and greens. And randomly placed around the room were what Carmine called "lollipop" trees with hundreds of small white blinking lights intertwined among the branches.

The ceiling was covered with garlands of white and yellow roses that cascaded down the side walls of the room. A quartet consisting of a harp, two violins and a flute greeted the guests as they arrived, as waiters deftly greeted each with glasses of Cristal Champagne. In the alcove of the room, an ice sculpture of the bride and groom decorated a long table covered with gold and white linen fabric. It offered up a feast of caviar, huge prawns, oysters, skewers of steak and chicken along with an enormous round of hot brie cheese with assorted unique crackers and crusted bread squares.

I knew that Joe was doing well in his business, but I guess he is doing really well. The room is absolutely magnificent and the appetizers are heavenly. Carmine was busy juggling her champagne and her food while trying to chat with the many relatives she hadn't seen for so long. Everyone seemed happy to see her and there were so many to talk to, catching up on all their lives, she barely noticed that they been there for an hour and the bride and groom still hadn't arrived.

Finally, the flare of five French horns playing Lohengrin's *Wedding March* heralded the arrival of the bridal party. All the guests were told to take their assigned seats at their tables, so that the wedding party could make their grand entrance. Carmine's table was the "Joy" table. But as she hastily made her way, gave a sigh of dismay. The same man who had made her shiver at the church was seated at her table! Carmine looked around to see if there was any way she could sit at another table, but everyone had found seats and she didn't have time to see if there were any empty chairs available.

I can be courteous and polite.

Taking her seat, she noticed Laurence beside her. He told her "Be nice, and remember, everyone is a spiritual being." She tried not to show how she felt receiving that reminder and smiled, instead, at the gentleman.

"Hi, I'm Carmine and I'm a cousin of the bride and her family."

"Hi, I'm Mark and I am friend of Barry. I noticed you at the church."

They started talking and Carmine felt that she could endure the few hours that she had to spend at the table with him. Actually, he was a nice looking man; blonde with a round face, a little heavy-set, medium height. "Pleasant" would come to most people's minds. But Carmine still felt the shiver every time she looked at him; there was something about his demeanor that made her gut react negatively.

There were six other people at the table, all friends of the bride and groom. They all seemed very friendly. The conversation was animated with much joking and laughing. The toasts were made to the bride and groom, different relatives from each side of the family spoke about humorous incidents involving the newlyweds and then the dinner began. Carmine noticed that Mark focused on Chardonnay during the toasting. *Hey Bud! She's only 16!* She screamed inside.

One could die now and feel as though you have not missed anything in life. Carmine thought, after eating the six-course dinner. What a sumptuous feast! Starting with a cold cucumber and mint soup and an arugula, radicchio and baby endive salad, it was followed by a choice of either Swiss chard or lobster ravioli in a light tomato sauce. After clearing the palate with a lime sorbet, the main entrée was a choice of Beef Medallions with Cognac sauce or Chilean Sea Bass with a Mango sauce, served with sautéed baby vegetables. There was even a dessert of a flaming baked Alaska that was presented with a roll of drums and a parade of the white-jacketed waiters. Each course, including the dessert, had its own special wine to complement each dish.

I can't move. Carmine's chin fell on her chest and she had to shake her head to wake herself up. *A nap would feel so good,* as she felt her head start to fall again.

A very large band or very small orchestra, Carmine couldn't decide which, replaced the quartet that had entertained everyone during dinner. As it played such bright and gay music, Carmine bounded out of her lethargy. The conductor, or bandleader, was also the Master of Ceremonies and directed the bride and groom to the dance floor for the first dance. Lights were turned off and only the candles remained, giving the room a golden glow with floral shadows and delightful fragrances. Everyone applauded as they danced to the "Wedding Waltz" by Ialan Eshkeri, looking at each other with adoration and love. They were joined by the parents and then the maid of honor and the best man. The relatives soon joined them and before long, everyone was dancing. Carmine noticed that Mark was already dancing with Chardonnay.

As Carmine danced with her many uncles and cousins during the evening, her eyes furtively followed Mark and Chardonnay, noting that Mark never left Chardonnay. And Chardonnay looked at Mark as though there were no one else in the room; her eyes were riveted on his. *I feel no good coming from this.* Carmine excused herself from her current dancing partner saying she had to go to the powder room. On the way, with no one looking, Carmine started talking to Laurence.

"Can you believe that guy, Laurence? Chardonnay is only 16; he must be twice her age. What do you think? He's up to no good, right?"

"There seems to be an intent that may not be perceived as honest or moral, Carmine. However, everyone has free will, so it shouldn't be hard for Chardonnay to say no."

"Laurence, she is only 16! Do you think that she is not flattered that someone like him would be interested in her? Really!" Carmine shook her head in disgust.

As Carmine entered the ladies room, Chardonnay met her at the entrance.

"Oh, Aunt Carmine, I am so happy to see you." And with that remark, threw her arms around her and hugged her, just as she did when she was a little girl. Carmine hugged her back and smoothed her hair.

"So what's going on with you, little vino?" Carmine's nickname for her when she was a baby. "You look so beautiful today."

"Oh, Carmine, did you see that cool guy I'm dancing with. He wants me to go out with him after the reception. He has this incredible stereo, which is some high-tech system from Japan and a condo that overlooks the water in Long Beach that he wants me to see. He says we can see the harbor, listen to music and talk."

"And I suppose he wants you to see his art work and etchings, also," Carmine said with sarcasm.

"Please wait a minute, sweetie. He's much older than you," Carmine grasped desperately for a reason to dissuade her. "I understand there is a relative gathering after the reception and, of course, you have to be there."

"Oh, no one is going to miss me. I want to be with Mark. He is so handsome and so much more mature than the babies I usually date." Chardonnay frowned. "Don't be a spoil sport, Aunt Carmine."

Carmine hugged her. "We'll talk later!"

Carmine repaired her makeup and her hair while Chardonnay did the same. As soon as the child left, as Carmine thought of her, she ran out to talk to Laurence.

"You have to do something about that Mark. I have a terrible feeling about him and I am never wrong about people. Get him away from Chardonnay, please."

"Carmine, you know I can't do too much or otherwise I am interfering."

"Well, you can do something, so do it NOW. After all, you gave my car a flat tire that fateful night that I became pregnant. I want to make sure that the same thing doesn't happen to her! Please, Laurence, please?"

Laurence bowed his head. "Let me see what I can do."

Carmine made her way to her table. As she approached, she saw Mark with his cell phone to his ear and heard him shouting.

"What do you mean my water heater blew and my living room is under water? The heater is almost brand new."

She heard someone else talking very loudly. Finally, Mark hung up and grabbed his coat, which he had discarded during the dancing.

"I have to go home and take care of this water problem." He glanced hungrily at Chardonnay. "I don't know when I'll be back."

"I'm sorry," she forced herself to say with a concerned look on her face, trying not to smile. She closed her eyes and sent a silent, fervent thank you to Laurence.

"You're welcome," Laurence replied silently. "All the Angels work together for the highest good of all involved!"

When she opened her eyes, Mark was gone. Standing in front of her was a young man she had not seen in years. He had green, green eyes, black hair and stood at least six feet tall.

"Patrick Mahoney! How are you? Do you remember me?"

"Of course, Aunt Carmine. In fact, you are the reason I am here. My parents couldn't come because they are on a cruise in the Mediterranean and they left me the invitation to the wedding, asking that I attend to represent them. They mentioned you and Cassie would be here, so I thought I would do as they suggested."

"Well, you have grown up and you are absolutely gorgeous," Carmine exclaimed, as she reached up to give him a kiss.

With that remark, Patrick became very red. "Aunt Carmine, please. I'm nineteen years old."

"Ooops, sorry, Patrick. Cassie would be furious at me for saying something like that to her and I apologize!"

Hoping to change the subject so he would forget her lapse of manners when it came to young adults, Carmine asked, "Well, what are you doing these days?"

"I just finished the AIDS ride from San Francisco to Los Angeles yesterday. That was a highlight of my life; riding with 2600 other riders through all kinds of weather and knowing that you are raising money for a good cause. It was absolutely awesome and really inspiring. Other than that, nothing, except I'm enrolled in UCLA Law School starting next quarter."

"Well, I'm not surprised. You were always brilliant."

At that remark, Patrick again turned red, but did not respond.

"You know it's really strange that I am here today, because yesterday, I was so beat from that six day, 450-mile bike ride that I was going to be a couch potato today. I was lying on the couch listening to my iPod and reading and all of sudden, I had such a spurt of energy I didn't know what to do with myself. I thought of the invitation and decided to attend. But outside of you and Cassie, I probably don't know one other person here. So almost in spite of myself, I'm here, even though it is good to see you, Aunt Carmine," he said with a shrug of his shoulders, apologetically. "Where's Cassie?"

"Unfortunately, Cassie couldn't be here because of a class conflict. I wish she had skipped the class and come, because it has really been fun. She will be so disappointed to have missed you. But let me introduce you to someone right now."

She took Patrick by the arm and started toward the bridal table. Chardonnay was sitting alone, her head hung down, her lip trembling and with a look on her face that made Carmine feel conscience-stricken.

"Chardonnay, what's wrong?"

"Oh, Aunt Carmine," Chardonnay said with a sob in her voice, keeping her head down so she wouldn't show her tears. "That cool guy, Mark I was telling you about. He just left! Didn't even say good-bye, after all the nice things he said to me."

"Well, Chardonnay, I happen to know that he had an emergency and had to leave immediately. I know it had nothing to do with you. But maybe you can help me out. This gentleman is Patrick Mahoney and he came as a representative of his parents who couldn't attend. Do you think you could introduce him to some of your friends and relatives to make him feel at home? Patrick, this Chardonnay DeLucca."

Chardonnay only raised her head when Carmine made her introduction. She listlessly held out her hand for Patrick to shake. She didn't look up until he greeted her with a warm, deep, "Nice to meet you, Chardonnay. Are you named after a wine?"

When she looked up at that remark, she blinked her eyes. And then started a slow smile. "Yeah, isn't that extremely cool?"

"Patrick just returned from the AIDS bike ride from San Francisco to LA. I know you did some volunteer work a few years ago for an AIDS organization, so I think maybe you two might have some similar interests."

"Oh sure, Aunt Carmine, I'll be happy to show Patrick around." Chardonnay, whose countenance had changed from tragic to one of delight, took Patrick's hand and led him to a group of her friends, talking animatedly.

"Well, Laurence, I think we have taken care of that trouble spot. I have to assume you were the one who gave Patrick that spurt of energy to come?"

"Carmine," Laurence acknowledged, "I knew that Chardonnay had, as you humans say, fallen for Mark. So her Guardian Angel and I arranged it, along with Patrick's Angel, for him to be here. They would have met eventually, but because of you, it happened sooner. And are you really Patrick's Aunt or even Chardonnay's?"

Carmine laughed. "Of course not, Laurence, but when you are older and others are very young, they have to call you something, so Aunt is what I am called. I'm really not their Aunt, at all.

"But Laurence, Laurence, you are incredible and I truly love you and what you have accomplished." With that, Carmine sent him a kiss, which was seen by one of Carmine's uncles.

"Carmine, you certainly have been throwing those kisses around, young lady. I hope this isn't a habit with you?"

"Uncle Maurice, I am having such a fabulous time, I have thrown away all my inhibitions and I'm doing whatever I like. Come on, let's dance." And with that, she took her 80-year-old uncle, both laughing and giggling, to the dance floor. Carmine's uncle, who had been a professional dancer when he was younger, led her into the Quickstep, which was so spectacular that everyone stopped whatever they were doing to watch them. At the end of the dance, they both made deep bows to a thunderous round of applause.

Then bowing to her uncle, she said, breathing hard, "Uncle Maurice, I haven't danced like that in years! It was so much fun! Thank you," giving him a huge hug!

Time went very fast after that. There was the cutting of the cake, which looked like a large bouquet of flowers from a distance, but actually was a cake of individual miniature cream puffs, filled with various creams, with a different flower decorating each one.

There was the traditional Italian groom's cookie cake, a giant cake composed of multiple cookies, mainly macaroons and pine nuts. And then there was the money dance, in which each guest who wished to, danced with either the bride or groom, in exchange for a money gift.

As she pinned a $20 bill on his lapel, Carmine told Barry how much she enjoyed the wedding and how beautiful Chloe was. She finally had a chance to speak to Chloe longer than the few seconds she had after the ceremony. She hugged her and told her she was the most beautiful bride she had ever seen.

"Aunt Carmine, you say that to every bride, I have heard you."

"But it's true, Chloe, every bride is the most beautiful, until I see the next one," Carmine retorted, making both of them laugh.

A little after one in the morning, the bride and groom made their departure to their bridal suite in the hotel with all the guests throwing white and yellow rose petals at the delighted couple as they ran to the elevator.

After the bride and groom decamped, all the relatives who had been invited to a post reception party moved to another suite in the hotel. Carmine noticed, as she made her way to the elevator, that Chardonnay had her arm through Patrick's and each of them only had eyes for each other. Carmine smiled smugly to herself and thought, that contrary to what she felt earlier, having one's own Angel was even better than winning the lottery.

Chapter Four

It was late Sunday night, and Carmine was still recovering from the wedding and the post reception for family members that had lasted until four o'clock Sunday morning. Carmine had slept the day away, finally awakening at six that evening, to remember that she had her weekly English class writing assignment due the next day.

Even though she calculated she had only taken sips of all the wine, maybe drinking little more than a glass and one or two swallows of the champagne, she was still feeling as though she had been drinking all night—probably from the combination of the lack of sleep and the alcohol!

After taking two aspirins, drinking some orange juice and eating soft ice cream, (an antidote for hangovers given to her by a former boyfriend who always seemed to have hangovers) she looked over the criteria for the paper. It was to be a presentation on a subject that would be suitable in a corporate environment.

Carmine started musing out loud. "I'll use my presentation on how to interview applicants. I certainly have presented it to multiple corporations over the years. All I have to do is change it a bit to meet the requirements for the class. I can do this in thirty minutes!" Carmine completed the changes needed in her computer and expelled a huge sigh of relief, feeling her shoulders relax from the anxiety and stress.

Suddenly, Carmine had an overwhelming feeling that she should call Cassie. It hit her in the solar plexus of her stomach or her "gut" with a feeling of almost panic.

She looked around for Laurence and asked, "Laurence, is what I am feeling, true?"

"Yes, Carmine, you definitely should call Cassie."

Carmine grabbed her cell phone and dialed Cassie's cell, her hands shaking. "Oh God, please don't let it be anything serious."

The phone barely rang before Cassie picked up.

"Hi, Cassie," Carmine tried to make her tone low key and casual. "Thought I'd call you to say hello and tell you about the wedding."

Before she could complete the sentence, Cassie interrupted her, crying uncontrollably as she spoke.

"Oh, Mom, Kathy was in a serious accident and I just returned from the hospital. She's in a coma and they don't know if she will come out of it. I was just going to call you," she sobbed.

"My God, what happened?" She gave a silent apology to Laurence for the irreverent use of God's name.

"She was driving back to the dorm and she must have lost control of the car, because she hit a telephone pole and hit her head on the side of the window. She was even wearing her seat belt, but the impact was too hard. And somehow the airbag didn't prevent it. There's nothing we can do except wait and pray. I want you to pray for her, too."

"Of course Cassie. Are her parents there?"

"They are on the way up. I can't believe it. She was so happy this afternoon before she left. She had finished her paper and was meeting this new guy for coffee at Starbucks.

I don't know why she was coming back so late." Cassie started crying, again.

"Listen, Cassie, praying is the best thing we can do. Let's hang up and pray. If I think of anything else we can do, I'll call you back. And, remember, you have to have faith."

As soon as Carmine hung up, she attacked Laurence with questions. "Will Kathy be all right? What can we do? Can you make her well, please?" Carmine implored.

"Carmine, you know that I cannot do anything about this situation. But by praying for her and having many others pray for her, will help. Energy follows thought and then that energy is sent to wherever it is needed. The more people praying, the more energy is directed towards every cell in that individual. Spiritual energy has great power to heal.

"If she is in pain, then the energy helps minimize it so it is not felt as intensely. If she needs surgery, the prayers will minimize the bleeding and maximize the healing. And the prayers can come from anywhere in the world; distance is not a factor. The more prayers, the more healing and that is why sometimes there are what you humans consider 'miraculous recoveries'. If it is time for her transition, then it will also be helped by the prayers. I know that those who are called scientists on your planet have performed studies and even they validate that prayer makes a difference."

Grimacing, Carmine asked, "Is this her time?"

"I do not know that, Carmine. As you know, they only let us know at that time."

Carmine was already calling Cassie again.

"Cassie, while I was praying," Carmine cast a significant look at Laurence, "it came to me that we should contact everyone we know so that they can pray for Kathy. So e-mail everyone in your contact list and I'll do the same. It doesn't matter if they know her or not.

"Ask everyone to pray for her and if they feel comfortable doing it, to send it to all their own contacts. Together with everyone else adding their own contacts, there should be an enormous number of people praying! It's like dialing for prayers and healing, only by e-mail!"

"Mom," Cassie yelled, "that's not funny!"

"I'm sorry, Cassie, I wasn't trying to be funny, just honest. Anyway, I know that it will help."

"Okay, Mom, I'll start as soon as we hang up."

"Me, too, Darling. Have faith!"

Two hours later, Carmine had e-mailed everyone she had in her contacts and then had made phone calls to her dearest friends to ensure they sent out the message to everyone they knew. Many e-mails were sent back responding to the request and saying they would start praying immediately.

Carmine acknowledged how technology used for this purpose was like having hundreds of Angels praying and she marveled how quickly it could help manifest prayers by multiple recipients in a minimum of time.

"I am absolutely, utterly, terribly exhausted," Carmine declared to no one in particular. "If I don't get to bed now, I will fall asleep right here."

She teetered off to bed and fell on top of the gold and champagne bedspread. She didn't even have the energy to crawl under the sheets, but continued praying for Kathy's full recovery.

Carmine opened her eyes, it seemed, two seconds later. She was still dressed in her sweats. For a moment she thought it was Sunday. Then she realized that it was Monday morning, a school day and she had a paper due. She looked at the clock, saw that it was after seven. She flung herself out of bed and raced to the bathroom. She ran through her ablutions. *I must call Cassie and see how Kathy is.* As she picked up the phone, it rang. *It can only be Cassie.*

"Mom," she heard at the other end, "Kathy came out of the coma and they are doing tests. So, far, everything looks okay. She has some broken bones and ribs, but they think she'll have no memory loss."

"Cassie, that's so wonderful," Carmine said with tears in her eyes. "I know the prayers helped. I'll e-mail everyone to give them an update as soon as I can and to make sure they continue praying and to thank them. You too, Cassie. Remember to have everyone give thanks! I have to get to school! Call me tonight with her status. And if anything changes in the interim, call my cell because I will be in school."

"Sure, Mom. I love you, Mom, and thanks for everything."

Carmine kissed into the phone and told Cassie she loved her too. When she hung up the phone, she had tears in her eyes, again. *Time goes so fast. I know we have to value every moment, but it is so hard. The mundane of life takes over and one day you find that your child is 18 and you're 37. And you think where did the time go and then find it's been wasted on irksome chores, like cleaning house, grocery shopping, the cleaners. And what is really valuable, like spending time with family and friends, you squeeze in between the chores, when it should be the other way around. Too many 'shoulds' in our lives,* Carmine thought with despair, *and not enough pleasures.*

All of sudden, she gave a yelp. "My class!"

"Laurence," she yelled, "you have to get me to school, quick. It's almost eight o'clock and I still have to get dressed, do my hair.

"And please give me a good hair day," she whispered.

Carmine, who always had her clothes ready the night before each new day, reached for the first thing she could find to wear in her closet, which was a pair of stretch black jeans along with a rumpled black t-shirt. Thankfully, she found a knee length deep cranberry sweater coat that hid most of the wrinkles.

Carmine hurriedly did her make-up, giving her face what she thought was the absolute minimum including a very thick coat of concealer for under her eyes. Carmine's eyes always had dark circles under them, a less propitious inheritance from her hardy Mediterranean forebears. After a weekend with almost no sleep, they were at their worst. She said a quick, silent thank you to the inventor of the concealer and also acknowledged a thank you to Laurence for giving her hair a wispy and curly look after her shower.

Whenever Carmine had school, she took so much time dressing it was almost painful. She rose an hour earlier than normal so that every part of her was perfect; her makeup, her clothes, her hair! It was way beyond dressing for a special occasion. It was like New Year's Eve or the Academy Awards. And she was honest with herself—it was because of Jake, her English instructor.

"Today," Carmine sighed to herself, "old Jake will have to see Carmine as she really is. Hope he won't be too disillusioned."

With a last disgusted look in the mirror, she hurriedly grabbed her paper, her books, her laptop and all her other miscellaneous junk and threw it into her huge burgundy backpack. It was more like a miniature suitcase, but she didn't care. She always wanted everything with her because she hated to find she needed something and it wasn't there. She really believed in the Boy's Scouts' motto "Be prepared."

She ran out of the house with Laurence beside her. Jumping into her car, she turned to Laurence and said very quickly and emphatically, "I need to make it to school, find a parking place and have my paper ready to turn in all before nine a.m."

He nodded in agreement. Carmine smiled. It was fantastic to have your own Angel that you could see and talk to. Maybe she had done something right in her life, after all.

"You know," she spoke to herself, "What more can I do with him that would really make life easier? This is going to take some thought."

Laurence kept his promise and Carmine was in class before 9:00 a.m., re-reading her paper to be sure she had it just right. She noticed Leslie hadn't shown up yet and she remembered she had missed the last class. *I hope she's okay.* She and Leslie had become very close, even though there was a wide difference in their ages. Age seemed to be irrelevant in their relationship and neither of them thought about it. They had a mutual admiration and respect for each other.

Carmine was turning to ask Laurence if he knew anything when Leslie walked through the door. Leslie, who always seemed to have an aura of radiance around her with her vivacious personality and dazzling looks, was now somber and grave. She was wearing sunglasses, but her face, which was always fresh and radiant, with almost no makeup, now had so much foundation on she looked like a Halloween character. There were some dark spots on her neck and puffiness around her mouth and lips, which was covered with dark red lipstick. She walked with her head hung low and almost shuffled to her seat. Dressed in all black and covered from head to toe, it was as though she aged twenty years since the last time Carmine saw her.

As usual, when Carmine became frightened, her voice became loud, "Leslie, what's wrong? You look absolutely terrible. Take off those sunglasses. Are you practicing for a new part?" After she said it, Carmine scrunched up her face and bit her lip, as she realized that the other students were now also staring at Leslie. "I didn't mean it quite that way, Leslie," she said softly. "I'm so sorry!"

"No, Carmine, don't apologize. I look a wreck, because I feel like one and it doesn't have anything to do with a new part. Do you have a minute after class? I need your advice. And I can't take off my sunglasses."

Carmine nodded as Jake had started talking.

Jake had some papers in his hand and started talking about the last assignment, which everyone had turned in last week. Carmine was still focused on Leslie and what was wrong with her. So when she heard Jake say her name, she quickly looked up and saw not only Jake looking at her, but everyone else in the classroom.

Carmine tried to keep a neutral look on her face as she briefly smiled, wondering why he called her name.

"As I said, Carmine's response to the assignment last week was one of the best I have ever seen," Jake was talking to the class, but looking at her.

Carmine tried not to look surprised and slightly nodded her head at his acknowledgment. Carmine rapidly went over the assignment in her head. The class had to write a one-page memo to a hypothetical employee population from a three-page document that contained information that may or may not have been relevant to the actual subject of the memo. The crux of the assignment was to eliminate the irrelevant material and to streamline the rest so that it could be easily read and understood. Because Carmine had done so much of this in her actual work, it had been one of her easier assignments.

Ahh, so there are some advantages of being older and wiser! So maybe she felt a little arrogant, but it was so seldom that she felt pleased with herself.

Then Jake proceeded to read the memo to the class. After finishing, he handed her the paper with a big "A" written on it and smiled at her. She smiled sweetly, she hoped, back to him.

"Carmine, could I please see you after class?"

"Of course," Carmine replied demurely, but her heart was beating rapidly and she felt herself flushing. She quickly turned her head away and saw Laurence grinning at her.

"Did you have anything to do with this?" Carmine hissed at Laurence.

"Of course not, Carmine. You never asked me to do anything for you, even though you seemed most interested in him; far more than a student admiring a beloved teacher."

"I am not interested in him," she hissed to him again while giving him a scowl and turning back to her seat.

"But Carmine," Laurence continued, "how about all those mornings you took hours to dress and what about . . ."

"Laurence, let it alone," she hissed again through her clenched mouth so no one would notice.

Out of the corner of her eye, she saw that even Leslie was eyeing her with a little smirk on her face.

"I guess I'll be a little late seeing you after class, Leslie," Carmine whispered. "Can you wait for me? I don't think it will be that long."

"Sure, I'll go get a cup of coffee and meet you outside by the bookstore. No worries," Leslie said as she gave her a small smile.

"Watching your reaction to Jake is making me feel a little better," Leslie whispered back.

It was the longest hour and a half Carmine had ever sat through, waiting for the class to end. The class could have been conducted in a third world language for all of the content she understood. She couldn't concentrate because she was focusing on her appearance. How this was the absolutely worst she ever looked, the possibilities of what he would say to her, how she would respond. Her thoughts were all-consuming and she looked at her watch every few minutes praying for the time to move faster.

Get a grip, Carmine. You are 37 years old. Not 12! Act your age!

After what seemed like endless hours, the class finished. As usual, there were at least five students surrounding Jake waiting for their turn to ask questions. She wanted to talk to Leslie and couldn't bear to wait the fifteen minutes it would probably take till he got to her. She impatiently looked at her watch.

"Carmine, you are deceiving yourself," she heard Laurence say. "You can't bear to wait the fifteen minutes to talk to Jake. Leslie has nothing to do with it."

Carmine turned to Laurence with a snarl on her face and gave him a look that made him step back from her. Unfortunately, there was another student behind Laurence, who thought the look was meant for him. He also stepped back with an incredulous, hurt look on his face. Stammering, he asked Carmine, "Did, did I do something to offend you?"

"Oh, gee, Jack, of course not! I was thinking of a paper that is due, which I absolutely don't want to do and I guess that look was for the distaste I have for the subject matter, not you. I am so sorry," she said with a very red face, very flustered.

Carmine gave herself a mental slap as she turned away from him. "Carmine," she said to herself, "don't let Laurence get to you." Even though, she admitted to herself, she was agitated because Jake wanted to speak to her.

Finally, it was Carmine's turn. She was the last one and wondered if he arranged it this way intentionally.

She smiled with what she hoped was a neutral look on her face.

"Carmine, that was an excellent paper! I was wondering if you would like to perhaps give me some insight on how you were able to compose it like you did so I could discuss your approach with the class. That memo was everything a corporate memo should be; short, brief, informative and to the point."

Carmine started to explain the process, when Jake interrupted, with his face flushing. "No, not now, Carmine. I was thinking, maybe, seeing you in the evening sometime this week or next; whatever would be convenient. As a trade, I'll take you out to dinner and you can give me your suggestions."

It was Carmine's turn to blush. "Ah, sure, that sounds more than fair. Actually, I'm free almost every evening this week. What would be convenient for you?"

"How about Wednesday night at about seven?"

"Perfect. Where do you want to meet?"

"I can either pick you up at your home or, if you are not comfortable with that, I can meet you at a restaurant of your choice," he said with some hesitation. His face was now bright red and his voice was a hoarse whisper.

"My home is fine. Here's my address and cell number and she gave him a business card. If you need directions, call me," Carmine said as calmly as possible, even though her heart was racing as fast as a car engine at the end of a drag race.

"Great. But I will Google it. Is there a restaurant around where you live that you would like to eat?"

"There is this great neighborhood Italian restaurant close by. It's within walking distance but they don't take reservations. We could meet at my condo and then walk. Is that all right?"

"Why don't we do that? I'll be looking forward to it."

Both their faces were now so bright red that they could have been used as signal lights. Jake's face was worse because he was also perspiring heavily.

"I'll see you in class Wednesday," Carmine said in a strangled voice and walked out of the classroom.

Walking as fast as she could, she made it to the ladies room where, upon entering, stood against the wall with her head back and began breathing deeply. She looked across at the mirror at herself and saw that her face was very flushed and very, very shiny.

"Oh, my gosh," she whispered to herself, "I think I have a date with Jake. I can't believe it."

She closed her eyes as she replayed their dialogue in her head. She began berating herself. *How come I said I was free all week? How come I didn't pretend I had something going? And I look a mess, of all days. What were you thinking, Carmine?*

All of a sudden she heard what seemed like an animal grunt. She quickly opened her eyes to see Laurence shaking his head at her with a sad look on his face.

"Carmine, Carmine you did well. Why, oh why, can't you accept yourself and your behavior without judging it and talking negatively to yourself? You are a spiritual being and you are an old soul. Your instincts are valid. You told the truth, which is always good. Positive self-talk will help you so much more than these judgments."

"Laurence," she said with a long sigh, "I know you mean well, but it is too much for you to forgo giving me feedback on my behavior, especially in a delicate situation like this?"

"Carmine, I'm here to help you in all situations and to encourage you to feel good about yourself. It's very hard for me if you are always judging yourself and your situation. Don't judge, Carmine, accept what happens. You seem to focus on the negative possibilities of a situation instead of the positive ones. This behavior occurs often with you humans. Be kinder to yourself, Carmine. When you judge, it is time for compassionate self-forgiveness. It will release any negativity and give you positive energy to go forward."

"Laurence, you have no idea how much I wanted Jake to notice me and now that he did, I don't want to do anything that makes me look bad to him." She stopped as she remembered, "Oh my gosh, Leslie is waiting for me. I completely forgot!"

She splashed some water on her face, ran her hands through her hair and ran out of the door hoping that she would not see Jake.

Almost jogging to the bookstore, she looked for Leslie at one of the outdoor tables. *I hope she didn't get tired of waiting for me and leave. I could see she needed someone to talk to.* Carmine scanned the tables one more time.

Out of the corner of her eye, she saw Laurence pointing to a table. Leslie had her head down on her arms so it was easy to miss her. Carmine hurried to the table as soon as she could catch her breath. "I am so sorry, Leslie, it took so much longer than I thought. I apologize for keeping you waiting," she said as she sat down.

Leslie slowly raised her head and took off her sunglasses. Her beautiful blue eyes were very red, and puffy, her black mascara was smeared below and above her eyes, her lipstick was everywhere, except on her mouth and her hair was stringy and dirty. Leslie looked up at Carmine and said pitifully, "I know! I look a mess!" and then started sobbing.

"Leslie," Carmine said with tears in her own eyes, "What happened? What's going on? What can I do to help?" Leslie moved her mouth to speak but before words came out, her sobbing turned into silent tears.

Carmine stretched her hands across the table and took Leslie's cold, shaking hands. "Leslie, please let me help you," she pleaded.

Leslie was now crying harder, but talking. Carmine tried to follow what she was saying about her boyfriend. Pathologically jealous, accusing her of seeing someone else in her acting class. Came over when her family was away on vacation and started hitting her.

"Do you mean that he beat you up? Is that what the bastard did to you?" Leslie slowly nodded her head.

Carmine spoke loudly with fury, "Did you report it to the police? Is he in jail? What did your family say and do?"

"Carmine, please, I can't keep up with your questions." Leslie wept pitifully.

"My dear, I'm so sorry," Carmine apologized with tears in her eyes. "How much did he hurt you and is he in jail? When did this happen?"

"I'm black and blue all over, but I haven't gone to a doctor. I don't think anything is broken. The only reason I came to class is because I had to turn that paper in and I wanted to see you. In the mess that he made in my room, I misplaced your telephone number. My family isn't back, yet. If my brothers find out, they'll kill him!"

"I wouldn't blame them but I'd say he deserves to be maimed rather than killed. He should feel your pain. I am so sorry that this happened to you, love," Carmine stroked Leslie's hair back and caressed her bruised face gently as Leslie's whole body shook with sobs.

Laurence interrupted, "Carmine, how can you say that? He is a spiritual being who has lost his way. You can't go around killing or maiming people."

"Look at her Laurence! How can you take that bastard's side?" she hissed at him.

"Carmine, Carmine, I'm not taking his side. What he has done is wrong and will hinder him immensely on his spiritual path, but revenge isn't helpful. This should be left to the proper authorities here on Earth and in the spiritual world."

"And talking about the proper authorities, what about his Angel, Laurence? How come he wasn't stopped?"

"His Angel did try to stop him and Leslie's Angel tried to stop her from seeing him. How many times have I told you people have free will? Angels are here to assist in providing a better life, but humans have to pay attention to us. We do everything we can within the limitations placed upon us by our spiritual agreements when we come to Earth, but you humans have to be responsible for your actions. Remember, how I tried to stop you with a flat tire the night you got pregnant. You went right ahead and took your parents' car, insistent on seeing him. I tried! You chose differently!"

Leslie had lifted her head from Carmine's hands and was looking at Carmine with a puzzled look on her face. "Carmine, who are you talking to?"

"I am talking to myself, Leslie, about this dreadful situation and what you should be doing," Carmine ad-libbed without pausing, as though it were perfectly natural to have this type of conversation. "It's my way of handling stressful situations."

Because of Leslie's emotional state, she seemed to take the answer without questioning it and laid her head down on her arms. As soon as Leslie looked away, Carmine attacked Laurence, unleashing a stream of thoughts: *Don't you dare remind me of that night! This is about Leslie's problem. Now, what are you going to do about that asshole?* Without pausing, she continued. *Never mind, don't answer. We'll talk about it later.*

"Leslie," Carmine said gently, "What are you going to do about this situation? You must report it."

"Carmine, I can't. I don't think I love him anymore, but I don't want to get him in trouble."

Carmine swallowed and closed her eyes before she replied, silently praying that she would be guided to say the right things. "Leslie, this man beat you up and you say, 'you don't think you love him anymore!' And why do you care if you get him in trouble? Maybe the next time he attacks a woman, he'll maim or kill her!"

Leslie said slowly through her tears, "He couldn't help it; he was so upset. He hasn't been selected for any of the parts he auditioned for and then he thought I was cheating on him and . . ."

"Leslie, are you making excuses for this guy? This same guy that hurt you and made you the way you are right now. You are giving him a reason for beating you? Leslie, let me ask you this, has any one in your family ever hit you?"

"No. Why?"

"Because when women make excuses for something like this, it is usually because they are used to it or they think they deserve this type of treatment. You have to understand, Leslie, there is never any justifiable reason for any behavior that gives someone the right to beat you up. There are no reasons that can possibly make it appropriate.

"I want to take you to your doctor to have you at least examined and see that everything is as it should be."

"No, no!" Leslie was almost hysterical in her reply. "I'm fine! There are no broken bones. I look and feel terrible! But it is mostly emotional, I'm a wreck inside. The bruises will go away."

"I'm not going to argue with you, Leslie," Carmine said with a sad smile. "Whatever makes you comfortable. If, after you think it over and want to go a doctor or press charges, I'll be happy to go with you. I'm your friend and I don't want to make you more miserable than you are now." Taking a tissue from her purse, she gently started wiping away Leslie's tears and the mascara from around her eyes.

"What are you going to tell your parents and your brothers?"

"I'll say I went motorcycling with a friend and we were in an accident. There's nothing they can do about that."

"Whatever you want to do. However, how about coming to my house tonight and let me take some pictures of how you look, for the record? This way, if you change your mind, at least you will have some proof. Please, Leslie. Stay the night so I can take care of you. I have an appointment in the late morning with a client, so you will be by yourself until the afternoon. The only thing is I don't have any clothes that could possibly fit you."

Leslie gave a huge sighed and closed her eyes. When she opened them, there were tears. "Thank you, Carmine, I'm so grateful. I was dreading going home alone. I'll go home now and get some clothes. You give me the directions to your house and I'll be there whenever you want me to be."

"Absolutely not! I'll go with you to your house and make sure the ass…, I mean the creep," Carmine amended, as Laurence gave her one of his looks, "isn't there waiting for you. Okay?"

"Thanks, Carmine. I was reluctant to ask you, but I didn't want to be by myself."

Carmine gathered her backpack and Leslie followed her as they both stood up to leave. Carmine placed her arm around Leslie and said while hugging her, "I'm glad you are staying with me tonight, Leslie and I promise I won't talk about this situation or what you should do, unless you ask me. The only thing I'll insist upon is taking your picture. Then it's up to you!"

Leslie hugged Carmine closer and put her head down on her neck and sniffed back her sobs.

Chapter Five

Carmine followed Leslie to her home in Monterey Park, a small suburb of East Los Angeles. During the drive, Carmine reviewed the last forty-eight hours' events; the wedding, not getting enough sleep, Kathy's accident, Jake, Leslie!

I can't believe all that has taken place in the last two days. I really need an Angel to give me support. Although, I don't know if Laurence is that much help. Somehow, when you think of an Angel in your life, you think everything is going to be smooth and easy and you can have almost anything you want. What a delusion that is!

Out of the corner of her eye, she saw Laurence frowning, almost pouting. *Oops! I always forget he can understand my thoughts.* Carmine sighed and shook her head with disgust. *Now I have to be careful about offending an Angel. My life gets more complicated, not less.*

"Laurence, please forgive me?" Carmine said with an almost saccharine sweetness. "You have to admit it has been a complicated, emotional two days and I'm not coping well, even with your help. I assumed that with an Angel, my life would be easy, if not easier."

"Carmine, I can't change the events in your life. You know that. There will always be obstacles because that is what you are here on Earth for, to learn. Angels make the learning easier. You have to pay attention to what you are given.

"It is so important to meditate and to have silence in life because that is when suggestions and direction are given to humans. If they listen, then the obstacles or challenges become easier and what could be a major challenge is diminished because of the help received from the Angel. It is easier to fulfill your spiritual contract. But you have to listen and be aware of the messages. It can't be done on a random basis. It must be practiced at all times. Otherwise, the message doesn't get through."

"Okay, Laurence, enough! I truly understand and am grateful for what you are sharing. But right now I'm exhausted and I need to help Leslie as much as I can." Carmine drove into Leslie's driveway.

Two hours later Leslie and Carmine were at Carmine's condo. It had taken them that long to clean up Leslie's room so that her parents would never know what happened.

Leslie parked her car in the second space of Carmine's underground parking garage and Carmine helped Leslie carry her small bag of clothes, books, and a variety of miscellaneous personal items. Leslie had brought enough to stay for two or three days, depending upon how she felt. As they walked into the condo, Carmine directed Leslie to the second bedroom while she walked to the refrigerator in the kitchen.

"Leslie, how long has it been since you have eaten?" she shouted.

Leslie walked into the kitchen and said with a puzzle in her voice, "I can't remember. It seems ages and I am starving. Let me order some food and I'll pay for it."

"Leslie, don't be foolish. I have some homemade lentil soup that I have frozen, as well as an eggplant sauce for pasta. I can have a great dinner on the table in about forty-five minutes that will include a salad, some olive bread and a good bottle of Chianti, which I have been saving for a special occasion. I think this could be called special, for a variety of reasons."

Carmine pulled the ingredients out of the freezer, placed them in the appropriate pots, along with water for the pasta, made the salad and dressing and opened up the wine to let it breathe. In ten minutes, the kitchen was warm, smelling of garlic and tomatoes.

As Leslie was setting the table, Carmine took a closer look at Leslie, and started silently berating herself for not noticing how wan and tired she looked. "Listen, Leslie, why don't you wash that makeup off your face and don't worry about how you look.

"In fact," she said, going into the bathroom and bringing out towels and a washcloth, "why don't you take a long, hot bath while everything cooks? Anything you need of mine, feel free to use. There are all kinds of aromatherapies for the bath and my cosmetics are under the sink." Leslie started to protest, but Carmine gently pushed her into the bathroom and closed the door. Carmine stood outside the bathroom door until she heard the water run.

Returning to the kitchen to stir her sauce and lower the gas on the soup, she suddenly remembered Laurence. Turning around, she saw him standing by the refrigerator.

"Laurence, are you going to help or not?" Carmine demanded. "We have got to do something about Leslie's situation."

"Leslie has free will. I certainly can't interfere and her Angel is doing everything he can to assist Leslie in this recent challenge. She knows what she needs to do. Certainly, you may guide her and assist her as best you can. Angels welcome any support they can receive from humans."

Carmine, eyes narrowed, considered Laurence, thinking how she could manipulate his help somehow, when the phone rang.

It was Cassie and before Carmine could say anything other than "Hello," Cassie started speaking very rapidly. "Kathy is so much better. They have taken her out of the ICU and she is now in a private room and wanting pizza. Isn't that great, Mom?" And then Cassie immediately started crying.

In all of the events of the day, Carmine had totally forgotten about Kathy. "How could you forget?" she scolded herself. "What kind of a mother am I?" She saw Laurence about to say something to her, but she gave him one of her "don't you dare" looks and he quickly shut his mouth.

"Cassie, darling, why are you crying?"

"I am so relieved about Kathy. I was so frightened for her. Neither of us have even started to accomplish what we want to do yet. In fact, Mom, I made a decision I need to talk to you about. I want to drive home this weekend to talk to you. Will you be around?"

"Cassie, darling, for you I'll always be around, even if I had the whole weekend scheduled, I would un-schedule it for you. I can't wait to see you! Now, should I worry or should I not worry?"

"Mom, you always worry, no matter what. No, this is something that I think you will approve of."

"Okay, it'll be hard for me to wait, but I will. Please send Kathy some flowers and balloons from both of us and then have them send me the bill. Or you can use your credit card that your Father gave you and I'll pay you back. Okay? And don't forget to e-mail everyone who prayed for Kathy, letting them know how well their prayers worked. I'll do the same with the people I e-mailed, too."

"Okay, I'll be sure to do that. And Mom, you are so great. Thanks for everything. And I'll take care of the flowers and balloons right away."

"So, I'll see you Friday night, probably around six. Let's plan a great weekend and can we go to my favorite Italian restaurant for dinner and then my favorite deli for breakfast? And will you make me one of your special dinners?"

"Sure, sweetie, anything you want." After blowing kisses to each other through the phone, Carmine hung up. She said a silent prayer thanking the Universe, God, and everyone else who had helped Kathy through her accident.

When she looked up, there was Laurence looking at her and, as she opened her mouth, he boomed, "Carmine, you are not a bad mother. Stop it. Do not be so hard on yourself. The fact that you forgot is understandable. This unnecessary negative energy impacts all your cells. Remember you are a magnet and attract what energy you emit! All you humans need to be more forgiving and loving to yourselves. You will find that in doing this for yourself, you will be more forgiving and loving towards others, too."

"Laurence why are you shouting? I can hear you just fine, Thank you!"

"I'm sorry Carmine, I'm used to shouting at you to get your attention when you can't see me."

"So, Laurence," Carmine said with a resigned sigh, "if I couldn't see you right now, you'd still be saying this to me?"

"Yes, Carmine, but you would not hear me because you choose not to. Even Angels get frustrated when we want you to hear something. We are on your side. Now, with me being available to you on this level, it is much easier to get your attention. But I forget that I don't have to shout."

Just as Carmine was going to comment, Leslie came out of the bathroom, wrapped in a white terry cloth robe. Her long black hair had been washed and was cascading around her shoulders and her face was scrubbed clean. Carmine kneaded her lips with her teeth, so she wouldn't give away what she was feeling when she saw Leslie without the makeup. Her eyes were puffy, there were bruises on her cheeks besides a scratch on her face and her lips were swollen. But her coloring was better and she was smiling.

"Leslie, you look squeaky clean and your cheeks are glowing. I think the bath gave you an attitude adjustment," Carmine said with a lightness she did not feel, as she poured a glass of wine for both of them. Handing one of the crystal wine glasses to Leslie, she picked up the other one and touched it to Leslie's. "I always loved the Jewish toast 'L'chaim - To Life,'" Carmine said, "and I think it is appropriate to make that toast now. You have so much to live for, Leslie. Please don't throw it away," she urged.

Tears came to Leslie's eyes as they both took a sip of the Chianti. Carmine hugged Leslie quickly and then said laughing, "I hope you are hungry because I have enough food for eight people. You know, in an Italian household, if you don't have lots of leftovers, then you haven't cooked enough and that is very embarrassing. I can't seem to get away from that notion, no matter how hard I try, so I always make more than anyone can possibly eat. I truly think it is genetic."

Still laughing as she poured the soup into the soup bowls, Carmine spread the eggplant sauce over the pasta, placing it in a huge bowl so that they both could help themselves. She had finished the dressing for the salad and the buzzer went off to remind her to take the olive bread out of the oven.

"This is a feast," Leslie exclaimed, looking over the pile of food on the table. "But you know what, I think I could eat it all by myself. I can't remember when I ate last."

She served herself the pasta and immediately started eating. Alternating with sips from the soup and wine, Leslie managed to eat two bowls of pasta while Carmine was still sipping her soup. The wine helped them relax and they chatted to each other about nothing in particular until Carmine brought something up about class.

Immediately, Leslie became more animated, "Carmine, I almost forgot. What did Jake want when he asked to see you? It took you so long. I thought you had forgotten to meet me."

Carmine lowered her eyes as she felt her cheeks flushing. She didn't want to say anything to Leslie, but she had shared so much about her crush on Jake that Carmine felt compelled to say something. She hesitated, "He liked my last paper and wanted my opinion on how he could teach his students to do the same thing I did."

"Then, I guess it didn't take that long, considering the subject matter," Leslie yawned. "I am really tired," she yawned again, as she took another bite of her salad, alternating with the olive bread and finished the last of her soup.

"Actually, I didn't have an opportunity to tell him because time was short, so we are meeting Wednesday evening to discuss it," Carmine whispered, hoping that Leslie wouldn't hear her. And before Leslie could say another word, Carmine jumped up from the coffee table and said, "Look before you go to bed, I have to take your picture to show your bruises and everything," and Carmine ran out of the room.

Leslie was sputtering into her salad, "You mean you're going out with Jake this Wednesday? Carmine," she yelled after her. "You mean you have a date with Jake?" And Leslie started giggling and pounding on the table. "Yes.s.s.s.s! How absolutely terrific," she said catching her breath between the giggles. And she started giggling once again.

"Leslie," Carmine said with a stern tone, "please stop giggling so I can take your picture with my phone and then I am going to use yours. This way there will be a copy in case something happens to yours." Carmine moved around Leslie taking pictures of the right and left side of the face. As Carmine started taking the pictures, Leslie became very serious. "Look, Carmine, is this necessary? I mean, I'm not going to press charges or anything and I would rather forget everything that took place; it's too painful."

"I understand, Leslie," as Carmine continued taking the pictures. "Leslie, look straight at me so I get a full face shot. After she had taken four pictures of Leslie's face, she asked Leslie where her phone was and when Leslie indicated the bedroom, Carmine retrieved it and duplicated the pictures she took on Leslie's phone. Finally finished, she held up Leslie's phone to her so she could see the photos.

"Leslie, this is how you look. I'm not even going to take any of your body, because I think this is enough. I promised you I wouldn't say another word about you pressing charges and I'm not. But I want you to have the pictures for two reasons. The first one is to remind you that should you ever think about going back to this creep, you have the pictures to refresh your memory. The second reason is, after you have a few days to think about this, and you want to change your mind, at least you have some proof. Okay?

"These are for you to do with what you think best. Promise me you won't delete them," as she handed Leslie's phone back to her. "And even if you do, she said with a sardonic smile, I have the same photos in my phone so it won't do any good. Understand?"

"Okay," Leslie said with downcast eyes. "I promise." She put the phone in her robe pocket and then took a gulp of the wine.

Carmine started cleaning up the dishes from the table and Leslie helped her. "Leslie," Carmine mumbled, "I don't need your help. I am going to throw everything I can in the dishwasher. I am so exhausted; it has been such a wild three days!"

"Carmine, I am so sorry that I added to your exhaustion. Please forgive me," Leslie responded with tears in her eyes again.

"Leslie, my dear, don't you dare even think that. You're my friend and I am here for you. Everything seemed to happen all at once and I am cranky. Please forgive me for upsetting you," Carmine pleaded, as Leslie sobbed again.

Carmine took Leslie into her arms and hugged her while she looked around for Laurence. Turning her head slightly to the right she saw him. "Help me" she mouthed over Leslie's shoulders. Laurence nodded and Leslie's sobs subsided immediately. "I am so sorry, Carmine, I feel so terrible about everything that anything seems to make me want to cry."

"Leslie, you have been through one of the worst situations a woman can go through, so, give yourself time. Your reaction is normal. Be kind to yourself and allow yourself to feel all those negative feelings. They are real and valid and if you don't cry, and hold them in, it will be hard for you to heal."

Carmine paused and stepped back so she could see Leslie's face before she continued. "You know, Leslie, this is just a suggestion, but maybe you should see someone that could help you, like a therapist. You know, this type of situation is so traumatic, it wouldn't hurt to talk to someone professionally. I have read that there is always guilt felt by the victim and you told me earlier you felt it was somewhat your fault he hit you. So it sounds as though you fell right into the guilt trap."

Leslie became very still as she listened to Carmine and didn't move or even blink for a few moments. "You know, Carmine," she said at last, "you may be right. Let me sleep on it and I'll tell you in the morning. But I don't even know a therapist to go to, if I should decide to do that."

"I do and a very good one! I have recommended him to several clients who have this type of issue arise for employees. I've been told he is excellent and have heard only raves from the employees that have been sent to him. I'll leave his telephone number on the kitchen table for you and you can call him if you want. I promise I won't bug you about it." After a look from Laurence, she laughed and said, "I'll amend that statement and say maybe not too much."

Leslie laughed and gave Carmine a tight hug. "Thank you, Carmine."

"Go to bed now and try to sleep. I'll finish up here and then I am going to take a bath and go to bed myself. I need to be out of here by 9:30 tomorrow morning to see one of my clients and I won't be back until 4:30. So you have that whole time to be by yourself. If I don't see you before I leave, be sure to help yourself to anything you want. Promise me you will indulge yourself by doing nothing except caring for yourself. I'll leave an extra house key and the remote to the garage on the kitchen table so you can come and go when you wish."

Leslie gave Carmine another hug, yawned and said good night as she went into the bedroom and closed the door.

Carmine waited a few minutes then hurried towards the closed door and put her ear to it. She heard the bed squeak and saw the light go out under the door.

She ran to the kitchen and turned to Laurence, "What did you do to stop her crying and calm down so fast?" she demanded.

"I had her Angel speak to her more intently than he was," Laurence said, "and she was able to hear the message that time. Her Angel has been hard at work for the past two days, but Leslie hasn't been able to hear him. She has been in such turmoil and so angry and upset that it was impossible for her to listen to what he was trying to tell her.

"When you humans desperately need our help, you can't hear what we are saying because there is too much agitation in the body that is created by turmoil, stress and negative emotions. It is like sending an e-mail and the message is delayed or returned because there is a problem on the receiver's end. When a situation arises that causes these overwhelming harmful emotions, sit down, be calm and try to meditate or go into silence. Then the Angel's message can be heard and the human then knows what to say and do. It is quite easy that way. But, alas, very few humans do this.

"However, her Angel was able to get through to Leslie at that particular moment in time, not only due to the intensity of his message, but because of your love and compassion for her, Carmine. Love is such a strong antidote for almost everything on Earth that causes pessimism or unhappiness or any negative situation. It heals and it places the human into positive energy. When a human picks up, even on a subtle level, that someone truly cares for and loves them, then the person responds to all the goodness that is flowing to her or him at that time. It is quite remarkable the impact that human love has."

"You know, Laurence, what you are saying makes sense because I know when I meditate and feel calm within, I can almost always find an answer to a problem or situation. But it is not easy because the turmoil and negativity takes over and that is all one can focus on." Carmine sighed as she began to ask another question; there was so much she wanted to learn. "I can't ask any more questions, tonight, Laurence, I am too exhausted. I wish you could help me with this mess," she pleaded, though she knew what the answer would be.

"Carmine," Laurence said softly, "you know I can't do that."

Carmine dropped her shoulders in resignation and then loaded the dishwasher with everything they had used for dinner so she wouldn't see the mess and could clean it up when she had more time. She looked up the therapist's name and number that she had mentioned to Leslie, copied it on a large piece of paper and left it on the kitchen table along with the remote from the garage and the house key.

She shuffled tiredly into the bathroom and took a long hot bath. She had just enough energy to light the candles and use some of her oils. Ten minutes later, with considerable effort, she dragged herself out of the tub and performed her usual bedtime rituals.

As soon as Carmine walked into her bedroom, she sank into her meditation chair. It felt so good to focus on peace and serenity, which is what meditation brought her. Out of the corner of her eyes, she noticed that Laurence was already meditating. *One of these days, I am going to ask him why he meditates. It seems so strange that an Angel meditates.*

"Carmine," Laurence started to say, "I meditate because . . ."

"Laurence, no! Please, can we postpone this conversation for another time?"

Laurence looked hurt, but Carmine ignored him and continued to meditate, focusing on a spot between her eyes and above her nose. This was her "third eye" where intuitive awareness merged with her consciousness and where clarity and peace automatically occur, if she did it right. At least that is what Laurence had taught her and she had to admit he was right. After the last three days, she needed it terribly. After fifteen minutes of meditating, Carmine found herself swaying and catching herself falling asleep on the chair. She stumbled to bed and within seconds, was asleep.

Chapter Six

Carmine was surprised that she was awake by five-thirty the next morning. But she had a good night's sleep and felt energetic and didn't have that tired hangover that she seemed to have many times in the past. She felt happy and ready to go for whatever the day had to offer.

Wow, why do I feel this good when I was so tired last night? She looked around for Laurence, thinking that he had to have something to do with her state of mind. Since she always started her morning with a meditation, he was waiting for her by her chair.

"Laurence, did you have anything to do with how good I'm feeling today?"

"Carmine, I always try to have you focus on the positive and many times you do, but not always. But last night even though you were tired, you were relaxing because you are happy that you and Jake will meet for dinner and that your daughter will be here with you this weekend. The human subconscious mind has much to do with one's state of energy and has an effect on one's everyday mental outlook, even if they are not aware of it."

At the mention of Jake's name, Carmine's face became flushed and she ignored what Laurence said about him.

"You're right, Laurence, I'm overjoyed that Cassie will be home this weekend. Our times together are so rare now that it is a special treat. But you mean that an underlying thought like that helps my moods and helps me sleep? Even if I meditate before sleeping which calms me anyway?"

"Very much, Carmine. Your mind is not as calm as you may think as there are always underlying thoughts that interfere with sleeping. Focusing on joy as well as a great deal of laughter during the day contributes to a person's ability to sleep."

Carmine smiled. "These conversations are so enlightening, but I can't spend the time, fascinating as it is," Carmine congratulated herself on her diplomacy. "Right now, I have to get ready," as she hurried to the bathroom.

"Carmine, you are always in a hurry and this is what is important." Laurence was talking to Carmine's back as he said this and she never turned around. Laurence gave a sad sigh and said, hoping Carmine would hear him. "Humans have all the wrong priorities. What is important, they don't even think about and what isn't, they spend all their short, precious time on Earth worrying about. Sometimes it is so hard being an Angel for humans."

Carmine turned her head, gave him an irritated look, and continued getting ready. Within fifteen minutes, she had showered, towel dried her short hair and put on a minimum of makeup, along with her black stretch jeans, a deep red cotton turtleneck and a short plum-color jacket. She felt almost overdressed, as her client was a high-tech computer company, which had the most informal business culture she had ever seen.

There was no dress code, so sweats and jeans were the usual attire. And there were no walls or formal offices, even for the president. Dogs, birds and other miscellaneous animals, as well as children, accompanied their various owners and parents to work. There was a child care room for the children and a large indoor and outdoor area for the animals. The company provided a huge gym with every conceivable item of equipment one could possibly use, along with an Olympic swimming pool for adults and a smaller pool for the children.

Everyone had to be at work by a certain time every day and stay for at least four hours; but other than that, employees could come and go as they pleased, as long as they got their work done. Everyone seemed to enjoy working there. Turnover was so low she couldn't remember the last time someone left. She went in to help the regular Human Resource Manager complete special projects that always were put off for a less busy day, which never seemed to happen.

Carmine loved working there and was looking forward to the day. Since she had awakened earlier than she had planned, she was able to catch up with her ever long list of chores. No matter how many tasks she was able to delete from her list and how she much she accomplished every day, the list seemed to remain at the same length. This morning she paid bills, cleaned the condo, including the kitchen, folded clothes, and made a grocery list so she could make Cassie her favorite dinner one of the nights she would be home.

Carmine concluded her tasks by quietly opening the second bedroom door to check on Leslie. She determined by Leslie's loud snoring, that she was sleeping well. She shut the door and then collected everything she needed, especially the all-containing burgundy backpack.

Carmine looked at the clock, saw that it was ten o'clock, locked the door and ran the three flights of steps with Laurence following her to the garage. As she opened the car door, she threw her backpack into the backseat. She buckled her seatbelt and started the car, looking over to see if Laurence was with her.

"Of course he is," Carmine admonished herself for even daring to think that he might not be there. "Hey, Laurence, you have been unusually quiet this morning. How come?"

"Actually, Carmine, I've been the same as usual for you; guiding you, advising you, helping you to do the best you can. But you have been so busy with your list of what you humans call chores and so engrossed with your own thoughts, that you did not hear me and I decided I wasn't going to shout," Laurence said with a petulant look on his face. "You humans become so caught up in the trivial and the mundane that what is most important to you in this lifetime is many times forgotten."

"Laurence, you are such a pain in the 'you know what,'" Carmine roared at him, thinking that everyone on the freeway could hear her. "The trivial and the mundane need to be done. It would be great if I could tell all the people that I owe money to that I didn't have time to pay them this month because I was too busy taking care of the important parts of my life or that my clothes are dirty because cleanliness and good hygiene are not high enough on this lifetime's list of importance, or that the dirt in my house is not dirty enough to take my time away from what matters.

"Darn it, Laurence," Carmine said with her voice softening, "I do agree with you, but much of this life is spent doing repetitious, boring, but absolutely essential chores. And if one doesn't do them, your life deteriorates rapidly into chaos." At this point, Carmine was quietly sputtering and her driving was becoming erratic. "Because you can flip your wings, and everything is done, doesn't mean I can do it. And, by the way, where are your wings? I have been meaning to ask you that ever since we came back to Earth together."

Laurence interrupted her, "Carmine, please, pay attention to your driving," Laurence begged, as he held lights on green longer, much to the puzzlement of the other drivers and pedestrians, so Carmine wouldn't crash into something or someone, if she had to stop suddenly. "Remember, if there is an accident, there is only so much that I can do. And stop taking your anger out on me. I'm trying to help you.

"To answer your question about my wings, Carmine, is it is up to the observer if the human's Angel has wings. Many humans would not believe that someone was an Angel without its wings. You, however, are a human where it doesn't matter whether the Angel has wings or not, so it is easier for me not having them."

"Laurence, I'm sorry. I know I'm being grouchy and cranky and everything else but there has been too much happening and I'm feeling stressed, once again. I haven't been giving as much time and concentration to my meditation and I guess it shows when I react so strongly to stupid statements, like the one you just gave me." Carmine realized she had used the word 'stupid,' and immediately retracted her statement. "It wasn't stupid, Laurence. I understand you simply see things differently than we humans."

"That may be, Carmine, but truly, you are not expected to get 'everything done' each lifetime. Trying to get everything done is an illusion for humans. One of the purposes of human life is to learn what is truly important to you and to help make the planet you live on a better place because you have been there. Each human must know what is truly important rather than urgent. Urgent is usually other people's needs or insignificant duties. If you get wrapped up in these insignificant and trivial routines, rather than your larger and true purpose in life, your most important spiritual contract is obscured." Carmine nodded absently.

Carmine drove into the company parking lot and parked the car. "Please stay out of my way. I've a lot of work to do and I can't be distracted," she said, focused on her client. Laurence nodded. She noticed that he was now wearing a green warm-up suit. *He will fit right in with the employees!* Carmine thought, but did not mention anything about the outfit as she walked into the building.

Six hours later, with a lot less energy than she had when she went in, Carmine walked out to her car, got in and breathed a sigh of relief. Even though she enjoyed working there, she had to operate at such a fast pace and there seemed to be so many distractions with the animals and the children and the no walls, she always felt she had run the L.A. Marathon. But it was fun and it was different so she couldn't complain about any part of it.

She glanced at Laurence, sitting in the passenger's seat and she laughed to herself because he looked as exhausted as she felt. Before she could say anything, he said, "Yes, Carmine, I look exhausted because I reflect you and your feelings. Angels try very hard to diffuse the negative feelings of humans by absorbing them, so that humans don't become so burdened and overwhelmed by their feelings." Carmine placed her hand over her heart and gave a grateful smile.

"I never thought about all that Angels do for us, Thank you! We both are tired. I am going to drive to the grocery store, pick up the food that I'll need for the weekend, drive home, take a long, long hot bath and go to bed. You'll get a break too!" Laurence placed his hand over his heart and grinned. As she was saying this, she thought about Leslie. "I'd better get more food for Leslie too." Carmine sighed deeply as her shoulders sank into her chest. *I want to be there for her as long as she needs me, but it is draining.*

"Maybe she won't need you to cook for her," Laurence said tentatively. Carmine looked at him for a moment, but then let his comment pass as she spotted her favorite organic grocery store.

She picked up fruit, vegetables and some of Cassie's favorite snacks and miscellaneous tasty items for the weekend. She also bought one-half of a roasted chicken for Leslie and her for that night. Carmine rushed through the checkstand and threw the three grocery bags into her trunk. With a sigh of relief, she drove home trying to keep herself awake by slapping her face at random times.

She didn't see Leslie's car when she drove into the garage. *I wonder where Leslie is. Maybe she had a late appointment and still isn't home.* She emptied the car of groceries and lugged them in the grocery basket from the garage on to the elevator and then the three floors to her condo. She couldn't wait to throw the groceries into the refrigerator, make a salad, and have a glass of wine and the chicken. She was too hungry to wait for Leslie to return.

As she took the groceries from the basket to the refrigerator, she noticed a large yellow piece of notebook paper on the kitchen table where she had left Leslie's note in the morning.

Dear Carmine,

I can't thank you enough for sending me to the therapist you recommended, Steve. He was great and has given me a lot to think about. My parents came home and I called them, told them everything, as Steve suggested and they asked me to come home. I'll tell you all when I see you at class. Thanks for everything Carmine. I don't know what I would have done without you.

Hugs and love,
Leslie

Carmine read the note twice. "So what am I going to do with the chicken?" Carmine asked herself. "I guess I am really tired if that's all I can think of." She remembered about what Laurence had said in the car about maybe she wouldn't have to cook for Leslie.

"Laurence," she grumbled, "did you know that Leslie wasn't going to be here?"

"I couldn't tell specifically, but there was some indication that she might return to her permanent home. But you know, Carmine, everyone has free will and it was only at the last minute that she decided."

"I'm glad of that," Carmine started raising her voice, "because if you knew for sure and still let me buy the chicken, I would be very upset with you."

Carmine cut some of the chicken up and threw that in a salad she was making. She poured herself a half a glass of Pinot Grigio, turned on her favorite classical radio station and then sat down at the small round glass kitchen table. She silently said a quick prayer and then slowly started eating. She looked up and there was Laurence sitting on the other chair watching her eat.

Not wanting to have any kind of conversation with him, Carmine ignored him and sat silently and ate her dinner. When finished, she stuffed all the dishes into the dishwasher, along with the previous night's and headed for the bedroom.

Halfway to the door, she gave an exclamation of horror. She looked at Laurence and they both said "JAKE" at the same time.

"Tomorrow is my date with Jake. I have no idea what I am going to wear. I was planning to go through my wardrobe tonight thinking I was going to have time and energy. What a laugh!"

Carmine was in her walk-in closet madly throwing clothes out on the floor, mumbling as each article of clothing landed on the soft purple carpet. "That's too dressy" to a black dress.... "that's too professional" to a linen pants suit... "too dark and too cool for this time of year" to another pants suit.... "too summery" to a print blue dress and "much too tight" to a pair of silk green slacks.

At that point, Carmine began heaving most of her clothes onto the closet floor in desperation, trying to find the perfect outfit.

Laurence shook his head, as he watched Carmine walk through the clothes she had thrown, disconsolately holding random pieces of clothing up to her face, Carmine fell on top of all of them and wailed, "I absolutely do not have a thing to wear tomorrow night!"

Laurence sat down on the closet floor next to Carmine and looked at her with a combination of puzzlement and pain in his face and said, "But, Carmine, I count 639 articles of clothing in your closet. How could you possibly not have anything to wear?"

"You are like every other man in the world and simply do not know how a woman thinks!" Carmine stopped crying suddenly, sat up, squinted her eyes at Laurence and asked in her most authoritative voice, "And how did you come up with that ridiculous number of clothing, Laurence? I know I don't have anything close to that exaggerated amount." And she stared at him with her arms crossed against her chest.

"Carmine," Laurence almost stuttered when he answered, startled by Carmine's tone of voice and her sudden transformation from the crying Carmine to almost adversarial Carmine. "I counted every article of attire in your closet."

"There is no way that I have that many clothes, unless you counted all my shoes, my belts, and all the rest of my accessories including my old nightgowns."

"Carmine, I counted whatever was in your closet"

"You are definitely clueless," giving a sardonic laugh. "There are different clothes for different occasions and shoes and belts and nightgowns do not count. They are things that go with the actual clothing and …" and then Carmine broke off. "This is useless! It will take days to explain the nuances of attire to an Angel— a male Angel at that.

"Look Laurence. I need something perfect to wear for tomorrow night. This is my first date with Jake and it's a supreme emotional event. What I wear has to feel right and be appropriate for the occasion. But it has to give the impression that I threw it together and that I don't care what I'm wearing. And it has to look fabulous on me so that Jake is captivated and dazzled by my mere presence."

Laurence looked at her in puzzlement. "Isn't that's an inordinate request to ask from a few pieces of clothing?"

"I don't know why I would expect you to understand," as Carmine sniffed at Laurence. "A man is a man is a man whether he is an Angel or human being. I thought Angels, whether male or female, would be different."

"Carmine, remember I told you that your perception of Angels as to whether they are male or female is based upon an individual's belief system. You happen to believe in male Angels so that is how I appear to you. However, Angels do not have a sexual identity as you know it on Earth. My understanding of women's attire would be the same whether I appear to you as either male or female."

"You are behaving exactly as any human male on Earth. It would be hard to believe that a female Angel would be as dense as you are right now." And Carmine rose regally from the pile of clothing she was sitting on in the closet, shut the door so she wouldn't see the mess of clothing on the floor and flung herself on the soft lavender comforter on the bed.

I am way too tired to think tonight so I'll meditate before going to sleep and maybe my subconscious will design the perfect outfit to wear tomorrow night.

Feeling better thinking about it, she did her regular nightly ritual, including her yoga and then threw on her favorite white cotton nightgown. As she sat down in her meditation chair almost asleep, she noticed the nightgown. *I think this is the same one I wore when I met Laurence. Maybe it will bring me luck for tomorrow evening.*

Carmine was almost through with her meditation when she suddenly sat up straight and opened her eyes. Her subconscious mind, while she was meditating, had, indeed, created the perfect outfit. Carmine smiled at herself. *I know meditation is supposed to place you in touch with the Universe and God, but it assists you in the mundane area as well. I don't know why I didn't think of putting those pieces together myself.*

"So easy," she said to herself as she thought of the deep plum boot-cut slacks, light lavender round neck silk blouse and the knee-length plum sweater jacket. "I'll look colorful, but casual and I'll wear some thin gold hoop earrings, a gold chain belt and black strappy booties."

With those thoughts, she ended her meditation by saying a heartfelt "thank you" and fell into bed. As she was falling asleep, she thought she heard Laurence say, with a chuckle in his voice, "You're welcome."

Chapter Seven

Carmine heard her Zen alarm clock chime three times before she opened her eyes and looked at the time: 4:45 a.m. She decided there was no way she was going to the gym and pressed the reset button for another hour and went back to sleep.

Five minutes later, or so it seemed, the clock chimed again. Carmine jumped out of bed as soon as the alarm went off and, as fast as possible, practiced her yoga exercises followed by fifteen minutes of meditation. No matter what the circumstances or how she felt, she reserved five to fifteen minutes in the morning for this special time to be alone with her thoughts and to find her inner balance, especially since Laurence confirmed the benefits of meditation.

On those rare days that she couldn't meditate, she always found that the day did not go as well as she needed. However, when she did meditate, she found no matter how much time she spent in meditation, that, somehow, not only were those minutes were given back to her and everything went more smoothly, but she had gained additional time somewhere in the day.

As she went through her morning ritual getting ready for school, Carmine scolded herself for not going to the gym regularly, as she had done BL. BL were the initials for "Before Laurence." Her life had been changed so dramatically since the very eventful night that she had been pretty negligent about that aspect of her life. "But," she resolved, "I promise I'll start going regularly next week. With Cassie being home for the weekend and with the date with Jake and.... *Oh, my gosh,* she thought, almost in a panic, *that's tonight.* Carmine rapidly finished putting on her makeup and combing her hair and went to the closet. She pulled out the slacks, blouse and sweater jacket she had meditated about last night and looked at them in relief. All three pieces were unwrinkled, clean and in completely wearable condition. "Thank you, God," Carmine said gratefully, "one less thing for me to do this evening."

She pulled on her black jeans, a black t-shirt, wrapped her lime green sweater on her shoulders and she was ready. Grabbing her backpack, she ran through the day's agenda. She had her English class with Jake and she wanted to see Leslie after the class. She had her other two classes, but maybe she could skip the one in Communications. This way she could start getting things ready for Cassie's arrival Friday afternoon and still have time to leisurely dress for tonight's date. She was working late on Thursday and knew that she wouldn't have time to do all the tasks she needed to do before Cassie arrived.

"Carmine," she told herself in a stern tone, "this is just a date. It's not like you're getting married, which is how you are behaving. Act your age! What are you? Twelve years old? It's a date, nothing more." As she said this, she heard a chuckle. She turned and there was Laurence trying hard not to show how amused he was at her conversation. Carmine had been so busy with all her thoughts and her activities of the morning, she had not even noticed Laurence, or, as she noted to herself, the lack of Laurence.

She said with a bright and gay voice, grabbing her keys and heading to the door, "Where have you been this morning? Oversleep?"

"Actually, Carmine, I've been here, but you've been so busy, again, with your thoughts and chores, you never even saw or heard me."

"Today is a big day so let's get started. No traffic, right Laurence?" Carmine's tone reflected her happiness.

"If this meeting with your instructor Jake does this for you, Carmine, perhaps you should see this person every day. You are filled with light and your whole being emanates a positive energy," Laurence said to Carmine as she was walking to her car.

"Laurence, I feel so good and excited about this 'meeting' as you call it. Maybe that is what you see in me."

"When humans are happy and joyful that energy actually radiates from the inside to the outside. And it is noticeable, not only to Angels, but to everyone. That is why when you feel good, good things happen. It is like a magnet."

Driving on to the freeway, Carmine was deep in thought about what Laurence was saying. The traffic, as usual, was moving very nicely. Carmine said a silent thank you to Mother and the Director for giving her Laurence. "How about me, Carmine? Are you going to say thank you to me? I'm the one that is doing this for you," Laurence asked.

"Yes, Laurence, thank you! I do appreciate everything you do but I do take you for granted sometimes don't I?" Laurence wistfully nodded in acknowledgment.

"I'm going to have to thank him more," Carmine told herself. She thought about all the times she would coach her HR clients on giving their employees positive feedback and prizing them for their accomplishments. She hadn't been doing so well with Laurence, not that he was an employee, but she knew how important it was to appreciate those you worked with. Laurence sat up taller, smiling at her with one of his kindest smiles.

"Hey, Laurence, I am thinking of what you said about when you feel good, you attract good things. Does that work in reverse? When you feel bad, you attract bad things? Because I know that some days start out bad and become worse, much worse!"

"Yes, Carmine, you are very perceptive. That is exactly true. You are always a magnet and it is energy. And it is very simple to attract good things all the time! You simply have to focus on the good and the positive and what you want and truly feel it. If you do that, you will have those things you focus upon. And that is true, too, about words you speak. Energy follows thoughts and words. What you speak and think, if you do it enough, will materialize. So you must think, feel and speak only the things that you want to create that are good. But it seems it is very difficult for humans to do this as they seem to focus on the negative."

"I know, Laurence. It is such a challenge; the negative always seems to be much more powerful than the positive," Carmine said as she sped into the college parking lot and had her usual close parking space. "Today, I am focusing on the positive and I know it will be a wonderful day. Thank you for the great ride in!"

Carmine's joy was evident in her walk as she almost danced to her classroom, bringing smiles to some of the students that she passed on the way. She was oblivious to this and almost everything else around her as she was trying to arrange a normal look on her face. She didn't want to give away her excitement over the date to Jake. She was determined that he wouldn't see any difference in her today. However, the minute she walked into the classroom, she spotted Leslie. Before Carmine could say a word, Leslie laughed and said "Boy, you are glowing. Does that look have anything to do with Jake and tonight?"

Carmine looked at Leslie with several caustic comments in mind, but, instead, commented, "you look so much better today, Leslie, I hardly see any bruises and you seem in better spirits, too." *Good, get her off my date and onto her needs.*

"Thanks, Carmine. I want to talk to you after class and tell you what happened yesterday. Do you have time?"

"For you, Leslie, always. You seem like my daughter and I can't refuse her, either."

Just then, Jake came into the class and turned bright red when he spotted Carmine. Carmine smiled weakly at him and felt herself grow hot. *This class today is going to be a nightmare. Please, let me stay cool and act normal.*

"Of course, I will help you," she heard Laurence say.

Carmine refused to comment back, but stared hard at him, thinking how much she would enjoy throttling his spiritual neck!

"But, Carmine," Laurence said teasingly, "I thought you wanted my assistance and that you were going to appreciate me from now on."

Carmine tossed her head as she glared at him, trying to keep a smile on her face for everyone else.

Leslie looked at her with concern in her eyes. "Carmine, you look rather strange, are you okay?"

"Yes, Leslie, don't even think about me. I'm thinking about tonight."

"You'll have an absolutely fabulous time with Jake," Leslie almost shouted. Carmine's face turned bright red and she surreptitiously looked around to see if anyone had heard Leslie. Because Jake was speaking to a student, everyone else in the classroom was talking and no one seemed to have heard their conversation, thank goodness!

Relieved, Carmine scooted down in her seat, hunched her shoulders, pretended she was reading her book, and said very quietly through clenched teeth, "Leslie, Please! Shut Up!"

Before Leslie could reply, Jake called the class to order and started the day's lesson. *This is going to be the longest hour and one-half of my life.*

Actually, the time went very quickly as Carmine was trying to decide what makeup she should wear, if the outfit she chose was the right one, the sequence of tasks she would accomplish once she arrived home, and devise several topics of conversation she could use this evening if there were silent moments. Jake did not look at her once during the class hour. Carmine was partly relieved and partly annoyed. *He could have at least smiled at me.*

As Carmine rose from her seat to leave, Jake walked over to her and said very softly, "I'll pick you up tonight about seven? Is that good for you?"

Carmine nodded her head yes. She cleared her throat a couple of times and then said, "That will be perfect. Do you need directions to my house?"

"I already Googled it. I'm looking forward to it."

"So am I," Carmine said, with what she hoped, was the right amount of enthusiasm. "It's a gated condo community; hit the buzzer next to my name and I'll unlock the gate as soon as I hear it, or you can text me."

Jake smiled and said, "I'll see you later," as he turned towards a student who had called his name. Carmine, as rapidly as possible, walked out of the classroom and saw Leslie waiting for her with a wide grin on her face.

"Leslie, if you say one thing, I swear I'll never speak to you again."

Leslie laughed and kept on grinning, but, thankfully, did not say anything else. They found a table by the bookstore and sat down. Leslie began telling Carmine about the events that took place, especially her visit to the therapist yesterday.

"So, Steve was fabulous! He helped me sift through my perception of my relationship with Bart and defined what was the truth about that relationship. I had confused possessiveness with love. Bart wanted to control me and put me down because it made him feel good, since his self-esteem was very low. And I allowed him, because my brothers seemed to treat me the same say way; you know, asking 'where are you going, what are you doing?' things like that. But Steve said that was where I became confused because my brothers did it out of love and concern and because they cared. Bart did it out of a need to feel superior. I didn't know the difference."

"How do you feel about everything today, then?" Carmine was trying to be gentle with her questions. "How are you going to handle the situation with Bart? Are you going to report this abuse to the police?"

"Steve recommended that I get a temporary restraining order, which means he can't be within a certain distance from me. I have to file the paperwork with the appropriate agencies, first to the city that I live in and then give a copy of the paperwork to anyplace else that I might be, for instance at work or school. But if he works at the same place or goes to the same school, then it can't be placed there. Bart doesn't go to any of the places that I do, so it shouldn't be an issue. Then, while the restraining order is in place, we will go in front of a judge to determine if the order is valid; and if it is, the judge will make it permanent and determine how long it should be.

"Steve said that the order is given for about three years on the average. The fact that I have the pictures that document how he hit me will give the police what they need to do the paperwork. And, of course, my brothers will make sure that he never gets close. It was all I had to do to stop all four of them from going after him and doing him damage. Even though my parents were very upset about what he did to me, they threatened my brothers with eviction from the house and worse if they went after Bart. They want it handled properly and they don't want to exacerbate this situation.

"Steve wants to see me a few more times," Leslie continued, "to make sure that this never happens again. He said the sessions will facilitate my commitment to myself and it demonstrates self-love, self-respect and self-trust. And I'm sure it won't happen again. But I want to understand completely how I allowed it to happen." Leslie was emotional, but was able to smile as she said the last sentence.

Carmine reached over to her and hugged her. "You are a brave and courageous woman, Leslie. By facing and acknowledging this horrible situation, you are taking responsibility for your part of it. I'm not blaming you. We have to understand how we might have, inadvertently contributed to situations like this, even unconsciously, so we don't create it again. Rightly so, many women are fearful for their or their children's lives, and it makes some kind of horrible sense to tolerate the situation, for a time. But thank goodness that this wasn't the case with you. You are out. I wouldn't want to see this pattern repeat for you.

"It seems to me, and this is only an observation, that you didn't speak up for yourself when Bart constantly put you down in so many areas of your life. I know you were unhappy about it, but you never told him that you resented his negative comments and criticism. Perhaps if you had, he would have seen you as someone who wouldn't tolerate this type of behavior. He possibly would have left you to pick on someone else who would. Instead, he thought you were easy prey and you gave him license to continue. He accelerated his behavior by hitting you. Instead of verbal abuse, it became physical. Hurrah for you for going ahead with the restraining order!"

"You should have been a psychologist, Carmine, because Steve said about the same thing," as Leslie nodded her head while Carmine was speaking.

"I'm going to skip out on my next class and go home. Cassie is coming home Friday afternoon and I'm going to do some cooking and other chores this afternoon so I can spend quality time with my daughter this weekend," Carmine said, as she began to gather herself to leave.

Leslie's face broke into a wicked grin as she interrupted Carmine, "Who are you trying to kid, Carmine? You want to go home and give yourself plenty of time to prepare for your hot date tonight."

Carmine felt her face turn red at Leslie's loud remark, but instead of retorting, she looked at Leslie with what she hoped was a disgusted look. Carmine couldn't hold the look for a more than a second, because she started giggling and said, "Leslie, you are so right. I am giggling like an adolescent. I should know better." But she couldn't help herself and went right on with the laughter.

She hugged Leslie good-bye and almost skipped to her car, with Laurence following her, wearing almost the same grin as Leslie had.

As Carmine started the car, she turned to Laurence and said, "Okay, Laurence, I know that you are as amused by this 'date' as Leslie, but I would appreciate your keeping your thoughts to yourself and not interrupting what I am thinking, as I plan for this event. Is that agreed?"

"Of course, Carmine," Laurence replied with compassion, "I will do whatever you wish."

"Thank you, Laurence."

Carmine was barely conscious of her drive home. She was busily thinking about what she was going to do as soon as she walked through her door. A long, slow bath, five or ten minutes' meditation followed by twenty or thirty minutes of a nap, and then plenty of time to dress. She congratulated herself on what she was wearing. Even though it was mid-October, it was very warm, in the high 80's, and she felt that the outfit she had planned would be perfect for the evening.

So intent was she on the plans for that night, she never noticed the police car behind her. She left the freeway for her off-ramp. She drove right through a yellow light that changed red as she drove through the intersection. Almost immediately, she heard a siren behind her and snapped her attention back to the present.

Looking at the rear view mirror, she saw the police officer motioning her to get over. Being Carmine, she became agitated. "Oh, my God, I am going to get a ticket. I never noticed he was behind me. Please, Laurence, you have to help me. I can't afford a ticket or the time it takes. Please," she pleaded with tears in her eyes, "you can't allow this to happen."

"Don't worry, Carmine," Laurence said in a hushed voice, "I will do the best I can to minimize the difficulty."

"You mean you are going to show yourself?"

Laurence gave her a quizzical look. "No, of course not!"

At that point, the police officer was beside her window. She smiled at him as she turned her window down with what she hoped was a sweet, innocent look.

"I'm not sure what I did, Officer."

"You practically went through a red light. It was yellow! Then it turned red."

"I'm so sorry. This light is new at this off-ramp and I guess I haven't adjusted," Carmine said with a puzzled look on her face. "I can't believe that I went through a red light, but if you say so, I guess I did," as she gave the officer a hesitant smile.

"May I see your license?" the officer asked as though he had not heard anything she had said.

Carmine carefully pulled out her driver's license as well as a copy of her insurance card. As she was doing this, she gave a silent plea to Laurence, "Do something!"

The officer looked at her driver's license, looked at the insurance receipt and then looked at her. Carmine had now arranged a look on her face that she hoped said, "I'm really sorry. It was a mistake. Please don't give me a ticket."

The officer handed back her license and said, "Okay, Lady, I'm not going to give you a ticket this time. But understand, the light is there to help you and to keep you out of trouble. Please pay attention in the future."

Carmine nodded her head at everything he said, and trying not to gush with gratitude, "I appreciate the warning officer and I will be careful from now on."

"Be sure that you do," the officer said as he turned toward his car. Carmine waited until the police car pulled away and then turned to Laurence.

"I don't know how you did that, but I want you to know that I am eternally grateful. But, how did you do that?"

"First I saw his loving essence and radiated it back to him. Then I spoke to his Angel who reminded him that his wife expected him home on time tonight, because they have tickets to a play. He was at the end of his shift and he had some paperwork to do at the station before leaving. We both reminded him of all the things he had to do, so he felt he didn't have the extra time to do your ticket."

"Laurence, you're a wonder and I can't thank you enough." With that statement, Carmine headed her car back into traffic, very carefully noting the speed limits and the lights and drove guardedly to her condo. Once inside, she dropped everything and tore off all her clothes and put on the same ragged white nightgown she had worn when she met Laurence.

She then took the next hour or more to "enhance her assets" as she used to tell Cassie when she was dressing for an important occasion. She took a long steaming bath, drank lots of water and then slathered her face with her most expensive face mask. The mask was so thick that only Carmine's two brown eyes and teeth showed. Carmine's reasoning was, if a little was good for you, then much more was better and fewer flaws would show when removed, at least on a temporary basis. Noticing that Laurence was watching all of this activity, she said without rancor, "I hope you are seeing me in the energy pattern. No one should be able to see me do this."

"Yes, Carmine, you are a vortex of moving energy. I will believe you are going to relax only when I actually see you do it."

"I'm going to relax," Carmine replied with a smile. "I'm going to do some yoga, a little meditation and then take a nap, something I haven't been able to do for weeks. What a luxury! I want to be very calm, centered and balanced tonight so I appear as though this is an everyday event in my life and be very blasé about it."

As she spoke, Laurence's face went from its usual composed and non-judgmental façade to one that looked like a Santa Claus countenance about ready to laugh. "Carmine," Laurence almost choked on not laughing out loud, "Are you not deceiving yourself? You have been consumed by this event since it was made."

"Laurence, Laurence, Laurence, I don't expect you to understand. Even though you are an angel, you are a male Angel and therefore anything I say wouldn't appear rational to you. It's girl stuff!" Carmine replied as she walked into the bedroom with her nose in the air, a haughty look on her face trying not to laugh at the absurdity of explaining first date anxieties to an angel.

She shut the door and then tried to do yoga and meditation, but her stomach was in turmoil. Finally, she threw herself on the bed, covered herself with the quilt and, almost without any effort, fell asleep.

Carmine was awake by 5:30 and started the final steps for the "DATE." She shampooed and dried her hair and noted it was unusually flattering. A super hair day! She gave Laurence mental thanks, with a twinge of guilt for being so short with him earlier.

Before she began her makeup, she took another look at the outfit she had assembled the night before. Yes, it was definitely right for the occasion so now she could concentrate on "enhancing" her face.

After slathering on a new moisturizer that had promised a moist young look, which she knew in her heart, was something she wanted to believe, and not a fact, she furiously worked for forty-five minutes with various cosmetics to magnify the good and eliminate or hide, in her judgment, the bad to give her a natural look. Carmine laughed as she thought of the disparity of the natural look and how long it took her to achieve "natural."

Laurence, who had been watching with acute fascination, tried to speak, but each time he would start, Carmine hissed at him with a look on her face that made him think it better to leave her alone.

After putting on her clothes, Carmine added the thin, gold-hooped earrings, the black strappy booties and took the sweater jacket out of the closet and placed it on a bedroom chair near the door with the small Coach purse that she had filled with a few necessities.

She then inspected each room in the condo to be sure that is was presentable, which it was, except for the bedroom. *But there was no way he was going to see that room,* she promised herself.

Laurence interrupted that thought with "Are you sure, Carmine?"

Carmine sniffed and tossed her head, "After all these lifetimes with me, Laurence, you have to ask that question?"

"Carmine, Carmine" Laurence said quietly, "I'm not judging you and I'm not joking with you. I'm reading your deeper thoughts. Perhaps you are not even aware of them."

The gate buzzer rang. "On my gosh! That's Jake! Laurence, I don't want to see, smell or hear anything to do with you tonight. Keep out of my way and out of my mind. Do you understand?" she asked him with the tone of a Marine Sergeant at a boot camp.

She buzzed the gate to let Jake in while speaking through the intercom in a low modulated voice, far different than the one she had used on Laurence. "Take the elevator to the top floor, Jake, and turn to your left. You'll see me at the door."

She squinted her eyes to spot any apparent flaws as she surveyed herself in the full-length mirror by the front door, took a huge breath, tried to arrange a relaxed smile on her face and opened the front door. As she waited for the elevator to open, she thought to herself, mimicking the Olympic opening words, "Let the games begin."

Chapter Eight

Jake's face was flushed when he came out of the elevator wearing an olive green short sleeve knit shirt with a matching sweater tied over the shirt and beige slacks. As soon as he spotted Carmine in the doorway, he almost ran the short distance towards her holding out both hands. One hand held a huge bouquet of multi-color flowers including roses, daisies and lilies, while the other held the largest box of Godiva Chocolates she had ever seen.

Carmine's smile turned to a wide grin of utter amazement which reflected in her eyes, as she looked from Jake's face to the flowers and to the candy and back to the flowers and candy.

She started with a low giggle, which turned into deep laughter because she couldn't think of anything to say. Jake looked puzzled for a moment and then he started laughing and there they were, the two of them, laughing delightedly, at her front door.

"Jake," she finally managed to say as their laughter subsided. She took the floral bouquet in one hand and the box of candy in the other, she ushered him inside nodding her head towards the door. "Please come in" she finally managed to say, "and how very thoughtful and kind to bring my two most favorite things, flowers and chocolate. How could you possibly know?" she asked him as he stepped into her hallway and followed her to the living room. "I'm almost overwhelmed with your thoughtfulness. I hope you understand why I laughed! I was so astonished to see them. I have never had anyone make such a lovely grand gesture. They are so both so large, I couldn't help myself. I love them!"

Jake nodded his head, continuing to laugh. "I guess I went overboard," he said with a sheepish look on his face. "I was so happy about seeing you that I wanted to bring something that conveyed that to you. I have been looking forward to this since the first day of my class when I saw you."

Carmine was astounded with his honesty and total lack of guile; she already liked him because of it. She realized she was staring at him and he seemed puzzled. She shook her head and said, "Please forgive me, Jake, what you said has further thrown me. Now I have that to digest along with the flowers and candy." And she startled to giggle, again, realizing what she said. "No pun intended," she said through her giggles, "or maybe there is."

Carmine started talking very hurriedly, "Please sit down," as she pointed to the couch. "Let me put the flowers in water; I think I have the perfect vase for these. It isn't used that much, but now I am glad I have it. As for the chocolates. . ." Carmine said as Jake put the box down on the kitchen counter, "I adore chocolate and if you don't mind, I'll have one as soon as the flowers are taken care of. I am one of those people who believe that dessert should be eaten any time one wants it."

Jake chuckled as he followed her into the kitchen for the vase and commented, "You sure talk fast. Do you know that?"

Carmine nodded her head and replied, "I do talk fast and when I am nervous, I talk faster."

"Don't be nervous around me! I am very easy going," he said with understanding in his eyes. Before she could reply, he said, "Here, while you arrange the flowers, I'll open this box. I absolutely agree with you, chocolate should be eaten whenever you want it."

The flowers were nicely arranged within a few moments in a very tall Waterford vase that she placed on her black teak coffee table, in the living room. She then turned to the open box of chocolates in Jake's hands. There were several layers and Carmine took a cursory peek at each one, noting the different kinds and how they tasted.

"Carmine, it appears as if you know each piece personally."

Carmine bent her head, looking a little ashamed. "I buy myself one every time I can and I always have something different so I know the selection they have by heart. I could never afford to buy a five pound box, so this is a real luxury."

"Actually, it is four pounds which is the largest they have available for sale at the store. If I had known they were your favorites, I would have had made a special order."

As Carmine continued her search for the right chocolate for the moment, Jake smiled at her, "You are so serious, about your selection. You can have more than one now, you know."

"Yes, but then I won't be able to eat dinner. You know when I was younger, I used to each lunch at whatever was my favorite candy store, at that time," she laughingly admitted with a shake of her head. "I think I'll take a small one right now as she chose a chocolate star. How about you? And how about a glass of wine to go with it?"

"I'll take the chocolate now," as he popped a white truffle in his mouth," but I'll wait for dinner for the wine. I'm really hungry," he acknowledged.

"I need to grab my jacket and we can leave right now. It is only three or four blocks to the restaurant and the walk is pleasant and easier than finding a parking place," Carmine spoke very fast as she opened the door to her bedroom in a way that would not allow Jake to see the mess.

While Carmine was getting her jacket and purse, Jake was inspecting her condo. "This is really very nice. It is functional, but yet attractive. I like the way you have it decorated. I particularly like the Oriental accents and the art work is fascinating! It looks all original," he said with a question in his voice.

"Thank you," Carmine gave him her most dazzling smile. "The art is created by my daughter, Cassie. She is an extremely talented artist as well as an actor, so she had a hard time deciding what to pursue in college. She decided upon the acting, but I think that was because her best friend also wanted to be an actor and they decided to go to the same college and room together. I don't know if she is going to be happy with that decision, but we'll see."

"Her art is amazing! I am very impressed," Jake said as he turned back towards Carmine.

"And you look lovely," Jake added shyly.

Carmine smiled and nodded her head, relishing the compliment in silence. She took Jake by the arm and directed him towards the door. "Let's get started," she directed, "we can talk as we walk. If we don't leave now, there will be a long wait."

As she was closing the door, she thought about Laurence. *I haven't heard one word from him and I haven't even seen him. I wonder what happened.*

Immediately, there was Laurence and she heard him say, "Carmine, I have been with you every second as always, but you asked me to not intrude, so I made myself scarce."

Carmine made a comic face at Laurence that Jake caught as he turned his head to her. "Is something wrong, Carmine?" he asked with concern.

"Just the opposite, Jake, everything is perfect," she said with a smile.

I can't believe I said that. Somehow Jake has made me feel really comfortable with how I feel. He seems so authentic that I respond in the same way. Carmine was silent as she was contemplating that thought.

Carmine noticed a beautiful, new, four-door silver Jaguar parked about a half block from her condo as they walked to the restaurant. "Wow," she exclaimed with amazement, "that is the first time I have seen such a luxury car parked here. I wonder whose it is?" she asked absently, looking at the various homes and apartments on the street. "That is my dream car! If I could have any car I wanted, this would be it," she declared with a sigh.

Jake's color rose from pale to red and he smiled at her with another sheepish look.

"That's my car, Carmine. It's my one luxury. It was also my dream car. And I made it come true."

Carmine looked at him, puzzled. She was trying to phrase her next question in a diplomatic manner, but Jake answered as though she had already asked the question.

"You are wondering how a college instructor could possibly afford a luxury car like this. Right?"

Carmine apologized. "Ummm, I hate to admit it, Jake, I was thinking that. It's none of my business really."

"Teaching is my second career; an avocation, really. I write books and that is my primary income source. I love to teach and English is something that I almost feel compelled to do, so I do that, too. It's my way of making a personal contribution to society in general."

"I am impressed, Jake," Carmine looked at him with admiration in her face. "Do you write textbooks, or what?"

"I write mysteries," Jake said a little self-consciously. "I noticed that you had a few in your bookcase."

Carmine looked puzzled. "I don't remember any books that I have with you as the author, Jake. I'm sure that there are no books by Jake Steiner in my bookcase."

Jake hesitated, and then took a deep breath and rushed the rest of his words. "I write under somewhat of a fictional name of Jake. I used the first two letters of my first name as the first and second letters, and then used the last two letters together, so that it is J. A. Ke. I like the idea that it has an Asian feeling."

"J. A. Ke," Carmine interrupted him, "you write those wonderful, humorous mysteries? How exciting! I can't believe it. I adore your books; they are absolutely my favorite. They are so complex, yet have so much humor in them that I laugh out loud while I am reading them. I think I have read every book you have ever written."

Jake's face blushed red as Carmine carried on.

Carmine heard Laurence warn, "Carmine, you are out of control."

Carmine immediately stopped speaking, turned to Jake, whose face was now neon red and lowered her voice, "I am so sorry, Jake, I truly don't want to embarrass you. When I get excited, my voice becomes loud and I seem to go out of control. It is a terrible habit that you would think that I would have outgrown at this age, but, unhappily, it is still there."

"You didn't embarrass me, Carmine. I love your excitement and the way you are able to express how you feel. I know my face was red but that seems to happen to me quite often. I'm very happy that you enjoy my books. I enjoy writing them so it's wonderful to have someone like them as much as I do."

"Jake, you are famous. Your books are well known, at least in mystery circles. You must love to teach knowing how much time it takes and how little financial income it generates. Teachers are paid so little in comparison for how much that they contribute to the whole of society," Carmine said with an apologetic tone.

"I do love teaching. It's so satisfying to know that I am helping others. I only teach one class a quarter, so it isn't that big a deal and my salary is donated to several charities I support in the area. I feel it is only fair, since my royalties from my books are almost embarrassing. But much of that goes to charities, also.

"I founded a school in East Los Angeles that takes students with potential from the first grade through the eighth grade and it has become a powerhouse learning center. Once the student is enrolled, we take care of everything, and I mean everything . . . clothes, transportation, books, spending allowances. We even contribute to the parents' income with our scholarships. I try to ensure that once a student has been accepted by the school, that he or she stays for the full length of time that is available. We have had amazing success and most of our students graduate from high school and are accepted to the colleges of their choice, most with scholarships!"

"That is incredible. What a service you are doing!" Carmine interjected.

"That is one of the reasons I write anonymously. I don't want people to know who I am because I want to be able to use my time and resources for what I believe are the greatest and highest good."

"I think it is so important to give back. I want to help underprivileged women when I graduate. Something that helps them find the resources to get out of poverty," Carmine enthused.

"I usually don't share what I do with many other people. It's just so easy to talk to you. I hope you'll keep what I shared between us."

"Jake, of course. You can have confidence that I will keep your secret. What you are doing is so impressive!"

"Aw, shucks, Mam, it's nothing," Jake said, mimicking John Wayne.

At that, Carmine started giggling and Jake joined her. By the time they had reached the restaurant, they were both gasping for breath from laughter and grinning non-stop at each other.

Carmine gave her name to the maître d' of the restaurant, who welcomed her warmly, as she was one of the regulars.

"Ms. Carmine," he said with slight Italian accent, "it will be a few minutes. We are very, very busy tonight and I know you want a table very far away from the front door so you will not feel drafts or any cold, even though…" he gestured upwards with his hands, "it's warm tonight." Carmine laughed at this, "Germino, you know me so well."

Carmine continued to ask Jake questions about his book as they waited for their table. "I interrupted you when you were telling me about your name, Jake. What were you saying about being Asian?"

"I seem to have a strong leaning for anything Asian. That is why I liked the way you furnished your condo, it has many far-eastern touches. And I like my name for my books because the last name is Ke. I don't know if you believe in reincarnation, but I do and I know that I had several lifetimes as an Asian."

Carmine raised her eyebrows at that statement and her words jumped out of her mouth, almost without her control. "Jake, I absolutely believe in reincarnation and, in fact, I know that there is reincarnation."

Carmine was interrupted by Laurence, warning sternly, "Careful, Carmine, remember your promise!"

Carmine grimaced, which caught Jake's attention immediately.

"What's wrong, Carmine?"

Carmine laughed and said "I was thinking how funny I sound when I say I know that there is reincarnation. But, sometimes you know things, in your heart, even if there is no proof. Don't you agree? And I know I was Chinese at least one time, maybe more."

"Yes, I agree with you one hundred percent, Carmine, that you can know things without proof, but how can you be so sure about being Chinese?"

Carmine smiled, trying to think of an answer that made sense without giving away information. Just as she opened her mouth to blurt out something, Germino called her name, "Ms. Carmine, your table, it is ready" as he grabbed two menus and ushered both of them to follow him.

Laurence had something to do with that interruption as Carmine pointedly looked at him. He simply nodded his head and shrugged his shoulders as though to say, "What would you have expected?"

Carmine raised her nose into the air and decided to ignore him no matter what took place for the balance of the night.

"This is my favorite table, Germino, Thank you." Carmine gave him a kiss on his cheek as he sat them at the corner table in the back of the restaurant.

"Carmine, this is nice. Very comfortable, not too noisy and it smells delicious! I'm starving, so maybe it's me."

Carmine laughed, told him to look at the menu and shared her impressions of the many items on the menu. They both decided on what they wanted and then Carmine continued to ask Jake about his family and where he lived.

By the time the waiter came for their order, she found out that he was an only child whose parents had been killed in an auto accident when he was nine and that he was raised by his maiden aunt, Sophie, who adored him.

His parents had left a very large trust fund and his Aunt, who had no other relative in the world, was leaving him her estate, which was quite enormous. She was still alive and lived with Jake in Pasadena at the family mansion. He told her briefly about attending college at Berkeley for his undergraduate degree, then transferring to Northwestern University for his Masters because he wanted to write and teach.

The waiter took their order, a wild mixed lettuce salad for her, minestrone soup for him and a potato and Italian broccoli ravioli with a garlicky red sauce, along with a glass of Chianti wine for each of them.

Before Carmine had an opportunity to ask Jake more about himself, he asked her questions and she found herself talking extensively about her life in general, Cassie, and her own most private dreams.

Usually it's me asking all the questions and listening, Carmine thought to herself as she was talking, *he seems genuinely interested.*

She told him all about her ex-husband, why they got married and how they were the most incompatible couple she knew, but how he was an excellent father to Cassie.

She described her relationship with Cassie and went into far too many details; how much she loved her, how important Cassie was to her, how hard it was when Cassie was growing up but the relationship was much better now and how she knew she was going to be a fabulous artist.... until she heard Laurence strong reproving "Ahem, Carmine."

She stopped abruptly and started talking about her parents, who had also died in an auto accident, only when she was twenty-five. She then told him about her business and where she wanted to go with her degree.

The waiter served their salad and soup, but Carmine and Jake hardly noticed, they were so involved with their conversation. Carmine told him about the many years she didn't date, because she wasn't interested and when she did, how disappointing it was.

Jake told her about his fiancée who had been killed in a skiing accident in Aspen trying to keep up with him. He felt that she had died trying to prove that she was as good as he was and how he blamed himself, even after seven years.

He then told her about his last relationship with a beautiful and brilliant woman, Giovanna, who owned her own international technology company that was very successful. He was heavily involved with her for more than two years and really thought, initially, that she was the one he would spend the rest of his life with. But there was a huge conflict between them and it was on and off so many times he finally gave up.

When asked about the conflict, all that Jake said was that Giovanna was raised with a European concept of love and fidelity which he found he couldn't live with and so he broke it off, even though she wanted to continue the relationship. But he felt it was for the best for both of them, especially now, as he smiled at Carmine.

Carmine was very curious about Giovanna, much more than the fiancée, but didn't ask any more questions, although she promised herself that if they went out again, she would try to find out more about that relationship and the actual conflict.

Not knowing how to respond to Jake's history, Carmine started expressing her feelings about aging and the pressure placed upon women to be young. That somehow led to conversations on politics (both voted for the best candidate, not the party) and religion, where Carmine started talking about the other side with such authority that Laurence had to warn Carmine with a strong, "Carmine, careful!" before she changed the subject.

What amazed Carmine was she could express her feelings on anything she spoke about to Jake and she wasn't afraid of offending him or having him laugh at her or feeling that "this is the last time he's taking me out." He was sincerely interested and gave appropriate comments. And, he was able to express his feelings on any subject, almost as well as she could hers. When she commented on this, he reminded her that he was, after all, a writer and an English teacher.

"You know," Carmine admitted a little hesitantly, "I have never spoken to any man like this in my life. I must feel very comfortable with you and trust you to do this. Which is remarkable for just going out with you once." And, Carmine teased, "Weren't we going to discuss my paper?"

Jake turned red again. "Actually, Carmine, as I am sure you realize, that was an excuse. I have never taken any student out and thought I never would because I don't think it is ethical or professional. The minute I saw you in my class, I felt something very special about you; it was some kind of connection. I thought if I waited too long, I would lose my chance. And if you said No, it would give me a little more time in the classroom for you to reconsider, so that's why I asked you in the way that I did. I hope you don't mind?"

Carmine bowed her head to conceal how happy she was to hear what he said. "Jake, how could I mind? I am delighted that you did it. You have been on my mind a lot," Carmine heard herself say. And then she gasped when she realized the implication. "I can't believe I said that," Carmine confessed to Jake.

Now Jake bent his head so it was at the same level as Carmine's and looked straight into her eyes and said softly and kindly, "Carmine, telling the truth about how you feel is never anything to apologize for. I value that trait highly in my friends!" And then he took her hand and held it for a few moments while they gazed at each other.

Finally, Carmine withdrew her hand and said lightly, "I value that, also, Jake. My bluntness and emotions haven't always been appreciated. Thank you. It is so great to be with someone where it is easy to be real." And then the conversation returned to its previous conversation as they shared their views of anything and everything that came into their heads.

Sometime during their conversation, they had eaten their first course and their entrée had been served. They both ate but neither of them seemed to paying any attention to the food.

It seemed only an hour later, but Carmine heard a soft cough and looked up to see Germino at the table. "Ms. Carmine, I am so sorry, but we are closing. May we give you the check?" he asked with an apology in his voice.

Carmine looked around as did Jake and both were surprised to see that they were the only diners left. Carmine vaguely remembered eating her dinner and drinking her wine, but couldn't remember when she started eating and when she finished. Noting that the plates had been removed without her noticing had her shaking her head. Had she been so engrossed in the conversation, she didn't remember if she ate or not? I'm not hungry, so I guess I did eat, she thought. Laurence gave her a smile that she could only be defined as a smirk and nodded yes, she had eaten.

"I'm so sorry, Germino, I hadn't noticed," Carmine apologized profusely and Jake took the check and left a $100 bill, saying sincerely, "Please excuse our tardiness, Germino. The food was delicious and we had no idea it was so late." Jake shook hands with Germino and Carmine saw him palm a $20 bill discreetly into his hand.

Germino smiled happily and turned to Carmine, "He is very nice, Ms. Carmine; be sure to bring him again."

Carmine and Jake practically ran out of the restaurant. Carmine started laughing the moment they were on the sidewalk.

"Jake," she accused him, giggling; no wonder he wants to see you back. "I am sure that you left at least a $40 tip and then gave another $20."

Jake blushed shyly and said, "Aw, shucks, Mam, it is 11:30 and they close at 11:00. It was the least I could do."

Jake took Carmine's arm and propelled her towards her condo. He was walking very quickly and speaking almost as fast as he was walking.

"I'm sorry that it's so late, Carmine; if I had known that we would still be out at 11:30 at night, I would have driven!!"

"Jake, it's okay."

"It was a great restaurant and the food was delicious. Everything seemed very fresh, which I love. I am an amateur cook and I only use fresh ingredients . . . and organic at that, whenever I can."

Carmine stopped walking and turned to him. "Jake, you are the most amazing individual I have ever known. So you cook and write and teach. Is there anything else that you do that I should know about you?" she asked, laughing softly.

"I feel that you know much more about me than I know about you."

"I play the piano and guitar and I sing. But I play the piano much better than I sing... but I love to sing, so I do it."

Carmine's laughter pealed through the quiet neighborhood, as Jake had taken her arm and started running with her. "Stop, Jake, I can't keep up! My shoes keep coming off."

Jake immediately stopped walking and asked solicitously, "Are you all right?"

"Of course, but I need to catch my breath. I haven't been exercising as I should and it shows. Boy, starting next week, I am getting up at 5:00 a.m. to hit the gym. These last two months have been so hectic! I've truly neglected that part of my life. I'd start Saturday, but Cassie is coming down tomorrow night for the weekend and I won't have time."

Carmine groaned, "I remembered that Cassie will want to come to this restaurant Friday or Saturday evening because it is her favorite and I promised that we would eat here. That should help my waistline," she lamented.

"Carmine, there is nothing wrong with your waistline," he said with admiration! "Your daughter is coming for the weekend?"

"Yes, she said she had something important to talk to me about so she is driving down so we can talk. I hope it is nothing too serious; but she told me not to worry! But I worry anyway; it is one of my many bad habits."

"I can't believe you have that many bad habits, Carmine," Jake said with a twinkle in his large hazel eyes.

Carmine almost sputtered as she said, "If you only knew! You should ask my Guardian Angel and he could tell you . . ." Carmine turned bright red when she said that and heard Laurence utter a stern and loud warning "Carmine!"

Jake turned to her with a strange look on his face, "I have heard of asking other people about someone's habits, but never a Guardian Angel."

"It is a way of speaking," Carmine started to explain rapidly and breathing unevenly. "You know, it's a mythical person, sort of like the imaginary large rabbit, Harvey. Do you think I'm crazy?"

"Carmine," Jake said softly, placing his arm around Carmine's shoulder, "there is nothing that you can ever do that I would think you're crazy. If you feel there is a Guardian Angel in your life that is real to you, why not," Jake said as he circled Carmine's shoulder closer as she shivered when he was speaking.

"Are you cold, Carmine?" Jake asked in a concerned voice, as he pulled Carmine closer to him. "I wish I'd driven; it seems to be a much longer walk at this time of night."

"I'm one of these people who are always cold, Jake, so don't worry about it. Besides, it gives me an excuse to have your arm around me," Carmine said with a shy smile. "And don't worry about the walk, I can't tell you how many times Cassie and I have walked this route late at night when she was home and I worked late. Instead of cooking, we would come here."

Jake laughed. "So, you are coming back Friday or Saturday again?"

"Yup," she said wickedly, mimicking Jake. "But they have incredible food so I don't mind at all. This was Cassie's very favorite place to eat before she left for college and since she has not been down to LA since August, this is where she wants to come."

"If Cassie is going to be home for the weekend, how about both of you joining me at the Getty on Sunday? They have a new art exhibit that I have been wanting to see and then we can eat at their wonderful restaurant that has a view of the Santa Monica mountains and the ocean beyond. I'd love to meet Cassie since you have told me so much about her."

"Jake, I would love to, but Cassie will leave about noon to return to Santa Barbara and there wouldn't be time. But thank you so much."

"Well, then, how about you joining me. We could go later in the day."

"Jake," she said sighing, "that sounds fabulous, it does, but could I take a rain check on it? I have made commitments to myself to take care of this weekend, including Cassie, and I need to honor them. It's very tempting, but it is important that I honor those commitments. Sounds crazy, I know. But when I broke commitments to myself in the past, I became very unhappy and angry with myself. So I have learned."

"No, Carmine, I don't think it is crazy. And I acknowledge you for honoring yourself and your choices. It's actually very inspiring. You know, the exhibit is running another month, so how about next weekend some time?"

Carmine gave him a delighted smile. "I think that sounds like a good plan. Let me check my calendar. I can text you tomorrow and let you know for sure!"

Just as Carmine finished speaking, they had arrived back at her condo complex. Jake started walking her to the locked front gate as she pulled the keys from her purse.

"Let me open the gate for you, Carmine," Jake requested.

Carmine looked at him for a moment with a puzzled look on her face. "Whatever for, Jake? I do it all the time."

Jake said with a red face, "It looks heavy and I thought I would do it for you."

"Jake, you are so sweet. Look, you don't have to walk me to the door. I am a big girl and come home alone all the time."

"Not really, Carmine, I am always with you," Carmine heard Laurence say to her.

Carmine gave Laurence her usual look of impatience when he spoke when he wasn't supposed to and Jake's face immediately became a deeper red.

"I didn't mean to offend you, Carmine, I wanted to help," in an apologetic tone.

"That look wasn't for you. Please don't be offended," Carmine stammered. "I sometimes have flashbacks to other times with other people and respond to that thought," Carmine improvised quickly trying to explain her reaction to Laurence's intrusive, unwelcome comment.

"I think we are both tired. It has been fun, but it's after midnight, and, frankly, it is hard for me to be up this late. It has been a hectic week," Carmine went on speaking rapidly and emphatically.

"Whoa, Carmine, it's all right. You don't have to apologize. Here, let me walk you to your front door so I know you are in safely and then I'll leave. Okay?"

"Of course, Jake." Instead of taking the elevator, they walked up the three flights of stairs. As they stood in front of Carmine's front door, Jake put his arms around her, gave her a gentle hug, told her how much he enjoyed the evening and that he would wait to hear from her about the Getty and handed her his business card with his cell phone number.

Before Carmine could gather her thoughts to respond, Jake was already walking down the stairwell.

Carmine slowly opened the front door and saw Laurence standing in front of her.

She pushed past him and continued into the dark living room where she paused to switch on a light. She sat down heavily on the couch and threw her head back against the cushion.

"You know," Carmine started speaking to herself, "I feel I have known Jake forever. I am so comfortable with him and I feel I can be me and he seems to like who I am."

"Carmine," Laurence started speaking, "Jake is someone you have known in various past lives in different significant roles that you both have played on Earth. Most of the time, it was a very good relationship; a few times, it didn't go well at all. But this is an on-going relationship for you both in this lifetime. The reason it feels so comfortable is that because you have deep unconscious memories of him. That actually is why some people feel so familiar and comfortable to you— it's old memories from different lifetimes that you are reacting to. And on a spiritual level, you could be considered soul mates as the Director defined that night you died."

Carmine looked at Laurence, almost without seeing him, as she tried to understand what he was saying.

"You mean that Jake and I have been together in past lifetimes and we are soul mates? And the reason that I am so comfortable with him is because I unconsciously remember our relationship from other incarnations?" Carmine asked with a wide smile.

"Laurence," she exclaimed as she rose from the couch and danced around the living room. "You have made me so happy. It's so marvelous having my own Angel to tell me these things. Does this mean that Jake and I will be together in this lifetime? Tell me," she begged.

"Carmine, you know I can't do that. I can't predict the future. Remember you have free will."

"You told me that we were together in several lifetimes and how good it was most of the time, so what difference does it make to tell me the rest?"

"I didn't tell you anything that someone that you describe as having second sight wouldn't tell you."

"Second sight? You mean a psychic?" Carmine asked with a puzzled tone in her voice.

"Yes, if you went to one of these people, they would tell you the same thing. And I can't predict the future because you and Jake have free will."

"Sometimes you can be so maddening! I can be so irritated with you; other times you are so sweet. You are like the older brother I didn't have! Tonight I am so happy, it doesn't matter." Carmine bent to smell the huge bouquet of flowers that Jake had given her. "These roses and lilies smell so heavenly. Actually, they remind me of heaven, now that I think of it."

Walking into the bedroom, Carmine hurriedly got ready for bed performing only the minimal of her usual bedtime routine. Sitting down to meditate and within a few minutes, she felt an overwhelming feeling of joy and happiness and her body felt as though it was floating.

She heard Laurence say, "Carmine, the way you feel right now is the way you should feel every day. Because you have experienced much happiness tonight your very cells are filled with light and joy. The time that you took to talk to God with your heart, as you do when you meditate, has culminated in what you are experiencing right now. This is something that can happen on a daily basis if you can constantly focus on the positive and feel appreciation and gratitude for all that is around you. And when you do that, only good things will come to you because your feelings act as magnets so you attract that exact, positive vibration into your life."

Carmine silently thanked Laurence for the beautiful illuminating message and acknowledged how blessed she was to have him in her life. She blew him a kiss. He responded by placing his hands together in prayer gesture and bowing.

The last thing Carmine remembered thinking, as she crawled into her comfortable, soft, warm bed, was how much sense Laurence made and how she could apply it to Jake. Within seconds, she was deeply asleep.

Chapter Nine

Carmine woke up very slowly the next morning, relaxed and calm as if she had slept for days. She peeked with half closed eyes at the Zen clock on her dresser and saw that it was, unbelievably, only quarter to six. She could stay in bed a good half hour longer before she had to get up and get ready for work. With Cassie coming tomorrow, she wished she could stay home and catch up on everything, but she knew that her client was expecting her. The minute she thought of Cassie, she became happy. She hadn't seen her since she dropped her off at college in August and it had been almost two months. She missed her, even the pouty, defiant, I-know-it-all Cassie. Carmine raised her head and shoulders, stretching her whole body very languidly and glanced at the clock again.

She let out a shriek when she saw she had misread the short and long hands on the clock. It was actually 9:30 a.m. She gave a piteous groan. She had to be at work no later than 10:30 and there was no way she could make it.

As she jumped out of bed, she noticed that her cell phone on the night stand was blinking. Picking it up she saw two text messages. Hoping that Cassie wasn't changing her plans, she looked. The first one was from Jake, saying how much he had enjoyed their evening and reminding her to check her calendar for next Saturday. He mentioned he would call that evening to see if she could make it.

The next one was from Cassie telling her she would be leaving around 11:00 a.m. on Friday and should be at home no later than 2:30 that afternoon, if traffic was good. She also asked if they could go to her favorite restaurant, La Penne, that evening.

Carmine sat down on the bedroom carpet and decided her plan of action. *Okay, I choose to not get upset and beat myself up that I overslept.... That's done! I will call work and let them know that I'll be late and I'll work late tonight. What I was going to do tonight, I'll do tomorrow morning.* Pleased with herself, Carmine called her employer. He sounded almost relieved as he said it was perfectly okay as they were running late and had to finish an essential project that would need to run over her scheduled time, anyway.

Carmine said a silent thank you when she hung up the phone and started rushing around getting dressed and getting things together for work, performing the minimum needed to have her look professional and fresh. She was ready to put on her clothes when, suddenly, she realized she hadn't seen or heard from Laurence.

"Why didn't Laurence wake me up?" she asked, looking around for him and saw him standing in front of her.

"I tried to, but you chose not to hear me because you were sleeping so deeply and so happily. You were absolutely ecstatic. I can only do so much. Remember you have free choice and...."

"Laurence, please no time for a spiritual lesson." But listening to what he said, Carmine smiled. She started reliving the whole wonderful evening before she realized what she was doing. "Laurence, I am sorry I always seem to run out of time when you speak, but you are such a distraction."

"Carmine," Laurence almost shouted, taking her quickly out of her reverie, "I do want to congratulate you on the way you handled this situation about being late. You did not judge or criticize yourself as you would have done in the past. I want you to be aware of that and acknowledge the great progress you are making."

"Oh, Laurence, thank you. And I mean it sincerely. I could not have done it without your help and I am so very grateful," as she bowed to him with hands in prayer gesture and a beautiful smile. Then she remembered the time.

"STOP!" she sternly told herself as well as Laurence. "I can't do this now."

Running to her closet, she snatched a light gray linen pants suit, expertly combining it with a deep red shell top, and dressed with the speed that she compared to an Olympic gold-medal runner. She was ready in less than a minute. She grabbed her backpack and plunked in the leftover chicken from the refrigerator and some miscellaneous fruit for lunch and was almost out the door when the gate buzzer rang.

Carmine looked at the time; it was 10:15; who could it be? "Yes," Carmine said into the speaker box. "Hi, delivery for Carmine Craig," a man's voice announced.

"Okay," Carmine said as she buzzed him in. "I'm on the third floor." Waiting at the door, Carmine wondered what it could possibly be. She couldn't think of anything that she had ordered that had to be delivered.

A man in a green floral uniform stepped off the elevator carrying a long gold box emblazoned with "The Fairy Garden."

The delivery man gave her the gold box, asked that she sign a receipt and was gone.

Carmine was too curious to go back inside the condo or even close the door as she opened the box. There, wrapped in gold paper was one gorgeous lavender sterling rose and a note that read, "A perfect rose to match the perfection of you and the evening! Thank you. Jake."

Carmine stood very still. No one in all her life had done something as romantic as this. She felt she was in some beautiful dream and wanted it to last forever. She closed the door and almost levitated to the living room. Sitting down on the couch, she stared into space with a delighted smile on her face.

"This could be serious," she said out loud as she hugged herself, "I must call him and say thank you. But it might be inconvenient, if he is teaching." Taking her cell phone out, she found the text he had sent and thought about how to reply.

Looking at Laurence, Carmine silently begged for his help. He looked back at her. No response. But suddenly, she found what she wanted to say. "This gorgeous rose symbolizes the beauty of the evening that we created between us. Thank you for your dazzling thoughtfulness! Big hugs, Carmine." Before she could change her mind about the message, she pushed the send button, took a deep breath, and smiled happily.

Opening her china cabinet, Carmine found her best Steuben crystal vase and carefully placed the rose in it. She looked around for the ideal place she could display it, but with the huge bouquet of flowers from last night, there was no place to make it stand out. "I'll put it on my nightstand so I can smell the flower first thing in the morning and the last thing at night."

When Carmine finished arranging her night stand so she could place the vase on it, along with the note, she noticed Laurence looking at her with a knowing look on his face.

"I have no idea what you are thinking, Laurence, and I don't want to know. Leave me alone, with a fantasy that has come true. I mean all women dream about this type of thing, but do you know how rarely it happens? I can't believe it is happening to me. And by the way, she smiled, were you the inspiration for the message?"

Laurence was beaming. "I can't take credit for that, Carmine. It was all you! And happy fantasies can come true or heartfelt dreams, as that is what they truly are! You have to believe in them, acknowledging, exploring and honoring what you feel and want. Somewhere deep in your unconscious, you felt that there was someone who would fulfill your dream of what would be the best companion for you. But what you humans don't realize is that you, yourself, make dreams come true by believing in them and making them seem real to you. This isn't always easy to do. It takes time and practice but this has been an underlying thread in your belief and you were able to manifest it."

"Are you telling me that I can have anything I dream about, as long as I feel them to be true?"

"Of course, Carmine, deep in your heart you know that. You have made several dreams come true for yourself."

"But I had to work hard to do that, Laurence, and had to make many sacrifices."

"I know, Carmine, but that is what you believed you had to do."

"Now wait a minute, Laurence, are you trying to tell me that I could have had the same things without working so hard?" Carmine asked incredulously.

Laurence sighed. "Carmine, Carmine, yes. It is a matter of allowing these dreams to happen. Most humans ask, but don't believe it will happen. The difference is believing and feeling that it will happen. In fact, acting as though it is already there makes it happen even faster. Many of your sages tell you this. But there are so many reasons humans don't allow it to happen. Maybe they think they don't deserve it or they feel guilty about it or whatever. It's very strange, I must say. Remember what I said before, you are a magnet, attracting good or bad?"

Carmine sighed, quickly forgetting her irritation. Bringing herself back to reality, she shook herself, breathed deeply, adjusted her clothes and with one quick glance at the clock, started running out the door.

"Okay, okay, Laurence, you have my complete attention and I guess what you say makes sense; I have to think about it. But I have to get to work and fast. Let's go and no traffic, okay!? With any luck, I could be there on time."

Carmine gave Laurence a silent thank you as she arrived at work a little before eleven o'clock. She just had time to place her bag in her office and transfer her lunch to the company refrigerator when the CEO asked to see her to give her the project.

"Carmine," he explained, "I need to have an analysis of all my employees' salaries as they relate to today's market to see if they are over- or under-paid. Here is a copy of each person's salary and his/her job description. We have reviews next week and I want to ensure that we are paying fairly. I don't want to underpay, but I don't want to overpay either. So if you could look at each person's job description and do some research on what is being paid for these same jobs by other companies, I would appreciate it. Do you think you could finish by this evening?"

Carmine did a quick calculation. There were only about fifty employees, which meant some jobs were performed by multiple employees. So maybe that would give her about thirty-five job descriptions to check. By using the internet, she thought she could have a good approximate figure for each position. "Yes" she told the CEO, "but it will probably take me until about seven or eight tonight. Would that be all right?"

"Excellent! I know I can always count on you," the CEO replied with a smile. "Leave everything on my desk and if I have any questions, I can call you. It will probably be early on Monday because I have a conference I am attending tomorrow in Long Beach. That's why I want the numbers in tonight. I'll review them over the weekend. If there are any issues that need to be addressed, I'll discuss them with you then."

"Feel free to call me anytime, even if it is over the weekend. You have my cell phone number in case you can't get me at my office number," Carmine said with a smile.

"I appreciate that, Carmine. I hope that won't be necessary."

Carmine started the research on the internet as soon she returned to her desk. She reviewed the numbers he gave her, organized the data into groups so she could work more efficiently and effectively and started searching. "Maybe this won't take as long as I think it will," Carmine said to herself as she quickly found what she was looking for with the first job description.

"It's going to take you at least until tonight," she heard Laurence say. Carmine looked up and saw him standing with his arms crossed. "It couldn't possibly," she almost whined, "I have so much to do tonight with Cassie coming tomorrow and I am already starting to get tired. Can you help me?" She begged.

"Of course, I will as much as I am allowed to, Carmine. But even with my help, it will take some time."

Some hours later, at 8:30 p.m., Carmine finished her memo to the CEO summarizing the job salaries and what she recommended. He wasn't going to be too disappointed, as most of the positions seemed to be fairly compensated and compared favorably with what other companies were paying. There were a few that needed some attention and she told him not to hesitate to call her if he wanted some additional information.

As she shut down her computer, Carmine smiled wearily at Laurence. "I don't know how much you helped me, Laurence, but all the information for each position was there when I accessed it, so I want to say thank you. I am sure that it would have taken me twice as long without you." Carmine gave a long tired sigh as she gathered all her possessions together and walked out of the building, knowing the door would automatically lock behind her.

"Lady, do you have a buck or so to help me find a room tonight?"

Carmine jerked herself up and stopped shuffling her feet when she heard the voice. Standing beside her was a homeless man with a cart full of his meager possessions. *I'm too tired to become upset or scared. Besides, Laurence is here if I need help.* She noticed that Laurence nodded his head as she had the thought.

Balancing everything in her hand the best she could, she reached into her purse and extracted a $5 bill. "Please be sure you spend it on a room or food, Okay?" she said with a smile. "God bless you."

"And you too, Miss. Many Blessings and thank you."

As she continued walking to the car, she told Laurence, "I don't care what people say about giving to the homeless. I have so much in comparison and they don't have anything, so I do what I can."

"Whatever you can do, Carmine, to help make someone's life a little better is always good."

"Laurence," she asked in a low and tired voice, "please get me home fast and safe. I can barely stand up."

Twenty minutes later, she walked into her front door. She dropped everything in the hallway, proceeded to the bedroom where she undressed and let the clothes fall on the floor where she had taken them off.

Heading into the bathroom, she heard her cell phone ring and ran back into the living room. Removing it from her purse, she saw that it was Jake.

"Hi Jake, how are you?"

"Carmine, you sound so tired. Is this a good time to call? I can always call back tomorrow."

"Absolutely not. I just got home and am feeling the effects of a long day, but I am so glad you called."

"And a late night! I apologize."

"Oh, please! No need to!"

"I wanted to respond to your kind text, but wanted to call instead of texting and thought I would wait until you were home from work."

Before he could say anything else, Carmine interrupted, "Jake, that was such a beautiful and thoughtful gesture. It made me feel so special and what a lovely way to start the day! I'm speechless. Saying thank you seems so inadequate."

"Carmine, you are special," Jake said with a chuckle in his voice. "But, I can hear how tired you are. Why don't I call you tomorrow morning so you can go to bed? I can wait until then to plan next week. What time is Cassie coming in?"

"Anytime from Noon on. So I am going to go to bed as soon as we hang up and then I'll get up early tomorrow and catch up on all the things I haven't had time for. I'm too tired to do it now."

"I'll call you sometime in the late morning, Carmine, and if I miss you, I'll try Sunday afternoon. I don't want to interfere with your time with Cassie."

"Don't worry about it, Jake, but thanks again for being so thoughtful. I'll talk to you tomorrow."

With that, Carmine hung up the phone and trudged slowly to the bathroom. "This is going to be the shortest bath in history," she yawned to herself noting that it was almost 9:30, "but it will help me calm down."

Five minutes later she was dressed in her comfy, white, torn nightgown, literally falling into bed. "I can't meditate in my chair tonight," she said as she pulled the covers over herself. "I'll meditate lying down." That was her last thought before she fell asleep.

What seemed like thirty seconds later, Carmine awakened suddenly and sat straight up in bed. *Today is the day Cassie is coming home and I have so much to do,* she excitedly told herself as she swung her legs onto the carpet and stretched. She glanced at the clock on her nightstand, which was partially hidden by the vase with Jake's rose. She smiled to herself when she saw it and started thinking about Jake. Realizing what she was daydreaming, she shook herself, like a dog shaking water off, and looked again at the clock. It was 7:45. Carmine had slept for ten hours straight, something she had not done for years.

Wow, after ten hours' sleep, you think I would be ready to fly, but with working and socializing late, I am still tired. Carmine started to do her morning yoga but found that she couldn't focus on the exercises because her mind was telling her how many other things she had to do. And she kept wondering what Cassie wanted to tell her.

Carmine started thinking about all that had transpired since Cassie left. She had been so busy, that she and Cassie hardly had time to talk. Cassie would call her at random moments, ask how Carmine was and then say she couldn't talk because she was too busy. This made Carmine feel like saying, "Why bother calling?" If she called Cassie, there would always be some excuse. She would be studying or just about to go out or someone was with her and she couldn't talk.

Weekends were practically impossible because Cassie had a class on Saturdays. After the class, she was never available as there were always activities and hanging out with friends.

Cassie usually ignored the calls from Carmine. Cassie had even told her mother when she called, that she would not answer her cell unless she was alone or with someone she felt comfortable with when speaking to her mother, which never seemed to happen. So if Cassie was coming to tell her something, it had to be huge.

"Hey, Laurence, why is Cassie coming and what is she going to tell me?"

Laurence materialized in front of her, "You don't really want me to tell you, Carmine. She'll be here shortly. You've waited this long, what are a few more hours?"

Carmine was about to give a sharp reply, but was too tired to bother. She stopped exercising and sat down in the meditation chair. "Ten minutes meditating might be of more value."

"That always helps," Laurence said. She opened her eyes and there he was, meditating with her. "Go away, Laurence," she said as she yawned widely. "I don't want to hear or see you. Please?"

"Of course, Carmine." And Laurence disappeared.

Gee, I hope I didn't hurt his feelings. Thirty minutes later she felt renewed and ready for anything that Cassie could tell her. Well, almost anything and then she started worrying about all the possibilities. When the worrying went to "Maybe she's pregnant," she yelled for Laurence.

"Laurence, tell me that it is not true. I can't bear to wait. I have been so busy that the possibility did not even occur to me until now. I wouldn't want to have what happened to me happen to her. I could not live, to have history repeat itself."

"Carmine," Laurence scolded, "you are making yourself ill when you have no facts and are projecting a fantasy without any evidence. Why do you humans, when you have an unknown situation, always think of the worst possibilities that could befall? Why don't you think of the happiest or best events? It is a puzzle," Laurence declared with a sigh.

Carmine immediately stopped her whimpering and stared straight at Laurence.

"You know," Carmine bit her lips and squeezed her eyes shut as she pondered Laurence's observation, "you are right. I do that a lot and so does everyone else. You tell me why that occurs? I mean she might be driving down here to tell me she won the lottery and we're millionaires."

"I do not know, Carmine, except maybe humans are afraid of happiness or being disappointed. It is very strange. I do know that many times when you have been thinking of unhappy circumstances that you sometimes draw them to you. Remember, you, indeed, are a magnet! You attract what you think and focus upon. So it is always much better to think and have your attention on the positive. You will then always draw goodness to you."

"Do you know how hard that is, Laurence, to always focus on the positive. There are so many horrible, tragic, terrible events that take place every day! How could anyone keep positive?" Carmine asked.

"That is your perception, Carmine, because what you humans call 'media' focuses on all the worst things that go on! All your newspapers, television, radio and anything else that informs your Earth population are fraught with negativity. Believe me, Carmine, there are many, many positive and happy events that happen every day that you don't hear about. But if you keep yourself focused on what makes you happy and keep that feeling within you, then you will find that you don't have to focus on what the world is drawing to itself. You can make your own world by giving attention to what is happy, joyful and in harmony with everything good."

"Laurence," Carmine admonished, "do you know how absolutely difficult that would be? When the world is going crazy with all ugly stuff, just to focus on what is happy and joyful? Laurence," she scolded, "Get real! At least real to this world."

"You are quite right, Carmine," Laurence said with considerable sadness. "You have the ability to do it, but it does take concentration and work. It seems it is easier to go along with the world thinking. But I promise you that if you can work on positive self-talk and giving attention to what is good and feels good, your life would be more joyous, peaceful and fulfilling.

"Do try, Carmine," Laurence's tone almost commanded. "Start with a few minutes a day and increase just a little with each passing day. You will see the results immediately."

Carmine looked at Laurence for one full minute, trying to comprehend how she could do it. "I have to give this more thought, Laurence, when I have more time. But let's see what I can do, starting today."

Carmine began attacking her to-do list for the day, including paying her bills, that always seemed to pile up on her desk, even though she tended to them every week. "I wonder what it would be like not to have bills? I guess I could try to use Laurence's suggestion about feeling good no matter what I am doing. Yeah, trying to feel good while paying bills is certainly an exercise in futility," she grumbled. *One couldn't have much of life without some of the things the bills pay for like having dependable water, electricity, phones and so on. I guess I could count myself lucky, with most of the world going without what we consider necessities. Actually, bills are blessings in disguise.* And Carmine realized that this was actually very true.

"Excellent, Carmine," Laurence said. "Excellent reframing! That is exactly what I mean. By always giving your attention to the positive side of anything, you keep yourself in harmony with what feels good. Paying bills in your world is normal, but understanding and acknowledging why they are there allows you to pay them with joy and allows you to keep yourself harmonized with positive energy."

"Okay Laurence, I hear you," Carmine said between clenched teeth. "But please do me a favor. Starting right now, this moment, please, do not comment to me unless I request it. I become so distracted and I can't focus!

"And when Cassie is around, you are absolutely, categorically, not to let me see or hear you. I want you to go back to pre-Carmine life when I didn't know you were around. Cassie knows me too well and she will know that something is different. So, please, promise me. Okay?" Carmine's tone was tinged with worry. "Who knew that an Angel can be such a challenge sometimes," Carmine mumbled to herself.

"Carmine, Carmine, I will do anything you ask. Remember, I'm here to help and assist you. Whatever you want, I will do." Laurence's tone was kind, but he looked disappointed.

"Listen, Laurence, don't be hurt. I am worried about the situation and I want to make sure that nothing gives itself away. Okay?"

"I understand, Carmine and I'm not hurt!"

"Well, good!"

Carmine finished her last bill with an enormous sigh of relief, which changed immediately to a huge groan. She had forgotten to call Leslie. She found Leslie's cell number in her phone and called. It went immediately to voice mail. "Leslie, it's Carmine. I wanted you to know I'm thinking of you and hope that you are feeling better and everything is going well or as well as can be expected. Call when you can. Cassie is going to be home for the weekend, so I'll be in and out, but do call me when you have a moment. Or at least text me to let me you're doing okay! Hugs!" And she hung up.

"Great! She will know that I am thinking of her and that she can call at any time."

Just when Carmine thought she might have a few moments to relax, the door opened and closed with a loud bang and Cassie noisily entered the condo.

"Hi Mom," Cassie yelled with a huge smile on her face, "I'm home."

Carmine turned to Laurence and mouthed, "Disappear" to him. She then ran to Cassie and with a whoop of delight, hugged her to her chest and started smothering her with kisses all over her face.

"Mom, Mom, stop. I can't breathe. Mom, control yourself! Carmine! Carmine, stop!" Cassie yelled to her mother. Using Carmine's actual name was Cassie's way of getting her Mother's immediate attention and to also let her know that she was doing something Cassie disliked. "It's okay, Carmine! I'm going be here for a couple of days," Cassie managed to say as she struggled to get away from the choking hold.

Carmine started giggling. "Cassie, I missed you so much. You look so good," as she stood away from her and looked up at Cassie's 5'6½" frame. "I think you grew and you look thinner. I hope you are taking care of yourself," Carmine heard herself say in a scolding voice. As she saw Cassie's face drop from a smile to a frown, she immediately apologized. "Sorry, hon, I know, I'm being a Mother."

Carmine threw her arms around Cassie's waist and looked up at her daughter. "Cassie, your hair is lovely," she exclaimed. Cassie's hair, which had always been light brown and worn in one length, was now done in dozens of blonde and golden brown highlights and was cut in a Heidi Klum style. "It suits you."

"Thanks, Mom," Cassie said in a bored voice, as though it was inconsequential that she had completely revamped her hair. But Carmine saw by her expression that she was pleased with the compliment.

"Hey, Mom," Cassie said as she went back to the door to bring her duffel bag inside. "I'm hungry! What do you have to eat? Not too much, because I want to go to Penne tonight and splurge. That is one place I have missed!"

"I can stir fry some rice and broccoli and I also have some leftover soup, but I'll make you anything you want. I'm so happy you are home."

"Let me think about it," Cassie said, as she lugged her bag to the second bedroom through the living room. Abruptly, she stopped and stared at the arrangement of flowers.

"Carmine, that's the biggest bouquet of flowers you've ever had," Cassie said with a suspicious tone. "Where did they come from?" she asked with a voice that was heavy with accusation. "I know you didn't buy them because you always buy one or two stems; never this many." And then as she turned back to the coffee table, she dropped her bag and ran and picked up the box of Godiva chocolates sitting next to the vase.

"Mom," she said, her eyes narrowing, with raised eyebrows, "I know you love chocolates, but I know you would never, ever buy this large a box. Who gave them to you? Was it a man?" she asked now in a demanding tone.

Carmine started laughing at her daughter and her skeptical tone of voice. "Cassie, isn't it possible that your

Mother, albeit, as old as she is, could have an admirer, perhaps even a beau?"

"A beau? Isn't that a little old fashioned? You mean you have a boyfriend?" Cassie asked in an incredulous voice.

"Could it be possible that someone might find me attractive and want to date me? Do you find that out of the realm of possibility, Cassie?" Carmine asked with a bemused look on her face.

"No, Mom, but you know, you haven't dated that much the last few years and I kinda thought," and now Cassie was turning a little red, "that maybe, well, you were too old for that kind of thing."

"Cassie, I am 37, not 87," Carmine said testily.

"You mean you actually have a boyfriend? I'm so excited for you! Really!" Cassie said, recovering herself. "I can't believe this. I want to hear all about him."

"Cassie, Cassie, of course, I'm going to tell you all about him. And note, he is not my boyfriend, just someone I went out with for dinner. But I need to hear what you want to tell me. I've been imagining all kinds of possibilities and not all of them good. So please, before I have a nervous breakdown, tell me. Tell me, please." Carmine sang the last three words, singing them to the tune from *My Fair Lady*.

"Mom, you worry too much. But it's good, maybe even great! I thought I'd tell you at dinner tonight."

Seeing Carmine's facial expression, she said, "Okay, okay, I'll tell you now. Let me unpack and use the bathroom. If you will make me the rice and broccoli, I'll eat and talk at the same time. But don't make me too much," Cassie warned, "because I want to eat all my favorites at Penne tonight."

As Carmine prepared lunch for Cassie, she tried to think what it could be. She didn't sound as though she had a boyfriend. Cassie had never been big on one-to-one boy relationships, even though there had been a few which had caused some of the biggest arguments between Carmine and Cassie. Thinking of those past relationships caused Carmine to have anxieties.

Cassie came out of the bedroom and opened the refrigerator door looking for something to drink. Taking some grape juice, she poured herself a glass.

"Hey, Mom, that smells good. I think I'm pretty hungry," she said as though she was surprised to find out.

"Cassie, you never know when you are hungry, just like me, until food is put under your nose. I thought college might change that."

"Mom, if you could see what they serve. It's nothing like I have here. Maybe that's why I've lost weight."

"One of the great educational values of college is that your child suddenly appreciates that which was taken for granted earlier," Carmine said with a knowing tone and a smile to Cassie.

"Carmine, that is condescending," Cassie said with considerable irritation. "I always appreciated your cooking. Didn't I always bring my friends here for dinner, because none of their mothers cooked as well as you?"

"Sorry, Cassie. Couldn't resist," Carmine said, blowing a kiss to Cassie as she served the stir-fry.

"Okay, kiddo, what is it that you have to tell me?"

Cassie took a deep breath and then looked right into Carmine's eyes and started talking very fast and with great animation.

"Mom, remember when Chloe got married and I couldn't come because of my class. The reason I couldn't skip my class, is that I had already missed it once. And that was two weeks before Chloe's wedding when I left school on a Thursday and went up to San Francisco to see Dad."

As Cassie said this, Carmine raised an eyebrow. "I didn't know how you would feel about my taking two days off plus my Saturday class to go up there, so I didn't mention it. But the other reason I didn't say anything is because I took my art portfolio to the San Francisco Art Institute and interviewed with them. I wanted to see what they would say about my work. Actually, I had sent it up earlier, along with a copy of my transcripts to Dad. He has a connection with one of the Board members, who had the President of the school review it. And he liked it! The Board member told Dad that the President would love to talk to me.

"So, I went up to meet with the President and one of the Admissions' Counselors. They said they felt that I had talent and would be a welcome addition to the Institute! And the reason I wanted to do this is because it became very clear to me after the first two or three weeks of school that I didn't want to do theater. I want to focus on being an artist.

"I know you thought I should do that before I applied at Santa Barbara, but I thought I wanted to be with Kathy and it would be fun in theater arts. But I found that I wasn't as happy as I thought I would be. When I talked to Dad about it, he suggested that I send up the portfolio and that's how it started. And then when Kathy had her accident, it made me realize that I should do what makes me happy because maybe I'm not going to have as much time available to me in life as I think I have.

"So I've already sent in the formal application. Dad is having the Board member write a letter of recommendation and my art teacher from high school is writing the other. But, the President said, at the end of my interview, that unless something was different than what I presented in my portfolio or in the paperwork that I officially submit, then I should consider myself accepted. Because the portfolio is 75% of the admission requirement. And I can get my Bachelors of Fine Art in three years if I go summer and winter, as they have classes all year round.

"Mom, it's so cool, because they are considered the third best school in the nation for photography and the fourth for painting. And you know how much I love photography and I'm so excited and. . . ."

Noticing Carmine's pained expression, Cassie stopped talking.

"Mom, aren't you going to say something? Are you upset with me?"

Carmine had sat quietly saying nothing while Cassie spoke. This behavior was the antithesis of Carmine's usual actions when Cassie presented some complex situation that Carmine had to handle.

Cassie was disturbed at her Mother's lack of reaction to a statement she thought would have her yelling and screaming. But Carmine wasn't as shocked as Cassie thought she would be because of Carmine's discussion of Cassie with Mother about Cassie the night she died.

"You are doing very well," Laurence said with pride in his voice.

Carmine took a big breath and then started speaking in a very soft tone, which was so different from Carmine's usual response to questionable news. "I guess I'm hurt, Cassie, that you couldn't tell me about this sooner or discuss it with me, but it's something I will get over. It's just hurt my pride that you told your Father without informing me. But, darling, I do understand. Your art has always been very important to you. Up until your junior year, you were going to art school. Then you were in the high school play and you decided to be an actor and thus, your choice of Santa Barbara.

"But one of the issues we discussed was the cost of art school. And the fact that San Francisco is a very expensive place to live. Your Father has always been very generous with you, but there is a huge difference in tuition between a state school and a private one."

"Mom, that's what's so cool," Cassie said excitedly. "Dad said he would pay for everything and he means everything. Tuition for the school, books, supplies, all my expenses. And it is expensive, but he said that it would be worth it, because he felt that it would give me the direction I need to become a respected artist. The only thing, and this is where I hope you understand and don't get too upset," Cassie was flushing as she spoke, "but Dad says I can live with Danielle, Emily and him. He will give me the guest house and this way he doesn't have to pay for an apartment or my living in the dorm. He'll let me keep my car, but I probably won't be driving it much because I'll take buses most of the time."

Cassie started to speak faster as she began describing how the classes were structured and how Danielle and her father were really excited about her staying with them, but not as excited as Emily, their twelve-year-old daughter, who adored Cassie.

All of sudden Cassie realized her mother had not said one word for the past ten minutes while Cassie had been rambling about school, living with her father and all the other details of her new life.

"Mom? Are you okay with this? You know, I was concerned about how you would feel about this and now you haven't said a word for the last ten minutes. I can't remember when you've been this quiet! Are you that upset with me?" Cassie asked with a quiver in her voice.

As Cassie spoke, she was looking at her mother, who seemed to be staring out into space.

"Please, Mom, are you okay?"

Carmine heard Laurence speaking to her with a warning in his voice, "Remember Carmine, all of Earth's children are loaned to parents to assist them to grow and become the individuals they were intended to be when they signed their contract to come to this planet. This is truly

Cassie's curriculum for this lifetime and she will achieve her objectives by making this school move. It will place her on the appropriate path. Do you understand? It has nothing to do with your ego!"

Carmine gave a small nod of her head, dropped her shoulders in resignation and gave a deep, huge sigh.

"Mom?"

"Cassie, of course, I'm okay! I was stunned about your changing your major so quickly without giving Theater Arts much of a chance and without discussing it with me. But it is all right, because if you feel you have to change, it is better to change your major as early as possible. And, of course, I don't mind you living with your Father."

Carmine heard a "Good for you, Carmine" from Laurence as she continued, "It comes as a shock. The fact that you did not let me know any of this while you were making all these changes. I guess I'm a little upset and hurt—not about the changes, but about not making me aware that you wanted to change. We have always been so close. To make such monumental changes in your life without me involved in the decision process makes me sad."

As Cassie started to speak, Carmine put her arms around her and hugged her. "It's okay Cassie! I understand. Your Father has a tendency to eliminate me from decisions relating to you. He wants to be in control so I don't interfere with his plans. But this is great for you, sweetie. It is something you have always wanted, but it was such an expensive major to choose, especially if you weren't sure if you wanted to pursue art or theater.

"But as long as your Father wants to do this for you, it's great. And I think it is terrific that your Father wants you to live with his family. It's something you have always wanted to do and I know that Emily, who absolutely adores you, is probably in a state of ecstasy. If it's okay with Danielle, where it definitely makes a difference if she approves or not, then I am happy with it. Honest!"

Cassie was glowing by the time Carmine finished speaking and gave her mother a big kiss on the cheek. "Mom, you are so cool. I was afraid that because Dad didn't consult you that you would be against it and angry. I tried to tell him to call you, but you know how Dad is about you, Mom!"

"Cassie, I understand and yes I would have loved to be included in the decision, but I am not blaming anyone, especially you. Your happiness is my main concern and if you feel this is what you want to do, then I am one hundred percent for it. And I also want to commend you, Cassie, for making this decision especially after you just started school. And I want to acknowledge and congratulate you on the courage you displayed as well as your initiative and following your heart. I am very proud of you and even though it was undertaken differently than I would have preferred, the outcome is perfect for you!"

As Carmine finished speaking her cell phone rang. She gently untangled herself from Cassie who was still draped around her and ran to pick it up.

"Hi Carmine, it's Jake. Am I calling at a good time?"

The minute Carmine heard Jake's voice, she felt herself blush. Cassie was looking at her and knew her mother too well not to notice.

"Who is it, Mom," Cassie asked in a wicked, loud voice, "is it your beau?"

Carmine gave Cassie a dirty look and continued speaking to Jake. "Actually, Cassie is here and we were talking. But I did check my calendar and next Saturday for the Getty is fine. I'm looking forward to it."

"Perfect. You sounded so tired last night I wanted to see if you were feeling better. And of course knowing you can do the Getty is good, also."

All the time she was talking, Cassie was making signs to her to put the call on hold. "Jake, can you hold on a minute, please?" she asked as she muted the call. "Cassie, what is it?" Carmine asked with annoyance in her voice.

"Mom, I'd love to meet him! Ask him to join us for dinner tonight, okay?"

"Cassie, I thought you wanted just the two of us to spend time together?"

"But, Mom, I want to meet him. PLEASE," Cassie begged.

Carmine raised her eyes to the ceiling as though asking for heavenly guidance. "I don't even know if he's available tonight."

"How about tomorrow night then? We can have dinner home and you can cook."

"Gee, thanks, Cassie!"

"Jake," she said removing the mute button, "Cassie said she would love to meet you. Would you be available tonight or tomorrow night? Actually, tonight would be better," Carmine said, thinking they would be shopping tomorrow and running errands and she didn't want to take the time to cook a special dinner.

"Sure, I am free tonight. I would love to take you both out! Wherever you want to go."

"Cassie wants to go to La Penne where we were Wednesday night. So maybe you won't want to come."

"Hey, Mom, I'll go anywhere. We could to Penne on Saturday night."

"Jake, you heard that. Whatever you want to do."

"La Penne is fine. What time should I pick you up?"

Carmine looked at the time. She saw that it was 2:00.

"Cassie, how about 6:30," she asked "for dinner."

"Make it six, Mom, I'm hungry and I didn't eat that much lunch."

"Jake, how about 6:00? You could meet us here about 5:30 and then we can walk over again."

"I'm looking forward to it, Carmine. See you then," he said as they hung up.

"Cassie, I am not sure this is a good idea. I have only gone out with him once and that was just two days ago. He's going to think I'm desperate."

"Mom, he won't. Look at you! You have a nice figure, good skin and you don't look your age at all."

"Yeah, well, Cassie, having you along will certainly give him an idea of how old I am. After all, you are not exactly twelve years old," Carmine quipped.

"Mom, it's okay," she said, as she hugged Carmine again. "You can always tell him you had me when you were fourteen." Carmine's dubious look on her face started Cassie laughing. "Look, Mom, I have an intuitive feeling that he is the right one and I want to meet him. And you know how good my intuition is!"

"Cassie's right, you know, Carmine, she has good intuition," Carmine heard Laurence say. "She doesn't fight her intuition like you do."

Carmine couldn't reply because Cassie was looking at her.

"Mom, you look a little strange. Are you all right?"

Carmine decided she wouldn't acknowledge Cassie's comment and ignored it by asking, "Sweetie, do you want to do anything special this afternoon? We don't have much time because we told Jake to be here at 5:30, but maybe we can do a little shopping or perhaps you want to rest and watch TV. Whatever you want to do is fine with me!"

"You know, Mom, I would love to have a mani-pedi. My nails are a mess," Cassie said as she held up her hands. "And my feet are worse. Do you think we could find someone on such short notice? Otherwise, I think I would love to take a long, hot bath and a nap. Maybe I could do both."

Carmine was already on the phone calling the nail salon to see if she could get Cassie an appointment.

Cassie was always amazed on how fast her mother could hear something that needed attention and then implement the appropriate action instantly. Within two or three minutes of Cassie's request, Carmine had an appointment for her.

"Okay, Cassie," Carmine directed with a drill sergeant's voice and demeanor, "Penny can take you at 2:30, which is exactly fifteen minutes from now. Luckily, it is just up the street. Why don't you take a quick bath or probably shower is faster and when you are finished with your appointment, you can come home and lie down. You can take my car unless you want me to drive you and you can put it on my credit card."

"Mom, calm down. You are going too fast for me. Two minutes ago I said I wanted a manicure and pedicure and now I have both, plus a bath and a nap. It is almost too much for my brain to comprehend!"

When Cassie saw her Mother's face drop into a frown, she started laughing. "Carmine, it's okay. I forgot what an organizer you were and how fast you can arrange things. You are very unique and I love you. I'll take a quick shower now and when I come home, a nap," and she quickly went into the bathroom.

As soon as she safely could without Cassie hearing her, Carmine attacked Laurence. "Didn't I tell you to keep out of my way with Cassie here? She knows me too well and when you make your comments, I react." Carmine was near tears now and trying not to yell. "Laurence, please, you don't want anyone to know about you, but you can't be my conscience and talk to me when Cassie is around. If I give you away, it is because of your behavior, not mine."

Laurence started to reply, "Carmine, I am still your Guardian Angel and need to guide you. And…"

Cassie emerged from the bathroom with a smile. "Carmine," she asked knowingly, as she pointed her head towards the nightstand in the bedroom where Jake's note and flower were displayed. "What is this 'perfect' nonsense?"

Carmine turned red as Cassie was speaking and couldn't contain herself between Cassie making fun of her and Laurence interrupting her. She started crying.

"Mom," Cassie said biting her lip with worry frowns on her face, "I was teasing. I think it's a little corny, but it's okay for you. Don't cry."

"I'm sorry, Cassie, I guess I'm a little sensitive about everything. Maybe because it has been so long since I have been interested in a man and . . ." Carmine suddenly stopped what she was saying. "Cassie, you are going to be late if you don't leave right now. We will talk about it later. Here are my car keys and the credit card." And Cassie grabbed them and her purse and ran out the door, slamming it hard.

Carmine shook her head at that interchange and then turned to Laurence with a determined look on her face. "Okay, Laurence, I want to know about Jake and me and about that comment about Cassie's intuition."

"Carmine, you know that you have free will and I can't tell you the future. But, I ask you this, how do you feel about Jake? You know your feelings are there for a reason; to guide and help you in your adventure in life. Don't discount them, ever. So, Carmine, I repeat, how do you feel about Jake?"

"When I think about him, I have this excited and joyful feeling in my stomach and that makes me so happy. And I've never, ever felt this way about anyone. I'm so comfortable with him and I feel I can be myself and he doesn't judge.

Even though we have only gone out once, but it is as if a lifetime was spent with him in that one evening."

"So what does that tell you, Carmine? What is the message your feelings are giving you?"

"You know, I never thought about my feelings in that way, but I guess they are telling me to develop the relationship and to not be afraid and, maybe, like my mother used to say, 'Go for the gusto!'"

"Excellent, Carmine. You are learning on a conscious level to explore and accept your feelings and to follow what seems right for you. Usually, you go with your intuition, which is your feelings, but on an unconscious level. Acknowledging and accepting your feelings, connects your intuition and your consciousness so you can make an effective decision. Of course, I, as your Guardian Angel, am always there guiding and assisting you, but if you can bring your intuition to a conscious level in this way, you will find that your decisions will help you manifest what you desire."

"Laurence, that is so true. So many times, I have felt something was right or wrong, but couldn't define it. So, acted, hoping that it would work out. And most times it did, I guess with your help, even though I didn't know it was you. So, thank you, Laurence," Carmine said with real gratitude in her eyes.

Suddenly, Carmine snapped back to attention and startled Laurence with a wail. "Oh my gosh, I am seeing Jake tonight." She started having a conversation with herself, as she rapidly went to her closet. "I need to find something casual to wear, that fits in with what Cassie is wearing, which I know will be jeans. And the weather is so much cooler today, so I need something that I can keep warm in."

Selecting a long black cotton skirt, a black wrap-around tee shirt and an aquamarine and gold coat sweater, Carmine felt it would meet all her criteria. Deciding to get ready for the evening before Cassie returned, she did her hair and makeup, slipped on her underwear and a robe. She'd finish dressing when Cassie got home. Finding she had time to relax, she decided to do a short meditation. She did this whenever she could, for she found that she always felt more in balance and life seemed to fall into place easily and smoothly.

It seemed she had only been in meditation a minute, before she heard Cassie come in. "Hey Mom, where are you. Look at my nails – don't they look cool?"

Carmine went out to greet Cassie and to look at her nails.

"I'm sorry Mom, did I disturb you? You look like you were sleeping."

"No, I was meditating. That has a better effect on me than sleeping. Your nails are so sweet," she exclaimed as she looked at Cassie's thumbs and big toes polished in light blue and decorated with a floral design of white and yellow daisies.

"Look, it's about 4:00. Why don't you go take a nap and I'll wake you about 5:00. Jake will be here at 5:30 so that will give you a half hour to get dressed. Okay?"

Cassie nodded yes with a yawn, as she headed to the guest room. "Mom, it's okay if I wear jeans tonight, right?"

"Of course, Cassie. I'm going to be casual, too."

"Mom, you are never casual. Your casual is everyone else's dress up, but it's okay with me." She blew her mother a kiss and then shut the bedroom door.

Carmine stood a moment thinking about Cassie's comment and acknowledged that she was right. She wasn't a casual person and was always more dressed up than other people. *It used to bother me, but now it is the way things are. I think I am becoming more comfortable with myself.*

"Laurence," she whispered, "did you have anything to do with this change?"

"You are more confident in yourself and maybe that is because of many of the conversations we have had. I also think it is because of Jake and how he accepted you totally the way you are. When one has a relationship with someone who accepts them unconditionally, no matter who it is, Mother, Father, spouse, child, it is very powerful.

"However," Laurence emphasized, "it certainly is not any different than what I was trying to tell you before you were able to see me, and before you met Jake. Maybe, after all these lifetimes, you finally are believing in yourself. It is hard for all Guardian Angels to understand the low self-esteem that most humans have. If you could believe that you are all divine beings having a human experience, your world would be so different. It would be so much more full of love, kindness and peace. Many times individuals behave badly and cause problems because they feel they are not loved, or are fearful of losing love or threatened in some way where love will be taken away and they don't believe in their magnificence or their uniqueness. It is very puzzling, indeed."

"Thank you, Laurence! It is always enlightening what you have to say about our human existence. It always makes so much sense after I sit with it a while and I absorb it on a deeper level. I know I don't always say it, but I am learning a lot, having you with me.

"Now, Laurence, I want to emphasize to you," and Carmine pronounced the words with great and heavy deliberation, "that you cannot, I repeat, cannot say anything to me tonight unless it is an emergency like the building is going to collapse on us. Okay? And you must be out of my sight so that you don't set me off. With both Jake and Cassie here, I know it will take all my reserves to get through the evening with both of them. If you say anything, I don't know how I will react, so try to stay out of my way tonight! Is that very clear?"

"I understand, Carmine, but remember I'm there to take care of you. I can always go back to the previous arrangement and become invisible with you not aware of me at all."

"No, I don't think so," Carmine said with hesitation. And then shook herself.

I can't believe I would even begin to entertain the possibility of giving up Laurence. But he does get in the way at times. I also can't believe I am introducing my daughter to Jake after one date! Tonight I don't need to look crazy because he is talking to me.

"Laurence" she said, "Please stay out of my way!"

Carmine finished dressing and promptly at five o'clock, Carmine woke Cassie up with a kiss and told her softly, "It's time to get up, kiddo."

Cassie yawned and opened her eyes. "Hey, Mom, you look nice."

"Gee, Cassie, you sound surprised. I think I'm still at an age, with some time and effort, I can look pretty good," she said in an acerbic tone, but with a smile on her face. "Let me finish putting on my lipstick and then the bathroom is all yours."

Waiting for Cassie, Carmine looked at herself in the hallway mirror to reassure herself about how she looked. Turning to Laurence, she said, "If anyone saw what I was doing, the opinion would be that I am vain and that is all I think about is how I look. And actually, right now that is exactly what I am thinking. Does that make me shallow or egocentric?" she asked with a frown.

"No, it doesn't Carmine. It is all right," Laurence said, as she turned towards him. "As long as you're happy and joyful within, you don't have to feel guilty about what you are thinking. You are much too hard on yourself Carmine, as are most humans. Human life is here to be enjoyed and to make the most out of each glorious day. You humans take the small things in life far too seriously."

"Laurence," Carmine whispered loudly, "Cassie will hear us talking and I don't want you to intrude on my thoughts unless it is IMPORTANT." Just as Carmine finished with Laurence, Cassie came out of bathroom, "Mom, who were you talking to?" as she glanced around.

"No one, Cassie, I guess I was talking to myself and giving answers too." She gave what she hoped was a sincere smile.

"That's okay Mom, I do it too."

While Cassie was finishing dressing, Carmine raced around the rooms picking up stray things, straightening the pillows on the couch and righting anything else that didn't seem perfect. She even did a quick washing of the kitchen floor asking herself if this meant she was REALLY compulsive.

She gave Laurence a look that said "don't you dare" as she saw him ready to reply.

She took a minute to look at the box of Godiva chocolates. *Mmm, one won't hurt me,* she thought as she picked up a round coconut crème. *How can something that tastes this good be so bad for you? I refuse to believe it.*

"Actually, Carmine," Laurence said with authority, "your belief that something is good or bad can influence how that substance impacts you. If you believe that chocolate is good for you, and you truly believe it and it doesn't bother you, then it probably is not going to have a negative impact. Conversely, if you feel that it is bad for you and you feel guilty, then it will have a negative effect on you."

"Laurence, that is crazy! The medical industry would absolutely crucify you for saying that. But you know," she said thoughtfully, "it has never hurt me as far as I can see and it doesn't do anything to my weight because I have always believed that chocolate was good for you. It makes me feel so good!"

As Carmine was staring into space thinking about Laurence's insights, she heard the door buzzer.

"That's Jake! He's a little early," she exclaimed as she ran to the door. She released the front gate to let him in and then turned around to look at herself in the mirror behind the front door. Studying herself in the mirror, she felt she looked okay; better than okay, maybe attractive. She was looking intently in the mirror to see if her makeup was on correctly, when she heard Jake walking from the elevator.

As she opened her front door, Jake appeared with a small nosegay of baby white roses in each hand.

"Hi," he grinned happily at Carmine. "I am glad to be here tonight and thought white roses for both of you would be appropriate. I hope your daughter likes roses?" he said with a question in his voice.

"Jake, she will love anything you give her. That is so sweet of you to think of her and of me," Carmine said, as she led Jake from the front door to the living room.

He handed both to her and she handed one back to him. "I think it would be nice if you give it to her, Jake. However, I will take my nosegay and place it in a vase. It's a good thing I have so many vases because they are certainly being used these days," Carmine said as she pointedly, and with good humor, looked at Jake.

Placing the roses in a miniature heart-shaped crystal vase, Carmine placed the vase next to the Godiva candy box. "I have to admit that I ate one right before you buzzed. It's been a hectic day and I haven't eaten anything till now."

Jake laughed. "I'm glad I could supply you with appetizers!" he teased. "You look lovely," Jake added. "But you always do."

Carmine blushed and started to say thank you when Cassie walked out into the living room. Dressed in skinny blue jeans with a red cotton turtleneck and an embroidered jean jacket with black riding boots, she walked over to Jake and held out her hand. "Hi, Jake, I'm Cassie and I am glad to meet you."

"I am glad to meet you, too, Cassie," he said as he handed the rose bouquet to her. "Your mother has told me so much about you that I feel I know you. It was all good," he spoke quickly as he saw Cassie's face start to frown. "I hope you like roses? These are white, but if you look closely as they open, you will see that there is pink in the center."

Cassie's eyes smiled widely and she blushed somewhat as she said, "Thank you, that is very nice of you."

Firmly clasping her nosegay, Cassie then stood very straight and looked up at Jake with a determined look on her face.

"Jake, I want you to know that I would like to know all about you so I am going to be asking you some personal questions, if you don't mind," Cassie said in a shaky, but challenging tone. "My mother is very important to me. I love her so much and I only want the best for her, so I hope that is all right," Cassie said with tears in her eyes. "Mom says if I have people's permission, then I can ask something of them that maybe wouldn't be permitted otherwise."

"Cassie, I am impressed. It takes a lot of guts to say what you said and I'll be happy to answer any and all questions you may have." And Jake led her gently to the couch so that they both could sit down.

Carmine listened to this interchange between the two of them and was almost apoplectic. There was Cassie telling Jake, someone she hardly knew, how she felt about her Mother, which made Carmine wildly ecstatic and yet she was asking personal questions of someone Carmine cared for, but didn't know that well. Carmine didn't know whether to yell at Cassie to stop or keep her mouth shut, which was almost an impossibility.

No, it was an impossibility because before Carmine could help herself, she let out a mortified "Cassie, darling!"

Then before she could say another word, Cassie said "Mom, I know this is embarrassing you, but I don't want you to get hurt and no one ever defends you. You're always defending and helping others and now I want to do that for you. And Jake understands," she said looking at him for confirmation.

Jake nodded his head yes and said softly to Carmine, "I truly understand and I have only high regards for Cassie for doing something that I know is difficult. Cassie must love you so very much to do this for you, Carmine."

By this time, tears were rolling down Cassie's cheeks. Jake took a white handkerchief from his pocket and wiped her face. "Cassie, what you've done is very brave and courageous. Please feel good about yourself for doing this for your mother. I'm here at your disposal and will answer each and every question truthfully and to the best of my ability. And no more tears, because I'm happy to do it," he said with compassion and understanding.

Carmine was so touched by the scene between Cassie and Jake that she couldn't find any words to express what she was feeling. She kept looking at the two and felt tears coming to her eyes. And then an intense jolt of what felt like electricity went through her body and there was a flash of insight or of 'knowing' that she and Jake had been together in other lifetimes. The feeling was so overwhelming that Carmine felt herself staggering and was saved from falling by sitting down in the gold chair facing the couch. Both Cassie and Jake looked at her and both said at the same time, "Mom, Carmine, are you all right?"

Carmine slowly nodded her head yes. She then heard Laurence say, "Carmine, that is the first time you have allowed yourself to consciously know the truth about the past, or what you humans call using your intuition or what is direct knowing independent of any reasoning."

While Carmine was trying to comprehend what Laurence was saying to her as well as what she had felt in that moment and trying to juggle the two emotions, Cassie ran to her and gave her a hug.

"Mom, you are absolutely white. I hope I haven't made you that angry with me."

Carmine shook her head, "Of course not, sweetie, I felt very strange all of a sudden. Maybe running around like a fool for the last week has caught up with me."

Carmine raised herself up from the chair, gave Jake a warm smile, placed her arm around Cassie's waist and said, "I think it's time that we walked over to Penne. Cassie, you can start asking your questions of Jake now or wait until we eat dinner. It is up to you and Jake, and as long as Jake doesn't care what you ask, neither will I. And I mean it," she said with a laugh.

After grabbing her coat and locking the front door, the three took the elevator down and walked out of the locked front gate. With Carmine in the middle, all three of them walked abreast on the sidewalk, holding hands and smiling.

Chapter Ten

They arrived at the restaurant around 6:15 and found that there was already a wait.

"Ah, Ms. Carmine, so nice to see you and, you also, sir." Then he saw Cassie and with a warm smile and a slight bow, kissed her hand. "It has been too long since we saw you, Ms. Cassie. How do you like college?"

"Germino, it is nice, but I am going to be transferring to another college in San Francisco. One where I can focus on artistic courses and obtain a degree in some area of art." Germino looked puzzled, but said, "Sounds nice, Ms. Cassie. I know you are a very talented artist.

"Ms. Carmine your favorite table will be ready in twenty-five minutes. Is that acceptable?"

"Of course!"

Jake asked if Carmine would like a glass of red wine while waiting and she told him only if he would share it with her. Cassie asked for a Coke. As soon as the drinks came, Cassie started asking her questions.

"First, Jake, how old are you?"

"I'm forty-three, Cassie."

"Well, that's great because my Mother is . . .," she began, until Carmine interrupted her.

"I'm sorry Cassie, you are forbidden to tell my age, at least at this time," Carmine laughed. "Actually, it is a very practical belief. I feel people put you in boxes if you tell them your age. If they don't know, they treat you as young as you behave. Otherwise, people are always telling you that you are too old for this, too young for that, etc. So I just don't tell my age. But I'm sure I'll eventually tell you. It's pretty obvious what age I'm probably close to because of Cassie's age, but I still want to keep to that philosophy. Is that all right?"

"It's fine. My Aunt Sophie thinks the same way. But whatever you like. If I didn't know you had a daughter Cassie's age, I would think you were twenty-five."

"You certainly have a way with words," Carmine gave him her brightest smile. "That makes me very happy."

In the twenty minutes that they waited for the table, Cassie continued her questioning while Carmine just stood back and listened. He told Cassie the same story about his fiancée that he had told Carmine and also the one about his relationship with Giovanna just touching on it and saying there were conflicts between them so it had ended.

"So, Jake, what were the conflicts with Giovanna?"

"Oh my God, Cassie! Please! Stop! These are personal questions!" Squinting her eyes, Carmine gave Cassie a warning look that Cassie knew from past experience meant big trouble from her mother.

Ignoring Carmine, Cassie looked directly at Jake and said, "You know I really would like to know. Maybe my mother has the same characteristics!"

Jake smiled at both the ladies, "First, Carmine, it's all right and, second, Cassie, I doubt if your mother has that particular issue."

Carmine then shrugged her shoulders and made a gesture letting Jake know that it was up to him, even though she admitted to herself that she really would like to know too. Laurence nodded his head in agreement!

"Giovanna was raised by her European father who taught her that there was no need to be monogamous in any relationship, including marriage." Jake went on to explain that he had tried to understand Giovanna's point of view, as he felt she was his soul mate, but could not convince her to change her behavior. She had tried several times, but couldn't seem to really want to be with just one man. After two years of an on-and-off again relationship (because Jake would always break up with her when he found out she was seeing someone else) he broke it off completely. Giovanna was very willing to continue being with him and wanted to marry him, but would not or could not change how she felt about just being with one man for the rest of her life. She still wanted to be with Jake, but could not understand his intolerance of behavior she felt was normal.

Carmine's mouth was wide open as she listened to his explanation. She kept on looking at Laurence, who was behind Jake. She couldn't wait to discuss the revelation with Laurence, but he silently kept on shaking his head.

"Gosh, Jake, that was quite an explanation," Cassie said in a high and apologetic voice. "Thank you for being so honest. I truly apologize for asking. I really had no idea it would be so personal."

"No apologies necessary! I really wanted you to understand. I have dated several women since then and none of them seemed to be right, either. Until now," he said in a low tone, looking directly at Carmine. "I know it sounds trite and contrived, but even though I have had only one date with Carmine and have only known her though my class, I feel something for her I have never experienced before. Even when I was with Giovanna!"

Carmine felt her body temperature rise so high she started perspiring and started fanning herself as she gave a big gulp.

"Mom, are you all right?" Cassie asked with a worried tone and even Jake looked concerned.

"I just swallowed the wine wrong. I'm fine," she said with a contrived cough to cover her embarrassment.

Other than that, Cassie's questions elicited merely miscellaneous pieces of information that Jake loved to ski, which he did well, and played golf, which he never did as well as he thought he should. He told her he loved to read and dance, and mentioned that he wrote a few books, implying that they were technical.

When Cassie asked what his "fatal flaw" was, he said that he had a huge tolerance for letting things go undone much longer than he should, unless it was his school or his philanthropic duties. Then he was almost obsessive. Otherwise, he could be very passive about things. "I guess I procrastinate a lot, which bothers me, but not enough to change too much." Cassie had laughed at this and said that he and her mother would make a good pair because Carmine never procrastinated. In fact, she was a step ahead of everything, which could make Cassie crazy sometimes.

"You have to know, Jake, Carmine has a control issue," Cassie said in a matter-of-fact tone.

Just as Carmine was going to defend herself against that statement, Germino came and told them the table was ready.

As they walked to the table, Carmine took Cassie aside and said with annoyance, "That is really enough! Cassie! I am sure you are making Jake uncomfortable with these questions."

As they were seated, Jake looked at Carmine and said, "I heard you and I'm not uncomfortable with Cassie's questions. In fact, I'm enjoying our conversation and am happy to answer as many questions as Cassie wants to ask."

Cassie gave her mother a triumphant look and said, "Jake, I have only one more question to ask and I can ask it little later. I'm really hungry and I want to see if they have anything new," she said, preoccupied with reading the multi-page menu.

When the waiter arrived, everyone had their order ready. Cassie ordered the seafood salad and then her favorite dish, gnocchi with a marinara sauce. Jake had the bean soup and then the pasta with clam sauce. Carmine decided that pasta three out of four days was just too much pasta for her body as she would be making Cassie's favorite pasta dinner the next night. She ordered a radicchio and arugula salad and salmon on a medley of root vegetables. For wine, Jake and Carmine had both ordered a glass of Pinot Grigio while Cassie had another Coke.

While they waited for their order, Cassie said, "Okay, Jake, I'm ready to ask that question. Is that okay?"

"You have all my attention, Cassie."

Giving her Mother a strange look, she said, "Just what are your intentions towards my Mother?"

"Cassie!" Carmine said in a shocked whisper. "Oh, my God, Jake, I'm so sorry." Carmine didn't know whether to laugh or cry, she was so outraged at the question.

"Carmine," Jake said, reaching across the table to take her hand into his, "I would love to answer that question."

Turning to Cassie, Jake said with quiet determination, "My intentions, Cassie, are for a very long-range commitment. I have watched your Mother in my classroom for two months and I feel I know her much better than I should, considering we have only been out once. But there is something between your Mother and me that transcends the element of time.

Perhaps we have Karmic ties. But I truly want to be a part of her life, if she will allow it."

Carmine was stunned into silence. Looking at Jake, she didn't know how to respond. But Cassie did. Clapping her hands with delight, and then lifting up her Coke glass in a toast, she said with glee, "I'll drink to that. Anytime someone mentions Karmic and my mother, I know that they're meant to be together."

Jake raised his glass with one hand while the other hand still clasped Carmine's hand, and said, with a shy smile on his face, "I'll certainly drink to that, too."

Carmine just looked at each of them shaking her head, speechless. All of a sudden, she heard Laurence warn her, "Accept what is being said, Carmine, they both love you and want the best for you. You can either laugh with them or become angry, which is not necessary or helpful. So laugh and be joyful in their love for you."

Carmine was saved from responding by the interruption of the waiter asking if they wanted dessert. *Thank God, I don't know what I should say or do. What was Cassie thinking? And Jake answered with such clarity.*

Before anyone had a chance to answer, Cassie said no. "Mom, please can we go to the Milking Cow for ice cream? That would be perfect."

Carmine laughed and said if Jake agreed. "The Milking Cow," Carmine explained, "has the best ice cream in all of Los Angeles, at least that's our feeling and it's within walking distance."

"Sounds perfect. Ice cream is my favorite dessert," Jake said.

The waiter arrived with the bill and Carmine gestured to him to give it to her. Taking out her credit card as Jake started speaking about paying for the dinner, she said sternly, "Jake, this is the 21st Century and women pay for dinner when they are out with a man and for all sorts of other things. This is my treat tonight, so please allow me to do this." And she handed the credit card to the waiter.

Jake looked at her and said, simply, "Okay, Carmine, if you insist. I'd prefer to pay, but I certainly don't want to offend or fight with you. But, in the future, this is something that we have to resolve."

Carmine smiled and said it would be something they would have to negotiate.

Cassie was silent, watching the two and nodding her head. *I know Jake is perfect for my mother. That really makes me feel relieved for I know now that she will have someone in her life to look after her.* And with that thought, Cassie hugged herself with pleasure.

The six block walk to the ice cream store went quickly as there was much talking and laughter. Scanning the ice cream menu displayed above the counter, Cassie and Carmine selected a vanilla and mint hot fudge and marshmallow sundae that they shared. Jake chose a raspberry swirl and vanilla ice cream cone. Enjoying their treats, they did minimal talking as they slowly made their way back to the condo.

Cassie let out a loud exclamation just before they approached the condo gate.

"Look at this cool Jag," she said peering into the window of Jake's car that was parked just in front. "This is so beautiful!"

"You know, Jake, this is both my mother's and my favorite car. We both agree if we could have any car, this would be it."

"Cassie," Jake said a little embarrassed, "That's my car. It is my choice of cars, also, so I decided that this would be my one vice. Would you like to drive it?" he asked as he handed her the keys.

"Oh, do you really mean it?" Cassie squealed excitedly. "I'd love to."

"Jake, are you sure?" Carmine asked. "Cassie is a very safe driver, but I would hate to have anything happen."

Jake put his arm around Carmine's waist and said, "Spoken like a true mother. I am sure it'll be fine."

Cassie unlocked the door and jumped into the seat. Starting the car, she beamed with rapture at Carmine and Jake.

"Cassie, you can drive it for five minutes and not one minute longer. And don't go on the freeway. Please! I'm looking at my watch right now."

"Don't worry Mom, I'll be really, really careful," she yelled out of the window as she drove away.

"I hope you don't regret this, Jake. It is a beautiful car and Cassie is very responsible, but she is still a teenager."

"Don't worry, Carmine, nothing will happen."

Then he took her by the waist with both arms around her and said softly, "I hope I didn't upset you in the restaurant about my intentions. That is something I wanted to do at the right time. But I felt that Cassie deserved an honest answer and I didn't want to lie. But I want you to know that I meant every word I said and I also want you to know that what I said is not something I do or say every month or every year to someone. There is a connection between us that is different from any other relationship I've had. It doesn't have to do with the time that we have known each other. I know that this is right for me, but I don't want to make you uncomfortable."

Carmine closed her eyes and took a deep breath. "This is difficult for me to say this, Jake, because I always hide my feelings so I can't be hurt, but," and here Carmine hesitated a moment, "I feel the same way about you. There is definitely something going on between us that transcends time. My only request is that we go very, very slowly because I've a tendency to run the other way if something goes faster than I think it should or seems to be out of my control." Carmine giggled a little. "Cassie was right when she said I had a control issue," she admitted.

"Carmine, we will go as slow or as fast as you want and feel comfortable with. I promise you," Jake said with a hint of emotion in his voice. And he very gently kissed Carmine on the lips for a brief moment and hugged her close to him.

Carmine felt so safe and warm in Jake's arms she just stood there with her eyes closed and hugged him back and completely forgot about Laurence, who was always there. Finally, she lifted her face to his and kissed him on the lips. This time Jake's response was not so gentle, but more aggressive and felt utterly delicious to Carmine. Just as she felt herself responding the same way, there were several car honks and Cassie was back.

"Hey Mom, you said five minutes. If I had known this was going on, I would have taken an hour," Cassie called out of the car window, with a knowing look.

Jake and Carmine separated so quickly that Carmine almost fell over and both their faces were flushed.

Carmine didn't know what to say to Cassie and started sputtering something about feeling cold and faint.

"Hey, Mom, it's all right, really. You don't have to make up an excuse. I'm grown up, remember," she said as she handed Jake the car keys.

"Thank you, Jake, that was so cool. Anytime you want me to do errands and I can drive your car, let me know.

"I'm going to go to bed," she said unlocking the front gate, "so you guys can come in and not worry about having me around."

"Why don't I walk you and Cassie to your door now," Jake asked, "and let you two sleep? It's late and it's been a long day."

"Jake, I think Cassie and I can get ourselves to our front door safely. It's less than a minute's walk if we don't use the elevator. Really, Jake, we will both be fine," Carmine said as she waved him towards his car.

"Well, I always like to walk a lady or ladies to their door, but if you insist, I'll let you do it this time. Thanks for a really wonderful evening and, Cassie, it was truly a pleasure to meet you. You're very special and I'm glad you love your mother so much," he said as he shook Cassie's hand.

He lightly kissed Carmine on the cheek, then got into his car and waved out of the window as he drove away.

Carmine and Cassie stood watching his car until it turned the corner.

"Mom," Cassie said, "I really liked him and I think you do too. Mom, I know this is the one for you. I just know." Cassie jumped up and down, like a little kid.

"You know, Cassie, I think you're right. And I also think you can calm down. But this has gone so fast for me I have to slow down and try to understand what has happened. It's hard for me to jump into a relationship in such a minimal amount of time. And, I want to make sure that he is over his girlfriend. She sounded spectacular to me and he even considered her as his soul mate once, so it must have been really serious."

"He sounded pretty final about ending the relationship and didn't seem to have any regrets, so I wouldn't worry! Mom, how many times have you told me when I became confused, to follow your heart, go with the flow, don't fight it. All those nuggets of advice you gave me when I was overwhelmed. Are they not true for you, too?" Cassie asked as they walked up the steps to the condo.

"You know, Mom, I am so relieved," Cassie said as she closed the door and double locked it from the inside. They made their way to the living room couch where they collapsed almost upon each other.

"What do you mean, relieved?" Carmine asked, puzzled.

"Well, Mom, Dad has Danielle and Emily to look out for him and I'm your daughter so I can watch out for you and take care of you, but I'm in college and now I am going to be even further away than Santa Barbara so it's harder to, you know, to kinda keep tabs on you. And when I graduate from college, I want to travel to study art and then who is going to take care of you? This way, with Jake around, I don't have to worry about you."

"Cassie," Carmine exclaimed with surprise in her voice, "you don't have to worry about me. I'm the one that worries about you. I'm the mother, remember. I take care of you!"

"But, Mom, you don't have anyone and if I'm gone or not around, who is going to take care of you? That's why I am so relieved about Jake. He is really cool and I know that he will watch out for you."

"Oh, Cassie, Cassie," Carmine said with a heart so full of love as she hugged her daughter. "You're so sweet and caring, darling. But truly, Cassie, I can take care of myself and you don't have to worry about me for years and years yet; with or without Jake."

"Mom, you don't understand what a responsibility it is to be the only child, no sibling, with a Mother who is alone. I know how hard you worked to ensure that I had a great childhood and that there wasn't too much difference between me and kids who had two-parent families. So I feel now that I am older, that I want and should take care of you."

"Cassie, don't you think that is a huge responsibility you are taking on yourself which isn't necessary? Do you really think I can't take care of myself?"

"Mom, that's not what I am saying," Cassie protested.

"Carmine," Laurence interrupted, "listen to what Cassie is trying to say. Really listen!"

Carmine closed her eyes and told herself to have patience with both Laurence and Cassie.

Then she said very quietly to Cassie, "Sweetie, are you trying to tell me that by having Jake in my life you feel that I have someone who cares for me and, therefore, it lessens the responsibility that you feel is yours, because you are the only one in my life who is close to me and truly cares?"

"Yes, Mom! You are reflecting exactly how I feel. I worry about you all the time."

"And Cassie, is that why I would receive those short telephone calls from you checking to see how I was? You were just making sure I was okay?"

"Yes."

"Cassie, that is truly beautiful of you, to worry and care that much. Even if Jake wasn't in my life, and who knows what is going to happen there, you don't have to worry or take responsibility for me. I'm not even forty so I think I've some good years ahead of me to take care of myself and do all the things I always wanted to do.

"But I thank you from the bottom of my heart. What you told me is incredibly kind and thoughtful. I'm very lucky to have such a beautiful, compassionate, conscientious and caring daughter. So, please remove that worry from your head and go forward to do whatever you wish, knowing that all will be well." And with that she kissed Cassie on her blonde hair and hugged her very hard.

"Look, kiddo, it has been a long day so let's go to bed. We can plan tomorrow when you wake up. But thank you again, darling, for your heartfelt concerns," as Carmine hugged her again.

Cassie unwound herself from her mother's embrace, blew her a kiss as she made her way to the bedroom, waved to her mother and said, "I love you Mom" and then closed the door.

Carmine walked into the bathroom and while getting ready for bed, went over the conversation with Cassie in her head. "What a difference a few years make from the time she was a teenager and it seemed nothing I ever did was right or to her satisfaction."

"Laurence, you didn't put this thing about taking care of me in Cassie's head, did you?" she asked accusingly.

"No, of course not, Carmine. I am not Cassie's Guardian Angel."

Carmine started to meditate, but found she was too tired, put herself to bed and was asleep before she pulled all the covers over her.

Both Carmine and Cassie slept late on Saturday morning and it was after eleven by the time they chatted together about the previous evening and everything else under the sun, had a light breakfast and decided what they would do for the day. They both happily agreed it would be shopping.

Carmine commented on the time and told Cassie to hurry so they could use their time effectively.

"Mom," Cassie yelled in an exasperated voice, "this is supposed to be fun, not for time efficiency."

Carmine smiled sheepishly to Cassie and admitted she was thinking work, not fun! They decided they would go to the Beverly Center in West L.A. and see what the best stores were featuring. Then they would each have a body scrub at Carmine's favorite spa at the end of the day.

That agreed upon, they both left with a clothes agenda; Cassie needed underwear and a pair of black ankle boots.

She also wanted a really funky pair of jeans for herself and to buy a pair for Carmine so she could look a little more casual.

At the premier trendy mall, it was a marathon of clothes on and off at several different stores. Finally, Cassie decided on a pair of deep purple straight leg jeans with a crystal design on each back pocket. It was fun as well as flattering and Cassie loved them. Carmine liked them so much she tried them on, only in black. Much to her surprise, they also looked good on her. Carmine said she would treat Cassie to the jeans as she knew that Cassie's allowance from her father covered the necessities and some clothes, but certainly not these jeans. Cassie hugged Carmine for her generosity and admitted that she was a little nervous about charging the jeans on her father's credit card.

The ankle black boots she found on sale were perfect, as well as the two beige bras, which were not beautiful, but really comfortable. Cassie beamed with happiness as she told her mother her purchases were exactly what she had envisioned. Well, not exactly, like the purple jeans, but even better!

Laurence couldn't resist commenting to Carmine, even though he knew he was supposed to keep silent, "When you ask for something that is so clear, and truly believe that it will happen, it will manifest. And this occurs with all your beliefs, positive or negative. So that it is why it is so important to keep strong and be positive."

Carmine tried to ignore what he said and told him silently, "We will talk about it later."

After splurging on an enormous shared hot fudge sundae, which they called a late lunch, Carmine and Cassie spent the rest of the afternoon at the Spa, getting their bodies scrubbed, sitting in the wet sauna and relaxing in the hot tub.

Several times Laurence tried to interrupt their conversation, but Carmine refused to acknowledge anything more he said. She only listened once when she was trying to make a left hand turn, when he warned her not to turn at that moment. A car had run a red light and they would've ended up being in a serious accident. She mentally thanked him and told him how grateful she was and let him know that only in situations like that was he supposed to converse with her.

When they finally arrived home, they collapsed on the couch with their packages thrown on the floor. "After spending so much time at the spa and with that body scrub, I feel like a beached whale. I can't move from here for the rest of the evening," Carmine moaned.

"Carmine, you promised to make me my favorite dinner, remember," Cassie pretended to whine.

"Okay, kiddo, you got it, but you, my love, will do all the dishes. Agreed?!"

"No problem, Mom. For you cooking, I would do a thousand dishes," then amended her statement with, "Well, maybe ten!"

Carmine heated a Swiss chard sauce and served it over homemade spinach fettuccine, both of which Carmine had stored in the freezer, along with a hard-crusted Italian bread and a mixed baby green salad. There was much conversation and laughter and merriment during dinner as they thoroughly discussed men in general, Jake, school, art, Cassie's father and stepmother, the political situation and Cassie's dates at college.

The conversation became serious when Carmine told Cassie about Leslie and how she hoped Cassie would never have to endure a situation like that. Cassie made a firm promise to her mother that she would allow no man to ever abuse her, physically or mentally.

They cleaned up the kitchen and, by nine o'clock, they were both ready for bed, early as it was. Carmine asked Cassie if she would accompany her to church the next day and then go out for breakfast before returning to school. Cassie readily agreed, as long as she could depart early in the afternoon.

Carmine felt sad thinking about Cassie leaving as she kissed her good night and gave her a big hug, which Cassie warmly returned.

"You know, kiddo, it seems as though you have been here only two minutes instead of two days. I really miss you. But I am also very proud of how you are taking responsibility for your life and making decisions that will help you in the future. You were able to identify and clarify your dream and now you are making and honoring that specific commitment to yourself. That is huge, especially in someone as young as you are. Sometimes adults have issues with doing that. So I truly acknowledge and congratulate your decision and wisdom on this choice."

"Gee, thanks, Mom. I really, really appreciate your understanding and accepting my new plans for school. You know you are extremely cool and I love you."

Cassie flung her arms around her mother the way she had done when she was four and gave her a big kiss. Then almost embarrassed by her "toddler moment," Cassie abruptly stopped and walked away to her bedroom.

"Good-night, Carmine. I'll count on you to wake me in the morning," she said as she shut the bedroom door.

Preparing for bed, Carmine noticed Laurence, who was very quiet. He almost looked like a kid who was sulking because he had been ignored.

"Laurence, thank you for behaving yourself today. You saved our lives in that car episode and you allowed me to be with Cassie with very little of your direction. Thank you! I'm so grateful!"

"Carmine, I am just performing my Angel duties. But it's difficult when you tell me you can't be bothered because people will notice when you react to what I am telling you. I think it was easier when you didn't see me and I could give you all the assistance that you need every day."

"Laurence, don't be silly. This is working out really well. But I have to go to bed. Can we please discuss this after Cassie leaves tomorrow?"

"Of course, Carmine."

With that, Carmine hurried through her nightly rituals for bed, meditated for five minutes and poured herself into bed. She was asleep before Laurence could say "God Bless You."

The next day, Carmine and Cassie slept late and barely made it to the 11:00 a.m. church service. They had a quick breakfast at the Pacific Dining Car in LA. Leaving the restaurant, Carmine told Cassie, "After this week, I'm going to go on a mini diet! Eating like this could become an addiction because all the food is prepared so well. But I just cannot keep eating as we have the last three days; it is ridiculous!" Cassie said she certainly understood. She would probably watch what she ate, too, even though it would be easy to do that with the food served at school. "Oh, Mom, the last few days have been the best meals I've had since I left home, with the exception of a few dates where we ate out."

Before she knew it, Carmine was walking Cassie to her red Civic. Carmine was telling her that, because of the building project at Cal State, she would have extra time off during the Holidays and could help her move.

"Oh, Mom, that would be great. Dad said he would hire a mover, but I would have to pack everything. Maybe you and Jake could come up and make it a vacation as well as help me pack."

"Cassie," Carmine said mortified, "I've only been out with Jake twice and already we are taking vacations together as well as helping you move."

"Well, Mom, you know this is the one for you," Cassie said in a matter-of-fact tone.

Carmine just ignored the comment and as Cassie drove out of the garage, she blew her a kiss with a request to call when Cassie arrived at her dorm.

Waving and throwing return kisses, Cassie left Carmine standing in the driveway, with tears in her eyes.

"Don't be sad, Carmine," Laurence said with kindness. "Be happy that she was here and you both enjoyed yourselves!"

"Oh, Laurence, I'm happy and sad; happy that she was here and sad that she has to leave. This really tells me that Cassie is on her own and that our relationship, even though it is good, has changed. It is less like Mother and daughter and more like, well, I guess sisters or friends. Which I guess is good, but it is different. Maybe I just don't like change that much."

"The childhood part of her life is over. So it is good that you see Cassie as a sister or friend rather than your child. That is a sign that you have completed your part of the contract to help her get her start in life. You did well. Enjoy the next phase."

"Well, look, Laurence, there is no way that I am going to give Cassie up as my child. She will always be my child and I am sure that I will worry about her always."

"Of course, Carmine, but in reality, Cassie is an adult and you must allow her to be that by treating her and respecting her as that adult. Don't you think most of your planet's parent issues regarding children are caused by the parents' feeling that they possess their children, instead of understanding that they are a loan, and that each child needs to go forward and take responsibility for him or herself? Making the child's decisions and trying to control the child, once he or she has reached young adulthood is not helpful, practically and spiritually. One of your beautiful poets said it so well, Khalil Gibran—

> *Your children are not your children. They are the sons and daughters of Life's longing for itself. They come through you but not from you, And though they are with you, yet they belong not to you.*

"That is so beautiful. Thank you, Laurence, for such a lovely reminder. I guess many parents feel that, since they are their children, they have the right to give them advice or even tell their children what to major in, where to live, all the things they themselves have learned. But I'll have to think about it later. Right now, I have to catch up on everything, including studying for finals as they are coming up soon. What I really want to do instead is take a long nap." Carmine closed her eyes, anticipating how glorious that would feel.

Laurence nodded. "Carmine, do what your body is telling you to do. It is talking to you for a reason. When you listen, it demonstrates self-respect, self-trust and self-love as it honors a commitment to yourself and your highest good. I promise you everything that you need to do will be completed."

Carmine grinned happily. "Hey, Laurence, I can think of a thousand reasons and arguments why that wouldn't work for a lot of people, but you know what..., I'm going to do it!"

Having said that with emphasis, Carmine marched into her bedroom where she undressed, pulled on her comfy white nightgown and threw herself onto the bed and under the covers. She was instantly asleep and didn't awake until Cassie called her two hours later to tell her she had arrived safely.

After telling Cassie she loved her and to be sure to rest, Carmine lay down on the bed and thought of all the things she had to do. Not able to put it all off any longer, she became a motion machine: picking up the house, studying in snatches, doing laundry and trying not to think about how much she missed Cassie.

By eight that evening, Carmine felt she had her homework under control, everything else in the house done and was ready for her usual nightly ritual of bath, yoga and meditation.

Just as she was filling the bath tub, her cell rang. Picking it up on the first ring, she heard Jake say, "I hope you don't mind me calling, Carmine, but I thought you might be lonely after Cassie left so I thought I would just say hello."

"Jake, how thoughtful. And you are right. I have been a little sad ever since she left. Isn't it silly?"

"Of course not. Carmine, I'm not a parent, but I have several cousins whom I adore and miss them terribly every time they leave. I can imagine how much harder it is for a parent."

"Thank you, Jake, for your understanding."

They chatted for a few minutes about what each had done since they had seen each other. Carmine then mentioned she was getting ready for bed. After a hectic weekend, she was looking forward to a simple full night's rest.

"Carmine," she heard Jake say hesitantly, "I would really like to see you before next Saturday. Is there a possibility we could go out to dinner next week? You have to eat, and, if I pick you up and we go out somewhere casual, it wouldn't take more than maybe an hour and a half."

"Jake, I'd love that, but I'm not sure of my schedule," Carmine replied as she felt a little shiver of happiness. "Maybe we could go Tuesday evening, but I'll know better tomorrow. Is that okay?"

"Perfect. I'll see you at school tomorrow, but I'll call you tomorrow evening. Anyway, have a delicious sleep and God Bless." With that, Jake said goodnight and hung up.

That is the first time any man has said God Bless. What a lovely way to end the conversation.

The next day was frenetic. She saw Jake at school, where they overtly ignored each other, but kept glancing at one another surreptitiously. She spoke to Leslie to find out what was happening with her. Leslie promised she would call during the week to give Carmine a current update on her life. Carmine also contacted her Tuesday client to make sure that her schedule would allow her to leave by 4:30 that day.

She spoke to Jake that night, confirmed their date for the next evening and started studying for finals, which would be beginning soon.

"I can't wait for these weeks to go by. I feel as though I am carrying a zoo-load of animals on my shoulders, including an elephant," she told herself as she gave a huge yawn. Then she gave herself words of comfort, "Carmine, as it always does, the time will fly and then you will have that delightful six weeks of vacation."

But later, even in her meditation, Carmine couldn't concentrate. She was so busy thinking of classes, finals, her consulting regular work and Jake. And Laurence couldn't help her concentrate, much as he tried. "Carmine," she told herself, "calm down, focus on your third eye and try to feel the peace and serenity that everyone has inside of them." And, after thirty minutes of intense concentration, the chattering in her mind stopped and she entered a state of true meditation, in silence and tranquility.

Chapter Eleven

Two and a half weeks later, Carmine sat on the couch on a Friday evening reminiscing about their Getty date and the magical days that followed, including their romantic walk on Santa Monica beach. She and Jake had been almost inseparable since that first Getty outing.

Even though Carmine was busy with school, they had enjoyed dinner together, sometimes just grabbing a quick bite. They had gone bowling and roller skating—things she hadn't done in ages. They had walked in the park near her home enjoying the little bit of nature along with the assorted L.A. characters that frequented the park. Jake introduced her to an Argentine dance class because she once mentioned wanting to learn to tango. They had laughed helplessly, as they tried to strike and maintain the style and attitude of the dance. She observed Jake's Tae Kwon Do class and noted he was very skilled and sexy in his martial arts uniform.

One night, aware that Carmine was busy, and wouldn't be able to see him, Jake had surprised her by dropping off a chicken potpie that his cook had made. "I didn't want you to have to stop to cook," he said with a shy smile on his face. He had given her a quick kiss on the cheek and told her to get back to studying. Another night, the intercom rang and, it was a delivery person from La Penne delivering broiled salmon with potatoes and a salad.

On several nights, they had made a quick dinner at home and Jake brought out his laptop and worked on his current story while she studied. They chatted briefly, but were comfortable working on their individual tasks.

Carmine usually disliked having a man around too often; she was surprised that Jake didn't affect her that way. They were both astonished at how comfortable they were with each other and how, with almost no effort, they were able to blend into each other's lives. She realized she was doing so much more with Jake and still had time for school.

Laurence had tried very hard to keep himself from commenting on Carmine's behavior and thoughts when Jake was there. When he forgot himself, Carmine had given him a squint-eye, gritted-teeth look which meant "STOP whatever you are going to say," which had caused Jake to comment on how much he loved the look she made when she was concentrating hard while studying.

"I am blessed," she told herself so many times. Laurence had agreed with her. "By having good Karma in other lives, you and Jake have earned each other in this life." Laurence told her. Carmine had pestered Laurence for more information. "I'll tell you more when the time is appropriate. It's not the right time for you to know." Laurence had said firmly. No amount of cajoling, threatening or whining on Carmine's part could pry any more information out of him.

Saturday Jake had shown up with his staff, a man and a woman, who cleaned her condo better than it had ever before been cleaned. "You told me that you couldn't go walking on the beach today because you had to clean," he said, in answer to Carmine's protests. "This way, your house is clean and you can relax and have some fun without worrying about your 'dirty house,' even though it looks pretty clean to me. It may be selfish on my part to arrange this so I can have you with me without feeling guilty that I am keeping you from doing things you need to do."

This was a man who definitely could be the 'one,' she thought to herself. Carmine put her arms around him and gave him the biggest hug and kiss she could muster with his staff and Laurence looking on. "You are incredible and I don't know what to do about you. You have been so wonderfully kind and thoughtful," Carmine said with tears in her eyes. "Thank you."

Jake had looked into her eyes, leaned in and kissed her until he remembered they weren't alone.

"Okay," Jake smiled as he pulled back from the gentle kiss. He turned to the man and woman. "Carmine, this is Rinaldo and Angela and they have been with my Aunt and me for thirty-five years. They are very trustworthy. If you have anything special they need to do, let them know. Otherwise, we are heading for Santa Monica beach for a long walk, some sightseeing and an early dinner."

Carmine and Jake had walked on the beach for hours, talking about their past, what they wanted from life, the mistakes they both had made, their spiritual beliefs—which were almost identical—Cassie, types of entertainment they both enjoyed and how they would change the world if they were running it. There was never a break in the conversation, because they had so much to say to each other and one topic would bring them to another. There were some good-natured heated arguments about subjects they disagreed upon like deep-dish pizza versus New York style, or important issues such as who should be the next U.S. President, but they always ended up laughing. It was easy to talk to each other, no matter how difficult the subject matter.

They had an early dinner at one of the hotels on Santa Monica beach. Their corner table looked out on the ocean.

There was no one else in the dining area. After so much conversation and debating earlier, they both sat quietly, Jake holding her hand across the table, watching a spectacular sunset. As the sun sank to the horizon, Carmine saw the green flash that sometimes occurs at that second when the sun falls just below the ocean's horizon.

"Jake, I just saw a green flash. Did you see it? I can't believe that I actually saw it! It's supposed to be good luck. Darn, I'm sorry that you missed it," Carmine exclaimed in a disappointed tone. "But I'll share my good luck with you," she promised.

"I don't need more luck! I'm already lucky because I am sitting here with you," he had said as he took her hand, bringing it to his mouth, and kissed her fingers gently. "It may be too soon to say this. I fell in love with you the first time I saw you. Standing at the front of the class, my breath caught when I looked at you sitting in front of me. I never thought love at first sight was possible. But now . . . I know it is. I can't stop thinking about you. I want to make your life better by being in it. I know I hardly know you, but at the same time I feel like I've known you forever. It is as if we've been together for several lifetimes already." Carmine said nothing, gazing at him with an incredulous, almost silly look on her face. Jake shifted uncomfortably and added, "I know I should have waited—given you time. But I wanted you to know how I feel."

Carmine tried to hold back tears. Jake reached out to Carmine and then pulled his hand back, "Carmine, did I overwhelm you? Say too much? Carmine, where are you?" She started stammering. "Ja, Ja, Jake, I don't know what to say. I feel that I've known you forever, too. I know that my feelings go very deep, but when the word love comes up, I shut down. I'm so terrified to explore what I feel because the few times I thought I was in love, I've been hurt. I've built up a wall around me so I can't be hurt again."

"Carmine, look at me," Jake coaxed.

"Do you think I would do anything to hurt you? There have only been two other women in my life that I have mentioned love to, but the feelings that I have for you are deeper and different. Give me an opportunity to help you feel safe enough to let down those walls."

Carmine saw the love and compassion for her in his eyes. She answered, "My heart is so full right now with your love. You are the first person that I have ever felt this way about. I feel terrified that if I commit to you, something will go wrong and we will lose each other.

"I don't have anything special to offer you," Carmine went on. "I'm an ordinary person with a very average, boring and, yes, kind of narrow life. And I have so many flaws. You haven't been around long enough to see them. And some of them could be 'fatal.' That's what Cassie calls them. Deal breakers! Once you see them, you'll want out."

Jake leaned forward. "Maybe you think that, but I see lots of special things about you. You are lovely and bright and have such a beautiful soul. You care about people, you raised a loving and compassionate daughter, you want to devote your life to helping others and you are fun and entertaining to be with. Forget about the flaws. Do you think that I am perfect? Let me tell you, my Aunt and my past girlfriends all agree, I have many flaws. You haven't seen them because you truly bring out the best in me. But none of us are perfect, Carmine.

"There is something about you and me together that transcends day-to-day drudgery and takes our relationship to another level. You can call it Karma, chemistry, or whatever, but I think you feel it too, Carmine. I am not asking you to commit to anything. I want you to know how I feel, and that I am committed to you."

Before she could comment, Laurence had entreated Carmine, "Respond out of love, instead of fear, Carmine."

Thank you, Laurence, I needed to hear that she replied to him in her head, speaking from her heart.

"Jake, you are the first man that I feel I could be with for the rest of my life. You are an incredible human being, whatever your flaws are. Why I'm hesitating is so rooted in me and my psyche. Just give me some time to assimilate everything. I'm a person who doesn't react well to change and it takes me more time to adjust."

She then took his hands in hers, looked straight into his eyes and with trembling words, said, "I care for you so much I'm scared. It's frightening to me."

He caressed her hands with his lips and smiled. "There's nothing to be scared of, but I understand. Knowing that you care gives me relief and hope. I promise I will not bring this up again until you feel comfortable about it and then we can discuss it further. Now let's have dinner and some fun," and he called the waiter over to order.

Two and a half amazing weeks! Shaking herself to bring herself back into the present, Carmine felt exhaustion in every muscle. *So much has happened in the last few weeks, I'm almost catatonic. Studying for finals, working more hours than planned and seeing Jake every evening makes for a very intense, busy life!*

Carmine had briefly spoken to Cassie a couple of times and Cassie seemed more interested in Jake than in anything else Carmine had to say, which made her laugh. She knew this was Cassie's way of ensuring Jake was still in her life. She had made time to have lunch with Leslie, who was back to being Leslie, relieved because Bart had moved to New York to act in some off-Broadway play. He had found a new girlfriend, whom Leslie ruefully pitied. Carmine still had finals and had not even thought about the Holidays. *Thank goodness for those six weeks off before the next quarter.*

Yawning, she stretched herself out on her couch with her head on one of the rose and gold throw pillows. "I hope Jake brings something over for dinner or we could order from La Penne. I am too numb to do anything except eat," she mused.

As though hearing her wish, Jake arrived with some soup and salad—a perfect light meal. As he kissed her on the cheek, he looked at her, noticing how tired she looked, "Honey, I can leave the food and get out of your way so you can study and then go to bed early."

"No Jake. Please stay. You can keep me focused on my homework. If you leave, I might fall asleep before I finish everything. You can help me stay awake."

"Okay. It's a deal!" he kissed her on the forehead and then helped serve up the soup and salad.

Jake sat on the couch with his computer on the coffee table and Carmine sat at the dining room table with her homework, both of them working while eating the simple dinner.

Suddenly, Carmine heard Jake gasp. She looked up and saw Jake holding his cell phone, his face pale.

"Jake, what's wrong?"

"Remember, Giovanna, my ex-girlfriend, the one I mentioned when we first met. She just sent me a text saying she may have breast cancer. She doesn't have any family here and wanted someone to be with her for some tests next week. I don't know what to say. I don't want to do anything that will hurt our relationship and at the same time, I don't think she should be alone."

"Of course, you need to be there. You are going to be there as a friend, right? Unless, of course, you still have feelings for her and then, yes, that would cause some huge problems," Carmine said with emphasis on the huge and looking directly at him.

"It would be a friend helping a friend. Nothing more."

"Jake, please, give her whatever help she needs. That's what friends are for, right?"

"You are such a beautiful and understanding soul. If it is okay with you, I am going to call her rather than text. Actually, I don't understand why she didn't just call me and ask," Jake said shaking his head.

"Maybe she wasn't sure of your reaction and thought that this might be safer. If you said no, then it wouldn't hurt as much."

"That is very insightful, Carmine. I think you're right."

Carmine looked at Jake, and with a little frown on her face, asked, "Do I have to worry about you getting involved with her or . . .?" Laurence stood close to Carmine as though to give her support, watching the conversation unfold, but holding his tongue.

"Carmine, no! Remember when I told you how we broke up? We both agreed it wouldn't work. It was on and off for two years. I felt I was on a merry-go-round when we were dating. It was impossibly hard to stay in the relationship. Please don't worry. If it bothers you, I won't do it. You mean too much to me."

"You know how much I worry and I so enjoy being with you." Carmine blew him a kiss as she finished speaking.

"Would you mind if I call her now? It shouldn't take that long and I want to get the details."

"No, of course not."

Jake nodded and went into the kitchen and shut one of the designer doors that separated the kitchen from the dining room.

As soon as Jake went into the kitchen, Carmine bombarded Laurence with questions. "Is this going to be okay? Is Giovanna trying to get Jake back? Does he want to go back? You know, I care for Jake and . . . ."

"Carmine, please! You know I can't answer these questions. Everyone has free will. You must have faith that everything will work out. Try to go with the flow, Carmine and release the need to control things. The Universe knows what it is doing. Everyone has his or her own contract to work out, Carmine."

"I don't want to be hurt and I don't want to have to worry that Jake might still have feelings for her. I want..."

"You want reassurance that it will work out exactly how you picture it in your head. No one can give you that, not even an angel. What's that saying you humans have, 'Nothing in life is guaranteed with the exception of death and taxes!' It is very odd that one is spiritual and the other something that man imposes on one another."

"Pleeeasse, don't try to change the subject. I'm not interested in speaking on a philosophical subject right now. I want to know that it will all work out the *right* way."

"Carmine, I assure you, the Universe always works out for the highest good of all concerned."

As Carmine shot Laurence a look of impatience, Jake walked back into the living room. "Are you okay? I thought I heard you talking with someone."

"I'm fine. I was going over my notes and trying to make sense out of them." Carmine cringed, because she hated lying. "So, what happened?"

"Next Tuesday she is having another biopsy that will be different than another one she had. Her other tests have not been consistent; some have shown positive, others negative and that is why the doctor feels there is a chance that it might be cancer. She is extremely fearful and wants someone with her."

"I understand. Well, I guess I'm trying to understand. But doesn't she have a girlfriend or someone close other than an ex-boyfriend to help her through this process? How about someone from the other relationships she has had?"

"Carmine, as I said, if you are uncomfortable, I won't do it."

"I think she was crazy to give you up! Maybe she has changed her mind and is using this as an excuse. I know that sounds kinda of bitchy of me, but it's what I am thinking. And yes, I am thinking that it might impact our relationship. I feel so much for you and when you said how beautiful and how bright she was, I feel insecure. But I'd hate for anyone to have to go through something like that alone."

"Please, don't. Trust me! She is not interested in me anymore from a romantic standpoint." Jake gently put his arms around Carmine and kissed the top of head. Carmine relaxed into the hug and sighed.

"Thanks so much, Jake, for your reassurance. I feel so much better!"

"Are you sure? You don't seem so to me," Jake said, while Laurence looked at her knowingly.

"Jake," Carmine said while giving her 'look' to Laurence to stop, "would you mind if we shut everything down so I can go to bed? I am probably oversensitive because I'm so tired."

"I understand, Carmine, as long as this doesn't have anything to do with the Giovanna situation. I know you were tired when I got here. I don't want you to go to bed and worry."

"Of course not. A good night's sleep is what I need."

Jake quickly gathered his belongings, gave Carmine a quick kiss and was out the door with his usual "God Bless."

Carmine, almost as quickly, got herself to bed, skipping her usual nightly ritual, even with Laurence reminding her to meditate.

Chapter Twelve

"Giovanna should be home and Jake long gone," Carmine said anxiously to herself as she looked at the clock and noted that it was 7:30 p.m. "I'm sure it will be fine," Carmine said in a positive tone as she looked at herself in the hallway mirror, a very wide, fake smile on her face. "Jake will call and let me know how it went. Hopefully, this episode will be over. Right, Laurence?"

"That is up to Jake, Carmine. He has free will."

Ignoring him, Carmine paced the house, tried to do homework; threw laundry in the washer, started dusting the house. She went from one chore to another without focus.

"Laurence, what is going on?" she cried. "Where is he and why hasn't he called? Come on, Laurence, I need you to help and you are not doing or saying anything. Make him call me!"

Carmine's cell phone immediately started ringing and as she picked it up, the display read Jake. "Thank you!" Carmine whispered to Laurence. With that, and a big fake smile, Carmine answered the phone.

"Hello, Jake. How did it go? I was worried as I haven't heard from you and, of course, anticipating the worst. I am trying to be honest with you. This situation has me reeling emotionally."

"Really sorry Carmine, but everything took longer than we thought. And then she needed to rest and after that, I took her out to dinner so she would have something in her stomach, as she wasn't able to eat before.

"But the good news is that the initial tests indicate that it is benign and the doctors feel that it won't change with the full biopsy results."

"Jake, what a relief for both of you. I'm happy for her, truly. What time are you going home?" she asked in a voice she hoped sounded concerned and sweet.

"She asked that I stay the night just for support; I couldn't say no. She was so shaky after the procedure. She is already in bed. Don't worry, Carmine, we are not sharing the same bed. I want to assure you of that."

There was a long silence before Carmine responded. "Thanks, Jake, for that reassurance. I'm not happy about you spending the night. I feel kinda mean about it, but I guess I can't help it."

"I'm so sorry Carmine. I don't know what to say. I'm trying to help and you are reading too much into this. Please, Carmine, I don't want to start an argument about this."

"Okay, Jake, I apologize. I guess I am scared you will go back to her and that will hurt a lot."

"No apologies necessary. You are making this into something big and it isn't. Truly, sweetie. I need to get some rest, so let me go. God Bless." Jake hung up.

Carmine slowly put her phone back in her purse. Looking at Laurence, she asked, "Do I have to worry? Somehow, this doesn't sound right to me. Why would she have him spend the night? She wants him back, I just know it!" Carmine put her chin down on her chest and sniffed several times. "Laurence, what am I going to do?"

"Carmine, wait! Don't jump to conclusions. You may be projecting something based on the hurts of your past. Don't make up a story that hasn't happened yet. I know it is very human behavior and you are scared. But don't misinterpret the reality of this situation."

"I am very realistic and everything sounds a little too contrived." Carmine heaved a sigh and seemed to study something in the distance. "I might as well get ready for bed. I can't concentrate." She threw all her homework into a pile and closed down the computer. She performed her nightly rituals and tried to meditate in her meditation chair, but gave up after fifteen minutes, unable to still her mind.

"Carmine," Laurence said authoritatively, "You need to do meditation the most, when you are so agitated and upset. Get back in the chair. Try again! Once you connect with your inner self, your mind will be still and you will be able to rise above the upset and find the peace and calm you want and need."

"Okay Laurence, I will try." Partly closing her eyes, she raised them to focus just above her nose and in between her eyebrows. Carmine found that she was actually meditating. When she opened her eyes it was ten o'clock. She sleepily got into bed whispering softy, "Thank you, Laurence, it's so nice to have you guide me" as she drifted off to sleep.

"My pleasure, Carmine. Sweet dreams!" Laurence whispered.

Next day was a workday and Carmine was so busy with her technology client that she did not realize that she had not heard from Jake until it was after 3:00 p.m. But with that realization, she couldn't keep her mind on anything. She sent an e-mail to the CEO and said she had an emergency and would have to leave. Fortunately, she had finished the critical work and what was left was not urgent. She could finish it next time.

She got into her car, noting that Laurence was with her, but did not say a word to him. She tried to drive in her usual cautious way, but she was trying so hard not to cry, she knew she was being careless. "Laurence, please just take care of me."

"Of course, dear one," Laurence said with sympathy.

Finally, reaching her condo parking space with a sigh of relief, she hurriedly parked, ran inside and hurled herself onto the couch, unable to hold the tears in any longer.

"Carmine, what has you so upset?" Laurence was hovering near Carmine with a concerned but puzzled look on his face.

"Jake hasn't called and I know something is going on. He didn't say it overtly, but he seemed to be wildly in love with her and then he broke it off. What if she has changed and wants him back and then he goes back with her? It will be so painful for me and I feel I will never find anyone like him again."

"Is that the issue?"

"Of course that is the issue! Why are you asking?"

"Many times the issue is how you respond to it, not the actual issue itself, not what is upsetting you."

Carmine stopped crying and felt anger replacing the tears. "Oh, the fact that Jake hasn't called, is with his former girlfriend whom he almost married, and who he admitted still wanted to marry him, if that is not upsetting me, then what is, Laurence?"

"Carmine, you feel rejected and it makes you feel you are unimportant to him and not worthy; isn't that the true issue? You are responding to your thoughts. Aren't you projecting something in the future that has no basis for the projection—that he will leave you and go back to Giovanna? And then, based on that thing that may not happen, you are deciding to feel badly about yourself, aren't you?"

Carmine laid her head back on the couch. After a long silence, "Laurence, you're right! I went right into the future with all those negative thoughts. I was responding to what I felt was the reason he did not call, not the fact that he did not call."

"Excellent, Carmine. It is something for you to think about. You humans are very seldom in the present—you are either in the past or in the future. Mindfulness or being in the present can eliminate so much stress and unhappiness. Stay focused on what is present in that moment!"

"It still bothers me that he hasn't called," Carmine admitted. "But maybe I am less upset. I am not going to let an unrealistic perception upset me. Well, I guess not too much."

As she was speaking, her cell phone rang and it was Jake. Taking a big breath, she answered the phone with what she hoped was a neutral voice.

"Hello Jake. What's going on? You haven't called and I am imagining …"

"Carmine, I apologize for not calling sooner. I need to see you to explain. Do you have time now?"

There was so much hesitation before Carmine replied, that Jake asked, "Carmine are you still there?"

"Yes, I'm here, Jake. All kinds of scenarios are going through my mind on why you need to see me. But, yes, I have time."

"Give me ten minutes." Jake hung up without his usual "God Bless."

"Laurence," Carmine whispered, "tell me what has happened. What is he going to tell me? This can't be good news! He is going to go back to Giovanna because she is not only beautiful, but brilliant and wealthy. Right?"

Laurence looked at Carmine with such compassion and love, she started crying.

"Carmine, you don't know what he is going to say and you are projecting a negative outcome. Could the real issue be that you don't feel you deserve to be in a loving and beautiful relationship and this situation is triggering that fear?"

"That could be it," she said slowly. "I feel so good being with him and it feels so right. I guess I have told myself that it won't last because I feel I am lacking so much that he would find fault with me, get bored with me, you know, all those insecurities I have."

"Let's see what he says before you make any more projections!"

At that moment, there was a knock on the door and when Carmine opened it, there stood Jake. "Someone was coming in and I went through the gate at the same time."

He took Carmine in his arms and gave her a big hug. Jake noticed that she let her arms hang down to her sides.

"I should have called, but things came up and I needed to understand them so I could explain what is happening to you very clearly and honestly."

Carmine motioned for him to sit down on the couch.

"Do you want something to drink?" Carmine finally asked.

"No, not now!"

Jake took Carmine by the arm and made her sit down beside him.

Clearing his throat several times, Jake spoke in a low, hoarse quivering voice, "Let me tell you everything that has happened and what I need to ask of you. You were right Carmine! Giovanna was using this as an excuse to start up the relationship again. Not that she didn't have to go through the procedure or that she wasn't frightened, but she said she had made a huge mistake when she was with me, by being involved with other men at the same time. She said she is ready to change her views of marriage and be monogamous because she loves me so much and knows how good we were together. I mentioned to her that I had heard this before, several times when we were in our relationship. Whenever I broke it off, she had made the same promises."

Carmine bit her lips and clenched her mouth shut as Jake spoke. She didn't say anything to him and nodded her head as a way of asking him to continue.

Speaking rapidly and intently while looking directly into her eyes, "There has always been a seductive quality about Giovanna and I do react to her whenever I see her. Nothing sexual took place, but I did talk to her about the possibility of starting up the relationship again. I owe you that honesty. I love you, and I couldn't understand why I was even entertaining the possibility of taking her back."

The tears started silently rolling down her face as Carmine swallowed and braced herself. "I can't believe this is happening..."

"Let me continue, please. I needed some time to think. So I took the day to weigh what I wanted in life. I decided a life with Giovanna was wrong. It didn't work multiple times before, why should it now? So I told her no, that it was in the past and I couldn't do it.

"What I need now is time and an experienced therapist to understand why I even considered it when I have these deep feelings for you. It is very confusing. I am asking for your understanding and patience to give me that time so that we can go forward as we planned in the future. And I don't know how long that will take. It should only take a few sessions and a few days, but I'm not sure and I want to be honest with you."

Carmine looked at him and shook her head.

"Does that mean No?" Jake asked.

"No! That means I don't understand. So what you are asking me is to wait around until you have the reason why you chose to explore the relationship possibilities with Giovanna and then we can go forward?"

"I guess you could say that. Yeah! Sounds really bad, when put it in that context," Jake admitted sadly.

"You know, Jake, I understand where you are coming from and I hear what you want! Of course, you should do whatever is necessary for your wellbeing. I do support you in that. But I think we should not see each other while you are going through this exploration, as you call it, and then see what happens. I can't promise anything at this point. Right now to say I am upset is an understatement. I don't want to get angry with you, even though I am, but I am trying to control it. I need to think about it and decide what is best for me and for my future."

Laurence put his hands together in prayer gesture, bowing to Carmine, acknowledging that she was right.

In a soft, but firm voice, Carmine continued, "From what you are saying, you have no idea how long this is going to take. And I am not sure I want to be around when you 'finally have understood your behavior.' Jake, you say you love me and then your ex-girlfriend calls you and makes you an offer. You are so dazzled by the offer that you are almost sucked into it and you say you are confused. I am sorry. I just can't understand, nor do I think I want to—at least not for now. It is going to take some understanding on my part too. Maybe I should also see a therapist," Carmine added, almost to herself.

"Carmine, I am so sorry that you feel that way and it breaks my heart so to put you through this. But I have to understand why this happened. Honestly, I am doing it so we can have the relationship I know is ours and we deserve.

You don't deserve a man who is confused. I don't want to hurt you! That is my greatest fear and I know I am doing it!"

"Do what you must, Jake. But don't have any expectations about me," Carmine said spiritedly, with a toss of her head.

"I won't," Jake said with dejection. "I want you to know, Carmine, that we will keep the student/instructor relationship that we have had in the class on the same level. There will be no change in that."

"No worries, Jake. There certainly won't be any change in my behavior. It is probably best that you leave now." And Carmine opened the front door and waved her hand for him to leave. Jake tried to give her a kiss on the cheek, but Carmine turned her head to avoid it.

"I understand how challenging this is for you, Carmine, and thank you for being as understanding as you have been. I am so grateful. I know you could have made this so much harder for me. I truly love you Carmine, I want you to know that," Jake said, with quiet resoluteness. And with head down, shoulders slumped and tear-filled eyes, he left.

As soon as the door was closed, Carmine started weeping, shaking her head, "I can't believe this. I knew it was too good to be true. Why did I allow this to happen? What am I doing wrong?"

Laurence tried to interrupt Carmine, but she continued venting.

"Carmine, you did nothing wrong and you did not allow it to happen. Everyone has free will and Jake is taking responsibility for his emotional reaction to this. That is very courageous and very healing. He is not blaming anyone but himself for his feelings and his behavior. He has emphasized that he is fully responsible."

"It hurts so much. I am so sad and depressed as well as angry."

"Take a moment to explore those feelings. You are sad and depressed because . . ."

Carmine said, thinking deeply, "I guess because he felt some reason to contemplate the relationship which makes me feel unworthy and not good enough for him. I want to feel that no matter what comes his way, he truly loves me and wouldn't even consider another alternative."

"So you are blaming yourself as well as Jake."

"Yes, I guess."

"Carmine, could you put this into another context? Perhaps see it from another perspective so you don't feel like a victim and have the opportunity see it as a learning experience to help you heal that part of you that wants to blame and doesn't think very highly of herself."

"I'm not sure what you mean, Laurence."

"Can you reframe this situation in such a way that it supports you so you can see this challenge as a blessing in disguise?"

"I am devastated. I can't think. All I want to do is cry. How am I going to get over this?"

"Maybe you won't get over it, Carmine, but instead see it and yourself in another perspective."

"This is supposed to make me feel better?"

"You can look at it in the way you are currently seeing it—devastating—or as an opportunity for growth and learning, for knowing yourself as a worthy, loving and a giving human being. You had a relationship with Jake and you still might have one, I might add. Jake fulfilled all your dreams and wishes you had about a man. You were able to open your heart in a way that it has not been open in the past, you enjoyed each other's company and you were able to grow. More importantly, you were able to be your authentic self and he loved you for exactly who you are, which gave you confidence in yourself. Remember, he said he loved you, not Giovanna, and he turned her down. So the blessing here is that you gained confidence in who you are. It made you understand, on a soul level, what a worthy and significant human being you are.

"You can do one of two things, Carmine. You can go forward, knowing that who you are is beautiful and worthy and forgive Jake for his issues. You can simply have no attachment to the outcome. You can also congratulate yourself on handling the situation with grace. You can go forward in your life trusting and accepting yourself as you are, because Jake validated all that was good in you. Or, you can look at yourself as a victim and blame him for how you feel. It is up to you. But this has been a beautiful, enlightening experience for you and you will recognize it once you are able to see it in the true light."

Carmine had become very calm while he was talking and quietly said, "Okay, Laurence, I hear you. Let me think about it. I know I don't sound like it, but I am grateful for your support."

She then went into the bedroom to get ready for bed. As depressed and sad as Carmine was, she did try to meditate. After ten minutes, she couldn't stay awake and pulled herself into bed where she eventually fell asleep, still trying to comprehend what Laurence had tried to tell her.

Upon arising the next morning, she was able to grasp what Laurence had said more fully. Carmine understood on a deeper level, that he was right. She was still sad, depressed and even angry, but she felt very confident about herself and congratulated herself on how she behaved.

The next week was hard with school and work, but when she saw Jake, he seemed to have lost some of his vitality and looked sad and down. She was able to see him as someone who was facing his own challenge.

Carmine heard Laurence say to her, "You've got it! I acknowledge and congratulate you for your ability to see his struggle even though you are in pain!" Since he was the instructor, there was no way she could ignore Jake so she tried very hard to keep her face neutral and he tried as hard to avoid looking at her.

When Cassie called and wanted to know if she and Jake were coming to help her pack, Carmine simply told her that the relationship was on hold and that Jake was out of her life, at least for now. Cassie started asking questions, but Carmine quickly drew the line. She wouldn't be discussing Jake until she had processed what she needed to process about the relationship.

"Carmine, look, it's okay. You don't have to come. Dad's hiring the mover and he said he would hire someone to help me pack. So I truly understand and I think it would be better if you take care of yourself. We'll be together for Thanksgiving and then we can talk."

"Cassie, my love, thank you for your understanding and your generosity. With all my heart, I am so grateful for a daughter with such a beautiful heart."

"Mom, I am so sorry about Jake, because I hear how sad you are. But I know it will all work out well in the end. I love you, Carmine." And with that, Cassie hung up.

"The last week of school," Carmine told herself on Sunday. "I can't wait and I can catch up with everything." She had not heard from Jake, but she had made peace in her heart that no matter what happened, it would be okay. It would hurt, really hurt, but still be okay.

Laurence had helped tremendously in supporting her. He also helped her to acknowledge that she had grown through the heartbreaking challenge, and had been able to separate herself from the victim mentality.

Her cell phone rang, and it was Jake. Hesitating for a moment, she took a big breath and answered the phone.

"Hi Jake, how are you?"

"Quite miserable without you, Carmine, but that is my issue, not yours. Would it be possible to see you tonight? I would like to talk to you."

Laurence looked at her, waiting to hear her reply with a knowing look on his face.

There was a long silence before Carmine said, "Sure, Jake, that would be okay. What time?"

"What about in ten minutes? I'm very close by."

"I'll be here."

Carmine looked at Laurence after hanging up the phone and impatiently asked. "Okay, Laurence, what's going on?"

"This is a very important discussion for you and how you handle it will impact your life going forward. Be sure you listen with your heart and see both yourself and Jake as loving essences having the inner resources to resolve this issue between you."

"You mean we will get back together?"

"Not necessarily, Carmine, it all depends on you, your perspective and your projections. We have discussed them on several occasions, and I hope you remember your strengths. But whatever happens, know that it will be the highest good for all concerned."

Carmine shook her head and gave a long sigh. Then she realized that Jake was going to be there in about five minutes and she was in her most grungy sweats, with no makeup and a scrambled head of hair which she had run her hand through numerous times. She thought about changing and throwing some makeup on. *Screw it. I don't really care at this point.*

Laurence gave her a "thumbs up." He had been rapidly incorporating what he learned on Earth in his expressions and behavior. He was more and more often dressing in various outfits he observed to be appropriate for different occasions. He said it made him feel more integrated in Carmine's life. "Plus it's fun. Playing with things in the physical form is something we Angels often don't get to experience," Laurence had told her. His behavior reminded Carmine of what the Director said before she returned to Earth, that Laurence might exhibit very human traits because of his visibility to her and the change of vibrations and energy. *That sure was happening*! Before she could look at herself in the hallway mirror to see how truly bad she appeared, the buzzer rang and she pressed the gate button to let Jake in. As she opened the door, Jake appeared, holding a huge, beautiful bouquet of white and lavender roses interspersed with hydrangeas set off by miniature silver sparkle hearts and angels.

Carmine couldn't help herself and cried out with delight, "Jake, that is so beautiful."

"I'm glad you like it, Carmine. I wanted to bring something and this reminded me of you and your loving essence and giving heart." He handed her the bouquet.

Carmine regained her composure and very formally said, "Do come in, Jake. What can I do for you?"

As they made their way into the living room, Carmine placed the flowers on the dining room table. Motioning to Jake to sit on the couch, she elected to stand, knowing from her many Human Resource workshops that whoever stands in a situation, or is taller, has the control. And control is what she wanted, God knows. *And God knows what he is going to say*, she thought. Carmine just wanted to be able to handle her feelings as well as possible while Jake was there. Standing gave her confidence.

Jake nervously cleared his throat. "First of all, Carmine, thank you for seeing me. I know I have disappointed and hurt you, and I appreciate your kindness in seeing me on short notice. I'm going to go right to the point, Carmine. This last week has been the longest in my life because of you and the way I hurt you. I have been going to a therapist every day to find out why I behaved as I did. I truly love you, so it was incredibly confusing. It was very evident after the first two sessions all this had nothing to do with my feelings about her or about you. It was gratification to my ego that someone like Giovanna wanted me—someone who is beautiful, intelligent and successful—and who, by the way, after the therapy sessions, I discovered I have no respect for at all.

"So after working with the therapist, I found that this behavior had something to do with my parents' relationship. I found out, listening to them argue one day when I was very young, my father had an affair with a beautiful, brilliant woman, apparently for no reason other than that he could—an ego thing. He truly loved my mother. So in a way, I was following in his footsteps, unconsciously, doing the same thing, trying to emulate him. But I was smart enough to be true to myself and had the strength to say no. I knew I loved you. I had to find the reason for that trigger that had me actually considering another relationship with her. I know now!

"I am here to ask your forgiveness and to ask you if we can continue our relationship. I know that it will be better and stronger because I know that this will not happen again, as I am now aware of the issue and it won't be triggered again. I know I hurt you and I so regret it. But will you consider it, Carmine? Give me a second chance. I love you so and will be heartbroken forever without you. I am committed to you and Cassie," Jake finished with tears in his eyes.

Carmine looked at Jake, trying not to cry. Laurence stood right next to her and said, "Carmine, don't let YOUR ego get in the way. This is about your life, your life together and both of your spiritual contracts. Make the decision from your heart! Without your ego or your mind! And think what the highest good is for both of you."

Carmine stood saying nothing for several minutes and looking at Jake. She went to sit on the couch with him and took his hands in hers, saying tearfully, "Jake I care so much for you. Yes, this truly hurt me. I hear that what you are saying is from your heart, which is never wrong. So, yes, Jake I want to continue our relationship and see what happens as we go forward. And I thank you for your honesty about your feelings in this situation, since it all began. I am so grateful and appreciative for that."

Out of the corner of her eye, she saw Laurence nodding his head and holding his hands in a prayer gesture.

"Carmine, I will be sure you will never regret this," Jake said softly as he enfolded her in his arms. "I know we are meant for each other and I will always be there for you and for Cassie in every way I can. Thank you for being so forgiving and compassionate."

Carmine laughed lightly and said, "It is for the highest good for both of us!" Jake looked a little puzzled about that statement, but nodded his head in agreement.

Still holding Jake's hands, she said, "Jake, this has been a very emotional night for me. I would love to continue, but I need some time to digest this and meditate on it. Would you understand if I asked you to leave now?"

"Carmine, you're not going to change your mind, are you?" he asked in a desperate voice.

"No, Jake, no for sure! But I need time to think everything through that has happened, to understand my reactions, too. And I am so tired. I think it is from all the feelings I have gone through this week. I would like to talk to you more about how I feel, but not tonight. Does that make sense?"

"Absolutely!"

Giving her a gentle and loving kiss, "I'll call you tomorrow! Wait! You have your final tomorrow in my class. I'll see you in the morning and call after that. We can continue the conversation whenever you are ready." Saying a quick "God Bless," he let himself out.

Laurence's face was wreathed in a wide smile. "Carmine, you were such a beautiful and loving soul tonight with the forgiveness and compassion you showed Jake. You truly have learned much these weeks we have been together and I congratulate you on your ability to put these learnings into effect. And I also congratulate you on following you heart rather than trying to get even or saying negative words to Jake."

"Thank you, Laurence. But it was your help that gave me the strength to get through this and you helped me learn so much. Truly, you are the world's best Angel! Oh excuse me, you are Heaven's best Angel."

Dressed as she was, without any of her night routines, including meditation, Carmine went straight to bed and to sleep.

Carmine woke at four-thirty the next morning, feeling happy and joyful for the first time, she thought, since forever, at least it seemed that way, she told herself. She knew she had made the right decision about Jake. After all, she told herself, he rejected Giovanna and had the honesty to tell her that he had considered it and then found out why. She couldn't think of another man she had dated or whom she knew to be that ethical and willing to take the full responsibility. And she admitted to herself, she truly did love Jake. After reliving the previous night's conversation, she looked at herself in the mirror and realized she was a mess. No condition in which to commence the rest of her life.

This is going to take some time. Carmine hastily went through her morning routine. By seven o'clock, she was finished, including cleaning herself up and looking, at least in her estimation, presentable. She used minimal makeup and dressed simply in a long sleeve red sweater, blue jeans and boots. "I need the energy of red," she told herself. She reviewed her class notes for the final that was scheduled for eight o'clock. Because it was finals, she just took a large red purse and stuffed in everything she thought she would need for the day. She was planning to come right home after the exam, relax and catch up with her sleep.

"And of course see Jake," Laurence told her with a loving smile. He was dressed today in a wizard's hat and long gown. Noticing her inquiring look, he said, "It's to help you with your final."

Shaking her head, but saying nothing, Carmine ran out the door and jumped into the car, heading out of the garage with Laurence in tow. She was used to traffic being light, so she was at school and in her seat for her final before eight. Leslie gave her a nod when she saw Carmine, but they were so stressed about the final, neither said very much to each other, except to wish good luck. Carmine told Leslie she was leaving right after she was finished, and would be in touch with her later in the week.

Jake arrived promptly at eight and handed out the tests. He told the class what he expected, informed them that everything had been covered in class, and that the exam should not take much more than two hours. He avoided looking at Carmine as much as he could throughout the class time.

Two hours and ten minutes later, Carmine, with Laurence, now in a graduation gown, because, he said, he was sure she had passed, made her way home. She parked the car, ran into her condo, peeled off all her clothes, went to bed and fell asleep. There she remained until her cell phone rang four hours later. It was Jake.

"Carmine, sweetheart. I want to see how you are doing and want to be sure you are comfortable with the decision you made last night. I hardly slept because I was so concerned that you might change your mind. When I can see you? The sooner, the better! If I can come over early this evening, that would be wonderful. And I would bring dinner." Jake stopped talking as he realized Carmine had not said a word, other than "Hello." "Carmine, are you still there?"

"Yes!" she finally piped up. "A little slow today! Too many things happening. You, finals, the last weeks. Kinda' overwhelming! But, yes, I would like to see you. Bringing dinner would be perfect. But it would have to be a short evening because I'm still exhausted. Hope that's alright with you?"

"I understand. I can't stay too long either because I have all my finals to correct and then I have to get the grades into the office as quickly as possible. So how about I come over about five and promise to leave no later than seven?"

Promptly at five o'clock, Jake was at the door with a box from La Penne. Carmine gave him a quick hug at the door. Then she took the box into the kitchen where she took out the contents—a roasted chicken that was cut into slices, mashed potatoes with chicken gravy and a salad, along with olive bread and a huge chocolate cupcake. She put everything but the cupcake on the plates on the kitchen table she had set earlier.

"Jake, this looks wonderful and I am starved. I realized I haven't eaten a thing all day."

Jake laughed and said, "The way you grabbed that box made me think you were much happier to see dinner than me."

"Sorry!"

"No worries! Please let's eat. Everything is hot and we can talk while eating."

"Carmine," Jake began, "I know last night's discussion was brief and you said you wanted to discuss it more. So whatever you want to ask and say, I am here for you."

"After thinking it over, I feel, if you agree, that it would be best if we put what happened in the past and just go forward to the future. Wherever that takes us. What happened is done and over and we both learned from it. I don't think it is necessary for us—for me—to relive it and discuss it. Everything has been said about it, as far as I am concerned."

She heard Laurence say, "Beautiful, Carmine. Well done!"

"Are you sure?" Jake said. "It's important to me that you feel secure about moving forward together. And I will do whatever it takes to make that happen."

"Jake, truly, I am okay. I am so appreciative for your concern." Carmine blew him a kiss across the table and continued eating.

"Thank you, Carmine. That is certainly a vote of confidence in my favor." And he happily blew her a kiss back. "Then if you feel that way, would you consider meeting my Aunt Sophie? She's my only family, as you know, and I want you to meet her right away as it is important to me. She has heard about you and would like to meet you. I think you both will love each other."

"I would love to meet her. When?"

"How about Wednesday night?"

"That works! I will have my second final over by then. Yea!" Carmine shouted with great enthusiasm, raising her hands wildly over her head, in celebration.

Then she collapsed on the chair. "I think I just used all my energy for that. Now I am ready for bed." Finishing her dinner, she eyed the chocolate cupcake. "Let's split this and then I am going to ask you to leave, Jake," as she took off some of the frosting with her fingers and stuck it in her mouth. "I am so exhausted I can barely eat this," she said with a giggle, "but I think I will manage."

"It's all yours!"

Gently kissing Carmine on her forehead and giving her a big hug, Jake told her, "I'll see you at five-thirty on Wednesday night, and I'll check in with you tomorrow." And then he left.

Carmine barely acknowledged that he was leaving, waved her hand wearily and blew him a kiss.

She turned to Laurence and said, "Thank you for not interrupting. It would have been too much to handle. I am going to bed now. Could I ask that we hold talking about this or sharing lessons till tomorrow? I need a little space."

"Certainly, Carmine, but may I say, I'm proud of you?" Laurence crowed as Carmine finished the cupcake, while she threw everything on the table into the dishwasher. "I'll clean up more in the morning," Carmine told herself.

Running through her nighttime ritual, she was on the meditation chair and within minutes was nodding. Realizing that there was no way she could keep awake for even a few minutes, she made her way to bed, barely able to pull the covers over her before falling asleep.

Chapter Thirteen

After polishing off her final on Wednesday, Carmine happily went home. She decided that she would spend the remainder of the day catching up on all the "weed patches" that had been ignored during the previous weeks.

She took time to rest and considered what she would wear to meet Jake's Aunt Sophie. *Would the Aunt like her? What should she wear that would be appropriate? What if the Aunt didn't like her? What if the Aunt hated her and didn't think she was good enough for Jake? Then Jake would have to choose. What if ….* A glance at Laurence, who was now shaking his head, made her immediately quash those questions.

"Carmine," Laurence cautioned, "you keep on going around in circles on your thinking. Remember what I keep on repeating to you. Focus on the positive and respond from love, not fear," Carmine said the last three words in unison with Laurence.

While contemplating meeting Jake's Aunt, Carmine managed to eat several of the remaining pieces of candy from the Godiva chocolate box. She felt that it was better to keep herself calm and focused with chocolate than with any prescription drug. *It was far less addicting and you never had to worry about admitting yourself into a detox center.*

There were a few times when Jake and she had gone beyond the sweet, good night kiss and a wild passion flared between them with all its sexual longings. Then Carmine would spy Laurence lurking. Bang! Those feelings would cease quicker than a candle snuffed out in the wind.

Jake would immediately sense her withdrawal, and ask if anything was wrong. Carmine would make up a dumb excuse. And even though Jake wouldn't say anything, she could feel that he thought there might be some sexual issues that Carmine wasn't acknowledging. But no matter how much Carmine yelled and screamed at Laurence to disappear when she was involved with Jake physically, he didn't seem to hear what she was saying.

It might be that I have to send Laurence back. I can't be with both Jake and Laurence, without telling Jake about Laurence. But maybe it wouldn't matter, if I marry Jake. Then I could tell him about Laurence. Carmine congratulated herself on her rational thinking.

"Laurence," Carmine said, with a rather petulant whine in her voice, "How about giving me permission to tell Jake about you? That would simplify my life and make it easier. How about it, Laurence?"

"Carmine," Laurence said with compassion, "you know you are not allowed to do that. It's not my authority that you must have, but rather the Council's, plus Mother's and the Director's."

"You could intercede, couldn't you?" she asked in a pleading voice. "It would be so hard to lose you, but it would be harder to lose Jake. And I will, because my behavior becomes so bizarre when you are talking to me and Jake is around. I have asked and asked that you not say or do anything when we are together, but you don't listen. Can't you disappear until I tell you it's okay to show yourself?"

"Carmine, you know I can't do that. And I seldom say anything! Most of the time I'm just there, like I am every day. I try to keep myself out of the way, but it is difficult to perform my duties and still keep you satisfied with my behavior."

"It is becoming harder and harder to keep your existence a secret. If Cassie was around, you wouldn't be a secret."

Cassie! I probably should call her and let her know that Jake is back in my life. Pulling her cell out of her purse, Cassie answered on the first ring. "Hey, Mom, I am on my way out to dinner with friends. I can't talk now."

"It's okay Cassie. I just wanted to let you know that Jake is back in my life and we will see what happens in the future."

"I'm not surprised. I just have this great feeling about your being with each other. But I am so happy for you, Mom. Talk to you later," Cassie said and quickly ended the call.

Turning to Laurence, Carmine said, "That certainly takes care of that. She certainly didn't seem surprised. And you are going to have to behave this evening! I do not want to see or hear you. There will be dire consequences if that happens, Laurence!" Carmine warned.

She told herself several times that it wasn't a big deal to meet Jake's Aunt. Finally unable to convince herself that it wasn't a big deal she finally acknowledged that it WAS a big deal. She wanted to look and feel perfect for the occasion. Contemplating her wardrobe and trying various clothes combinations, Carmine finally decided on black. Black was boring, but safe. And she wanted to feel safe, very safe.

Her final choice was a full-length black knit skirt, a black knit sweater over the skirt secured with a black belt and black boots and a black and silver pendant with Chinese characters on a silver and gold chain to wear around her neck. Looking in her mirror, she felt that maybe it was, perhaps, too boring, too safe and not her. Rummaging through her closet, Carmine found a three-quarter knee-length, deep blue antique silk kimono embroidered with gold and silver Chinese characters that she could wear as a long jacket. Better, she thought to herself. Jake will like it because of his affinity with Asian culture.

"Remember, Carmine," Laurence said, "your commitment to yourself is always the most important as it is what makes you authentic."

Carmine rolled her eyes, but nodded her head in agreement.

Promptly at five-thirty, Jake rang her buzzer and appeared at her front door in a black leather jacket over a gray and black sweater with a black t-shirt showing above the sweater and black slacks. He took one look at her, and as he caressed her arm and the silk jacket, he said, "You look extremely exotic and beautiful! Looks as though black was the color of choice for us tonight."

As he casually kissed her softly on the lips, he took a small box out of his jacket, which was wrapped in red and white paper with a thin red silk ribbon tied around it.

"What's this?" Carmine asked with a puzzle in her voice.

"Just open it, you'll see."

Tearing the paper and ribbon off, she opened the box lid and there was a miniature white china Angel, with gold silken wings and a beautiful angelic face. It almost looked like Laurence.

"It is truly lovely, Jake. With Christmas almost here, it will be perfect on my tree." Examining it further, she found a small button at the bottom of the base and when she pressed it, it played the song, "All I Ask of You," from *Phantom of the Opera*.

"It's just delightful, Jake. Thank you for your thoughtfulness."

"I know you said that this was one of your favorite songs, but it is also a reminder of how I feel about you."

She reached up to give him a quick kiss, but Carmine found that he held her and the quick kiss became very long..... she felt herself melting in his clasp. She closed her eyes and kissed him back. She opened her eyes, found herself staring directly at Laurence, and suddenly became very tense.

She pulled herself away and said breathlessly, "Jake, what are you doing?"

"Carmine," he asked grinning, "you have to ask? I love kissing you and I don't do it enough. Don't you enjoy it?" And then as though answering his own question, he said, "It seems as though you do and then suddenly you back off. I am confused! Can you help me to understand? If I am going too fast for you, just tell me. You know I'll understand."

Carmine became very red and with a bowed head she reached for his hand. "Of course, you're confused. You've every right to be. We need to sit down and talk about this. Trust me, Jake, it's not a simple explanation, but it has nothing to do with you."

As she was speaking, she received a warning glance from Laurence. "Carmine," she heard him say, "You CANNOT inform Jake about me." Trying to ignore Laurence, Carmine said, "Look, we have to leave now in order to arrive on time for dinner. Let's discuss this when we have more time. I promise we will do it soon." She then gave Jake a big hug and a light kiss as she led him out the door.

As she turned from locking the door to the condo, Jake held her and said in a very serious, almost desperate tone, "I'm going to keep you to your promise, Carmine. As soon as we can, we're going to sit down and discuss this. Okay?" Carmine nodded her head yes and quietly said, "Jake, thank you so much for understanding."

"I'm not sure I understand, Carmine, but I care for you so much, that I'm willing to be patient, for the moment, anyway."

They were very quiet as they drove the 134 Freeway to Pasadena, but in spite of the earlier upset, it was a companionable silence. Carmine had closed her eyes and was mentally reviewing what Jake had told her about his Aunt Sophie. She was over eighty. Jake wasn't sure, as she never told him her date of birth and he allowed her that secret because he felt it was important to her. She donated her time and a great deal of money, which she had inherited from her parents, to a multitude of charities. She had raised Jake since his parents had died, and she had never married.

Jake had thought it was because of him, but she had confessed the real reason to him one day. When she was twenty-one, Sophie had fallen in love with a married doctor who had been separated from his wife for five years. His wife had told him that she did not want to be married, but had not wanted a divorce because she liked the convenience of the marriage, and felt that it was best for the children not to have divorced parents. He had agreed to that lifestyle, mainly for the children's sake, until he met Sophie.

They had fallen very much in love and he had decided to ask his wife for a divorce. But when he did, his wife, unexplainably, decided that she wanted him back. Because of the children, he felt that he had to see if it would work. He would give it a year and if it didn't work out, he would divorce. They both had high levels of integrity, so they decided they would not see each other until that year had passed. However, because they had the same friends and frequented the same social gatherings, they saw each other numerous times, which had complicated their lives and their friendship. At the end of the year, the doctor had told his Aunt, sadly and tearfully, although he loved her, and would continue to love her for the rest of his life; because of the children he adored, he would remain with his wife.

Sophie had taken to her bed for a month. Then one day, she had decided that enough was enough. She had money and time and she would do whatever she could to make the world a better place. She had given enormously and many times, anonymously, to foundations and charities. And she had raised Jake, giving him all her love and attention.

Jake said that when Sophie was younger, she had been years ahead of her time and was considered a "dangerous women's libber," when few people even knew what that meant. She was constantly getting into trouble with her parents for her escapades. Jake said that she reminded him of Patrick Dennis's loveable but zany character in his book, *"Auntie Mame."*

Jake had interrupted her thoughts only once when he had turned to her and said almost with a question in his voice, "You know, Carmine, it seems when I am driving with you, there never seems to be any traffic and the freeways are always clear. It is remarkable. I guess that gives me another reason for having you around all the time." And, as he laid his hand on hers, she just shrugged her shoulders with a small, secretive smile, not knowing what to say.

The car slowed and Carmine opened her eyes. She was in long driveway that was covered by trees on both sides, spreading their branches so wide, it gave the driveway a canopy of multi-colored light and dark green. The car stopped in front of a huge gray English Tudor house covered with green vines and miniature white and pink roses.

Jake opened the car door for her and helped her out of the car and up the five gray long marble steps on to the porch of the house. Two giant wood teak doors with swirls of etched glass in each upper half greeted them. He rang the elaborate brass lions' head doorbell to the left of the doors, and there was a great ringing of chimes. "I wanted you to hear these chimes as well as letting Aunt Sophie know that we are here," Jake said. "How beautiful," Carmine remarked. "They remind me of music I have heard lately, but I can't remember when!" Then she saw Laurence, who gave her a meaningful look and recalled it was the night she had died. She smiled at him and then turned her head away so he could not distract her.

The door was opened by a tiny, roly-poly woman of indeterminate age with piercing green eyes, short, light blonde hair, a round, lined face that gave it interest and distinction. She was glowing with a wide smile. She wore a long moss green skirt, with a matching velvet loose blouse that came to her knees. Long, dangling green earrings that ended in cat silhouettes, played around her face.

"Hello, Carmine," she said gaily, "I'm so glad to meet you at last" and she reached up and enfolded Carmine in her small arms and gave her a tight hug! "And do come in" she trilled, as she brought Carmine inside a large hall with a multi-colored-glass dome high in the ceiling. In the center of the hall was an intricate teakwood carved curved staircase that, seemingly, circled up to the dome, but ended on a second floor.

Holding Carmine's arm, she turned to Jake and said with a laugh in her voice, "Aren't you going to introduce me properly, Jake?"

"Of course, Aunt Sophie. Carmine, this is Sophie Steiner, who is my Aunt, my mentor and my friend and I love her dearly." As he spoke, he bent to kiss her softly on her cheek. "Aunt Sophie, this is Carmine Craig, the woman I have been talking to you about for weeks."

"Carmine, my dear, I have not heard Jake talk this way about any one with the exception of Mickey Mouse when he was five." Even though she barely came up to Carmine's shoulder, Aunt Sophie firmly took her arm, and walked her though a long floor-to-ceiling window-lined hallway, talking all the time about details of the house.

"This house is enormous, as it has about 24,000 square feet on eleven acres of land, and was way too large for both of us. So when Jake went into business with his school and his other activities, we just had the house remodeled. Most of it is used for Jake's businesses and his school offices. Then the rest of the house we converted to a living area for us. We each have a suite of rooms, including a bedroom, a sitting room with a small kitchen and small office, and then a central family area with a living room, dining room, great room and library, where are going right now.

"In addition to the multiple offices and living areas for the staff, the balance of the house has a great ballroom and dining room plus a theater and a hotel-like kitchen. But those are only used for formal occasions or when the students from Jake's school visit. It also holds a multi-level gym and small spa, which Jake and the students use.

"Initially the house was built sometime in the late 1800's for my grandparents who wanted it for their children and their eventual spouses and, of course, for all the servants. I remember running through these rooms as a little girl and hiding from my nanny. Or I should say, nannies, because I had so many. They couldn't keep up with me and ended up quitting very quickly," she chuckled as she spoke. "I was certainly a naughty child and my parents could never understand what made me so wild. If I had been a boy, it would have acceptable, but certainly not for a girl, not in that era. Many times, I wish I had been a boy! My parents would have tolerated my behavior better! But I am grateful that times have changed and women can now be their true selves and there is no stigma.

"Here we are in the living room and the central family area," Sophie said, as they entered a very wide and long room, which was covered on two walls with tall wide colorful stained glass and leaded windows from floor to ceiling. Each side of the window held long, green heavy brocade drapes which curled onto a beautiful oak floor covered with a several oriental looking carpets in various designs and colors. The ceiling was a combination of columns and vertical carved woods, also of oak. The room was filled with an eclectic array of furniture, mainly oriental and antique. The predominant color was green, with touches of maroon, mahogany and black. The way the furniture was placed gave it a warm and inviting feeling.

"This is so lovely," Carmine exclaimed as she looked around, taking in the several large multi-colored couches, quilted chaise lounges, the grand piano and a variety of tables and lamps in different heights, sizes and styles. The other two walls were covered with built-in bookshelves, which held hundreds of books. Carmine heard water flowing from somewhere, but couldn't identify from what.

Sophie noticed Carmine's tilting of her head and answered her unspoken question, "Yes, there is a waterfall in the garden, along with a lap and full Olympic size pools and the greenhouse, which Jake should show you after dinner."

Jake, Carmine and Sophie spent an hour sipping a superb Chardonnay and chatting. Sophie asked Carmine one question which led to other topics. The discussion flowed, sometimes heated, with friendly differences of opinions, other times lively and entertaining. Everyone laughed and enjoyed each other's witty jokes. And Laurence kept his promise to Carmine, remaining silent and unseen.

At 7:15, Angela, whom Carmine had met previously, came in and announced that dinner was ready. Taking their wineglasses, she led them to a small dining room, in an alcove where a round teak table sat on a platform surrounded with tall teak ladder chairs. The table, set for three, overlooked a large curved floor-to-ceiling bay window. Squinting to see outside, Carmine saw large trees and what looked like water, but she couldn't be sure.

"I'll take you out to the garden later," Jake promised, as he seated Carmine in her chair.

"Your table looks lovely, just like a garden." Carmine complimented the exquisite floral china that rested on cranberry and gold chargers, with each piece crafted in a different flower pattern. Beside each ornate silver place setting, there were two different shapes of long-stemmed crystal wine goblets in addition to crystal water glasses.

Angela and Rinaldo served dinner and, while they ate, Sophie regaled Jake and Carmine with episodes of her childhood and youth and then shared her stories of well-known people and celebrities whom she knew intimately. Her reminiscences were never malevolent, but hilarious incidents worthy of *People Magazine* coverage, but which could never be publicly acknowledged.

As they finished their dessert—individual amaretto chocolate soufflés topped with a huge mound of whip cream—Sophie began yawning. "My dears, you must excuse an old lady. I can always tell when it is nine-thirty at night because my tongue gets tired. Then I know it's bedtime."

Rising from the table, Sophie stood in front of Carmine and took her hands into hers. "My dear, you are as lovely as Jake said you were. You remind me a little of Jake's mother when she was in her teens." As Carmine tried to rise, she stopped her. "Oh, please don't, this way we are eye level and it makes me feel tall. It is something I have aspired to be all my life.

"Carmine, it has been a delightful evening. I am so glad you have strong opinions and are able to express them. That makes life so much more interesting, don't you think?" And with that statement, she gave Carmine a hug and a kiss on her cheek.

"Sophie," Carmine said, as she hugged her back, "this has been a fabulous evening for me. The food was so incredible and the conversation captivating. I don't think I have ever laughed so hard. What a book you could write!"

"Yes, I have often thought of writing a book, but I think I would be sued the minute it was published. So that's not an option. And don't thank me for dinner, thank Rinaldo and Angela. They've been cooking for us for the past thirty-five years. I even sent them to school in France and Italy the first five years they were here so they could learn to cook like gourmet chefs. Now, they go occasionally, just to keep up on the newest and latest. They have to be very knowledgeable, as we do so much entertaining; I always leave everything to both of them to arrange the food and service, and choose any additional caterers, if needed. It works out beautifully for everyone."

Sophie continued, "That is how Jake learned to cook and where he got his love of food. Many a Saturday when Jake was growing up they would take him into the kitchen and have him assist them preparing that night's entrée or desserts. Sometimes he would ask how to do something and then they would teach him. He was an apt student and they loved showing him their best culinary skills."

Carmine had managed to rise out of her chair and was still holding Sophie's hands.

"Sophie, it has been such a memorable and delightful evening for me and you are a very special person. I now know why Jake's eyes sparkle when he speaks about you. And you might say you are an 'old lady' and I have no idea how old you are, but the person I see before me is very, very young." And she bent down and kissed Sophie lightly on the cheek.

Sophie laughed at that remark and told Carmine, "I have never told anyone my age because I feel, if you do, they tell you how you should behave just because that is how they think one should behave at that age. This way, people don't know, and I can do anything I want and people can't reprimand me because I am not acting my age! A phrase I absolutely loathe!"

"That is my philosophy also! I do believe we are kindred spirits!"

Sophie grinned impishly. "My dear, I see you have read the old book that was so popular in my era, *Anne of Green Gables*. She was my favorite heroine. Anne used that word often. But I agree with you completely!"

Returning Carmine's kiss, she then turned to Jake and directed, "You must show Carmine the rest of the house and the garden, before she leaves tonight; especially the garden." She gave him a quick kiss, "Don't keep Carmine up too late, Jake. I'll see you in the morning!"

Jake took Carmine's hand and asked her, "What would you like to see first, the garden or the rest of the house? I know it is getting late, Carmine, so I won't spend much time in either. I know how tired you've been."

"But, Jake, this is so exciting being here and seeing your Aunt and where you live, I couldn't possibly be tired now."

"Why don't I take you through the rest of the house first and I'll have Rinaldo light the heat lamps in the garden so it won't be cold for you. The garden looks vastly different in the evening than it does in the day. It is almost magical, so you can see it now and then come back during the day soon so you can see it both ways."

"Sounds perfect," Carmine said with a wide smile. "Lead away!"

They met Rinaldo as they were leaving the room, and he had heard Jake speak to Carmine.

"I will take care of that right away, Mr. Jake," as he went outside to turn on the lamps.

Jake took Carmine out to a hall and started walking toward where Rinaldo had exited. "Jake," Carmine asked, "where is the bathroom? Before I take this hike, I think I should use one."

Jake said it was a good idea for both of them and showed her one while he went across the hall to another.

Just as she was about to leave the bathroom, she saw Laurence staring back at her in the mirror. "Laurence," she demanded, "What are you doing here? I hope you have me as an energy pattern. Didn't I tell you I didn't want to see you in any bathroom at all?"

"Yes, you did, and you haven't seen me until now. I am appearing to you here, which is a private place, no? And yes, I have you as an energy pattern. Remember, I am always with you, whether you can see me or not. I wanted to say I am so happy you are enjoying yourself. When you are happy, I am happy. Happiness is an energy that is felt by all you come in contact with and people respond to it and feel good about you and themselves. The same is true if you are feeling unhappy; that is also energy, and it impacts people in a negative way. If you Humans understood that you are all connected to each other on a soul level, your world would be vastly different and it would eliminate so much strife and . . ."

"Laurence, Laurence, please no lectures! Jake is waiting for me. He will be wondering where I am. But, yes," she admitted with a lilt in her voice, "I am absolutely, positively, incredibly happy. So, please," she warned anxiously, "don't ruin it by letting me see you. Okay?" Laurence nodded. Giving him a-don't-mess-with-me look, she left the bathroom.

Jake was waiting for her in the long hallway, lounging beside a large green door. "Carmine, I thought I heard you talking to someone," he said, puzzled. "I was so impressed with the bathroom I had this wonderful conversation with myself," Carmine said lightly, trying to seem as though it was something she did every day; silently telling herself that she must be more careful. "Now, onto to the grand tour," she said, as she grabbed Jake's hand.

"My dear, I am only going to give you the mini tour of the house because it's so late and I do want you to see the garden. You can come back some other time and take the grand and more leisurely tour of everything else inside, Okay?"

Jake led her through several large rooms that had been converted to offices for his school and philanthropic work. "I had these redone when we remodeled because different staff members were at various locations. Now, everyone is here and it's much more efficient and convenient."

They walked down a hallway that separated the offices, through a magnificent double door that was decorated with raised figures, colored in blue, gold and green. When Jake threw open the doors, there was a ballroom as large as a football field, lined on one side with floor to ceiling mirrors, with a stage, room for a full orchestra, two grand pianos, tables, chairs and other furniture.

Carmine gasped, "This is magnificent. I could spend the rest of the evening here. It reminds me of Versailles, only in better taste."

"I promise we will come back soon, but not tonight." As they walked through the ballroom to the other end, he pointed out the hotel kitchen, and on the other side of the hallway, a dining room with an enormous table that could easily seat a hundred.

"We do all our philanthropic entertaining here. Yes, it's a little outrageous, but we use the space for some amazing charity events. Sometimes it seems a waste to have all this space and only use it three or four times a year. It really is from an earlier era. But it's part of the family legacy. I'll show you my suite of rooms and the rest of the living quarters when we have more time. I am sure that Rinaldo has set up the heat lamps and turned on the evening lights so you can see the garden. I want to show you the garden before you get too tired," he said, looking at the clock and noting that it was after ten.

Taking Carmine back through the great room, he opened the large double floor-to-ceiling doors to the outside and, with a small bow, gestured her to go through the doorway.

The first thing Carmine noticed was the splashing of water. She turned in that direction and saw a high multi-tier waterfall cascading down onto large, gray boulders emptying into a shimmering large pond, and surrounded by an array of plants and flowers. Tiny twinkling white lights adorned all the trees and shrubbery. Ceramic and clay figures of small angels and fairies dotted the brick path surrounding the pond. A low stone gray bridge with lamps of stone lights sculpted into a variety of flower shapes—lilies, irises and roses—stretched across the pond.

Beyond the pond were a garden, a green house and an Olympic-size swimming pool with diving boards and slides as well as a long lap pool. The white wrought iron tables and chairs, the enormous barbecue and stove on the large brick patio were perfect for outdoor dinners. Among the patio tables and chairs were outdoor heaters, all turned on to give the patio an aura of golden light.

Carmine gazed delightedly around the garden. Turning to Jake, she whispered, "You're right, this is magical! How lucky I am to be here. Thank you." She leaned in and gave him a soft kiss on the lips.

She tried to step away, but he caught her by the wrist. "Not so fast, my pretty lady." He took her hand and walked to the end of the patio where the barbecue was and found a switch hidden in the brick. Suddenly, the entire garden was filled with the music of violins and harps.

"Enchanting and so beautiful! It makes me want to cry. It ignites the beauty of my soul and makes it soar!"

"Carmine," Jake said, as he continued to hold her hand, but dug into his pants pocket, he pulled out a ring and said, "I want to show you something."

"This ring was my mother's." He showed her a heart shape large ruby surrounded by small heart-shaped diamonds on a wide gold band.

"It's breathtaking," Carmine stammered and she felt herself shaking. She heard Laurence say "Stay calm. It is not what you are thinking, Carmine," and at that, a small sigh of relief escaped her.

"Carmine," Jake said looking lovingly into her eyes, "I know what you have told me is that it takes time for you to become involved. And you want to go slow, especially after the episode with Giovanna and I truly understand that. But I want you to know that however long it takes for you to accept me and trust me, again, there is never going to be anyone but you in my life. I know that what happened with Giovanna harmed our relationship and your trust in me, but, truly, it was a blessing in disguise because it gave me such clarity about my feelings for you. I am committed to you, Carmine, for my lifetime and even beyond, he said with a shy smile. So I want you to accept this ring as a symbol of my fidelity and love and trust. I want you to wear it as a reminder to you that I will always be there for you, forever!"

And as he said that, he placed it on her middle finger of her right hand. As he finished, he said, "I feel that there is a connection with my mother and you because both of you were born in July and have the same birth stone, the ruby."

"Ja Ja, Jake," Carmine started stuttering, "I don't know what to say. The ring is gorgeous and I am so honored that you are giving me something that belonged to your Mother. And part of me wants to accept it, but another part of me is scared and says this is too fast. And you're right, especially after the episode with Giovanna, even though I know in my heart that it is in the past and it is over. I truly accept that and I do trust what you are saying."

Carmine took a big breath, biting her lip and then letting it out before asking the next question. "And, realistically, what does this mean, Jake, for both of us?"

"This is only the beginning of our relationship, which I want to make permanent. I want to have a lifetime together as husband and wife. I never believed in 'love at first sight.' I thought it was something poets and the entertainment industry dreamed up. But from the first moment I saw you in my classroom, I knew that you were someone unique and special. It was almost like being hit with the proverbial Cupid's arrow. It was all I could do not to ask you out after the first class. I thought I was crazy because this has never happened to me before. But as the weeks went on, I realized that it was something deeper.

"Take as long as you want. I know that you care for me, but you need more time, especially after what has taken place in the last week. If you feel, after giving it thought and time, it is not right for you, I'll understand!" Jake gave a strangled laugh. "If you decided against the relationship,

Carmine, I would probably jump off the nearest high mountain around here!"

Carmine heard Laurence gasp at that statement and she made a sound that Jake interpreted to mean that she was shocked.

"Carmine, I'm joking. It would devastate me, but I would try to understand. But I thought we could start by making a commitment to each other now and then proceed slowly or as quickly as you want to the next step. You set the pace. What do you say?"

Carmine's face was now wet with silent tears as she grasped Jake's hands in an impassioned grasp.

"Jake, I am so lucky to have a man who is so thoughtful and kind and understands my hesitation. I do care for you so much. When I think of you, it seems as though butterflies, fairies, angels and rainbows and everything beautiful surrounds me! I am that happy. Perhaps what happened with Giovanna also helped me see how much you meant to me. I don't have to think about it. Of course I will wear the ring and I am committed to you and the relationship!"

She stood on her toes and kissed Jake passionately with all the tenderness and love she felt for him. He returned the kiss with the same intensity and when they fell apart, Jake said softly, "Carmine, if your body is telling me what I think it is telling me, why don't we go to my suite of rooms right now?" And he picked her up in his arms and started walking towards the house. Over Jake's shoulder, Carmine saw Laurence following them.

Carmine blushed very red and asked Jake to put her down, which he did, but continued to hold her in his arms. Then, avoiding his eyes, she said quietly and with some hesitation. "Jake, I would like to do that, but not tonight. I need to talk to you first. Friday, as soon as my last final is done, why don't you come over and then I can tell you what

I think is important for you to know and then we can go from there."

Jake stood holding her for a few minutes, looking at her. Finally, much to Carmine's relief, because she thought she had offended him, he smiled, put her down and said, "Carmine, whatever you want. I can wait forever, and will!"

"Thank you for your understanding. I am so blessed when I am with you." And with that, Carmine kissed him again, deeply and fervently, and he responded the same way. They were both gasping for air when they stopped. They looked at each other and started laughing so hard, Carmine had to sit down in one of the white wrought iron chairs.

"You are going home right now or all bets are off about tonight." Taking her arm, Jake led her out through the garden entrance right to his car.

"I don't even have my purse."

"You stay here and I'll run in to retrieve it. Did you leave it in the great room? And what does it look like?"

Carmine nodded yes, "It's a small velvet black bag with a black bow on the front."

"I'll be back in a second; don't leave without me," he winked and then ran through the garden entrance.

Carmine smiled and turned on the overhead interior car lights and gasped at the brilliance of the ring in the light. "I can't believe this is happening to me," she said out loud in a voice filled with astonishment.

"It is, Carmine. And your energy pattern is something I have never seen in you before so you're experiencing an emotion that is new to you."

"Laurence, you are so right. I have never felt this way before. Maybe perhaps the night that Cassie was born, but this is different than that. With Cassie there was some sadness there; the relationship with her father and how I felt about becoming a mother. There were so many conflicts.

"Laurence, tell me, you said Jake and I had known each other in several lifetimes, but I am sure there are literally hundreds of other people we have known. I know I'm attractive and have certain attributes, but nothing that special. Certainly I'm no beauty queen or even that much of a beauty. We have a lot in common and it is easy for us to talk. And then there is my age, I am thirty-seven years old, not old, but certainly not young. I'm sure there are hundreds of women just like me whom he has also known in past lives, so why is Jake in love with me? I know why I love him, but there is something else going on between Jake and me that feels deeper. You said you'd tell me when the time was right. Please, let it be right now."

"I have permission to tell you now. You two have a very strong Karmic connection. In many previous lifetimes, you were with Jake. In two of the more current lifetimes, speaking in spiritual time, you saved his life. That is what makes the bond so strong. One time, you stopped an adversary from cutting off his head by offering yourself as that man's wife.

"The second time, Jake was a very prominent person in that society and you stepped in front of him to protect him from a bullet. As you lay dying in his arms, he promised you that he would never forget what you had done for him and that he would always love you. If you had not saved his life at that time, there would have been a different sequence of events in history, with a negative effect on the world. When someone makes a statement like that, it is forever engrained in his soul. When he saw you that first day of school, his soul remembered and he fell in love with you at that moment. It wouldn't matter whether you were attractive or plain, old or young! Jake would still fall in love with you. The connection is that strong."

Carmine sat very still with her mouth open, almost as though she were going to speak, but couldn't. Finally, as she was taking a trembling breath to reply to Laurence, Jake opened the car door.

"Carmine," he asked with concern, "are you all right? You look," pausing for a way to describe her, "you look as though you have had some kind of shock. What happened?"

Carmine started speaking rapidly, "Everything tonight has just moved me on a very deep level. So many feelings have just surfaced. I looked at the ring in the car light and it is magnificent. I am so honored that you want me to wear it. Knowing that it was your Mother's makes it very precious. I'm overwhelmed!"

All smiles, and blushing a little, Jake said, "If she were here, she would be happy that you are wearing it." He gently took both her hands and kissed each of them with tenderness. "But please don't feel overwhelmed. You were so pale when I opened the door, I thought you were ill! This is one of the happiest days of my life!"

He grinned, started laughing and relaxed a bit, and so did Carmine. Then he leaned over and gave her a hug and a kiss. "Hey, let me get you home. It is almost midnight now and you were tired to begin with." He handed her purse to her and started the car. "Why don't you put your head back and relax? This chariot will have you home quicker than you can say 'Aunt Sophie!'"

Laughing, Carmine did put her head back because she wanted to think about what Laurence had told her. Minutes later, Jake was softly calling her name as she suddenly sat up and looked around. "How did we get home this fast?" she whispered, as she shook her head, trying to get rid of the grogginess.

"For one reason, as usual, there was no traffic and for another, it took only fifteen minutes. But you were asleep before I was out of the driveway."

"I am such a fun date," Carmine exclaimed reprovingly, "You have been so understanding tonight. The least I could do is stay awake!"

"It is perfectly all right," Jake said as he bent over to kiss her. After the quick kiss, he jumped out of the car and ran around to open her door. "I am going to walk you to your door and then leave very quickly. Otherwise," he said with a mischievous look in his eye, "I'll probably stay the night."

"Give me a few more days. I'm still a little old-fashioned," Carmine pleaded as she took his hand and they walked up the three flights of brick steps to her condo door. Jake kissed her very softly and gently on her lips, took her hand in his and kissed it, as he opened the door and then waved good-bye as he left.

Waving back until he was out of her sight, she shut and locked the door and then leaned against it and sighed. *One of the best nights of my whole life! And the most difficult.* She had turned down Jake's offer to stay the night twice. "I'm old-fashioned!" Carmine snorted.

"You did the right thing. You have to be very clear on what you both want and expect. Many times relationships don't work out because of those two simple but very important criteria." Laurence was beside her again.

"Laurence," Carmine snapped with irritation, "PLEASE! I don't want to hear anything more about doing the right thing. I DO want to hear more about everything you told me in the car, like saving Jake's life twice and all those details. I am so intrigued." She walked into the living room, sat down on the couch, put her hand on her chin and looked at Laurence with anticipation.

"There are many components that go into a relationship which have been on-going for so many lifetimes. I've told you all that I could so that you would understand the attraction between you and Jake. I cannot discuss this in any more detail, so please don't continue to question me."

"Laurence, what am I going to do with you?"

Suddenly, Carmine stood up straight, looked directly at Laurence and wailed, "My God, what AM I going to do with you? There is no way I can have both Jake and you, unless I can tell Jake about you. I can't let Jake go and if he is here in my life to stay, there is no way you can continue to be a secret. Please Laurence, please let me tell him."

"Carmine, you know I can't do that. And if you do inform Jake of my presence, the penalties will be severe!"

"But, then ..." Carmine's eyes were filled with tears and she said with sharp pain, "I'll have to let you go. There is no way I can have both of you."

"You are right, Carmine," Laurence nodded his head in agreement and sighed, "I will have to remove myself from your physical presence and return to my unseen self."

Carmine sat for a long time, her head bowed in her arms, while Laurence watched her. Finally, her head came up and she said to him, "Laurence, I can't see any other way. I do love Jake with all my heart and I just want to be with him and make him happy. So if I can't tell him, you'll have to change back to your original role." The tears were now falling and there was a little hiccup in her voice. She couldn't help but notice that Laurence was wearing all black, as if he were in mourning.

Laurence came close to her and wiped the tears that were spilling on her cheeks.

"Laurence, that is the first time I remember you touching me, except when you took me to Mother."

"It is one of our cardinal rules that we can never touch our human charges, except when we leave them or take them with us."

"Does that mean you're leaving?"

"Yes, Carmine, you have made your decision that Jake is your love and that I must go."

"Laurence, I'm going to miss you so. I know numerous times I acted so ungrateful and that I did not want you around, but I did like having you here. You know that, right?" Laurence nodded with a knowing smile. "I can talk to you in the other dimension whenever I want to, right?"

"Yes and no," Laurence said with a concerned tone. "You will completely forget everything that had to do with this relationship on this physical plane. You will remember this particular period in your life, but without any memory of me. There will be times when a fleeting memory will occur, but nothing that you will actually be able to recall. And, as time goes by, even those thoughts will become obscure.

"But you will continue to speak to me on an unconscious level when you meditate or when you pray or when you reflect deeply on a problem and when you listen to your inner counselor, who will always give you the true answers. I will always continue to assist you in your life just as I did before I came into the physical realm. You won't be able to see and hear me like you do now."

"Laurence, what am I going to do without you?"

"Carmine, listen to what I have just said. You will NOT be without me."

"I know you're right," Carmine agreed listlessly. "It just seems that life will be so difficult without you. There are so many ways you made my life easier. You helped me to understand life in a new way, so that it can be happier and more joyful. I am so grateful and appreciative for that gift. And you kept me entertained and, it was nice just to have you around. You know, those discussions that gave me answers to all those unanswered questions I had about the Universe. I know it sounds silly and absurd, Laurence, but not having traffic when I drive is going to be almost as hard to give up as you!"

Laurence hesitated and then offered, "Perhaps I can give you good traffic Karma as a gift. What you Earth people call 'a going-away present.'"

"What a gift that would be! It wouldn't be nearly as good as having you here with me, but it would help immensely."

"Let me discuss it with the others." For a moment, everything was very still and Laurence had disappeared. But before Carmine could consciously verify his disappearance, Laurence stood before her.

"It has been granted. They have allowed other humans to have similar, but different Karma for a variety of things, like finding money or always having perfect weather when they travel, so this is not as unique as I thought."

"Thank you, Laurence, thank you."

And she got up on her toes, kissed her hands and then stretched her arms up and placed her hands on his lips.

Laurence seemed to be almost overwhelmed by the gesture and his face became very red.

Trying not to show that she had noticed, Carmine asked with eyes cast down and in a choked, constricted voice, "When will you leave, Laurence?"

"Tonight, Carmine, when you are asleep. Tomorrow you will awaken and you will not know that anything is different. Nothing will be changed in your mind regarding this period except that I'll not be remembered as part of it.

"I'll say good-bye now," Laurence said. "You will still be able to see me until you fall asleep. Then it will return to the usual Guardian Angel and human relationship that we have had for the past twenty lifetimes."

Carmine nodded as her lips pressed together to stop the tears. "I'll get ready for bed and then meditate. Will you meditate with me like you usually do, Laurence?"

"Of course, Carmine. You won't remember this, but I'll always be with you when you meditate."

Carmine hastily did her usual nighttime routine and within five minutes was back in the bedroom. She had thrown her clothes on the floor and put on the white tattered nightgown that she had worn the night of her transition. She took her usual place in her meditation chair, wistfully regarded Laurence, and waved a tiny good-bye to him with her right hand, before she closed her eyes.

"I'm so tired and sleepy. I know that I'll only be able to meditate for five minutes" she said with sadness as she yawned. "But I want to do this with you one last time."

Carmine prophesized correctly because within six or seven minutes of meditating, she was almost asleep. She crawled into her bed, sighing with the heaviness she felt.

"Goodnight and good-bye, Laurence," she said groggily; "I am truly going to miss you," and was asleep as she uttered the last word.

"Will miss being in your world, too, Carmine. Sweet dreams." Laurence hovered a hand over her. Instantly, there was a huge bang of thunder and the room was filled with a luminous white light that made the room as bright as noontime on a summer day—and then, complete and total darkness.

PART III

Chapter One

Carmine woke the next morning feeling relaxed and rejuvenated. She lay there enjoying the luxurious feeling of sleeping in and not rushing. She squinted at her Zen clock and shook her head several times in disbelief when she saw the time.

"Oh, my gosh, it's Noon. I can't believe I slept that late. And on a weekday. I am so grateful I had nothing scheduled for today."

As she lay back in bed, she had an uncomfortable feeling that something was amiss. She raised her head and looked around. Everything seemed to be in order, but it was just a feeling that was hard to dismiss. As she pulled the comforter up to her shoulders, she recalled a flash of her dream. Something about an Angel. Darn, she couldn't recall it. But dreaming about an Angel had to be good. She would look it up in one of her dream books.

She closed her eyes for a moment and was almost asleep when the phone rang.

"Hello," she said, as she yawned.

"Hey, Mom, you are still in bed at this time," she heard Cassie ask. "Are you sick?"

"No, darling, I was just tired and didn't wake up until a few moments ago."

"Mom, you never sleep until Noon. Never! I can't remember one time in my life you have slept that late unless you were sick, especially on a week day."

"I'm just fine, Cassie, so don't worry about me," Carmine replied in an irritated voice.

"Okay, okay, don't get mad! I called for two reasons. First, is it okay to ask about you and Jake?" she asked with some hesitation. "We haven't had to time to talk and I just want to know how it is going."

"Cassie, it certainly is okay to ask. It's going very well. I met his Aunt last night and she was so lovely. Very energetic, entertaining and spirited. I hope when I reach her age, whatever that is, I'll have half her stamina."

"Mom, you never stop now! So trust me, you will have as much energy as she does, if not more! Especially when you get old! And, meeting his Aunt sounds very serious. Wow!"

"Thanks, Cassie. I love your confidence in me." Ignoring the "serious comment," Carmine asked, "So what is the second reason for the call?"

"I wanted to tell you that Dad is having everything moved for me during Christmas break. All I have to do is pack. I wanted to know if you would like to help. Dad even said if you do, you could follow me up to San Francisco and stay at his house during Christmas. We could all be together and now you could even bring Jake, since he is back in your life!"

"That's sounds great, Cassie. All of us together under one roof! Danielle, Emily, your Father and Jake and myself. I can't wait," Carmine said with irony and shook her head at that imagined scenario.

"It would be fun with everyone there and you said you would help me unpack, which I would appreciate."

"Cassie, sweetie, I think deep in your lovely heart of hearts, you think that your father and I will get together and become one family again and then toss Danielle and Emily out on the street."

"Mom, of course not! At least not Emily," Cassie said laughing. "I thought that it was nice of Dad to offer."

"Honey, I will be happy to help you pack and unpack, but I will not stay at the house. Luckily, I have those six weeks of vacation, which is perfect to help you, and to get my life together before school starts in January. And maybe I will bring Jake with me," Carmine said almost defiantly.

"Gee, Mom, I was kinda kidding about your bringing Jake, knowing how you have been in the past about men. But if you're thinking of bringing him, it must be serious."

"Actually," Carmine swallowed a couple of times and said very softly, almost hoping Cassie wouldn't hear her, "he gave me a ring last night."

"You mean an engagement ring?" Cassie yelled so loud that Carmine had to put the phone as far away from her ear as possible. "Oh, my gosh, Mom, this is so sudden, especially for you!"

"Cassie, Cassie, calm down. No, it is not an engagement ring! It's a friendship ring stating his intent to become much more than a friend and that he is willing to wait for me as long as it is necessary."

"You mean he wants to marry you?" Cassie's voice was now so loud Carmine felt there was no need for the phone.

"Yes, he did say that." And then Carmine proceeded to tell Cassie about the prior evening.

At the end of the lengthy monologue, there was quiet on the other end of the phone.

"Cassie, are you there?" Carmine asked with concern.

Finally, Cassie said, "Mom, I don't know what to say, except that I'm very happy for you and it makes me want to cry." And then Cassie did just that!

"Cassie, please don't cry. Now I'm going to start crying." Through the sobs, Carmine started laughing. "We are two crazy women, Cassie. You know that?"

At that, Cassie started laughing and for a moment that is all that was heard on the phone, two women laughing and crying at the same time.

Finally, Carmine said, "You know Cassie, I had a strange dream last night, which I just remembered. It was about an Angel that came to Earth to be with me. And when I woke this morning, I felt that I was looking for him. Isn't that strange?"

"Mom, what does your dream book say? You always look at that when you have a dream you can't understand."

"I haven't had a chance to do that, but I will as soon as we hang up."

"Mom," Cassie shrieked, "I almost forgot about Thanksgiving. What are we going to do this year? Since I am spending Christmas with Dad, I definitely want to spend it with you and, I guess, now Jake. Are we still going to go to Aunt Maddie's like we usually do?"

"I'm not sure. Whatever we do, I want to include Jake so I will have to talk to him. But don't worry, kiddo, we will be together. Will you drive down Wednesday morning? Traffic on that day is the worst in the year! Maybe it would be a good idea to take the train and I'll pick you up at the L.A. station. This way you don't have to drive back and forth and can relax. Why don't you think about it? And if you decide, then we should make reservations pronto, because it will be packed, I'm sure."

"That's a good idea. I'll go ahead and make the reservation now and I'll just put it on the credit card and then you can write me a check. Okay?"

"Perfect! Let me know the time, as soon as you can so I can put it on my calendar."

"Have fun, Mom and don't study too hard," Cassie cautioned as she said good-bye. Then added, "Say hello to Jake for me!"

As soon as Cassie hung up the phone, Carmine ran to her bookcase and found her books on interpreting dreams. Looking up "Angel" in one of them, she read, "Dreaming of an Angel is like dreaming of your higher or ideal self; any message from an Angel may be a message from the super-conscious."

How interesting. I wonder what it meant because I don't remember anything like a message or my higher self. It sounds like a good omen so I'm going to make it mean that something wonderful is going to happen to me. She looked down at the friendship ring and amended the thought, *something wonderful has already happened.* She hugged herself with happiness.

The phone rang again and it was Jake. Almost shyly, she told him how excited she was about the ring and that she couldn't wait until Friday evening. He said he felt the same way and then he brought up Thanksgiving. She mentioned that Cassie had asked where they were spending the day.

"Carmine," Jake said hopefully, "Please spend the day with my Aunt and me. We always have a small group of friends and a few relatives. I'd like you and Cassie to meet them. I hope it is not too late, but I was so intent upon our relationship, I forgot about everything, including Thanksgiving. And don't forget Christmas, too."

"Jake, please, one holiday at a time," Carmine laughed. "Let's take care of Thanksgiving first. Cassie and I would love to come. What can I bring?"

"Rinaldo and Angela do all the cooking and then they join us for dinner. At one time, we had caterers cook the dinner so they could enjoy the day, but they were both so unhappy with the food, that they now do it. We just hire a few people to serve and clean up. But let me ask them if they would like you to add to their bountiful feast."

"It sounds lovely. I can't wait! And I don't have to bring food. I can bring something else, like wine or flowers. So let me know."

Carmine told him about her dream, the Angel and what her book said about it. She tried to explain how something felt amiss in her condo, but couldn't explain what.

"Knowing how intuitive you are, Carmine, is there something wrong in your condo? I can come right over, if you need me."

"No, it's not that. It just a feeling I have and I can't seem to grasp what it is. Like I'm missing something, but don't know what."

"If you need help, let me know. In the meantime, study hard. You know I can be there anytime. I can make dinner for you, help you do laundry, dust, etcetera, etcetera, etcetera."

Carmine giggled at that last part as he imitated the same tone and dialect as Yul Brynner used in the old movie, *The King and I.*

"No, Jake, I must be strong and try to be able to be without you for two days. It will be good for me; make a better person of me, etcetera, etcetera, etcetera," Carmine retorted in the same tone and dialect.

There was laughter from both ends of the line with that exchange. "Okay, Carmine, I am going to take you out for a celebration dinner on Friday evening in honor of finishing your finals, how about that? Then we'll have that conversation that you promised me."

"Jake, I promised you a very special dinner at the end of finals. So let me take care of everything, okay?"

"When you said you would cook a special dinner, I didn't think it would be on the day your finals end. But whatever you want, Carmine. It is not many women who would turn down a dinner, but then you are not like any woman I know. This makes you very special, no pun intended."

"I am blushing. I think you're very special, too."

"Now that we have shared our mutual admiration, I'd better hang up or you will never do the studying you need to do. Call me if you need anything," Jake gave her his lovely good-bye, "God bless, Carmine."

Carmine spent the rest of the day studying for her final and catching up with all her other chores. At different times during the day, she would find herself looking around for someone who she felt should be there and then become angry with herself.

"Who are you looking for?" she asked with annoyance.

She managed to have a quick lunch with Leslie and catch up with all her news. Leslie had a new "friend" who seemed to be the opposite of Bart, thank goodness, and who was encouraging Leslie to go for her Master's in drama. Carmine showed Leslie the ring and Leslie snickered. "Yea! Sure! Friendship Ring! That's an engagement ring if I ever saw one." But Carmine would not admit anything to Leslie, other than it was truly just a friendship ring.

After her last final on Friday, feeling good about how she did, Carmine gave an excited hoot as she got into her car. But then she had that feeling again that something was missing. Taking inventory of everything in the car, including her red purse, all seemed to be there. She looked around one more time and then, shaking her head, she drove off the campus.

"I'm so happy that everything is over, at least for this semester," she said to herself. "Six weeks of no school; just work." And there was going to be almost three weeks where all her clients would not need her. *This is Heaven. That's a strange word to explain how I feel.*

Carmine stopped at the organic store to pick up the food for that night. She had left a red lentil, basil and tomato soup cooking in her Crock Pot that morning before going to school. "What am I going to have for the main dish?" she asked herself as she pushed her grocery basket through the aisles. She looked at her watch, noting that it was only Noon. I think I have time to make homemade pasta with shrimp, clam juice, fennel, artichoke hearts, and garlic. I'll pick up a small brie cheese, and crackers for an appetizer. That, with olive bread and some salad makings, will complete a nice dinner. Jake said he would bring the dessert and wine.

There was no one waiting in the checkout line and by 12:50, she was home, and had put all the groceries away and had started making the pasta.

"One full recipe should be enough for both of us," she told herself as she manually cranked the old-fashioned pasta machine her parents had used, and then hung the wide noodles on the pasta rack to dry. As soon as she was finished with the pasta, she prepared the rest of the dinner so that the only thing she needed to do at the last minute was boil the water for the pasta, heat up the shrimp and artichoke sauce, and put dressing on the salad.

Carmine took some time to set the table with a dramatic motif of black and gold featuring her gold and white Havilland Limoges china, which her parents had given her when she married. She completed the table setting with ivy from her garden in a short crystal vase and gold candles.

Complimenting herself on how attractive the table looked, she turned on the stereo and inserted a Mozart CD. The music reminded her of something or someone, but she couldn't think of what.

It's good to feel good! Carmine acknowledged what she had accomplished, not "going crazy" about details, as she usually did when she was under time pressure and wanted to make a good impression.

Noting she still had two hours, she knew exactly how she would spend it. "I'm going to spend it indulging myself! A long bath, meditation, nap and taking my time to dress" she told herself as she danced into the bedroom. She envisioned the simple, long pseudo velvet emerald green robe she would wear. It was called a robe because she purchased it in the lingerie department, but, actually, it was a hostess garment. It was easy to wear and cook in, and it made her feel beautiful and glamorous, something she didn't feel every day or even, she thought raising her eyebrows, once or twice a year.

Lying in the bathtub, she thought to herself, "I'm so happy! I can't remember when I have been this happy. It's like a combination of Christmas when I was a kid and every other wonderful experience all rolled into one." Looking at the ring, her smile became wider. "There's Jake, whom I adore and if I admit it, love! Cassie has finally found her dharma or her work in life, using the Hindu word. I have six weeks off from school, and negotiated three weeks off from work with my HR clients. Other than having a few image consulting clients, I am free!"

Carmine closed her eyes and opened them to realize that the water had come up to her mouth. *I must have fallen asleep for a moment.* She raised herself out of the tub and threw on her favorite body lotion and her cotton nightgown with the holes in it.

"One of these days," she promised herself, "I'll discard it, but not yet. When I put it on it feels so heavenly. What's a few holes?" She started meditating, but after one minute she was nodding and moved to her bed. Pulling the deep lavender blanket over her shoulders, she was instantly asleep.

"Hello Carmine!"

"Laurence, I thought you left."

"I didn't leave, Carmine, you know that. You just can't see me as you did before."

"I can see you now."

"I know, Carmine, it's because you are asleep and your subconscious mind has taken over. It's like having a lucid dream, but you are not dreaming."

"I'm so happy to see you. I'm so happy right now in my life. I know much of that is due to you and I am glad that I can tell you that. It is such a glorious feeling! I feel I can do anything, be anyone and I just feel so much love toward everyone—the whole world, I guess."

"You are supposed to feel that every day of your life. It is what life is all about—to give and receive love."

"Is every day possible? I'm sure that my feelings have to do with Jake and Cassie."

"You humans think that good feelings have to depend on how other humans feel or act towards them or experience material conditions that are in harmony with what they feel is right for them. That's just not true, Carmine. It just depends upon you.

"You are the one in charge of how you feel. Accepting situations as they are rather than deciding to be upset will keep you in a loving and positive vibration. When you see the loving essence of each individual knowing that each one is a divine being having a human experience and doing the best it can, it will be impossible for you to judge. So it will keep you in the highest vibration possible on Earth and it will help keep you in this state of happiness and well-being.

"There is much good in your world; much more than bad. But your television, radio and written communications seem to focus only on the negative, so it is hard to understand that good truly predominates."

"Laurence," Carmine smiled. She missed his lessons. But couldn't resist teasing him, "Oh, my! You are lecturing again! I am excited about Jake and Cassie and the direction my life is taking and I want to tell you about that. I love Jake so much! He is so inspirational! I mean, look what he has achieved in his life. He has written books and has created this wonderful school and then he has done so much philanthropy and he teaches. And then I look at my life and, well, it is so boring and so uneventful! Thinking about it makes me so disappointed in myself."

"You are talking about Jake's work as though it is more important than yours and that is not true. Each person has his or her own contract or curriculum to fulfill and each one is unique and specific to that individual. You cannot compare yourself to others, for each lifetime has different objectives in order to learn the lessons that must be learned in that lifetime. When you return to the other side, your home, and leave Earth, you will be evaluated on the achievement of those objectives you set out for yourself. What is of interest and value in your daily life is not what truly matters when you change your dimension and time.

"The most important essence at the core of each existence is automatically included in each contract. It is so basic: how much love you have given and received. The love you have given each day and the love you have been able to receive are one of the most important aspects of your living.

"Many times you have been of service to others. This is also an important part of giving love. It has been much easier for you to give love, through service to others, than it has for you to receive it. Receiving has always been difficult for you, for on some level, for you feel you are not worthy.

Every person in your world is worthy of receiving love—there are no exceptions."

"It does seem it is easier to give love than to receive. And maybe on some level you are right, Laurence. I didn't think I was worthy. But after I died and we came back together, it seemed I learned much more about myself and it was easier just to be me, instead of trying to be someone else. I don't know if that makes sense, but I have been happier with myself. Maybe it was because of Jake or maybe it was because of you. But I am more comfortable with being me. Even with that loud, critical voice I hear when I become fearful, or I make mistakes, or do something that I feel is silly, I don't seem to be as afraid of how I feel. I'm able to forgive myself, using the compassionate self-forgiveness that I was taught. I understand there are no mistakes, just opportunities for learning. So maybe it was good that I died, even it was a mistake."

"We all learned from that experience, including myself, Carmine. You've taught this Angel things, too. I miss our chats. I think you had better continue with your nap. I just wanted to speak with you one more time."

"Will I remember this when I wake up?"

"Not really, Carmine, but maybe just a little. It will dissipate with time. In the future, there might be a few more of what you will consider dreams about me, but not as long as this."

"Something in me remembers you because, many times, I'm looking for something and now I realize it is you. But I don't know it when I am awake."

"I know, Carmine, there is a deliberate block so that you will not recall the previous events. Gradually, you will forget this and after time it will be like a subtle and blurred memory."

"That's too bad, Laurence, I would really like to remember. You've been a good friend."

"I always have been your friend. Your Angel. Go to sleep, Carmine, and remember I am always with you."

There was a sharp bright light and then darkness.

A loud noise awakened Carmine. Without opening her eyes, she tried to turn off the chime, but it continued to ring. Finally, she opened her eyes and turned over towards the nightstand. It wasn't her Zen clock, but the telephone.

Carmine, not quite awake, answered the phone, which was on her nightstand.

"Carmine," she heard Jake say, "are you all right? I have been buzzing your door with no response. I have been phoning you for several minutes and this is the first time you have answered. I was very concerned."

"Jake," Carmine exclaimed as she looked at her clock, it is almost 6:00. "I took a nap and overslept" as she ran to the door with the phone in her ear to buzz him in. "I must've been tired," she continued to talk, as she opened the front door.

"Heavens," she cried to herself as she looked down and saw that she was wearing the old cotton nightgown. Thinking she might change quickly before Jake arrived, she saw him run up the stairs, two at a time and walk towards her before she could even shut the door.

Jake carried a Poinsettia in a flower pot under one arm, a bottle of red wine under the other arm and a cake box in his hands. He leaned over to give her a kiss and said laughing as he gazed at her, "Gee, Carmine, you didn't have to dress up so much. It's just a casual date."

Carmine laughed wickedly, "Hey, guy, this is my favorite gown for entertaining at home. Be glad that you are special enough to warrant my wearing it for you!"

Jake, through his laughter, kissed Carmine on the cheek. He walked in, and placed the flowers, the wine and the cake box on the kitchen table. "This is a dessert that Rinaldo made. It's a chocolate cake with chocolate icing with a special filling in it. He knows how much you love chocolate, so he made this especially for you." He opened the box and placed the cake in the refrigerator.

"It sounds and looks absolutely wonderful, Jake. Maybe we should have dessert first?" As she registered Jake's reaction, she hastily replied, "Just kidding."

"Look, I need to change. So please excuse me so I can dress properly. I never sleep that deeply during the day.

"I had such a strange dream. It was about an Angel that I could see and hear on Earth because of some mistake about my death, but then he had to return to our former existence, where he became invisible to me.

"It was bizarre. I can remember that much. Isn't that interesting?"

"Yes, it is Carmine. Maybe you can write about it. People are always fascinated with tales like that. And you know, you write very, very well. If anyone can do it, you can."

"That is something I never thought about, but maybe I will think about it."

With that, she gave him peck on his cheek and left to change. "Jake, please, would you mind opening the wine and pouring it in the glasses on the table?" she asked just before shutting the bedroom door.

"Consider it done, Carmine."

Twenty minutes later, elegant in makeup and her emerald green gown, and the long, green and gold chandelier earrings dangling from her ears, Carmine reappeared.

"Carmine, you look absolutely beautiful." Jake drew her to him and gave her a deep passionate kiss. And for the first time, Carmine responded without any of her usual hesitation. They finally drew apart, both breathing hard.

"This is the first time you responded without what I perceived was fear. What has changed? You promised me that we would discuss this as soon as finals were over."

Carmine picked up her glass of wine and took a long sip. Breathing hard, almost hyperventilating, she took Jake by the arm while handing him his wine glass and led him to the couch in the living room.

Sitting facing him, she said when her breathing had quieted, "Jake, I don't know, for sure. I'd been hurt in the past with my husband and in one other relationship. I think I needed to be very, very sure that I was committing on a deeper level than just physical attraction. And I had to be sure that you were too, especially after the Giovanna episode."

Jake kissed her again, but more intensely and with so much passion that Carmine entirely melted into the moment and responded in turn. They reluctantly drew apart, looking deeply into each other's eyes.

"If this continues," Jake quipped, "we will have dessert first and I am not talking about the chocolate cake. Maybe we will never get to dinner!"

Carmine blushed, sat up determinedly and said softly, "Much as that sounds enticing, and it does, I think you will like dinner and delaying gratification can stoke the fire, don't you think?" she said rather saucily. She pointed to the Brie cheese and crackers she had placed on the coffee table, "*Bon Appétit*! Start with this, please."

Carmine noticed the Poinsettia. "The Holidays are already here and I've not done one thing to prepare. Going to school, along with working, seems to come first, second and third in my life. I'm so glad, however, that you have managed to become a part of it," Carmine said as she bowed her head, but with her eyes focused on Jake.

"Carmine, I'm planning on spending as much time with you during the next six weeks as you will allow. So please make time for me in your busy schedule. I'll help you in anything you need."

"Jake," Carmine replied as she ladled the soup in the soup bowls in the kitchen and placed them on the dining room table. "You are definitely included in all my plans. She started the water boiling under the pasta pot, heated the ingredients for the sauce, and found an igniter to light the candles on the table.

"Shall we sit down and eat?"

"This is a beautiful table, Carmine; it's so elegant," purred Jake, as he pulled the chair out for her sit and then seated himself.

"I'll say the grace," Jake said softly, as they both bent their heads to bless their food.

After a short prayer, Jake raised his wine glass and said, "To us, Carmine, today, tomorrow and always!"

Carmine picked up her glass and very seriously said, "Jake, I will happily drink to that."

And as they touched glasses, Jake raised his eyes and asked, "What are you telling me, Carmine?"

"I am committed to you, Jake, in spite of my fears. I know that we are meant to be together and I'm ready to take the risk of loving you."

Jake smiled glowingly, "I know that you were hurt very much when that episode, as you call it, happened with Giovanna and I wish it hadn't occurred. But you now know how much I care for you and that I am so committed to you and our relationship. So, I do understand your hesitation, but is there a risk, now?"

"Because I have found that when you love, you can be hurt. And there have been some hurts in my life that I don't want to repeat. Maybe that is why I never became involved with anyone in the last twelve years. I was hurt two out of two times and that doesn't count what happened with you. When you bat zero percent, you stop batting, if you know what I mean. I didn't want the number of strike outs to increase. And I made a commitment to myself that I was never going get involved with anyone because I wasn't going to get hurt. And then what happened with you and Giovanna just cemented my shield of protection."

"To love is a risk," Jake continued, "But only when you risk, are there great rewards. And, yes, there can be great losses. But if you don't love because you are afraid, you might as well be dead. Isn't that what life is all about? To go beyond what you know, to the 'divine unknown', so to speak. And especially with love! You know, the old adage, 'Tis better to have loved and lost than never to have loved at all.' It's trite, but it has been around for hundreds of years because it is true."

"Jake, I know all of this in my mind, but, emotionally, it was hard for me to make myself understand it that way."

"Carmine, I promise you, on my parents' grave, that I'll never do anything again that will cause you pain. I would never hurt you and if somehow I do, it would be unintentional. You're safe with me."

"Jake, no more apologies. Thank you for waiting until I was ready," and Carmine threw him a kiss.

He reached over and took her right hand in his and with his other hand started removing the ring on her finger. Then when the ring was half-way off, he stopped.

"I need to talk to Cassie right now."

"Right now?" Carmine asked almost with indignation, "But the soup will get cold."

"Yes," he said emphatically, "right now! It's important! Trust me, Carmine, Okay?"

"Okay, I'll call her on her cell phone," Carmine said a little reluctantly.

Picking up the cordless phone in the living room, Carmine dialed Cassie.

It rang only once when Cassie answered.

"Hi darling, it's me." And before she could continue, Cassie interrupted her, saying with irritation, "I'm with some friends and I can't talk. Can you call me tomorrow?"

"Actually, Cassie, it's Jake that wants to speak with you and he said it was important."

"Jake? Just a minute while I go outside."

Carmine heard Cassie excuse herself from her friends. Five seconds later, she said "Okay, Mom, put him on."

"Hi Cassie, how are you?"

"I'm good, Jake," but with a question in her voice.

"Cassie, I need to ask you something about your Mother. Is that okay?"

"Sure Jake." Cassie said with a note of puzzlement in her voice. "What is it?"

"I want to ask you for permission to marry your mother. I love her very much and I'll take very good care of her. I know how important you are to her so I want to make sure that you would be okay with the marriage. I promise you that I will never interfere between you and your Mother's relationship and will do everything I can to ensure that you two continue being the good friends you now are. I want to take care of your mother in every way possible and I will take good care of you, too, if you will allow it.

"It is important to me that you approve of the marriage because I know how important your mother is to you and I don't want you to think you are losing her. I'll never try to be your father and hope that you will look upon me as a good friend and confidant."

Cassie gasped, "What has my mother said?"

"I haven't asked her officially, even though she knows that's what I want to do," Jake said as he looked straight into Carmine's eyes.

"Jake, I think you are perfect for my mother and if she wants to marry you, and I hope she does, then I approve. This is so exciting," Cassie was yelling happily in Jake's ear. "And thank you for asking my permission. I can't believe anyone would do something like that for me."

"Cassie, let me ask her right now."

Placing the phone on the table with the conference button pushed so Cassie could hear, he took Carmine's right hand, slipped the friendship ring off her middle finger and then slipped it on her ring finger of her left hand. "Carmine, will you please marry me?"

Carmine, who had her mouth open in wonderment during the entire conversation, sat with tears running down her face.

"Jake," she sobbed, "of course. I am so touched that you asked Cassie for permission. She's so important to me and you understand the relationship between us. Thank you, thank you for your thoughtfulness and kindness."

Jake then picked up the phone with his free hand and asked, "Cassie, did you hear that?"

"Yes, Jake," Cassie said also sobbing. "It was wonderful and thank you for including me in the engagement. Can I talk to my mother now?"

"Mom, I'm so happy for you," Cassie said softly, but clear enough for Jake to hear. "And Jake is so perfect for you. After all this time and after all the flakes you dated, you deserve this happiness."

"Thank you, Cassie, I'll call you tomorrow, okay darling? Love you, sweetheart," Carmine said as Cassie said good-bye.

Jake left his chair and, in two steps, lifted Carmine out of her seat and tilted her head.

He took her in his arms, placed one hand on her hair and then he gently kissed her. Carmine responded with the same gentleness. "Carmine," he sighed. Carmine looked up at him and said shyly, "You have been so understanding, Jake, and words cannot begin to tell you how much I appreciate it. So tonight I want to ask you something."

"Anything…" Jake smiled.

"Please, I would like you to, to," she started out very softly and started to turn red, as she hesitated and then giggled, "spend the night."

Jake took both her hands in his and laughed with delight.

"Carmine, I'd be honored." He drew her in and kissed her with more passion and gently kissed her lips. She responded by matching his passion and kissed him back fervently, trying to express all the love she felt for him in that one kiss.

"You know," he said quietly in her ear and a smile on his lips, "we could always skip dinner."

"On no," Carmine exclaimed, "I made this absolutely wonderful dinner and you are going to eat it. And besides, that dessert that Rinaldo made looks incredible. There just will be dessert on top of dessert," Carmine said with a mischievous smile.

"Now go sit down! Let's eat this soup before we have to eat it chilled and let me finish cooking."

Jake praised the simple, but delicious flavors of the soup and placed the bowls in the dishwasher while Carmine finished up the pasta and sauce. Jake took one forkful of the homemade pasta with the shrimp sauce. "Carmine, this is so light and yet it has such a flavor. It is magnificent."

"Thank you, kind sir. I love to cook and to experiment with recipes. I created this recipe from a similar dish I had in San Francisco one year. I think it worked out well.

"Jake," Carmine said as she scraped the last of the pasta sauce with her bread, "I can't forget that dream about the Angel. It just seemed so real and had so much detail."

"Carmine, why don't you write it down? Maybe you could write it as a short story and or eventually turn it into a book. Right now, everyone is interested in Angels and such. I think you could do it and do it well. You know, you are going to be off work and school for six weeks. You could try writing it then."

"You know I'm going to go up to Santa Barbara and then San Francisco to help Cassie move during the Christmas holidays, so I don't know how much time I'll have."

"Carmine, let me help you do that. I can drive and you can write. I have a friend in San Francisco who has a beautiful suite at the Saint Francis and I know he would lend it to me. We could stay there and we could both help Cassie move."

"Jake, are you sure that you want to give up all that time? It would probably take a week or so! First, packing in Santa Barbara and getting things organized and then helping her move in at her father's. I know she is going to spend Christmas with her father's family, so we will be returning home before then."

"Carmine, it'll be fun. There are several charity functions I have to attend, but once we set a time schedule, I can coordinate it with the secretary who takes care of the philanthropic events so maybe I won't have to miss any one of them. I want to help you and Cassie and, besides, it will be fun to get to know her better and spend some time together that is not sandwiched between school and your work!"

"Jake, I would be so grateful for your help. Thank you," Carmine said, as she grasped his hand and squeezed it. "It does sound fun, even if it is moving! I don't think we will have to spend much time in Santa Barbara because with three of us working, we could wrap it up in a day or two at the most."

"Don't worry about it, Carmine! We can reserve a hotel room for a couple of nights so we don't have to rush. We could block off a week just to ensure that we get everything done. Just let me know the dates and I'll make arrangements, if that is okay with you?" Jake asked a little hesitantly.

"Oh, no, Jake, it sounds terrible," Carmine said laughing. "Spending time with you, Cassie and in Santa Barbara and San Francisco is something I think I can handle."

"Well, then," Jake said matter-of-factly, "when do you want to get married? January sounds good to me, but I know how women are about these things. I guess that would be too early, right?" he asked, but with a hopeful note in his voice.

"Jake," Carmine asked incredulously, "are you serious?"

"I am and I'm not. I would love to do it tomorrow, so January sounds like a long time from now, but I know that you would probably want more time," he replied a little sheepishly.

"Jake, my love. Yes! Even though I know I love you and you love me, we do not know each other that well. You know, I'm talking about the shadow side of our personalities, what Cassie called the 'fatal flaw.' You know those things that are not too bad, but maybe not the best side of us. I mean you need to know that I am terribly impatient and get myself into a lot of trouble with that behavior. And when I am excited or nervous or scared, I start yelling and it makes me seem angry, even when I'm not. And . . ."

"Whoa, Carmine, wait. I don't care. I know I love you and my love is unconditional; for better or worse, you are the one for me. And I certainly have enough 'fatal flaws' as you call them to match yours. But I understand you are still a little frightened about how you feel about me and marriage. Isn't that right? Especially after Giovanna?" he asked softly as he took her hand.

Carmine thought a moment and slowly nodded her head. "You're right, Jake, those are part of the concerns I have. But I think to be fair to each other and to know what we are getting into, we should wait until next summer. This way, we don't have to go too fast and we can spend as much time together as possible, but at least we will know each other. I have seen so many marriages where they didn't know each other, and then they got married and ended up hating each other.

"Besides, I have these horrible math and statistic classes to get through next semester, which I know will take their toll on me emotionally, besides being there for Cassie and whatever help she may need." Carmine heaved a long sigh. "Intuitively, summer sounds best. Is that okay with you?"

"Carmine, whatever you want. If you want to wait five years, I don't care. Just so we will be together."

"Thank you, for the hundredth time, for understanding, Jake," she said with a smile of relief as she pressed his hand tightly.

Jake, holding Carmine's hand, arose from the table and walked around to where Carmine was sitting. He gently pulled her up, and tucking his hand behind her neck, he bent down and ardently kissed her. Carmine responded with a fierce passion that she didn't recognize in herself and started undoing his belt buckle.

"Carmine, wait! Let's do this right," Jake said huskily. He leaned over the table and blew out the candles. "Is there anything that needs to be put away in the kitchen?"

"Not really," Carmine said breathlessly, as she continued to kiss his neck, his ears and anything else she could reach.

"Okay, Carmine, here we go."

He picked her up and walked to the bedroom, opened the door and said, "I have been waiting for this since the first day I saw you." Kissing Carmine hungrily as he closed the door with his foot, he placed her gently on the bed and lay down next to her. They looked at each other for a few seconds, then they furiously, and with gales of laughter, began peeling off each other's clothes. With sighs of giddiness and happiness, they fell into each other's arms.

"This is the way it should be," Jake whispered into Carmine's ears. Holding her away from him, but with his arms still around her waist, he looked deep into her eyes and said, "You are stunning, beautiful inside and out. Then with a happy note in his voice and drawing her to him, he again whispered, "This is going to be one memorable night!"

Chapter Two

Carmine awakened abruptly around four the next morning. She again had the reoccurring dream of the Angel and being on Earth with him. Every time she had the dream, it was more detailed. This time the Angel told her his name, which was Laurence, and he told her that he approved of Jake and their relationship. It was very strange. Shaking her head as though that would help recover the dream, she saw Jake next to her in bed, sleeping soundly and very happily. Sighing and leaning back with a wide smile, she thought of the night before and how responsive they had been to each other. Carmine had never felt this way about anyone in her life, ever, and she had savored every moment of it. She quietly bent over Jake and gently kissed him. He seemed to smile but continued to sleep.

Carmine thought of snuggling with him while he slept, but was much too awake to stay in bed with someone seriously sleeping. She thought of waking him up and decided against it. She very slowly left the bed, pulled on an old cranberry robe from the brass clothes tree in the corner, tiptoed to the bedroom door, opening and shutting it very carefully after her, so she wouldn't wake him.

When she walked into the dining room, there were the dishes on the table and everything else they used from dinner. She made a disgusted face. *I'll have to clean up some time, so I guess this is as a good a time as any.* Moving quietly and with as much speed as possible, she had the room back to normal within an hour.

She opened the refrigerator door and looked longingly at the dessert that Rinaldo had made. "Darn, that looks good. I wonder if Jake likes dessert for breakfast?" she asked herself. "For me it would be perfect," and as she said that, she took a finger and dragged it across the chocolate frosting and then licked the finger clean.

Heavenly.

Savoring the chocolate, she took a fork from the drawer and took a huge bite. After another bite, she chastised herself. *Better stop now before I eat it all.*

Noting that it was just five-thirty, Carmine decided to do her morning meditation before preparing for the day. As she meditated in the living room, she played the Mozart CD's very quietly. As she was meditating, she remembered the dream that had awakened her. "Maybe I should start writing it down as Jake suggested. It certainly couldn't hurt and maybe I could make more sense out of the dreams."

After finishing her meditation and doing her morning yoga, she looked in on Jake. He was still asleep with the same happy grin on his face. Carmine silently closed the door and went into the second bedroom where she had her computer. Opening it up, she stared at the screen for a good twenty minutes. She then wrote "Carmine's Angel" centered as the title. As she typed it, she shrugged her shoulders. "Why not?"

"How should I start this?" Sighing as she rubbed her nose and forehead for inspiration, she closed her eyes and tried to take herself back to the evening before school started and to the dreams that were harbored in her subconscious. Finally, she nodded her head as if agreeing with someone and started writing.

"The headache was getting intense, the worse she ever had, but not enough to stop her. Not now!..."

Epilogue

Carmine and Jake were married the following August in Jake and Sophie's garden at the foot of the rock falls, with a small group of friends and relatives. Cassie was her mother's maid of honor and Jake had his best friend from college, Rusty, as his best man. Rinaldo and Angela cooked for the event with all of Jake and Carmine's favorite foods. The cake, standing three tiers high, consisting of chocolate, raspberries, chocolate and white mousse filling, was covered in a hard chocolate frosting with a raspberry sauce. It was the *piece de resistance*. When asked why it was three tiers high, for only seventy-five people, Rinaldo said, "Ms. Carmine, you must have a piece each week for the first month, then a piece for each month of the first year and then a piece a year for the first five years, or as long as it lasts. Trust me, Ms. Carmine, it will last forever the way I wrap it for you." And it almost did.

After a honeymoon cruise to the Mediterranean, Carmine finished her college degree in June of the next year. Carmine and Jake lived in Jake's suite of rooms to stay close to Sophie who would never admit that she was glad to have them nearby. Jake and Carmine remodeled the suite to make it their home prior to the wedding.

When Sophie passed on, they built a small house, by Jake's standards, for the two of them next to the big house, which was then used exclusively for Jake's school and all of his other charitable activities.

Carmine finished her book, *"Carmine's Angel"* and it was published. Carmine was always surprised when she got a note from someone who said the book reminded them of the power of love and angels. Carmine found that she loved writing. Jake and she became a writing family. She found herself in demand as a speaker for women's groups and was able to become a spokesperson for women's rights. (No surprise, as this was part of that spiritual contract to help other people, as specified by Laurence and the Director, that long-ago fateful night when Carmine had died.)

She assisted Jake with his philanthropic responsibilities and his research for his J. A. Ke books. They remained committed to local and national charities. Their lives were extremely busy and hectic, but also fulfilling. They felt, in their small way, they were contributing good to the Universe.

Carmine's "traffic Karma" was a source of gossip. People couldn't help but notice that wherever Carmine drove, traffic seemed to be non-existent. There were times when Carmine would be driving to the same location as other individuals and she would reach that destination in minimal time while all the other drivers would take much longer. Those who loved and knew her said that it was the Universe saying thank you for all the good she did. Those who were not so kindly disposed said she was a witch, or worse!

When questioned about this, Carmine would only shrug her shoulders with a puzzled look on her face and tell the inquirer she had no idea why it happened and what caused it, but she was very grateful for this blessing, and hoped it would continue.

Cassie became a photojournalist after she graduated from her art school, traveling around the world. She was always at the epicenter of action, photographing critical world events and capturing the humanity of those moments. Carmine worried about her intensely, but Jake reminded her that Cassie had to do what made her happy, and that she had her own curriculum to fulfill.

Cassie married a newspaper owner who lived in Northern California and immediately started her family. Much to Carmine's relief, Cassie stayed home to take care of the baby and then, the three other children who followed. Carmine and Jake visited often with Cassie's family, enjoying being grandparents, tickled when sometimes people thought the grandchildren were their children. "I guess I don't look as old as I thought I did," Carmine would laugh to herself.

Cassie changed her artistic focus from photojournalism to creating unique marble sculptures of children of all countries and races who had lost their young lives in wars. They became a symbol for peace in the world and were sought after by governments, museums, and individual art lovers. This fulfilled the prophecy that had been revealed to Carmine the night that she died, that Cassie's work would enhance humanity.

Leslie became a world-famous stage and film actor, who was particularly known for her portrayal of Shakespearian women. She married a very successful lawyer who was much older than she, well-established in his profession. He helped her found free legal clinics throughout the United States to provide help and guidance to abused women. Supporting these clinics financially, and with her celebrity, was Leslie's way of saying thank you for her success and happiness. Leslie became a close friend of Cassie and her family and, remained Carmine's friend until Carmine's final transition.

Patrick and Chardonnay married after Chardonnay's graduation from her Master's Program. Patrick worked as a partner in his father's law firm and implemented a policy that all employees provide pro bono work for indigenous groups and individuals. The employees were paid for their volunteer work and the firm became known as the most profitable legal firm in the city, despite its significant unpaid legal work. This supported Laurence's teaching that the more you give, the more you receive.

Chardonnay received a Master's Degree in Spiritual Psychology and used it to coach individuals to help them achieve their career goals and to fulfill the parts of their curriculum to love and be of service. "Everyday life and spiritual life cannot be separated," Chardonnay always reminded her clients.

Carmine and Jake lived to their early eighties, in best of health, until the very end. Jake went first and then, as indeed the Heaven's computer had stated, at eighty-two, Carmine followed. Upon leaving her body, the first two "people" she saw were Laurence and Jake. "Laurence," she cried out, "I thought I couldn't see you anymore" and then she looked at Jake. "My darling," she gasped in delight, "I thought you had died."

"Carmine, welcome my love. I've been watching over you and waiting for you," Jake said reassuringly.

Laurence hugged Carmine and said, "Congratulations, we've completed your twenty lifetimes and now you've changed dimensions. The old is completed. Your Karmic debt for that suicide is cancelled." Laurence smiled, releasing Carmine to Jake. Jake kissed her and said, "I'm so glad to be with you again."

"Me too! Hello my love!"

Walking hand-in-hand with Jake, Carmine felt no different than she had on Earth, and she and Jake looked about the same age as the first time they met. Jake began telling her about the projects he had started, waiting for Carmine to help him. He enthused about how much Laurence had assisted him while waiting for Carmine to return Home.

"Wait, Jake," Carmine questioned, "I thought home was on Earth."

"No, Carmine, Earth is just a temporary place where we learn to grow spiritually. This is our true home where we return time after time, after our sojourn to Earth. You have just temporarily forgotten, Carmine," Jake laughed, as he hugged her. "I am so glad you're back and you have so many friends and relatives waiting to see you. Even though a minute here is like a year on Earth, it was still hard having you away from me."

"We're going to have so much fun together," he said, as he pulled her towards a group of people holding out their arms to Carmine to welcome her. "See, Carmine?" Jake said, "Here are the people who are special to you and who you most influenced and helped in your last Earth life." Carmine turned to Jake, gave him a loving kiss and then walked with hands out-stretched into the welcoming group, where she was enveloped in a feeling of pure love, peace, joy and happiness.

She truly was Home!

The Never Ending . . .

Acknowledgements

It is known that it takes a village to raise a child, but it certainly took a village in supporting me writing this book.

So thank you to my many wonderful villagers that include...

Carol Woodliff, my editor, who kept my vision about what I wanted to achieve and was able to enhance it using her spiritual and shamanic knowledge as well as her mastery of writing.

Jane Cook-Rashid, who reviewed the book word by word, line-by-line, taking hours editing the punctuation, grammar, and vocabulary and adding so much to the book's readability.

Trish Weber-Hall, who created the cover design, and then gave it as a graduation gift. She also supported me with her words of wisdom as well as knowledge and advice for self-publishing.

Pranic Healing's and Self Realization Fellowship's spiritual teachings, both added so much wisdom to my life and inspired me as I wrote *Carmine's Angel.*

University of Santa Monica Master's Program in Spiritual Psychology was the final impetus for writing the book, which incorporated many of its skills and tools that were given to Carmine by Laurence.

"The Hoodies," Susan, Karen, Laura, and Mary, who supported me with their understanding, kindness and encouragement.

My doctor, Sai-Ling, Coaches/Counselors Bonnie, Elizabeth and Steve, soul friend Maria, as well as readers Tracy and Margie who gave their time to read and give insight on the story.

All my other numerous friends who gave me ongoing encouragement and strength to finish during the writing process.

My supportive and understanding husband, Glenn. He was ALWAYS there for me, no matter what I said or did, listened to all my frustrations and complaints without judgment, patiently, lovingly and silently, taking all that occurred in his stride, showing me what unconditional love truly means in the context that Laurence defined it. Love you, Glenn!

And lastly, my sister Kathe, who was so sure that I was meant to write and complete this book and would never let up on reminding me about what my curriculum was in this life. I know, wherever she is, she is complimenting herself on my finally achieving it, and telling me, "I told you so." Thank you Kathe, for your faith in me. I miss you so much!